PRIZE STORIES 1976
The O. Henry Awards

PRIZE STORIES
1976

The O. Henry Awards

EDITED AND
WITH AN INTRODUCTION
BY

WILLIAM ABRAHAMS

DOUBLEDAY & COMPANY, INC.
GARDEN CITY, NEW YORK
1976

ISBN: 0-385-00829-5
Library of Congress Catalog Card Number 21–9372
Copyright © 1976 by Doubleday & Company, Inc.
First Edition

808.83
PRI
1976

76–11174

CONTENTS

PUBLISHER'S NOTE

THIS VOLUME IS THE FIFTY-SIXTH in the O. Henry Memorial Award series.

In 1918, the Society of Arts and Sciences met to vote upon a monument to the master of the short story, O. Henry. They decided that this memorial should be in the form of two prizes for the best short stories published by American authors in American magazines during the year 1919. From this beginning, the memorial developed into an annual anthology of outstanding short stories by American authors, published, with the exception of the years 1952 and 1953, by Doubleday & Company, Inc.

Blanche Colton Williams, one of the founders of the awards, was editor from 1919 to 1932; Harry Hansen from 1933 to 1940; Herschel Brickell from 1941 to 1951. The annual collection did not appear in 1952 and 1953, when the continuity of the series was interrupted by the death of Herschel Brickell. Paul Engle was editor from 1954 to 1959 with Hanson Martin coeditor in the years 1954 to 1950; Mary Stegner in 1960; Richard Poirier from 1961 to 1966, with assistance from and co-editorship with William Abrahams from 1964 to 1966. William Abrahams became editor of the series in 1967.

Doubleday also publishes *First-Prize Stories from the O. Henry Memorial Awards* in editions that are brought up to date at intervals. In 1970 Doubleday also published under Mr. Abrahams' editorship *Fifty Years of the American Short Story*, a collection of stories selected from the series.

The stories chosen for this volume were published in the period from the summer of 1974 to the summer of 1975. A list of the magazines consulted appears at the back of the book. The choice of stories and the selection of prize winners are exclusively the responsibility of the editor. Biographical material is based on information provided by the contributors and obtained from standard works of reference.

INTRODUCTION

IN THE INTRODUCTION to *Prize Stories 1967*, the first of these collections for which I had sole editorial responsibility, I began with a reference to dedicated readers and writers of short stories:

> By dedicated readers [I explained then] I mean those who read stories out of preference, as others read articles, who actively like them and seek them out and care enough to discriminate between the good, bad, and merely mediocre. By dedicated writers I mean those who *must* write, "the addicts," as Doris Lessing has recently called them, for whom the form is not only congenial but a necessity. "Some writers I know," Mrs. Lessing observed, "have stopped writing short stories because as they say 'There is no market for them.' Others, like myself, the addicts, go on, and I suspect would go on even if there really wasn't any home for them but a private drawer."

I no longer remember the source of the observation; perhaps it figured in a review by Mrs. Lessing in the *New Statesman*. In any event, it made an excellent starting point for one who had already discerned in the current state of short-story publication "cause for alarm," and it seems to me that I have been ringing doleful changes on that theme over the intervening ten years. But with no noticeable effect. The situation has not improved; it may even have worsened a bit: magazines, large and little alike, giving the major portion of their pages to articles and artwork, and as cool as ever to fiction (when not downright hostile to it), are themselves increasingly vulnerable in a time of spiraling costs and competition from the newer "media." On the publishing situation or market, then, I doubt that anything further need be said these ten years on except to utter the usual, annual, and I fear foredoomed prayer that it may improve.

And yet, paradoxically, the story has continued to thrive: adversity and indifference would seem to have discouraged only those writers whose need to write was rather tenuous to begin with, less a need, one might say, than a kind of whimsicality. Consider: 175 stories have been chosen for these collections from 1967 through 1976 from a total of more than ten thousand stories that got into print somehow, somewhere. Evidently the number of addicts (or dedicated writers) was (and is) vastly larger than might have been anticipated. With a fine disregard for the market, these addicted writers have written their stories and sent them out to their fate, and addicted readers have discovered them in familiar, less familiar, and sometimes virtually unknown periodicals, as a glance at the list of magazines consulted that is included in each of these volumes will suggest. At this point, as in the past, I must again pay tribute to all magazines publishing stories, but especially to those admirable little magazines—many of them knowing only the briefest existence—that have provided a home for so many stories over the decade.

Over the decade—the phrase would seem to authorize generalizations about the contemporary short story that one would hesitate to make on the basis of a single year's reading. Even so, I approach the task diffidently and tentatively, for when one is speaking of a form as loose and elusive of definition as the story has become in recent years—"any fiction not long enough to be called a novel"—and a form, besides, that encourages individuality and idiosyncracy, one knows in advance almost any generalization carries with it its built-in contradiction. Nevertheless, for one must begin somewhere, thinking back over the stories of the decade, I am struck by the increasing number that have been written, that continue to be written, in the first person—and the first person not in the traditional role of observer-narrator, but more often than not at the very center of the story, as its principal character. Does this mean, then, that we are entering an age of disguised autobiography? Conceivably: but I think a more plausible explanation is to be found in a comment made by George Orwell in the notebook he was keeping the year before his death: "In the first person *anything* can be made to sound credible."

The presumption of credibility, once so taken for granted as to require no comment at all, has become a matter of urgent concern (or revulsion) for many of the writers of this decade. Reluctant to accept as a condition of the story the suspension of disbelief that has been inseparable from the form virtually from the beginning, they ask: need a story be credible at all; how is it to be made credible; *can* it be made credible? And is not credibility, even supposing it to be achieved, itself an illusion? For what is one believing in, after all, but a fiction?

Questions of this sort are implicit in the work of such older masters as Borges and Nabokov, whose influence upon a younger generation of writers has been unmistakable, less for their practice (which is quite inimitable) than for the principles—or questions —upon which it is based. One does not find, now, overt neo-Borgesian or neo-Nabokovian "stories" to the extent that, twenty-five years ago, one came upon story after story in the manner of Hemingway, say, or, alternatively, Henry James, for influence in the case of Borges and Nabokov goes deeper than imitation, indeed exists on a level entirely apart from it. In one of Borges' brief, deceptively casual, profoundly suggestive essays in the collection *Other Inquisitions,* he reproduces a fragment from Coleridge's *Anima Poetae* that must resound in any discussion of the nature of reality in life and in art: "If a man could pass through Paradise in a dream, and have a flower presented to him as a pledge that his soul had really been there, and if he found that flower in his hand when he awoke—Ay!—and what then?"

At this point, it may be instructive to compare two stories written ten years apart, each awarded first prize in the O. Henry collection of its year, Joyce Carol Oates's "In the Region of Ice" (from *Prize Stories 1967*), and from this year's collection, Harold Brodkey's "His Son, in His Arms, in Light, Aloft."

Miss Oates's story, powerfully told and securely traditional in form, is among the most impressive achievements of what we must now think of as its author's early period. It tells of a nun, Sister Irene, teaching English literature in a "downtown" Catholic university, and her relation to a brilliant, troublesome, psychotic Jewish student:

> In meditation, alone, she often thought about him. When she tried to talk about him to a young nun, Sister Carlotta, everything sounded gross. "But no, he's an excellent stu-

dent," she insisted. "I'm very grateful to have him in class. It's just that . . . he thinks ideas are real." Sister Carlotta, who loved literature also, had been forced to teach grade-school arithmetic for the last four years. That might have been why she said, a little sharply, "You don't think ideas are real?"

Sister Irene acquiesced with a smile, but of course she did not think so: only reality is real.

The story is told from Sister Irene's point of view; hence the irony of a religious believing "only reality is real" is, of necessity, left unexplored, though it may be said to haunt the story. But Miss Oates's aim is to achieve credibility, which she admirably does, drawing upon all those techniques of "realism"—in dialogue, in setting, in a logical chronological pattern of scenes and events, leading to a dramatic, ironic, wholly credible conclusion—all those techniques that John Barth was presently to mock at, even as he made use of them, in his influential story "Lost in the Funhouse" (included in *Prize Stories* 1969), and which Miss Oates herself was gradually to abandon or alter in the stories of her middle period.

To turn from "In the Region of Ice" to "His Son, in His Arms, in Light, Aloft" is to be made vividly aware of the development or change in the story in this past decade, and to be reminded again of the varieties and possibilities of the form itself. No wonder—to echo Mrs. Lessing once more—it is a form that inspires addiction. Having proved himself a master of traditional techniques in "A Story in an Almost Classical Mode" (included in *Prize Stories* 1975), Mr. Brodkey has now jettisoned them entirely in this newer story. "His Son . . ." has been described as "luminous," and I think this is true, in the sense that the story is given to us in a succession of illuminations, as it were accidentally, much as a flashlight darts about in the dark, coming to rest on one object or another. Told in the first person, it is an attempt by the narrator, now a grown man, to remember himself as a small boy as he figured in the life of his father: the triumph of the story is the portrait of the father that emerges from these fragments, the more credible for being fragmentary, of the remembered past. At the beginning of the story, one assumes it to be no more than another exercise in disguised autobiography, but the narrator, almost immediately, as though to head off so easy and so natural a misconception, will have none of it:

> What if I am wrong? What if I remember incorrectly? It does not matter. This is fiction—a game—of pleasures, of truth and error, as at the sensual beginning of a sensual life.

At the end of Mr. Brodkey's fiction occurs the beautiful, memorable phrase "An accidental glory," and in the composition of his "fiction" he seems to have raised the accidental to an aesthetic principle. I say "seems" because consciousness, the conscious assembling of these "fictitious" glories, may play a larger part in the game than the author, that prestidigitator, is prepared to allow us to recognize.

"This is fiction"—that protest, that counterclaim, that challenge —is being heard ever more insistently from authors who appear to have grown weary of the traditional story and, departing from it, are exploring ever more adventurously the possibilities of "reinventing" the form.

It would be misleading, however, to exaggerate their number, for the majority of short-story writers continue to conduct their explorations within the hardly visible confines of the tradition itself. Few have done so as consistently, or with such rewarding results, as John Updike. He has appeared many times in this collection. His story, "Separating," characteristic of him in its maturity, control, stylistic ease, authenticity of emotion, and accuracy of observation, provides the occasion to honor him once again, this time with the Special Award for Continuing Achievement. His unflagging mastery is at once an example and a consolation for addicts of the short story, readers and writers alike.

WILLIAM ABRAHAMS

HIS SON,
IN HIS ARMS,
IN LIGHT, ALOFT

HAROLD BRODKEY

HAROLD BRODKEY has won first prize two years in a row
—his "A Story in an Almost Classical Mode" shared first
prize in last year's volume. He was born in Staunton, Illinois, and now lives in New York City. His stories have appeared in *The New Yorker* and *Esquire*. He is the author
of *First Love and Other Stories*.

MY FATHER IS CHASING ME.

My God, I feel it up and down my spine, the thumping on the
turf, the approach of his hands, his giant hands, the huge ram-
ming increment of his breath as he draws near: a widening effort.
I feel it up and down my spine and in my mouth and belly—
Daddy is so swift: who ever heard of such swiftness? Just as in stories. . . .

I can't escape him, can't fend him off, his arms, his rapidity, his
will. His interest in me.

I am being lifted into the air—and even as I pant and stare
blurredly, limply, mindlessly, a map appears, of the dark ground
where I ran: as I hang limply and rise anyway on the fattened bar
of my father's arm, I see that there's the grass, there's the path,
there's a bed of flowers.

I straighten up. There are the lighted windows of our house,
some distance away. My father's face, full of noises, is near: it
looms: his hidden face: is that you, old money-maker? My butt is
folded on the trapeze of his arm. My father is as big as an automobile.

In the oddly shrewd-hearted torpor of being carried home in the dark, a tourist, in my father's arms, I feel myself attached by my heated-by-running dampness to him: we are attached, there are binding oval stains of warmth.

In most social talk, most politeness, most literature, most religion, it is as if violence didn't exist—except as sin, something far away. This is flattering to women. It is also conducive to grace—because the heaviness of fear, the shadowy henchmen selves that fear attaches to us, that fear sees in others, is banished.

Where am I in the web of jealousy that trembles at every human movement?

What detectives we have to be.

What if I am wrong? What if I remember incorrectly? It does not matter. This is fiction—a game—of pleasures, of truth and error, as at the sensual beginning of a sensual life.

My father, Charley, as I knew him, is invisible in any photograph I have of him. The man I hugged or ran toward or ran from is not in any photograph: a photograph shows someone of whom I think: *Oh, was he like that?*

But in certain memories, *he* appears, a figure, a presence, and I think, *I know him.*

It is embarrassing to me that I am part of what is unsayable in any account of his life.

When Momma's or my sister's excesses, of mood, or of shopping, angered or sickened Daddy, you can smell him then from two feet away: he has a dry, achy little stink of a rapidly fading interest in his life with us. At these times, the women in a spasm of wit turn to me; they comb my hair, clean my face, pat my bottom or my shoulder, and send me off; they bid me to go cheer up Daddy.

Sometimes it takes no more than a tug at his newspaper: the sight of me is enough; or I climb on his lap, mimic his depression; I stand on his lap, press his head against my chest. . . . His face is immense, porous, complex with stubble, bits of talcum on it, unlikely colors, unlikely features, a bald brow with a curved square of lamplight in it. About his head there is a nimbus of sturdy wickedness, of unlikelihood. If his mood does not change, something tumbles and goes dead in me.

Perhaps it is more a nervous breakdown than heartbreak: I have failed him: his love for me is very limited: I must die now. I go somewhere and shudder and collapse—a corner of the dining room, the back stoop or deck: I lie there, empty, grief-stricken, literally unable to move—I have forgotten my limbs. If a memory of them comes to me, the memory is meaningless. . . .

Momma will then stalk in to wherever Daddy is and say to him, "Charley, you can be mad at me, I'm used to it, but just go take a look and see what you've done to the child. . . ."

My uselessness toward him sickens me. Anyone who fails toward him might as well be struck down, abandoned, eaten.

Perhaps it is an animal state: I have-nothing-left I-have-no-place-in this-world.

Well, this is his house. Momma tells me in various ways to love him. Also, he is entrancing—he is so big, so thunderish, so smelly, and has the most extraordinary habits, reading newspapers, for instance, and wiggling his shoe: his shoe is gross: kick someone with that and they'd fall into next week.

Some memories huddle in a grainy light. What it is is a number of similar events bunching themselves, superimposing themselves, to make a false memory, a collage, a mental artifact. Within the boundaries of one such memory one plunges from year to year, is small and helpless, is a little older: one remembers it all but it is nothing that happened, that clutch of happenings, of associations, those gifts and ghosts of a meaning.

I can, if I concentrate, whiten the light—or yellow-whiten it, actually—and when the graininess goes, it is suddenly one afternoon.

I could not live without the pride and belonging-to-himness of being that man's consolation. He had the disposal of the rights to the out-of-doors—he was the other, the other-not-a-woman: he was my strength, literally, my strength if I should cry out.

Flies and swarms of the danger of being unfathered beset me when I bored my father: it was as if I were covered with flies on the animal plain where some ravening wild dog would leap up, bite and grip my muzzle, and begin to bring about my death.

I had no protection: I was subject now to the appetite of whatever inhabited the dark.

A child collapses in a sudden burst of there-is-nothing-here, and that is added onto nothingness, the nothing of being only a child concentrating on there being nothing there, no hope, no ambition: there is a despair but one without magnificence except in the face of its completeness: *I am a child and am without strength of my own.*

I have—in my grief—somehow managed to get to the back deck: I am sitting in the early evening light; I am oblivious to the light. I did and didn't hear his footsteps, the rumble, the house thunder dimly (behind and beneath me), the thunder of his-coming-to-rescue-me. . . . I did and didn't hear him call my name.

I spoke only the gaping emptiness of grief—that tongue—I understood I had no right to the speech of fathers and sons.

My father came out on the porch. I remember how stirred he was, how beside himself that I was so unhappy, that a child, a child he liked, should suffer so. He laid aside his own mood—his disgust with life, with money, with the excesses of the women—and he took on a broad-winged, malely flustering, broadwinged optimism—he was at the center of a great beating (of the heart, a man's heart, of a man's gestures, will, concern), dust clouds rising, a beating determination to persuade me that the nature of life, of *my* life, was other than I'd thought, other than whatever had defeated me—he was about to tell me there was no need to feel defeated, he was about to tell me that I was a good, or even a wonderful, child.

He kneeled—a mountain of shirtfront and trousers; a mountain that poured, clambered down, folded itself, re-formed itself: a disorderly massiveness, near to me, fabric-hung-and-draped: Sinai. He said, "Here, here, what is this—what is a child like you doing being so sad?" And: "Look at me. . . . It's all right. . . . Everything is all right. . . ." The misstatements of consolation are lies about the absolute that require faith—and no memory: the truth

of consolation can be investigated if one is a proper child—that is
to say, affectionate—only in a non-skeptical way.

"It's not all right!"

"It is—it is." It was and wasn't a lie: it had to do with power—
and limitations: my limitations and his power: he could make it
all right for me, everything, provided my everything was small
enough and within his comprehension.

Sometimes he would say, "Son—" He would say it heavily—
"Don't be sad—I don't want you to be sad—I don't like it when
you're sad—"

I can't look into his near and, to me, factually incredible face—
incredible because so large (as at the beginning of a love affair): I
mean as a *face*: it is the focus of so many emotions and wonder-
ments: he could have been a fool or was—it was possibly the face
of a fool, someone self-centered, smug, an operator, semi-criminal,
an intelligent psychoanalyst; it was certainly a mortal face—but
what did the idea or word mean to me then—*mortal?*

There was a face; it was as large as my chest; there were eyes,
inhumanly big, humid—what could they mean? How could I read
them? How do you read eyes? I did not know about comparisons:
how much more affectionate he was than other men, or less, how
much better than common experience or how much worse in this
area of being fathered my experience was with him: I cannot say
even now: it is a statistical matter, after all, a matter of averages:
but who at the present date can phrase the proper questions for
the poll? And who will understand the hesitations, the blank
looks, the odd expressions on the faces of the answerers?

The odds are he was a—median—father. He himself had usually a conviction he did pretty well: sometimes he despaired—of
himself: but blamed me: my love: or something: or himself as a
father: he wasn't good at managing stages between strong, clear
states of feeling. Perhaps no one is.

Anyway, I knew no such terms as *median* then: I did not understand much about those parts of his emotions which extended
past the rather clear area where my emotions were so often
amazed. I chose, in some ways, to regard him seriously: in other
ways, I had no choice—he was what was given to me.

I cannot look at him, as I said: I cannot see anything: if I look at him without seeing him, my blindness insults him: I don't want to hurt him at all: I want nothing: I am lost and have surrendered and am really dead and am waiting without hope.

He knows how to rescue people. Whatever he doesn't know, one of the things he knows in the haste and jumble of his heart, among the blither of tastes in his mouth and opinions and sympathies in his mind and so on, is the making yourself into someone who will help someone who is wounded. The dispersed and unlikely parts of him come together for a while in a clucking and focused arch of abiding concern. Oh how he plows ahead; oh how he believes in rescue! He puts—he *shoves*—he works an arm behind my shoulders, another under my legs: his arms, his powers shove at me, twist, lift and jerk me until I am cradled in the air, in his arms: "You don't have to be unhappy—you haven't hurt anyone—don't be sad—you're a *nice* boy. . . ."

I can't quite hear him, I can't quite believe him. I can't be *good*—the confidence game is to believe him, is to be a good child who trusts him—we will both smile then, he and I. But if I hear him, I have to believe him still. I am set up that way. He is so big; he is the possessor of so many grandeurs. If I believe him, hope and pleasure will start up again—suddenly—the blankness in me will be relieved, broken by these—meanings—that it seems he and I share in some big, attaching way.

In his pride he does not allow me to suffer: I belong to him.

He is rising, jerkily, to his feet and holding me at the same time. I do not have to stir to save myself—I only have to believe him. He rocks me into a sad-edged relief and an achingly melancholy delight with the peculiar lurch as he stands erect of establishing his balance and rectifying the way he holds me, so he can go on holding me, holding me aloft, against his chest: I am airborne: I liked to have that man hold me—in the air: I knew it was worth a great deal, the embrace, the gift of altitude. I am not exposed on the animal plain. I am not helpless.

The heat his body gives off! It is the heat of a man sweating with regret. His heartbeat, his burning, his physical force: ah, there is a large rent in the nothingness: the mournful apparition of his regret, the proof of his loyalty wake me: I have a twin, a

massive twin, mighty company: Daddy's grief is at my grief: my
nothingness is echoed in him (if he is going to have to live without me): the rescue was not quite a secular thing. The evening
forms itself, a classroom, a brigade of shadows, of phenomena—
the tinted air slides: there are shadowy skaters everywhere; shadowy cloaked people step out from behind things which are then
hidden behind their cloaks. An alteration in the air proceeds from
openings in the ground, from leaks in the sunlight which is being
disengaged, like a stubborn hand, or is being stroked shut like my
eyelids when I refuse to sleep: the dark rubs and bubbles
noiselessly—and seeps—into the landscape. In the rubbed distor-
tion of my inner air, twilight soothes: there are two of us breathing in close proximity here (he is telling me that grownups sometimes have things on their minds, he is saying mysterious things
which I don't comprehend); I don't want to look at him: it takes
two of my eyes to see one of his—and then I mostly see myself in
his eye: he is even more unseeable from here, this holder: my
head falls against his neck: "I know what you like—you'd like to
go stand on the wall—would you like to see the sunset?" Did I
nod? I think I did: I nodded gravely: but perhaps he did not need
an answer since he thought he knew me well.

We are moving, this elephant and I, we are lumbering, down
some steps, across grassy, uneven ground—the spoiled child in his
father's arms—behind our house was a little park—we moved
across the grass of the little park. There are sun's rays on the
dome of the moorish bandstand. The evening is moist, fugitive,
momentarily sneaking, half welcomed in this hour of crime. My
father's neck. The stubble. The skin where the stubble stops. Exhaustion has me: I am a creature of failure, a locus of
childishness, an empty skull: I am this being-young. We overrun
the world, he and I, with his legs, with our eyes, with our alliance.
We move on in a ghostly torrent of our being like this.

My father has the smell and feel of wanting to be my father.
Guilt and innocence stream and re-stream in him. His face, I see
now in memory, held an untiring surprise: as if some grammar of
deed and purpose—of comparatively easy tenderness—startled
him again and again, startled him continuously for a while. He
said, "I guess we'll just have to cheer you up—we'll have to show

you life isn't so bad—I guess we weren't any too careful of a little boy's feelings, were we?" I wonder if all comfort is alike.

A man's love is, after all, a fairly spectacular thing.

He said—his voice came from above me—he spoke out into the air, the twilight—"We'll make it all right—just you wait and see. . . ."

He said, "This is what you like," and he placed me on the wall that ran along the edge of the park, the edge of a bluff, a wall too high for me to see over, and which I was forbidden to climb: he placed me on the stubbed stone mountains and grouting of the wall-top. He put his arm around my middle: I leaned against him: and faced outward into the salt of the danger of the height, of the view (we were at least one hundred and fifty feet, we were, therefore, hundreds of feet in the air); I was flicked at by narrow, abrasive bands of wind, evening wind, veined with sunset's suncrispness, strongly touched with coolness.

The wind would push at my eyelids, my nose, my lips. I heard a buzzing in my ears which signaled how high, how alone we were: this view of a river valley at night and of parts of four counties was audible. I looked into the hollow in front of me, a grand hole, an immense, bellying deep sheet or vast sock. There were numinous fragments in it—birds in what sunlight was left, bits of smoke faintly lit by distant light or mist, hovering inexplicably here and there: rays of yellow light, high up, touching a few high clouds.

It had a floor on which were creeks (and the big river), a little dim, a little glary at this hour, rail lines, roads, highways, houses, silos, bridges, trees, fields everything more than half hidden in the enlarging dark: there was the shrinking glitter of far-off noises, bearded and stippled with huge and spreading shadows of my ignorance: it was panorama as a personal privilege. The sun at the end of the large, sunset-swollen sky, was a glowing and urgent orange; around it were the spreading petals of pink and stratospheric gold: on the ground were occasional magenta flarings; oh it makes you stare and gasp; a fine, astral (not a crayon) red rode in a broad, magnificent band across the middlewestern sky: below us, for miles, shadowiness tightened as we watched (it seemed); above us, tinted clouds spread across the vast shadowing sky: there were funereal lights and sinkings everywhere. I stand on the wall and lean against Daddy, only somewhat awed and ab-

stractcd: the view does not own me as it usually does: I am partly
in the hands of the jolting—amusement—the conceit—of having
been resurrected by my father.

I understood that he was proffering me oblivion plus pleasure,
the end of a sorrow to be henceforth remembered as Happiness.
This was to be my privilege. This amazing man is going to rescue
me from any anomaly or barb or sting in my existence: he is going
to confer happiness on me: as a matter of fact, he has already
begun.

"Just you trust me—you keep right on being cheered up—look
at that sunset—that's some sunset, wouldn't you say?—everything
is going to be just fine and dandy—you trust me—you'll see—just
you wait and see. . . ."

Did he mean to be a swindler? He wasn't clear-minded—he
often said, "I mean well." He did not think other people meant
well.

I don't feel it would be right to adopt an Oedipal theory to explain what happened between him and me: only a sense of what
he was like as a man, what certain moments were like, and what
was said.

It is hard in language to get the full, irregular, heavy sound of a
man.

He liked to have us "all dressed and nice when I come home
from work," have us wait for him in attitudes of serene all-is-well
contentment. As elegant as a Spanish prince I sat on the couch
toying with an oversized model truck—what a confusion of social
pretensions, technologies, class disorder there was in that. My
sister would sit in a chair, knees together, hair brushed: she'd doze
off if Daddy was late. Aren't we happy! Actually, we often are.

One day he came in plungingly, excited to be home and to have
us as an audience rather than outsiders who didn't know their
lines and who often laughed at him as part of their struggle to improve their parts in his scenes. We were waiting to have him ap-
prove of our tableau—he usually said something about what a
nice family we looked like or how well we looked or what a pretty
group or some such thing—and we didn't realize he was the
tableau tonight. We held our positions, but we stared at him in a
kind of mindless what-should-we-do-besides-sit-here-and-be-happy-

and-nice? Impatiently he said, "I have a surprise for you, Charlotte—Abe Last has a heart after all." My father said something on that order: or "—a conscience after all"; and then he walked across the carpet, a man somewhat jerky with success—a man redolent of vaudeville, of grotesque and sentimental movies (he liked grotesquerie, prettiness, sentiment). As he walked, he pulled banded packs of currency out of his pockets, two or three in each hand. "There," he said, dropping one, then three in Momma's dressed-up lap. "There," he said, dropping another two: he uttered a "there" for each subsequent pack. "Oh, let me!" my sister cried and ran over to look—and then she grabbed two packs and said, "Oh, Daddy, how much *is* this?"

It was eight or ten thousand dollars, he said. Momma said, "Charley, what if someone sees—we could be robbed—why do you take chances like this?"

Daddy harrumphed and said, "You have no sense of fun—if you ask me, you're afraid to be happy. I'll put it in the bank tomorrow—if I can find an honest banker—here, young lady, put that money down: you don't want to prove your mother right, do you?"

Then he said, "I know one person around here who knows how to enjoy himself—" and he lifted me up, held me in his arms.

He said, "We're going outside, this young man and I."

"What should I do with this money!"

"Put it under your mattress—make a salad out of it: you're always the one who worries about money," he said in a voice solid with authority and masculinity, totally pieced out with various self-satisfactions—as if he had gained a kingdom and the assurance of appearing as glorious in the histories of his time; I put my head back and smiled at the superb animal, at the rosy—and cowardly—panther leaping; and then I glanced over his shoulder and tilted my head and looked sympathetically at Momma.

My sister shouted, "I know how to enjoy myself—I'll come too! . . ."

"Yes, yes," said Daddy, who was *never* averse to enlarging spheres of happiness and areas of sentiment. He held her hand and held me on his arm.

"Let him walk," my sister said. And: "He's getting bigger—you'll make a sissy out of him, Daddy. . . ."

Daddy said, "Shut up and enjoy the light—it's as beautiful as Paris and in our own backyard."

Out of folly, or a wish to steal his attention, or greed, my sister kept on: she asked if she could get something with some of the money; he dodged her question; and she kept on; and he grew peevish, so peevish, he returned to the house and accused Momma of having never taught her daughter not to be greedy— he sprawled, impetuous, displeased, semi-frantic in a chair: "I can't enjoy myself—there is no way a man can live in this house with all of you—I swear to God this will kill me soon. . . ."

Momma said to him, "I can't believe in the things you believe in—I'm not a girl anymore: when I play the fool, it isn't convinc- ing—you get angry with me when I try. You shouldn't get angry with her—you've spoiled her more than I have—and how do you expect her to act when you show her all that money—how do you think money affects people?"

I looked at him to see what the answer was, to see what he would answer. He said, "Charlotte, try being a rose and not a thorn."

At all times, and in all places, there is always the possibility that I will start to speak or will be looking at something and I will feel his face covering mine, as in a kiss and as a mask, turned both ways like that: and I am inside him, his presence, his thoughts, his language: *I* am languageless then for a moment, an automa- tion of repetition, a bagged piece of an imaginary river of de- scent.

I can't invent everything for myself: some always has to be what I already know: some of me always has to be him.

When he picked me up, my consciousness fitted itself to that position: I remember it—clearly. He could punish me—and did— by refusing to lift me, by denying me that union with him. Of course, the union was not one-sided: I was his innocence—as long as I was not an accusation, that is. I censored him—in that when he felt himself being, consciously, a father, he held back part of his other life, of his whole self: his shadows, his impressions, his adventures would not readily fit into me—what a gross and absurd rape that would have been.

So he was *careful*—he *walked on eggs*—there was an odd courtesy of his withdrawal behind his secrets, his secret sorrows and horrors, behind the curtain of what-is-suitable-for-a-child.

Sometimes he becomes simply a set of limits, of walls, inside which there is the caroming and echoing of my astounding sensibility amplified by being his son and in his arms and aloft; and he lays his sensibility aside or models his on mine, on my joy, takes his emotional coloring from me, like a mirror or a twin: his incomprehensibile life, with its strengths, ordeals, triumphs, crimes, horrors, his sadness and disgust, is enveloped and momentarily assuaged by my direct and indirect childish consolation. My gaze, my enjoying him, my willingness to be him, my joy at it, supported the baroque tower of his necessary but limited and maybe dishonest optimism.

One time he and Momma fought over money and he left: he packed a bag and went. Oh it was sad and heavy at home. I started to be upset, but then I retreated into an impenetrable stupidity: not knowing was better than being despairing. I was put to bed and I did fall asleep: I woke in the middle of the night; he had returned and was sitting on my bed—in the dark—a huge shadow in the shadows. He was stroking my forehead. When he saw my eyes open, he said in a sentimental, heavy voice, "I could never leave *you*—"

He didn't really mean it: I was an excuse: but he did mean it— the meaning and not-meaning were like the rise and fall of a wave in me, in the dark outside of me, between the two of us, between him and me (at other moments he would think of other truths, other than the one of he-couldn't-leave-me sometimes). He bent over sentimentally, painedly, not nicely, and he began to hug me; he put his head down, on my chest; my small heartbeat vanished into the near, sizable, anguished, angular, emotion-swollen one that was his. I kept advancing swiftly into wakefulness, my consciousness came rushing and widening blurredly, embracing the dark, his presence, his embrace. It's Daddy, it's Daddy—it's dark still—wakefulness rushed into the dark grave or grove of his hugely extended presence. His affection. My arms stumbled: there was no adequate embrace in me—I couldn't lift *him*—I had no adequacy yet except that of my charm or what-have-you, except things the grown-ups gave me—not things: traits, qualities. I mean my hugging his head was nothing until he said, "Ah, you love me. . . . You're all right. . . ."

Momma said: "They are as close as two peas in a pod—they are just alike—that child and Charley. That child is God to Charley. . . ."

He didn't always love me.

In the middle of the night that time, he picked me up after a while, he wrapped me in a blanket, held me close, took me downstairs in the dark; we went outside, into the night; it was dark and chilly but there was a moon—I thought he would take me to the wall but he just stood on our back deck. He grew tired of loving me; he grew abstracted and forgot me: the love that had just a moment before been so intently and tightly clasping and nestling went away, and I found myself released, into the cool night air, the floating damp, the silence, with the darkened houses around us.

I saw the silver moon, heard my father's breath, felt the itchiness of the woolen blanket on my hands, noticed its wool smell. I did this alone and I waited. Then when he didn't come back, I grew sleepy and put my head down against his neck: he was nowhere near me. Alone in his arms, I slept.

Over and over a moment seems to recur, something seems to return in its entirety, a name seems to be accurate: and we say it always happens like this. But we are wrong, of course.

I was a weird choice as someone for him to love.

So different from him in the way I was surprised by things.

I am a child with this mind. I am a child he has often rescued.

Our attachment to each other manifests itself in sudden swoops and grabs and rubs of attention, of being entertained, by each other, at the present moment.

I ask you, how is it possible it's going to last?

Sometimes when we are entertained by each other, we are bold about it, but just as frequently, it seems embarrassing, and we turn our faces aside.

His recollections of horror are more certain than mine. His suspicions are more terrible. There are darknesses in me I'm afraid of, but the ones in him don't frighten me but are like the dark in the yard, a dark a child like me might sneak into (and has)—a dark full of unseen shadowy almost-glowing presences—the fear, the danger—are desirable—difficult—with the call-to-be-brave: the childish bravura of *I must endure this* (knowing I can run away if I choose).

The child touches with his pursed, jutting, ignorant lips the large, handsome, odd, humid face of his father who can run away too. More dangerously.

He gave away a car of his that he was about to trade in on a new one: he gave it to a man in financial trouble; he did it after seeing a movie about crazy people being loving and gentle with each other and everyone else: Momma said to Daddy, "You can't do anything you want—you can't listen to your feelings—you have a family. . . ."

After seeing a movie in which a child cheered up an old man, he took me to visit an old man who probably was a distant relative, and who hated me at sight, my high coloring, the noise I might make, my father's affection for me: "Will he sit still? I can't stand noise. Charley, listen, I'm in bad shape—I think I have cancer and they won't tell me—"

"Nothing can kill a tough old bird like you, Ike. . . ."

The old man wanted all of Charley's attention—and strength—while he talked about how the small threads and thicker ropes that tied him to life were being cruelly tampered with.

Daddy patted me afterward, but oddly he was bored and disappointed in me as if I'd failed at something.

He could not seem to keep it straight about my value to him or to the world in general; he lived at the center of his own intellectual shortcomings and his moral pride: he needed it to be true, as an essential fact, that goodness—or innocence—was in him or was protected by him, and that, therefore, he was a good *man* and superior to other men, and did not deserve—certain common masculine fates—horrors—tests of his courage—certain pains. It was necessary to him to have it be true that he knew what real goodness was and had it in his life.

Perhaps that was because he didn't believe in God, and because he felt (with a certain self-love) that people, out in the world, didn't appreciate him and were needlessly difficult—"unloving": he said it often—and because it was true he was shocked and guilty and even enraged when he was "forced" into being unloving himself, or when he caught sight in himself of such a thing as cruelty, or cruel nosiness, or physical cowardice—God, how he hated being a coward—or hatred, physical hatred, even for me, if I was coy or evasive or disinterested or tired of him: it tore him apart literally—bits of madness, in varying degrees would grip him as in a Greek play: I see his mouth, his salmon-colored mouth, showing various degrees of sarcasm—sarcasm mounting into bitterness and even a ferocity without tears that always suggested to me, as a child, that he was near tears but had forgotten in his ferocity that he was about to cry.

Or he would catch sight of some evidence, momentarily inescapable—in contradictory or foolish statements of his or in unkept promises that it was clear he had never meant to keep, had never made any effort to keep—that he was a fraud; and sometimes he would laugh because he was a fraud—a good-hearted fraud, he believed—or he would be sullen or angry, a fraud caught either by the tricks of language so that in expressing affection absentmindedly he had expressed too much; or caught by greed and self-concern: he hated the evidence that he was mutable as hell: that he loved sporadically and egoistically, and often with rage and vengeance, and that madness I mentioned earlier: he couldn't stand those things: he usually forgot them; but sometimes when he was being tender, or noble, or self-sacrificing, he would sigh and be very sad—maybe because the good stuff was temporary. I don't know. Or sad that he did it only when he had the time and was in the mood. Sometimes he forgot such things and was superbly confident—or was that a bluff?

I don't know. I really can't speak for him.

I look at my hand and then at his; it is not really conceivable to me that both are hands: mine is a sort of a hand. He tells me over and over that I must not upset him—he tells me of my power over him—I don't know how to take such a fact—is it a fact? I stare at him. I gasp with the ache of life stirring in me—again:

again: *again*—I ache with tentative and complete and then again tentative belief.

For a long time piety was anything at all sitting still or moving slowly and not rushing at me or away from me but letting me look at it or be near it without there being any issue of safety-about-to-be-lost.

This world is evasive.

But someone who lets you observe him is not evasive, is not hurtful, at that moment: it is like in sleep where *the other* waits —the Master of Dreams—and there are doors, doorways opening into farther rooms where there is an altered light, and which I enter to find—what? That someone is gone? That the room is empty? Or perhaps I find a vista, of rooms, of archways, and a window, and a peach tree in flower—a tree with peach-colored flowers in the solitude of night.

I am dying of grief, Daddy. I am waiting here, limp with abandonment, with exhaustion: perhaps I'd better believe in God. . . .

My father's virtues, those I dreamed about, those I saw when I was awake, those I understood and misunderstood, were, as I felt them, in dreams or wakefulness, when I was a child, like a broad highway opening into a small dusty town that was myself; and down that road came bishops and slogans, Chinese processions, hasidim in a dance, the nation's honor and glory *in its young people,* baseball players, singers who sang "with their whole hearts," automobiles and automobile grilles, and grave or comic bits of instruction. This man is attached to me and makes me light up with festal affluence and oddity; he says, "I think you love me."

He was right.

He would move his head—his giant face—and you could observe in his eyes the small town which was me in its temporary sophistication, a small town giving proof on every side of its arrogance and its prosperity and its puzzled contentment.

He also instructed me in hatred: he didn't mean to, not openly: but I saw and picked up the curious buzzing of his puckered distastes, a nastiness of dismissal that he had: a fetor of let-them-

all-kill-each-other. He hated lots of people, whole races: he hated
ugly women.

He conferred an odd inverted splendor on awfulness—because
he knew about it: he went into it every day. He told me not to
want that, not to want to know about that: he told me to go on
being just the way I was—"a nice boy."

When he said something was unbearable, he meant it; he
meant he could not bear it.

In my memories of this time of my life, it seems to be summer
all the time, even when the ground is white: I suppose it seems
like summer because I was never cold.

Ah: I wanted to see. . . .

My father, when he was low (in spirit) would make rounds, inside his head, checking on his consciousness, to see if it was safe
from inroads by *"the unbearable"*: he found an all-is-well in a
quiet emptiness. . . .

In an uninvadedness, he found the weary complacency and self-
importance of All is Well.

(The women liked invasions—up to a point.)

One day he came home, mysterious, exalted, hatted and suited,
roseate, handsome, a little sweaty—it really was summer that day.
He was exalted—as I said—but nervous toward me—anxious with
promises.

And he was, oh, somewhat angry, justified, toward the world,
toward me, not exactly as a threat (in case I didn't respond) but
as a jumble.

He woke me from a nap, an uneasy nap, lifted me out of bed,
me, a child who had not expected to see him that afternoon—I
was not particularly happy that day, not particularly pleased with
him, not pleased with him at all, really.

He dressed me himself. At first he kept his hat on. After a
while, he took it off. When I was dressed, he said, "You're pretty
sour today," and he put his hat back on.

He hustled me down the stairs; he held my wrist in his enormous palm—immediate and gigantic to me and blankly suggestive
of a meaning I could do nothing about except stare at blankly
from time to time in my childish life.

We went outside into the devastating heat and glare, the blathering, humming afternoon light of a midwestern summer day: a familiar furnace.

We walked along the street, past the large, silent houses, set, each one, in hard, pure light. You could not look directly at anything, the glare, the reflections were too strong.

Then he lifted me in his arms—aloft.

He was carrying me to help me because the heat was bad—and worse near the sidewalk which reflected it upward into my face— and because my legs were short and I was struggling, because he was in a hurry and because he liked carrying me, and because I was sour and blackmailed him with my unhappiness, and he was being kind with a certain—limited—mixture of exasperation-turning-into-a-degree-of-mortal-love.

Or it was another time, really early in the morning, when the air was partly asleep, partly adance, but in veils, trembling with heavy moisture. Here and there, the air broke into a string of beads of pastel colors, pink, pale green, small rainbows, really small, and very narrow. Daddy walked rapidly. I bounced in his arms. My eyesight was unfocused—it bounced too. Things were more than merely present: they pressed against me: they had the aliveness of myth, of the beginning of an adventure when nothing is explained as yet.

All at once we were at the edge of a bankless river of yellow light. To be truthful, it was like a big, wooden beam of fresh, unweathered wood: but we entered it: and then it turned into light, cooler light than in the hot humming afternoon but full of bits of heat that stuck to me and then were blown away, a semi-heat, not really friendly, yet reassuring: and very dimly sweaty; and it grew, it spread: this light turned into a knitted cap of light, fuzzy, warm, woven, itchy: it was pulled over my head, my hair, my forehead, my eyes, my nose, my mouth.

So I turned my face away from the sun—I turned it so it was pressed against my father's neck mostly—and then I knew, in a childish way, knew from the heat (of his neck, of his shirt collar), knew by childish deduction, that his face was unprotected from the luminousness all around us: and I looked; and it was so; his face, for the moment unembarrassedly, was caught in that light. In an accidental glory.

I-80
NEBRASKA,
M.490–M.205

JOHN SAYLES

JOHN SAYLES was born in 1950 in Schenectady, New York. His first novel, *Pride of the Bimbos,* was published in 1975. He now lives in Boston and is at work on a second novel.

T HIS IS THAT ALABAMA REBEL, this is that Alabama Rebel, do I have a copy?"

"Ahh, 10-4 on that, Alabama Rebel."

"This is that Alabama Rebel westbound on 80, ah, what's your handle, buddy, and where you comin from?"

"This is that, ah, Toby Trucker, eastbound for that big O town, round about the 445 marker."

"I copy you clear, Toby Trucker. How's about that Smokey Bear situation up by that Lincoln town?"

"Ah, you'll have to hold her back a little through there, Alabama Rebel, ah, place is crawling with Smokies like usual. Saw three of em's lights up on the overpass just after the airport there."

"And how bout that Lincoln weigh station, they got those scales open?"

"Ah, negative on that, Alabama Rebel, I went by the lights was off, probably still in business back to that North Platte town."

"They don't get you coming they get you going. How bout that you-know-who, any sign of him tonight? That Ryder P. Moses?"

"Negative on that, thank God. Guy gives me the creeps."

"Did you, ah, ever actually hear him, Toby Trucker?"

"A definite 10-4 on that one, Alabama Rebel, and I'll never forget it. Coming down from that Scottsbluff town three nights ago I copied him. First he says he's northbound, then he says he's southbound, then he's right on my tail singing 'The Wabash Cannonball.' Man blew by me outside of that Oshkosh town on 26, must of been going a hundred plus. Little two-lane blacktop and he thinks he's Parnelli Jones at the Firecracker 500."

"You see him? You see what kind of rig he had?"

"A definite shit-no negative on that. I was fighting to keep the road. The man aint human."

"Ah, maybe not, Toby Trucker, maybe not. Never copied him myself, but I talked with a dozen guys who have in the last couple weeks."

"Ahh, maybe you'll catch him tonight."

"Long as he don't catch me."

"Got a point there, Alabama Rebel. Ahhhh, I seem to be losing you here—"

"10-4. Coming up to that Lincoln town, buddy. I thank you kindly for the information and ah, I hope you stay out of trouble in that big O town and maybe we'll modulate again some night. This is that Alabama Rebel, over and out."

"This is Toby Trucker, eastbound, night now."

Westbound on 80 is a light-stream, ruby-strung big rigs rolling straight into the heart of Nebraska. Up close they are a river in breakaway flood, bouncing and pitching and yawing, while a mile distant they are slow-oozing lava. To their left is the eastbound stream, up ahead the static glare of Lincoln. Lights. The world in black and white and red, broken only by an occasional blue flasher strobing the ranger hat of a state policeman. Smokey the Bear's campfire. Westbound 80 is an insomniac world of lights passing lights to the music of the Civilian Band.

"This that Arkansas Traveler, this that Arkansas Traveler, do you copy?"

"How bout that Scorpio Ascending, how bout that Scorpio Ascending, you out there, buddy?"

"This is Chromedome at that 425 marker, who's that circus

wagon up ahead? Who's that old boy in the Mrs. Smith's pie-
pusher?"

They own the highway at night, the big rigs, slip-streaming in
caravans, hopscotching to take turns making the draft, strutting
the thousands of dollars they've paid in road taxes on their back
ends. The men feel at home out here, they leave their cross-eyed
headlights eating whiteline, forget their oily-aired, kidney-jamming
cabs to talk out in the black air, to live on the Band.

"This is Roadrunner, westbound at 420, any you eastbound
people fill me in on the Smokies up ahead?"

"Ahh, copy you, Roadrunner, she's been clean all the way from
that Grand Island town, so motormotor."

(A moving van accelerates.)

"How bout that Roadrunner, this is Overload up to 424, that
you behind me?"

(The van's headlights blink up and down.)

"Well come on up, buddy, let's put the hammer down on this
thing."

The voices are nasal and tinny, broken by squawks, something
human squeezed through wire. A decade of televised astronauts
gives them their style and self-importance.

"Ahh, breaker, Overload, we got us a code blue here. There's a
four-wheeler coming up fast behind me, might be a Bear wants to
give us some green stamps."

"Breaker break, Roadrunner. Good to have you at the back
door. We'll hold her back a while, let you check out that four-
wheeler."

(The big rigs slow and the passenger car pulls alongside of
them.)

"Ahh, negative on that Bear, Overload, it's just a civilian. Fella
hasn't heard bout that five-five limit."

"10-4 and motormotor."

(Up front now, the car is nearly whooshed off the road when
the big rigs blow past. It wavers a moment, then accelerates to try
and take them, but can only make it alongside before they speed
up. The car falls back, then tries again.)

"Ah, look like we got us a problem, Roadrunner. This uh, Vega
—whatever it is, some piece of Detroit shit, wants to play games."

"Looks like it, Overload."

"Don't know what a four-wheeler is doing on the Innerstate this time of night anyhow. Shunt be allowed out with us working people. You want to give me a hand on this, Roadrunner?"

"10-4. I'll be the trapper, you be the sweeper. What we got ahead?"

"There's an exit up to the 402 marker. This fucker gets off the ride at Beaver Crossing."

(The trucks slow and the car passes them, honking, cutting sharp to the inside lane. They let it cruise for a moment, then the lead rig pulls alongside of it and the second closes up behind, inches from the car's rear fender. The car tries to run but they stay with it, boxing it, then pushing it faster and faster till the sign appears ahead on the right and the lead truck bulls to the inside, forcing the car to squeal off into the exit ramp.)

"Mission accomplished there, Roadrunner."

"Roger."

They have their own rules, the big rigs, their own road and radio etiquette that is tougher in its way than the Smokies' law. You join the club, you learn the rules, and woe to the man who breaks them.

"All you westbound! All you westbound! Keep your ears peeled up ahead for that you-know-who! He's on the loose again tonight. Ryder P. Moses!"

There is a crowding of channels, a buzzing on the airwaves. Ryder P. Moses!

"Who?"

"Ryder P. Moses! Where you been, trucker?"

"Who is he?"

"Ryder—!"

"—crazy—"

"—weird—"

"—P.—!"

"—dangerous—"

"—probly a cop—"

"—Moses!"

"He's out there tonight!"

"I copied him going eastbound."

"I copied him westbound."

"I copied him standing still on an overpass."

Ryder P. Moses!

On 80 tonight. Out there somewhere. Which set of lights, which channel, is he listening? Does he know we know?

What do we know?

Only that he's been copied on and around 80 every night for a couple weeks now and that he's a terminal case of the heebiejeebs, he's an overdose of strange. He's been getting worse and worse, wilder and wilder, breaking every trucker commandment and getting away with it. Ryder P. Moses, he says, no handle, no Gutslinger or Green Monster or Oklahoma Crude, just Ryder P. Moses. No games with the Smokies, no hide-and-seek, just an open challenge. This is Ryder P. Moses eastbound at 260, going ninety per, he says. Catch me if you can. But the Smokies can't, and it bugs the piss out of them, so they're thick as flies along Nebraska 80, hunting for the crazy son, nailing poor innocent everyday truckers poking at seventy-five, Ryder P. Moses. Memorizes your license, your make, and your handle, then describes you from miles away, when you can't see another light on the entire plain, and tells you he's right behind you, watch out, here he comes right up your ass, watch out watch out! Modulating from what must be an illegal amount of wattage, coming on sometimes with "Ici Radio Canada" and gibbering phony frog over the CB, warning of ten-truck pile-ups and collapsed overpasses that never appear, leading truckers to put the hammer down right into a Smokey with a picture machine till nobody knows who to believe over the Band anymore. Till conversations start with "I am not now nor have I ever been Ryder P. Moses." A truck driver's gremlin that everyone has either heard or heard about, but no one has ever seen.

"Who is this Ryder P. Moses? Int that name familiar?"

"Wunt he that crazy independent got hisself shot up during the Troubles?"

"Wunt he a leg-breaker for the Teamsters?"

"Dint he use to be with P.I.E.?"

"—Allied?"

"—Continental Freightways?"

"—drive a 2500-gallon oil tanker?"

"—run liquor during Prohibition?"

"—run nylons during the War?"
"—run turkeys during Christmas?"
"Int that the guy? Sure it is."
"Short fella."
"Tall guy."
"Scar on his forehead, walks with a limp, left-hand index finger is missing."
"Sure, right, wears a leather jacket."
"—and a down vest."
"—and a lumber jacket and a Hawaiian shirt and a crucifix round his neck."
"Sure, that's the fella, medium height, always dressed in black. Ryder P. Moses."
"Dint he die a couple years back?"
"Sheeit, they aint no such person an never was."
"Ryder P. who?"
"Moses. This is Ryder P. Moses."
"What? Who said that?!"
"I did. Good evening, gentlemen."

Fingers fumble for volume knobs and squelch controls, conversations are dropped and attention turned. The voice is deep and emphatic.

"I'm Ryder P. Moses and I can outhaul, outhonk, outclutch any leadfoot this side of truckers' heaven. I'm half Mack, half Peterbilt, and half Sherman don't-tread-on-me tank. I drink fifty gallons of propane for breakfast and fart pure poison. I got steel mesh teeth, a chrome-plated nose, and three feet of stick on the floor. I'm the Paul mother-lovin Bunyan of the Interstate system and I don't care who knows it. I'm Ryder P. Moses and all you people are driving on *my* goddamn road. Don't you spit, don't you litter, don't you pee on the pavement. Just mind your p's and q's and we won't have any trouble."

Trucks pull alongside each other, the drivers peering across suspiciously, then both wave hands over head to deny guilt. They change channels and check each other out—handle, company, destination. They gang up on other loners and demand identification, challenge each other with trivia as if the intruder were a Martian or a Nazi spy. What's the capital of Tennessee, Tennes-

see Stomper? How far from Laramie to Cheyenne town, Casper
Kid ?Who won the '38 World Series, Truckin Poppa?

Small convoys form, grow larger, posses ranging eastbound and
westbound on I-80. Only the CB can prove that the enemy is not
among them, not the neighboring pair of taillights, the row of red
up top like Orion's belt. He scares them for a moment, this Ryder
P. Moses, scares them out of the air and back into their jarring
hotboxes, back to work. But he thrills them a little, too.

"You still there, fellas? Good. It's question and answer period.
Answer me this: do you know where your wife or loved one is
right now? I mean *really know* for sure? You been gone a long
time fellas, and you know how they are. Weak before Temptation. That's why we love em, that's how we get next to em in the
first place, int it, fellas? There's just no telling *what* they're up to,
is there? How bout that Alabama Rebel, you know where that little girl of yours is right now? What she's gettin herself into? This
minute? And you there, Overload, how come the old lady's always
so tired when you pull in late at night? What's she done to be so
fagged out? She aint been haulin freight all day like you have. Or
has she? I tell you fellas, take a tip from old Ryder P., you can't
ever be certain of a *thing* in this world. You out here ridin the Interstate, somebody's likely back home riding that little girl. I
mean just *think* about it, think about the way she looks, the faces
she makes, the way she starts to smell, the things she says. The
noises she makes. Now picture them shoes under that bed, ain't
they a little too big? Since when did you wear size twelves?
Buddy, I hate to break it to you but maybe she's right now giving
it, giving those faces and that smell and those noises, giving it all
to some other guy.

"Some size twelve.

"You know how they are, those women, you see them in the
truck stops pouring coffee. All those Billie Raes and Bobbi Sues,
those Debbies and Annettes, those ass-twitching little things you
marry and try to keep in a house. You know how they are.
They're not built for one man, fellas, it's a fact of nature. I just
want you to think about that for a while, chew on it, remember
the last time you saw your woman and figure how long it'll be before you see her again. Think on it, fellas."

And, over the cursing and threats of truckers flooding his channel he begins to sing—

> In the phone booth—at the truckstop
> All alone,
> I listen to the constant ringing—of your phone.
> I'd try the bars and hangouts where
> You might be found,
> But I don't dare,
> You might be there,
> You're slippin round.

They curse and threaten but none of them turn him off. And some do think on it. Think as they have so many times before, distrusting with or without evidence, hundred-mile stretches of loneliness and paranoia. How can they know for sure their woman is any different from what they believe all women they meet to be —willing, hot, eager for action? Game in season. What *does* she do, all that riding time?

> I imagine—as I'm hauling
> Back this load.
> You waiting for me—at the finish
> Of the road.
> But as I wait for your hello
> There's not a sound.
> I start to weep,
> You're not asleep,
> You're slippin round.

The truckers overcrowd the channel in their rush to copy him, producing only a squarking complaint, something like a chorus of "Old MacDonald" sung from fifty fathoms deep. Finally the voice of Sweetpea comes through the jam and the others defer to her, as they always do. They have almost all seen her at one time or another, at some table in the Truckers Only section of this or that pit stop, and know she is a regular old gal, handsome looking in a country sort of way and able to field a joke and toss it back. Not so brassy as Colorado Hooker, not so butch as Flatbed Mama, you'd let that Sweetpea carry your load any old day.

"How bout that Ryder P. Moses, how bout that Ryder P. Moses, you out there, sugar? You like to modulate with a me a little bit?"

The truckers listen, envying the crazy son for this bit of female attention.

"Ryder P.? This is that Sweetpea moving along about that 390 mark, do you copy me?"

"Ah, yes, the Grande Dame of the Open Road! How's everything with Your Highness tonight?"

"Oh, passable, Mr. Moses, passable. But you don't sound none too good yourself, if you don't mind my saying. I mean we're just worried *sick* about you. You sound a little—over*strained?*"

"*Au contraire*, Madam, *au contraire.*"

She's got him, she has. You catch more flies with honey than with vinegar.

"Now tell me, honey, when's the last time you had yourself any sleep?"

"Sleep? *Sleep* she says! Who sleeps?"

"Why just *evrybody*, Mr. Moses. It's a natural fact."

"That, Madam, is where you are mistaken. Sleep is obsolete, a thing of the bygone ages. It's been synthesized, chemically duplicated and sold at your corner apothecary. You can load up on it before a long trip—"

"Now I just don't know *what* you're talkin bout."

"Insensibility, Madam, stupor. The gift of Morpheus."

"Fun is fun, Ryder P. Moses, but you just not making *sense.* We are *not* amused. And we all getting a little bit *tired* of all your prankin around. And we—"

"Tired, did you say? Depressed? Overweight? Got that run-down feeling? Miles to go before you sleep? Friends and neighbors I got just the thing for you, a miracle of modern pharmacology! Vim and vigor, zip and zest, bright eyes and bushy tails—all these can be *yours*, neighbor, relief is just a swallow away! A couple of Co-Pilots in the morning orange juice, Purple Hearts for lunch, a mouthful of Coast-to-Coast for the wee hours of the night, and you'll droop no more. Ladies and gents, the best cure for time and distance is Speed. And we're all familiar with that, aren't we folks? We've all popped a little pep in our day, haven't we? Puts you on top of the world and clears your sinuses to boot. Wire

yourself home with a little methamphetamine sulfate, melts in
your mind, not in your mouth. No chocolate mess. Step right up
and get on the ride, pay no heed to that man with the eight-ball
eyes! Start with a little propadrine maybe, from the little woman's
medicine cabinet? Clear up that stuffy nose? Then work your way
up to the full-tilt boogie, twelve-plus grams of Crystal a day! It
kind of grows on you, doesn't it, neighbor? Start eating that Sleep
and you won't want to eat anything else. You know all about it,
don't you, brothers and sisters of the Civilian Band, you've all
been on that roller coaster. The only way to fly."

"Now Ryder, you just calm—"

> "Benzedrine, Dexedrine,
> We got the stash!"

he chants like a high-school cheerleader,

> "Another thousand miles
> Before the crash."

"Mr. Moses, you can't—"

> "Coffee and aspirin,
> No-Doz, Meth.
> Spasms, hypertension,
> Narcolepsy, death.
> "Alpha, methyl,
> Phenyl too,
> Ethyl-amine's good for you!

> "Cause when you're up you're up,
> An when you're down you're down,
> But when you're up behind Crystal
> You're upside down!"

The airwaves crackle with annoyance. Singing on the CB! Sass-
ing their woman, their Sweetpea, with drug talk and four-syllable
words!

"—man's crazy—"
"—s'got to go—"
"—FCC ever hears—"
"—fix his wagon—"

"—like to catch—"

"—hophead—"

"—pill-poppin—"

"—weird talkin—"

"—turn him *off!*"

"Now boys," modulates Sweetpea, cooing soft and smooth, "I'm sure we can talk this whole thing out. Ryder P., honey, whoever you are, you must be runnin out of *fuel*. I mean you been going at it for *days* now, flittin round this Innerstate never coming to light. Must be just all *out* by now, aren't you?"

"I'm going strong, little lady, I got a bottle full of energy left and a thermos of Maxwell House to wash them down with."

"I don't mean *that*, Mr. Moses, I mean fuel *awl*. Int your tanks a little low? Must be runnin pert near empty, aren't you?"

"Madam, you have a point."

"Well if you don't fuel up pretty soon, you just gon be out of *luck*, Mister, they isn't but one more place westbound between here and that Grand Island town. Now Imo pull in that Bosselman's up ahead, fill this old hog of mine up. Wynch you just join me, I'll buy you a cup of coffee and we'll have us a little chitchat? That truck you got, whatever it is, can't run on no *pills*."

"Madam, it's a date. I got five or six miles to do and then it's Bosselman's for me and Old Paint here. Yes indeedy."

The other channels come alive. Bosselman's, on the westbound, he's coming down! That Sweetpea could talk tears from a statue, an oyster from its shell. Ryder P. Moses in person, hotdamn!

They barrel onto the off-ramp, eastbound and westbound, full tanks and empty, a steady caravan of light bleeding off the main artery, leaving only scattered four-wheelers to carry on. They line up behind the diner in rows, twin stacks belching, all ears.

"This is that Ryder P. Moses, this is that Ryder P. Moses, in the parking lot at Bosselman's. Meet you in the coffee shop, Sweetpea."

Cab doors swing open and they vault down onto the gravel, some kind of reverse Grand Prix start, with men trotting away from their machines to the diner. They stampede at the door and mill suspiciously. Is that him, is that him? Faces begin to connect with handles, remembered from some previous nighttime break. Hey, there's old Roadrunner, Roadrunner, this is Arkansas Traveler, I known him from before, he aint it, who's that over there? Overload, you say? You was up on I-29 the other night, north of Council Bluffs, wunt you? What you mean no, I had you on for pert near a half hour! You were where? Who says? Roadrunner, how could you talk to him on Nebraska 83 when I'm talking to him on I-29? Overload, somebody been takin your name in vain. What's that? You modulated with me yesterday from Rawlins? Buddy, I'm out of that Davenport town last evening, I'm *west*-bound. Clutch Cargo, the one and only, always was and always will be. You're kidding! The name-droppin snake! Fellas we got to get to the bottom of this, but quick.

It begins to be clear, as they form into groups of three or four who can vouch for each other, that this Ryder P. Moses works in mysterious ways. That his voice, strained through capacitors and diodes, can pass for any of theirs, that he knows them, handle and style. It's outrageous, it is, it's like stealing mail or wiretapping, like forgery. How long has he gotten away with it, what has he said using their identities, what secrets spilled or discovered? If Ryder P. Moses has been each of them from time to time, what is to stop him from being one of them now? Which old boy among them is running a double life, which has got a glazed look around the eyes, a guilty twitch at the mouth? They file in to find Sweetpea sitting at a booth, alone.

"Boys," she says, "I believe I just been stood up."

They grumble back to their rigs, leaving waitresses with order pads gaping. The civilians in the diner buzz and puzzle—some mass, vigilante threat? Teamster extortion? Paramilitary maneuvers? They didn't like the menu? The trucks roar from the Bosselman's abruptly as they came.

On the Interstate again, they hear the story from Axle Sally. Sally broadcasts from the Husky three miles up on the eastbound side. Seems a cattle truck is pulled up by the pumps there, left idling. The boy doesn't see the driver, all he knows is it's pretty ripe, even for a stock-hauler. Something more than the usual cow-shit oozing out from the air spaces. He tries to get a look inside but it's hard to get that close with the smell and all, so he grabs a flashlight and plays it around in back. And what do you think he sees? Dead. Dead for some time from the look of them, ribs show-

ing, legs splayed, a heap of bad meat. Between the time it takes
the boy to run in to tell Sally till they get back out to the pumps,
whoever it was driving the thing has pumped himself twenty gallons and taken a powder. Then comes the call to Sally's radio, put
it on my tab, he says. Ryder P. Moses, westbound.

They can smell it in their minds, the men who have run cattle
or have had a stock wagon park beside them in the sleeping lot of
some truck stop, the thought of it makes them near sick. Crazy.
Stone wild crazy.

"Hello there again, friends and neighbors, this is Ryder P.
Moses, the Demon of the Dotted Line, the Houdini of the Highways. Hell on eighteen wheels. Sorry if I inconvenienced anybody
with the little change of plans there, but fuel oil was going for
two cents a gallon cheaper at the Husky, and I never could pass up
a bargain. Funny I didn't see any of you folks there, y'ought to be
a little sharper with your consumer affairs. These are hard times,
people, don't see how you can afford to let that kind of savings go
by. I mean us truckers of all people should see the writing on the
wall, the bad news in the dollars and cents department. Do we
'Keep America Moving' or don't we? And you know as well as me,
there ain't shit moving these days. Poor honest independent don't
have a Chinaman's chance, and even Union people are being un-
saddled left and right. Hard times, children. Just isn't enough
stuff has to get from here to there to keep us in business. Hell, the
only way to make it is to carry miscellaneous freight. Get that per-
item charge on a full load and you're golden. Miscellaneous—"

(The blue flashers are coming now, zipping by the westbound
truckers, sirenless in twos and threes, breaking onto the channel
to say don't panic, boys, all we want is the cattle truck. All the
trophy we need for tonight is Moses, you just lay back and relax.
Oh those Smokies, when they set their minds to a thing they
don't hold back, they hump after it full choke and don't spare the
horse. Ryder P. Moses, your ass is *grass*. Smokey the Bear on your
case and he will douse your fire. Oh yes.)

"—freight. Miscellaneous freight. Think about it, friends and
neighbors, brothers and sisters, think about what exactly it is we
haul all over God's creation here, about the goods and what they
mean. About what they actually mean to you and me and everyone else in this great and good corporate land of ours. Think of

what you're hauling right now. Ambergris for Amarillo? Gaskets for Gary? Oil for Ogalalla, submarines for Schenectady? Veal for Vermillion?"

(The Smokies moving up at nearly a hundred per, a shooting stream in the outside lane, for once allied to the truckers.)

"Tomato for Mankato, manna for Tarzana, stew for Kalamazoo, jerky for Albuquerque. Fruit for Butte."

(Outdistancing all the legitimate truckers, the Smokies are a blue pulsing in the sky ahead, the whole night on the blink.)

"Boise potatoes for Pittsburgh pots. Scottsbluff sugar for Tampa tea. Forage and fertilizer. Guns and caskets. Bull semen and hamburger. Sweetcorn, soy, stethoscopes and slide rules. Androids and zinnias. But folks, somehow we always come back empty. Come back less than we went. Diminished. It's a law of nature, it is, a law—"

They come upon it at the 375 marker, a convention of Bears flashing around a cattle truck on the shoulder of the road. What looks to be a boy or a very young man spread-eagled against the side of the cab, a half-dozen official hands probing his hidden regions. The trucks slow, one by one, but there is no room to stop. They roll down their co-pilot windows, but the only smell is the thick electric-blue of too many cops in one place.

"You see im? You see im? Just a kid!"

"—prolly stole it in the first place—"

"—gone crazy on drugs—"

"—fuckin hippie or somethin—"

"—got his ass but good—"

"—know who he is?"

"—know his handle?"

"—seem im before?"

"—the end of him, anyhow."

All order and etiquette gone with the excitement, they chew it over among themselves, who he might be, why he went wrong, what they'll do with him. Curiosity, and already a kind of disappointment. That soon it will be all over, all explained, held under the dull light of police classification, made into just some crackpot kid who took a few too many diet pills to help him through the night. It is hard to believe that the pale, skinny boy frisked in their headlights was who kept them turned around for weeks, who pried his way into their nightmares, who haunted the CB and out-ran the Smokies. That he could be the one who made the hours between Lincoln and Cheyenne melt into suspense and tension, that he could be—

"Ryder P. Moses, westbound on 80. Where *are* all you people?"

"Who?"

"What?"

"Where?"

"Ryder P. Moses, who else? Out here under that big black sky, all by his lonesome. I sure would preciate some company. Seems like you all dropped out of the running a ways back. Thought I seen some Bear tracks in my rear-view, maybe that's it. Now it's just me an a couple tons of beef. Can't say these steers is much for conversation, though. Nosir, you just can't beat a little pa-laver with your truckin brothers and sisters on the old CB to pass the time. Do I have a copy out there? Anybody?"

They switch to the channel they agreed on at the Bosselman's, and the word goes on down the line. He's still loose! He's still out there! The strategy is agreed on quickly—silent running. Let him sweat it out alone, talk to himself for a while and haul ass to catch him. It will be a race.

(Coyote, in an empty flatbed, takes the lead.)

"You've probably all wondering why I called you together to-night. Education. I mean to tell you some things you ought to know. Things about life, death, eternity. You know, tricks of the trade. The popular mechanics of the soul. A little exchange of ideas, communication, I-talk-you-listen, right?"

(Up ahead, far ahead, Coyote sees taillights. Taillights moving at least as fast as he, almost eight-five in a strong crosswind. He muscles the clutch and puts the hammer down.)

"Friends, it's all a matter of wheels. Cycles. Clock hand always ends up where it started out, sun always dips back under the cornfield, people always plowed back into the ground. Take this beef chain I'm in on. We haul the semen to stud, the calves to rangeland, the one-year-olds to the feedlot, then to the slaugh-terhouse the packer the supermarket the corner butcher the table of J.Q. Public. J.Q. scarfs it down, puts a little body in his jizz, pumps a baby a year into the wife till his heart fattens and flops, and next thing you know he's pushing up grass on the lone pray-ree. You always end up less than what you were. The universe it-self is shrinking. In cycles."

(Coyote closes to within a hundred yards. It is a cattle truck. He can smell it through his vent. When he tries to come closer it accelerates over a hundred, back end careening over two lanes. Coyote feels himself losing control, eases up. The cattle truck eases too, keeping a steady hundred yards between them. They settle back to eighty per.)

"Engines. You can grease them, oil them, clean their filters and replace their plugs, recharge them, antifreeze and STP them, treat them like a member of the family, but poppa, the miles take their toll, Time and Distance bring us all to rust. We haul engines from Plant A to Plant B to be seeded in bodies, we haul them to the dealers, buy them and waltz around a couple numbers, then drag them to the scrapyard. Junk City, U.S.A., where they break down into the iron ore of a million years from now. Some cycles take longer than others. Everything in this world is a long fall, a coming to rest, and an engine only affects where the landing will be.

"The cure for Time and Distance is Speed. Did you know that if you could travel at the speed of light you'd never age? That if you went faster than it, you would get younger? Think about that one, friends and neighbors, a cycle reversed. What happens when you reach year zero, egg and tadpole time, and keep speeding along? Do you turn into your parents? Put that in your carburetor and slosh it around."

And on he goes, into Relativity, the relationship of matter and energy, into the theory of the universe as a great Mobius strip, a snake swallowing its own tail. Leaving Coyote far behind, though the hundred yards between stays constant. On he goes, into the life of a cell, gerontology, cryogenics, hibernation theory. Through the seven stages of man and beyond, through the history of aging, the literature of immortality.

(Through Grand Island and Kearney, through Lexington and Cozad and Gothenburg, with Coyote at his heels, through a hun-dred high-speed miles of physics and biology and lunatic-fringe theology.)

"You can beat them, though, all these cycles. Oh yes, I've

found the way. Never stop. If you never stop you can outrun
them. It's when you lose your momentum that they get you.

"Take Sleep, the old whore. The seducer of the vital spark.
Ever look at yourself in the mirror after Sleep has had hold of
you, ever check your face out? Eyes pouched, neck lined, mouth
puckered, it's all been worked on, cycled. Aged, Wrinkle City.
The cycle catches you napping and carries you off a little closer to
the ground. Sleep, ladies, when it has you under, those crows
come tiptoeing on your face, sinking their tracks into you. Sleep,
gents, you wake from her half stiff with urine, stumble out to do
an old man's aimless, too-yellow pee. It bloats your prostate, pulls
your paunch, plugs your ears, and gauzes your eyes. It sucks you,
Sleep, sucks you dry and empty, strains the dream from your mind
and the life from your body."

(Reflector posts ripping by, engine complaining, the two of
them barreling into Nebraska on the far edge of control.)

"And you people let it have you, you surrender with open arms.
Not me. Not Ryder P. Moses. I swallow my sleep in capsules and
keep one step ahead. Rest not, rust not. Once you break from the
cycle, escape that dull gravity, then, people, you travel in a
straight line and there is nothing so pure in this world. The Interstate goes on forever and you never have to get off.

"And it's beautiful. Beautiful. The things a sleeper never sees
open up to you. The most beautiful dream is the waking one, the
one that never ends. From a straight line you see all the cycles
going on without you, night fading in and out, the sun's arch,
stars forming and shifting in their signs. The night especially, the
blacker the better, your headlights making a ghost of color on the
roadside, focusing to climb the white line. You feel like you can
ride deeper and deeper into it, that night is a state you never
cross, but only get closer and closer to its center. And in the daytime there's the static of cornfields, cornfields, cornfields, flat mo-
notony like a hum in your eye, like you're going so fast it seems
you're standing still, that the country is a still life on your windshield."

(It begins to weave gently in front of Coyote now, easing to the
far right, nicking the shoulder gravel, straightening for a few
miles, then drifting left. Nodding. Coyote hangs back a little further, held at bay by a whiff of danger.)

"Do you know what metaphor is, truckin mamas and poppas? Have you ever met with it in your waking hours? Benzedrine, there's a metaphor for you, and a good one. For sleep. It serves the same purpose but makes you understand better, makes everything clear, opens the way to more metaphor. Friends and neighbors, have you ever seen dinosaurs lumbering past you, the road sizzle like a fuse, night drip down like old blood? I have, people, I've seen things only gods and the grandfather stars have seen, I've seen dead men sit in my cab beside me and living ones melt like wax. When you break through the cycle you're beyond the laws of man, beyond CB manners or Smokies' sirens or statutes of limitations. You're beyond the laws of nature, time, gravity, friction, forget them. The only way to win is never to stop. Never to stop. Never to stop."

The sentences are strung out now, a full minute or two between them.

"The only escape from friction is a vacuum."

(Miles flying under, North Platte glowing vaguely ahead on the horizon, Coyote, dogged, hangs on.)

There is an inexplicable crackling on the wire, as if he were growing distant. There is nothing for miles to interfere between them. "The shortest distance—between two points—ahh—a straight line."

(Two alone on the plain, tunneling Nebraska darkness.)

"Even the earth—is falling. Even—the sun—is burning out."

(The side-to-side drifting more pronounced now, returns to the middle more brief. Coyote strains to pick the voice from electric jam. North Platte's display brightens. Miles pass.)

"Straight—"

There is a very loud crackling now, his speaker open but his words hung, a crackling past the Brady exit, past Maxwell. (Coyote creeping up a bit, then lagging as the stock-hauler picks up speed and begins to slalom for real. Coyote tailing it like a hunter after a gut-ripped animal spilling its last, and louder crackling as it lurches, fishtails, and lurches ahead wheels screaming smoke spewing saved only by the straightness of the road and crackling back when Coyote breaks into the Band yelling Wake up! Wake up! Wake up! pulling horn and flicking lights till the truck ahead steadies, straddling half on half off the right shoulder in direct line with the upspeeding concrete support of an overpass and he speaks. Calm and clear and direct.)

"This is Ryder P. Moses," he says. "Going west. Good night and happy motoring."

(Coyote swerves through the flameout, fights for the road as the sky begins a rain of beef.)

ROSES, RHODODENDRON

ALICE ADAMS

Alice Adams grew up in Chapel Hill, North Carolina, and since then has lived mainly in San Francisco. This is her sixth appearance in the O. Henry Prize Stories. Her novel *Familes and Survivors* was published in 1975.

For Judith

O NE DARK AND RAINY Boston spring of many years ago, I spent all my after-school and evening hours in the living room of our antique-crammed Cedar Street flat, writing down what the Ouija board said to my mother. My father, a spoiled and rowdy Irishman, a sometime engineer, had run off to New Orleans with a girl, and my mother hoped to learn from the board if he would come back. Then, one night in May, during a crashing black thunderstorm (my mother was both afraid and much in awe of storms), the board told her to move down South, to North Carolina, taking me and all the antiques she had been collecting for years, and to open a store in a small town down there. That is what we did, and shortly thereafter, for the first time in my life, I fell violently and permanently in love: with a house, with a family of three people, and with an area of countryside.

Perhaps too little attention is paid to the necessary preconditions of "falling in love"—I mean the state of mind or place that precedes one's first sight of the loved person (or house or land). In my own case, I remember the dark Boston afternoons as a precondition of love. Later on, for another important time, I recognized boredom in a job. And once the fear of growing old.

In the town that she had chosen, my mother, Margot (she

picked out her own name, having been christened Margaret),
rented a small house on a pleasant back street. It had a big sur-
rounding screened-in porch, where she put most of the antiques,
and she put a discreet sign out in the front yard: "Margot—Antiques." The store was open only in the afternoons. In the mornings and on Sundays, she drove around the countryside in our
ancient and spacious Buick, searching for trophies among the area's
country stores and farms and barns. (She is nothing if not enter-
prising; no one else down there had thought of doing that before.)

Although frequently embarrassed by her aggression—she
thought nothing of making offers for furniture that was in use in
a family's rooms—I often drove with her during those first few
weeks. I was excited by the novelty of the landscape. The red clay
banks that led up to the thick pine groves, the swollen brown
creeks half hidden by flowering tangled vines. Bare, shaded yards
from which rose gaunt, narrow houses. Chickens that scattered,
barefoot children who stared at our approach.

"Hello there. I'm Mrs. John Kilgore—Margot Kilgore—and I'm
interested in buying old furniture. Family portraits. Silver."

Margot a big brassily bleached blonde in a pretty flowered silk
dress and high-heeled patent sandals. A hoarse and friendly voice.
Me a scrawny, pale, curious girl, about ten, in a blue linen dress
with smocking across the bodice. (Margot has always had a passionate belief in good clothes, no matter what.)

On other days, Margot would say, "I'm going to look over my
so-called books. Why don't you go for a walk or something, Jane?"

And I would walk along the sleepy, leafed-over streets, on the
unpaved sidewalks, past houses that to me were as inviting and as
interesting as unread books, and I would try to imagine what
went on inside. The families. Their lives.

The main street, where the stores were, interested me least.
Two-story brick buildings—dry-goods stores, with dentists' and
lawyers' offices above. There was also a drugstore, with round marble tables and wire-backed chairs, at which wilting ladies sipped at
their Cokes (this was to become a favorite haunt of Margot's). I
preferred the civic monuments: a pre-Revolutionary Episcopal
chapel of yellowish cracked plaster, and several tall white statues
to the Civil War dead—all of them quickly overgrown with ivy or
Virginia creeper.

These were the early nineteen-forties, and in the next few years the town was to change enormously. Its small textile factories would be given defense contracts (parachute silk); a Navy preflight school would be established at a neighboring university town. But at that moment it was a sleeping village. Untouched.

My walks were not a lonely occupation, but Margot worried that they were, and some curious reasoning led her to believe that a bicycle would help. (Of course, she turned out to be right.) We went to Sears, and she bought me a big new bike—blue, with balloon tires—on which I began to explore the outskirts of town and the countryside.

The house I fell in love with was about a mile out of town, on top of a hill. A small stone bank that was all overgrown with tangled roses led up to its yard, and pink and white roses climbed up a trellis to the roof of the front porch—the roof on which, later, Harriet and I used to sit and exchange our stores of erroneous sexual information. Harriet Farr was the daughter of the house. On one side of the house, there was what looked like a newer wing, with a bay window and a long side porch, below which the lawn sloped down to some flowering shrubs. There was a yellow rosebush, rhododendron, a plum tree, and beyond were woods—pines, and oak and cedar trees. The effect was rich and careless, generous and somewhat mysterious. I was deeply stirred.

As I was observing all this, from my halted bike on the dusty white hilltop, a small, plump woman, very erect, came out of the front door and went over to a flower bed below the bay window. She sat down very stiffly. (Emily, who was Harriet's mother, had some terrible, never diagnosed trouble with her back; she generally wore a brace.) She was older than Margot, with very beautiful white hair that was badly cut in that butchered nineteen-thirties way.

From the first, I was fascinated by Emily's obvious dissimilarity to Margot. I think I was also somehow drawn to her contradictions—the shapeless body held up with so much dignity, even while she was sitting in the dirt. The lovely chopped-off hair. (There were greater contradictions, which I learned of later—she was a Virginia Episcopalian who always voted for Norman Thomas, a feminist who always delayed meals for her tardy husband.)

Emily's hair was one of the first things about the Farr family that I mentioned to Margot after we became friends, Harriet and Emily and I, and I began to spend most of my time in that house.

"I don't think she's ever dyed it," I said, with almost conscious lack of tact.

Of course, Margot was defensive. "I wouldn't dye mine if I thought it would be a decent color on its own."

But by that time Margot's life was also improving. Business was fairly good, and she had finally heard from my father, who began to send sizable checks from New Orleans. He had found work with an oil company. She still asked the Ouija board if she would see him again, but her question was less obsessive.

The second time I rode past that house, there was a girl sitting on the front porch, reading a book. She was about my age. She looked up. The next time I saw her there, we both smiled. And the time after that (a Saturday morning in late June) she got up and slowly came out to the road, to where I had stopped, ostensibly to look at the view—the sweep of fields, the white highway, which wound down to the thick greenery bordering the creek, the fields and trees that rose in dim and distant hills.

"I've got a bike exactly like that," Harriet said indifferently, as though to deny the gesture of having come out to meet me.

For years, perhaps beginning then, I used to seek my antithesis in friends. Inexorably following Margot, I was becoming a big blonde, with some of her same troubles. Harriet was cool and dark, with long, gray eyes. A girl about to be beautiful.

"Do you want to come in? We've got some lemon cake that's pretty good."

Inside, the house was cluttered with odd mixtures of furniture. I glimpsed a living room, where there was a shabby sofa next to a pretty, "antique" table. We walked through a dining room that contained a decrepit mahogany table surrounded with delicate fruit-wood chairs. (I had a horrifying moment of imagining Margot there, with her accurate eye—making offers in her harsh Yankee voice.) The walls were crowded with portraits and with nineteenth-century oils of bosky landscapes. Books overflowed from rows of shelves along the walls. I would have moved in at once.

We took our lemon cake back to the front porch and ate it

there, overlooking that view. I can remember its taste vividly. It was light and tart and sweet, and a beautiful lemon color. With it, we drank cold milk, and then we had seconds and more milk, and we discussed what we liked to read.

We were both at an age to begin reading grownup books, and there was some minor competition between us to see who had read more of them. Harriet won easily, partly because her mother reviewed books for the local paper, and had brought home Steinbeck, Thomas Wolfe, Virginia Woolf, and Elizabeth Bowen. But we also found in common an enthusiasm for certain novels about English children. (Such snobbery!)

"It's the best cake I've ever had!" I told Harriet. I had already adopted something of Margot's emphatic style.

"It's very good," Harriet said judiciously. Then, quite casually, she added, "We could ride our bikes out to Laurel Hill."

We soared dangerously down the winding highway. At the bridge across the creek, we stopped and turned onto a narrow, rutted dirt road that followed the creek through woods as dense and as alien as a jungle would have been—thick pines with low sweeping branches, young leafed-out maples, peeling tall poplars, elms, brambles, green masses of honeysuckle. At times, the road was impassable, and we had to get off our bikes and push them along, over crevices and ruts, through mud or sand. And with all that we kept up our somewhat stilted discussion of literature.

"I love Virginia Woolf!"

"Yes, she's very good. Amazing metaphors."

I thought Harriet was an extraordinary person—more intelligent, more poised, and prettier than any girl of my age I had ever known. I felt that she could become anything at all—a writer, an actress, a foreign correspondent (I went to a lot of movies). And I was not entirely wrong; she eventually became a sometimes-published poet.

We came to a small beach, next to a place where the creek widened and ran over some shallow rapids. On the other side, large gray rocks rose steeply. Among the stones grew isolated, twisted trees, and huge bushes with thick green leaves. The laurel of Laurel Hill. Rhododendron. Harriet and I took off our shoes and waded into the warmish water. The bottom squished under

our feet, making us laugh, like the children we were, despite all
our literary talk.

Margot was also making friends. Unlike me, she seemed to seek
her own likeness, and she found a sort of kinship with a woman
named Dolly Murray, a rich widow from Memphis who shared
many of Margot's superstitions—fear of thunderstorms, faith in
the Ouija board. About ten years older than Margot, Dolly still
dyed her hair red; she was a noisy, biassed, generous woman. They
drank gin and gossiped together, they met for Cokes at the drugstore, and sometimes they drove to a neighboring town to have
dinner in a restaurant (in those days, still a daring thing for unes-
corted ladies to do).

I am sure that the Farrs, outwardly a conventional family, saw
me as a neglected child. I was so available for meals and overnight
visits. But that is not how I experienced my life—I simply felt
free. And an important thing to be said about Margot as a mother
is that she never made me feel guilty for doing what I wanted to
do. And of how many mothers can that be said?

There must have been a moment of "meeting" Emily, but I
have forgotten it. I remember only her gentle presence, a soft
voice, and my own sense of love returned. Beautiful white hair,
dark deep eyes, and a wide mouth, whose corners turned and
moved to express whatever she felt—amusement, interest, boredom, pain. I have never since seen such a vulnerable mouth.

I amused Emily; I almost always made her smile. She must
have seen me as something foreign—a violent, enthusiastic Yankee (I used forbidden words, like "God" and "damn"). Very
unlike the decorous young Southern girl that she must have been,
that Harriet almost was.

She talked to me a lot; Emily explained to me things about the
South that otherwise I would not have picked up. "Virginians feel
superior to everyone else, you know," she said, in her gentle (Vir-
ginian) voice. "Some people in my family were quite shocked
when I married a man from North Carolina and came down here
to live. And a Presbyterian at that! Of course, that's nowhere near
as bad as a Baptist, but only Episcopalians really count." This was
all said lightly, but I knew that some part of Emily agreed with
the rest of her family.

"How about Catholics?" I asked her, mainly to prolong the conversation. Harriet was at the dentist's, and Emily was sitting at her desk answering letters. I was perched on the sofa near her, and we both faced the sweeping green view. But since my father, Johnny Kilgore, was a lapsed Catholic, it was not an entirely frivolous question. Margot was a sort of Christian Scientist (her own sort).

"We hardly know any Catholics." Emily laughed, and then she sighed. "I do sometimes still miss Virginia. You know, when we drive up there I can actually feel the difference as we cross the state line. I've met a few people from South Carolina," she went on, "and I understand that people down there feel the same way Virginians do." (Clearly, she found this unreasonable.)

"West Virginia? Tennessee?"

"They don't seem Southern at all. Neither do Florida and Texas—not to me."

("Dolly says that Mrs. Farr is a terrible snob," Margot told me, inquiringly.

"In a way." I spoke with a new diffidence that I was trying to acquire from Harriet.

"Oh.")

Once, I told Emily what I had been wanting to say since my first sight of her. I said, "Your hair is so beautiful. Why don't you let it grow?"

She laughed, because she usually laughed at what I said, but at the same time she looked surprised, almost startled. I understood that what I had said was not improper but that she was totally unused to attentions of that sort from anyone, including herself. She didn't think about her hair. In a puzzled way, she said, "Perhaps I will."

Nor did Emily dress like a woman with much regard for herself. She wore practical, seersucker dresses and sensible, low shoes. Because her body had so little shape, no indentations (this must have been at least partly due to the back brace), I was surprised to notice that she had pretty, shapely legs. She wore little or no makeup on her sun- and wind-weathered face.

And what of Lawrence Farr, the North Carolina Presbyterian for whom Emily had left her people and her state? He was a small, precisely made man, with fine dark features (Harriet looked very like him). A lawyer, but widely read in literature, especially the English nineteenth century. He had a courtly manner, and sometimes a wicked tongue; melancholy eyes, and an odd, sudden, ratchety laugh. He looked ten years younger than Emily; the actual difference was less than two.

"Well," said Margot, settling into a Queen Anne chair—a new antique—on our porch one stifling hot July morning, "I heard some really interesting gossip about your friends."

Margot had met and admired Harriet, and Harriet liked her, too—Margot made Harriet laugh, and she praised Harriet's fine brown hair. But on some instinct (I am not sure whose) the parents had not met. Very likely, Emily, with her Southern social antennae, had somehow sensed that this meeting would be a mistake.

That morning, Harriet and I were going on a picnic in the woods to the steep rocky side of Laurel Hill, but I forced myself to listen, or half listen, to Margot's story.

"Well, it seems that some years ago Lawrence Farr fell absolutely madly in love with a beautiful young girl—in fact, the orphaned daughter of a friend of his. Terribly romantic. Of course, she loved him, too, but he felt so awful and guilty that they never did anything about it."

I did not like this story much; it made me obscurely uncomfortable, and I think that at some point both Margot and I wondered why she was telling it. Was she pointing out imperfections in my chosen other family? But I asked, in Harriet's indifferent voice, "He never kissed her?"

"Well, maybe. I don't know. But of course everyone in town knew all about it, including Emily Farr. And with her back! Poor woman," Margot added somewhat piously but with real feeling too.

I forgot the story readily at the time. For one thing, there was something unreal about anyone as old as Lawrence Farr "falling in love." But looking back to Emily's face, Emily looking at Lawrence, I can see that pained watchfulness of a woman who has been hurt, and by a man who could always hurt her again.

In those days, what struck me most about the Farrs was their extreme courtesy to each other—something I had not seen before.

Never a harsh word. (Of course, I did not know then about couples who cannot afford a single harsh word.)

Possibly because of the element of danger (very slight—the slope was gentle), the roof over the front porch was one of the places Harriet and I liked to sit on warm summer nights when I was invited to stay over. There was a country silence, invaded at intervals by summer country sounds—the strangled croak of tree frogs from down in the glen; the crazy baying of a distant hound. There, in the heavy scent of roses, on the scratchy shingles, Harriet and I talked about sex.

"A girl I know told me that if you do it a lot your hips get very wide."

"My cousin Duncan says it makes boys strong if they do it."

"It hurts women a lot—especially at first. But I knew this girl from Santa Barbara, and she said that out there they say Filipinos can do it without hurting."

"Colored people do it a lot more than whites."

"Of course, they have all those babies. But in Boston so do Catholics!"

We are seized with hysteria. We laugh and laugh, so that Emily hears and calls up to us, "Girls, why haven't you-all gone to bed?" But her voice is warm and amused—she likes having us laughing up there.

And Emily liked my enthusiasm for lemon cake. She teased me about the amounts of it I could eat, and she continued to keep me supplied. She was not herself much of a cook—their maid, a young black girl named Evelyn, did most of the cooking.

Once, but only once, I saw the genteel and opaque surface of that family shattered—saw those three people suddenly in violent opposition to each other, like shards of splintered glass. (But what I have forgotten is the cause—what brought about that terrible explosion?)

The four of us, as so often, were seated at lunch. Emily was at what seemed to be the head of the table. At her right hand was the small silver bell that summoned Evelyn to clear, or to bring a new course. Harriet and I across from each other, Lawrence across from Emily. (There was always a tentativeness about Lawrence's posture. He could have been an honored guest, or a spoiled and

favorite child.) We were talking in an easy way. I have a vivid recollection only of words that began to career and gather momentum, to go out of control. Of voices raised. Then Harriet rushes
from the room. Then Emily's face reddens dangerously, the corners of her mouth twitch downward, and Lawrence, in an exqui-
sitely icy voice, begins to lecture me on the virtues of reading
Trollope. I am supposed to help him pretend that nothing has
happened, but I can hardly hear what he is saying. I am in shock.

That sudden unleashing of violence, that exposed depth of terrible emotions might have suggested to me that the Farrs were
not quite as I had imagined them, not the impeccable family in
my mind—but it did not. I was simply and terribly—and selfishly
—upset, and hugely relieved when it all seemed to have passed
over.

During that summer, the Ouija board spoke only gibberish to
Margot, or it answered direct questions with repeated evasions:

"Will I ever see Johnny Kilgore again, in this life?"

"Yes no perhaps."

"Honey, that means you've got no further need of the board,
not right now. You've got to think everything out with your own
heart and instincts," Dolly said.

Margot seemed to take her advice. She resolutely put the board
away, and she wrote to Johnny that she wanted a divorce.

I had begun to notice that these days, on these sultry August
nights, Margot and Dolly were frequently joined on their small
excursions by a man named Larry—a jolly, red-faced man who
was in real estate and who reminded me considerably of my father.

I said as much to Margot, and was surprised at her furious reaction. "They could not be more different, they are altogether opposite. Larry is a Southern gentleman. You just don't pay any attention to anyone but those Farrs."

A word about Margot's quite understandable jealousy of the
Farrs. Much later in my life, when I was unreasonably upset at
the attachment of one of my own daughters to another family
(unreasonable because her chosen group were all talented musi-
cians, as she was), a wise friend told me that we all could use
more than one set of parents—our relations with the original set

are too intense, and need dissipating. But no one, certainly not silly Dolly, was around to comfort Margot with this wisdom.

The summer raced on. ("Not without dust and heat," Lawrence several times remarked, in his private ironic voice.) The roses wilted on the roof and the banks next to the road. The creek dwindled, and beside it honeysuckle leaves lay limply on the vines. For weeks, there was no rain, and then, one afternoon, there came a dark torrential thunderstorm. Harriet and I sat on the side porch and watched its violent start—the black clouds seeming to rise from the horizon, the cracking, jagged streaks of lightning, the heavy, welcome rain. And, later, the clean smell of leaves and grass and damp earth.

Knowing that Margot would be frightened, I thought of calling her, and then remembered that she would not talk on the phone during storms. And that night she told me, "The phone rang and rang, but I didn't think it was you, somehow."

"No."

"I had the craziest idea that it was Johnny. Be just like him to pick the middle of a storm for a phone call."

"There might not have been a storm in New Orleans."

But it turned out that Margot was right.

The next day, when I rode up to the Farrs' on my bike, Emily was sitting out in the grass where I had first seen her. I went and squatted beside her there. I thought she looked old and sad, and partly to cheer her I said, "You grow the most beautiful flowers I've ever seen."

She sighed, instead of smiling as she usually did. She said, "I seem to have turned into a gardener. When I was a girl, I imagined that I would grow up to be a writer, a novelist, and that I would have at least four children. Instead, I grow flowers and write book reviews."

I was not interested in children. "You never wrote a novel?"

She smiled unhappily. "No. I think I was afraid that I wouldn't come up to Trollope. I married rather young, you know."

And at that moment Lawrence came out of the house, immaculate in white flannels.

He greeted me, and said to Emily, "My dear, I find that I have some rather late appointments, in Hillsboro. You won't wait dinner if I'm a trifle late?"

(Of course she would; she always did.)

"No. Have a good time," she said, and she gave him the anxious look that I had come to recognize as the way she looked at Lawrence.

Soon after that, a lot happened very fast. Margot wrote to Johnny (again) that she wanted a divorce, that she intended to marry Larry. (I wonder if this was ever true.) Johnny telephoned —not once but several times. He told her that she was crazy, that he had a great job with some shipbuilders near San Francisco—a defense contract. He would come get us, and we would all move out there. Margot agreed. We would make a new life. (Of course, we never knew what happened to the girl.)

I was not as sad about leaving the Farrs and that house, that town, those woods as I was to be later, looking back. I was excited about San Francisco, and I vaguely imagined that someday I would come back and that we would all see each other again. Like parting lovers, Harriet and I promised to write each other every day.

And for quite a while we did write several times a week. I wrote about San Francisco—how beautiful it was: the hills and pastel houses, the sea. How I wished that she could see it. She wrote about school and friends. She described solitary bike rides to places we had been. She told me what she was reading.

In high school, our correspondence became more generalized. Responding perhaps to the adolescent mores of the early nineteen-forties, we wrote about boys and parties; we even competed in making ourselves sound "popular." The truth (my truth) was that I was sometimes popular, often not. I had, in fact, a stormy adolescence. And at that time I developed what was to be a long-lasting habit. As I reviewed a situation in which I had been ill-advised or impulsive, I would reënact the whole scene in my mind with Harriet in my own role—Harriet cool and controlled, more intelligent, prettier. Even more than I wanted to see her again, I wanted to be Harriet.

Johnny and Margot fought a lot and stayed together, and gradually a sort of comradeship developed between them in our small house on Russian Hill.

I went to Stanford, where I half-heartedly studied history. Har-

riet was at Radcliffe, studying American literature, and writing poetry.

We lost touch with each other.

Margot, however, kept up with her old friend Dolly, by means
of Christmas cards and Easter notes, and Margot thus heard a re-
markable piece of news about Emily Farr. Emily "up and left
Lawrence without so much as a by-your-leave," said Dolly, and
went to Washington, D.C., to work in the Folger Library. This
news made me smile all day. I was so proud of Emily. And I imagined that Lawrence would amuse himself, that they would both
be happier apart.

By accident, I married well—that is to say, a man whom I still
like and enjoy. Four daughters came at uncalculated intervals, and
each is remarkably unlike her sisters. I named one Harriet, although she seemed to have my untidy character.

From time to time, over the years, I would see a poem by Harriet Farr, and I always thought it was marvellous, and I meant to
write her. But I distrusted my reaction. I had been (I was) so
deeply fond of Harriet (Emily, Lawrence, that house and land)
and besides, what would I say—"I think your poem is marvellous?" (I have since learned that this is neither an inadequate
nor an unwelcome thing to say to writers.) Of course, the true
reason for not writing was that there was too much to say.

Dolly wrote to Margot that Lawrence was drinking "all over
the place." He was not happier without Emily. Harriet, Dolly
said, was traveling a lot. She married several times and had no
children. Lawrence developed emphysema, and was in such bad
shape that Emily quit her job and came back to take care of him
—whether because of feelings of guilt or duty or possibly affection, I didn't know. He died, lingeringly and miserably, and
Emily, too, died a few years later—at least partly from exhaustion,
I would imagine.

Then, at last, I did write Harriet, in care of the magazine in
which I had last seen a poem of hers. I wrote a clumsy, gusty letter, much too long, about shared pasts, landscapes, the creek. All
that. And as soon as I had mailed it I began mentally rewriting,
seeking more elegant prose.

When for a long time I didn't hear from Harriet, I felt worse and worse, cumbersome, misplaced—as too often in life I had felt before. It did not occur to me that an infrequently staffed magazine could be at fault.

Months later, her letter came—from Rome, where she was then living. Alone, I gathered. She said that she was writing it at the moment of receiving mine. It was a long, emotional, and very moving letter, out of character for the Harriet that I remembered (or had invented).

She said, in part: "It was really strange, all that time when Lawrence was dying, and God! so long! and as though 'dying' were all that he was doing—Emily, too, although we didn't know that—all that time the picture that moved me most, in my mind, that moved me to tears, was not of Lawrence and Emily but of you and me. On our bikes at the top of the hill outside our house. Going somewhere. And I first thought that that picture simply symbolized something irretrievable, the lost and irrecoverable past, as Lawrence and Emily would be lost. And I'm sure that was partly it.

"But they were so extremely fond of you—in fact, you were a rare area of agreement. They missed you, and they talked about you for years. It's a wonder that I wasn't jealous, and I think I wasn't only because I felt included in their affection for you. They liked me best with you.

"Another way to say this would be to say that we were all three a little less crazy and isolated with you around, and, God knows, happier."

An amazing letter, I thought. It was enough to make me take a long look at my whole life, and to find some new colors there.

A postscript: I showed Harriet's letter to my husband, and he said, "How odd. She sounds so much like you."

THE RICHARD NIXON FREISCHÜTZ RAG

GUY DAVENPORT

GUY DAVENPORT was born in Anderson, South Carolina, and teaches English at the University of Kentucky. He is the author of *The Intelligence of Louis Agassiz, Carmina Archilochi, Sappho: Songs and Fragments, Cydonia Florentia, Flowers and Leaves,* and *Tatlin!*

ON THE Great Ten Thousand Li Wall, begun in the wars of the Spring and Autumn to keep the Mongols who had been camping nearer and nearer the Yan border from riding in hordes on their przhevalskis into the cobbled streets and ginger gardens of the Middle Flower Kingdom, Richard Nixon said:

—I think you would have to conclude that this is a great wall.

Invited by Marshal Yeh Chien-ying to inspect a guard tower on the ramparts, he said:

—We will not climb to the top today.

In the limousine returning to The Forbidden City, he said:

—It is worth coming sixteen thousand miles to see the Wall.

Of the tombs of the Ming emperors, he said:

—It is worth coming to see these, too.

—Chairman Mao says, Marshal Yeh ventured, that the past is past.

The translator had trouble with the sentiment, which lost its pungency in English.

—All over? Richard Nixon asked.

—We have poem, Marshal Yeh said, which I recite.

> West wind keen,
> Up steep sky
> Wild geese cry
> For dawn moon,

Reprinted by permission of the author and the *Hawaii Review.*

For cold dawn
White with frost,
When horse neigh,
Bugle call.

Boast not now
This hard pass
Was like iron
Underfoot.

At the top
We see hills
And beyond
The red sun.

Richard Nixon leaned with attention, grinning, to hear the translation from the interpreter, Comrade Tang Wen-sheng, whose English had been learned in Brooklyn, where she spent her childhood.

—That's got to be a good poem, Richard Nixon said.

—Poem by Chairman Mao, Comrade Tang offered.

—He wrote that? Richard Nixon asked. Made it up?

—At hard pass over Mountain Lu, Marshal Yeh said. Long March. February 1935.

—My! but that's interesting, Richard Nixon said. Really, really interesting.

The limousine slid past high slanting walls of The Forbidden City on which posters as large as tennis courts bore writing Richard Nixon could not read. They proclaimed, poster after poster by which the long limousine moved, *Make trouble, fail. Again make trouble, again fail. Imperialist reactionary make trouble and fail until own destruction. Thought of Chairman Mao.*

The limousine stopped at The Dragon Palace. Richard Nixon got out. Guards of the Heroic People's Volunteer Army stood at attention. On a wall inside the courtyard four tall posters caught the eye of Richard Nixon.

—That's Marx, he said, pointing.

—Marx, repeated Marshal Yeh.

—And that's Engels.

—Engels.

—And that's Lenin and that's Stalin.

—Precisely, Marshal Yeh replied.

Richard Nixon went back to the second poster, pointing to it with his gloved hand.

—That's Engels?

—Engels, Marshal Yeh said with a worried, excessively polite look in his eyes.

—We don't see many pictures of Engels in America, Richard Nixon explained.

That man old Toscanelli put up to sailing to the Japans and Cathay westward out from Portugal, the Genovese Colombo, they have been saying around the Uffizi, has come back across the Atlantic. *Una prova elegantissima!* Benedetto Arithmetic would say. The Aristotelians will be scandalized, *di quale se fanno beffa.* The Platonists will fluff their skirts and freeze the air with their lifted noses. *È una stella il mundo!* But like the moon, forsooth, round as a melon, plump and green. Oh, he could see those *caravelle* butting salt and savage waves, the awful desert of water and desolation of the eye, until the unimaginable shorebirds of Cipongo wheeled around their sails and the red tiles and bamboo *pergole* of Mongol cities came into focus on capes and promontories. Inland, there were roads out to Samarkand, India, Persia, Hungary, Helvetia, and thus back to Tuscany.

He had completed the world journey of the Magi, it occurred to Leonardo as he moved the bucket of grasses that Salai had brought him from Fiesole. They had come from the East, astrologers, and Colombo's sails, in these days of signs wherein every moving thing must declare itself for God or Islam, would have worn the cross, which the philosophers of the Medes did not wait to learn would be forever, until the end of time, the hieroglyph of the baby before whom they laid their gifts in the dark stable. The world was knit by prophecy, by light.

Meadow grass from Fiesole, icosahedra, cogs, gears, plaster, maps, lutes, brushes, an adze, magic squares, pigments, a Roman head Brunelleschi and Donatello brought him from their excavations, the skeleton of a bird: how beautifully the Tuscan light gave him his things again every morning, even if the kite had been in his sleep.

Moments, hours, days. Had man done anything at all?

The old woman had brought the wine and the bread, the onions. He and Toscanelli, Pythagoreans, ate no meat.

The machine stood against the worktable, the *due rote*, unaccountably outrageous in design. Saccapane the smith was making the chain that would span the two *rote dentate*. You turned the pedals with your feet, which turned the big cog wheel, which pulled the chain forward, cog by cog, causing the smaller wheel to turn the hind *rota*, thereby propelling the whole machine forward. As long as the machine was in motion, the rider would balance beautifully. The forward motion stole away any tendency to fall right or left, as the flow of a river discouraged a boat from wandering.

If only he knew the languages! He could name his machines as Archimedes would have named them, in the ancient words. He called his flying machine the bird, *l'uccello*. Benedetto said that the Greeks would have called it an *ornitottero*, the wings of a bird.

Light with extravagance and precision, mirror of itself *atomo per atomo* from its dash against the abruptness of matter to the jelly of the eye, swarmed from high windows onto the two-wheeled balancing machine. The rider would grasp horns set on the fork in which the front wheel was fixed and thus guide himself with nervous and accurate meticulousness. Suddenly he saw the Sforze going into battle on it, a phalanx of these *duo rote* bearing lancers at full tilt. *Avanti, O Coraggiosi, O!* the trumpet called, *tambureggiandi le bacchette delli tamburi di battaglia.*

The scamp Salai was up and about.

—*Maestro!* he piped. You've made it!

Leonardo picked up the brown boy Salai, shouldered him like a sack of flour, and danced the long, gliding steps of a sarabande.

—*Sì, Cupidello mio, tutto sennonchè manca la catena.*

—And then I can make it go, ride it like a pony?

—Like the wind, like Ezekiel's angel, like the horses of Ancona.

Salai squirmed free and knelt before the strange machine, touching the pedals, the wicker spokes, the saddle, the toothed wheels around which the chain would fit, *i vinci.*

—*Como leone!*

He turned to the basket of flowering grasses, reaching for his silver pencil. Bracts and umbrels fine as a spider's legs! And in the thin green veins ran hairs of water, and down the hairs of water ran light, down into the dark, into the root. Light from the farthest stars flowed through these long leaves. He had seen the prints of leaves from the time of the flood in mountain rocks, and had seen there shells from the sea.

—Maestro, Salai said, when will the chain be ready?

—Chain? Leonardo asked. What chain?

He drew with his left hand a silver eddy of grass. It was grace that he drew, perfection, frail leaves through which moved the whole power of God, and when a May fly lights on a green arc of grass the splendor of that conjunction is no less than San Gabriele touching down upon the great dome at Byzantium, closing the crushed silver and spun glass of his four wings around the golden shaft of his height.

—The chain, Salai said, the chain!

Did man know anything at all?

Before flying to China, Richard Nixon ordered a thousand targets in Laos and Cambodia bombed by squadrons of B-52s. He sent one thousand, one hundred and twenty-five squadrons of bombers to silence the long-range field guns of North Viet Nam along the border of the DMZ. Richard Nixon was pleased with the bombing, knowing that Chairman Mao would be impressed by such power. Dr. Kissinger had recommended the one thousand, one hundred and twenty-five squadrons of bombers to Richard Nixon as something that would impress Chairman Mao. The bombs were falling thick as hail in a summer storm when Richard Nixon set foot on China, grinning. A band played *The March of the Volunteers*. Premier Chou En-lai did not walk forward. Richard Nixon had to walk to where Premier Chou stood grinning. They shook hands.

—We came by way of Guam, Richard Nixon said. It is better that way.

—You have good trip? Premier Chou asked.

—You should know, Richard Nixon said. You are such a traveler.

Richard Nixon rode in a limousine to Taio Yu Tai, outside the

Forbidden City. As soon as he got to his room, the telephone rang.

—Who would be calling me in China? he asked.

Dr. Kissinger answered the telephone.

—Yes? he said.

—Excellency Kissinger? a voice asked. You are there?

—We are here, Dr. Kissinger said.

—His Excellency the President Nixon is there?

—Right here, said Dr. Kissinger, taking off his shoes.

—Would His Excellency Nixon come to telephone?

—Sure, said Dr. Kissinger. For you, Dick.

Richard Nixon took the telephone, put it to his ear, and looked at the ceiling, where scarlet dragons swam through clouds of pearl.

—Nixon here, he said.

—Excellency President Nixon there?

—Right here, Richard Nixon said. To who have I the honor of addressing?

—Now you speak with Comrade Secretary Wang.

A new voice came on the line. It said:

—Chairman Mao invite you, now, come to visit him.

—Right now? Richard Nixon asked. We've just got off the plane. We came by way of Guam.

—Now, said the telephone. You come visit. Yes?

—OK, Richard Nixon said. Will do. You coming to pick us up?

The line had gone dead.

—Son of a bitch, Richard Nixon said.

Dr. Kissinger rocked on his heels and grinned from ear to ear.

Roses, buttons, thimbles, lace. The grass grows up to the stones, the road. There are flowers in the grass and flowers on her dress. And buttons down her dress, and lace on the collar and cuffs and hem. And buttons on her shoes. In the Luxembourg she wears a shawl from Segovia and Pablo says she looks like a Spanish woman of the old school, when women were severe and well-bred and kind, and I say that she looks like an officer in the Union Army. We sing "The Trail of the Lonesome Pine," which she plays on the piano, throwing in snatches of "Marching Through Georgia" and "Alexander's Ragtime Band." She has Pumpelly's nose, the hands of a Spanish saint.

In France she wears a yellow hat, in Italy a Panama. Alice, I say, Assisi, the grass of Assisi, and the leaves Sassetta. We walk comfortably over the stones, hearing the bells ring for the nuns and the girls in their school. It is so quiet, she says, being herself quiet to say that it is quiet. Spain is a still life, I say, only Italy is landscape. The birds there, she says. St. Francis, I say. The birds suffer their suffering each in a lifetime, forgetting it as they endure. We remember suffering from years and years ago. Do not talk of old things, she says. There is no time any more, only now. Not, say I, if you can hear as I can the bugles and see the scarlet flags.

And I could, I can, I always can. The officers sit in their saddles and the guidons with their Victorian numbers and faded reds move to the head of the column. It is an old way with men, it happened at Austerlitz and Sevastopol. The generals are high on their horses, listening to the band, to the shouts of the sergeants. It is glory. When Leo moved out, we trotted around the room like horses, and Basket went around with us. I was the general and Alice was the officer and Basket was the horse, and all together we were Napoleon. We were pickaninnies cakewalking before the elders on a Saturday in Alabama, we were Barnum and Bailey and the Great Rat of Sumatra going a progress to Chantilly to see the lace and the cream.

It is quiet, she says, and I say, Alice, look at the flowers. Yes, she says. Yes, I say. Is it not grand to say *yes* back and forth when we mean something else and she went behind a bush and loosened her stays and camisole and shamelessly stepped out of the frilly heap they made around her buttoned shoes and I said *yes*, here where St. Francis walked, Alice, you do realize, don't you, that the reason we came to Assisi is that you are from San Francisco and this is the hometown of St. Francis and she says I am wrapping my underthings in my shawl, do you think anyone will notice?

Red tile, moss, pigeons. We drink wine under the trees, though it is too hot to drink wine. Well, I say, we are here. Yes, she says, we are here, and her eyes jiggle and her smile is that of a handsome officer who has been called to headquarters and seen General Grant and is pleased to please, well-bred that he is.

This is not Fouquet's, I say. Certainly not Fouquet's, she says. I

touch her foot with my foot, she touches my foot with her foot.
The crickets sing around us, fine as Stravinksy. If Spain is a still
life, what is Italy? They came here, I said, the grand old poets, because the women have such eyes. Surely not to see the cats, Alice
says. No, I say, not for the cats. Henry James came here for the
tone. William might come here and never see the tone. William
if he came would take in the proportions, and would not look at
the cats. A princess and a cart go by, Henry sees the princess and
William sees the wheel of the cart how it is in such fine proportion to the tongue and the body.

When you talk, she says, I shiver all over, things flutter around
inside. When you smile, I say, I bite into peaches and Casals
plays Corelli and my soul is a finch in cherries. Let us talk and
smile forever. This is forever, Alice says. It is so quiet. Look at the
dust, I say. Would you walk in it barefoot? Another glass of wine,
she says, and I will fly over the bell tower. Did you have a rose-
wood piano in San Francisco? I ask. With a bust of Liszt on it,
she says, and a vase of marigolds.

Look at these colors and you can see why Sassetta was Sassetta.
Will we go to England again, she says, to sit in the cathedrals?
Look at these hills and you will know why St. Francis was St.
Francis.

The roses, she says, are very old. They are the roses of Ovid, I
say. They are the only roses that are red. If I knew the Latin for
red I would say it, if the Latin for rose, I would say it, the Latin
for the only red in the oldest rose, I would say it. Were I Ovid, I
would give you a rose and say that it is given for your eyes. I would
take it, she says. I am glad you would, I say, touching her foot
with my foot. Sassetta's rose, Pablo's rose.

Madame Matisse is a gentian, she says, touching my foot with
her foot. Are all women flowers, all girls? Henri Rousseau was
married to a sunflower, Cézanne to a pear tree.

Alice, I say. Yes, General Grant, she says. Pickaninny, I say.
Augustus Caesar, she says. Do you see those pines over there, the
ones that look like William McKinley addressing the Republican
Party? You mustn't mention McKinley to Pablo, she says, he
thinks he has trod on the honor of Spain. He has, I say, that is the
American way. But the pines, Alice, the pines. I see them, she
says, they have had a hard life. Do you, I say, see the bronze fall

of needles beneath them, and know the perfume of rosin and dust and old earth we would smell if we climbed there? The flutter has begun, she says. And now look at the rocks, the cubist rocks, down the hills from the pines, and the red tile of the roofs, and the chickens in the yard there, the baskets. I see all that, she says. and having seen it, Alice? I ask. It is there to see, she says. That is the answer, I say. It is also the question.

Mao sat in his red armchair looking benign and amused. Richard Nixon sank too far into his chair, his elbows as high as his ears. He beamed. He did not see the stacks of journals, the shelves packed with books, the bundles of folders, the writing brushes in jars. He beamed at Mao and at Dr. Kissinger, whom Mao had called a modern Metternich. The reporters had written that down.

The cluttered room was dark. What light there was came from tall windows which gave onto a courtyard as bleak as the playground of a grammar school. The translator said that Chairman Mao had asked about hegemony.

—We're for it, Richard Nixon said.

—Your aides are very young, Chairman Mao said.

—Are they? Richard Nixon asked.

—We must learn from you on that point, Chairman Mao said. Our government is all of old men.

Richard Nixon did not know what to say.

—Old, Chairman Mao said, but here, still here.

—The world is watching us, Richard Nixon said.

—You mean Taiwan, Chairman Mao said.

—No, Richard Nixon said, beaming, the world out there, the whole world. They are watching their TV sets.

Chairman Mao grinned and leaned back in his comfortable armchair.

—Ah so, he said, the world.

NEL BAGNO

JOSEPHINE JACOBSEN

JOSEPHINE JACOBSEN was the winner of the Prairie Schooner Fiction Award for 1974, and her book *The Shade-Seller: New & Selected Poems* was nominated for a National Book Award in 1975. From 1971 to 1973 she served as poetry consultant to the Library of Congress.

B EFORE MRS. GLESSNER SHUT HER LARGE SUITCASE, which she had just weighed, she went into the bathroom to get the final articles for her toilet bag. The open door impeding her in the small space, she thrust it to with her heel. The breeze from the open casement caught it at the same moment, and as it slammed shut, the knob fell off on the inside.

It was a glass knob, cut in facets, and it made a hard, thin sound as it hit the tile floor. Now it was possibly chipped, and the tile too, perhaps. Annoyed, Mrs. Glessner snatched it up; neither showed any sign of damage, and she took the knob with its projecting metal tongue and inserted it carefully back in its hole. But it refused to attach itself, and conscious of limited time, she kneeled on the tiles with their small blue flowers and put her eye to the hole. She couldn't make out anything, and she again inserted the knob's projection, but it only turned flaccidly, refusing to mesh with whatever rachet caused it to function; released, it would not even balance there.

She glanced furiously at her wrist, but it was bare. The tiny watch was propped a dozen yards away, on her bedroom bureau. How many minutes before the taxi? Fifteen? Ten?

She put the glass knob on top of the yellow wicker laundry-hamper, next to the Italian pocket dictionary and the box of Klee-nex. It was perfectly quiet in the bathroom, except for the sound of traffic from the parkway, coming faintly but steadily through the casement window, which the breeze, sucking back, had slammed shut. With a sudden uneasy movement she went to open it again. It resisted, and she had to yank hard on the handle; but then it flew open, revealing the small darkened screen, the tops of rusted, rosy maples and, far below, the edge of the little wood at the back of the school.

She was still not in the least alarmed, mostly because of the ludicrousness of the situation. The notion of her missing her taxi, her plane, Italy itself tomorrow, trapped in the most incidental of rooms, was the stuff of drunken parties.

But five minutes had certainly passed, and how, actually, would she get out? She sat on the edge of the tub for a moment, to get things straight.

She had, at most, ten minutes. She leaped up, went rapidly to the medicine cabinet—yes, scissors right where they belonged. Again she knelt before the door, the scissors closed, prying deli-cately for the hinge that would draw back the tongue. It yielded, slightly each time, but immediately something arrested it. By the fourth or fifth try, she knew it was no use. She knelt there on the floor, humiliated by the ineffable absurdity of her situation. Could she break down the door? She looked about her. Small toilet arti-cles ranged on three glass shelves; the toilet; a circular, bristly toi-let brush; the long narrow tub, with its porcelain soapdish; the wash basin; the medicine cabinet, filled with bottles, tubes, vials; a metal radiator, very shiny; on the wall, a small Haitian painting, next to it a wall clipboard with snapshots and a torn-out news-paper column; on top of the hamper, an Italian pocket dictionary and a tiny transistor radio—these put out conspicuously for her handbag—a blue quilted Kleenex-box, and the glass door knob, the sight of which brought her round again to the handleless door.

Her entire distress was concentrated on her plane. Something must happen before the taxi came. She took off her right shoe. It was a black leather pump, and looking at its heel, she at once knew better than to try; nevertheless, she swung her arm in a big arc and crashed the heel against the indented panel. The blow

sent a violent jolt all the way up to her neck, and made a raw scar
in the paint. The wood itself was not even marked.

She put her pump back on, with dignity, conscious of keeping
her head. She did not think for an instant of anything subsequent
to the taxi's arrival. All right, she would make her clownish predic-
ament public. She would yell for help. It would have to be out of
the window; old Mrs. Abernathy, below, was in Wisconsin, and
this was the top floor of the small condominium.

She went to the window and was struck by how narrow it was.
The screen prevented her leaning out. Genuinely furious, she
picked up her scissors and began to hack at the screen, feeling a
savage satisfaction as the blades burst through, the screen ripped
and curled. It scratched her hand badly, but she yanked a big
piece inward and back, and thrust her head cautiously through
the opening. For the first time, a curious twinge went down her
spine.

The window was too narrow to get her shoulders through, and
without leaning out, all she could see were the treetops, the
empty cinder path below with the wire fence along its boundary,
and far to the right, a tiny segment of sidewalk. The late September air was fresh on her face. She glared out at the empty afternoon; but, at first sheepishly and then louder, she called, "Anyone? Anyone!" She *would not* call, "Help!" It was still too
ridiculous. "Anyone?" she yelled. "Anyone there?"

Exactly in answer, a bell rang distantly in the kitchen. It was,
by the familiar tone, the downstairs front door. It was, she knew,
the taxi.

Mrs. Glessner stayed just where she was at the window, resisting with success an impulse to tears. The taxi would be by the
front door, on the other side of the building, parked in front of
the red brick steps and small white columns, a scene which she
now visualized. She had not heard the taxi pull up nor would she
hear its departure. The bell rang again, a long irritated peal. Mrs.
Glessner turned toward the door, stood close by it with the wild
conviction that an irascible driver would ride the little elevator to
the twelfth floor, seeking his delinquent customer. It was very unlikely; but that is what he did.

After a silence of some minutes, during which his customer en-
visioned the pumpkin-colored rear of the cab receding toward the

parkway, there was a short, sharp brring. Now she did yell, quite shamelessly. "Help! Help! I'm in here!" but the bell only rang again, and again, and then stopped.

Mrs. Glessner retreated to the edge of the tub, sat down, folded her hands, took a deep breath. She was, she had always cheered herself by thinking, a tough nut. But in the silence after the bell, the reality of the taxi, the plane, Italy, dropped from her mind. Why shouldn't she die here, slowly? Starve here? Die? Because, people did not starve to death in suburban bathrooms; because, nothing of the sort happened; because, people from the outside came—gas men, painters, Barnie the janitor, checking something. Because, people phoned repeatedly, and then wondered, and came. Because, from time to time, small boys walked along the cinder path at the back of the school, looking for lost baseballs.

Mrs. Glessner was by profession a writer of what she called non-fiction prose, and now she thought of this. Still torn between a sort of abashed amusement—she would dine out on this yet—and what she was afraid was the onset of fear, she said aloud: "All right, how would I sum it up? My immediate chances?" Gas men? The meter was in the basement. Workmen? She hadn't commissioned any. Barnie, checking? For what? She had already told him good-bye. He had a key, but why should he use it, except perhaps for a brief inspection before she got back at the end of the month? Friends? Oddly, only then did she think, Maury? Maury. But for weeks everyone would think her in Italy.

Still, the improbability of any real disaster under such circumstances encouraged her. Why she? If she were writing this . . . but suddenly she felt a chasm open, widen, between her own reporting and the thing reported. The thought was unpleasant, also irrelevant, and she skipped to the next consideration. Resources, immediate resources.

She looked around the small room, small, she supposed, as a cell. Such amount of wall space as rose to the high, narrow ceiling was papered with a water-resistant surface on which pale blue and lavender fish cruised in and out of deeper purple clusters of marine growth. The shower curtain was a scattering of purple shells on a sand-colored background.

Since there was nothing else she could immediately do, she was above all concerned with keeping cool, as she still phrased it to herself. She totted up her advantages.

She had electric light for when the dark came, (if she were still here). She need not soil herself, or her room. She had heat, if the night were cold. She had, above all, water. She had a radio. She could, she thought with dour mirth, go on improving her Italian. She could—but as she looked at the medicine cabinet, she got up, and without any clear idea of what she was going to do, opened the cabinet door, took out a round vial of yellow capsules, took them over to the toilet, emptied them in and pushed the handle. Immediately, she thrust her hand into the coiling water and tried to sieve up the capsules, but they rushed through her fingers, and she retrieved only one sticky tablet.

This totally unexpected performance shocked her literally off her feet; she sat down on the little rug, put her head on the hamper and tried to understand what had just happened to her. The implications of both her first, and then her second, action were insupportable because identical, and because both came straight up from some involuntary self knowledge that had not filtered through to her consciousness.

She had thrown away a perfectly good vial of sleeping pills in a melodramatic gesture, a committing of herself to the fight under any circumstance—inherited from heaven knew what fictional or cinematic conditioning, she thought scornfully. But then her hand, like the paw of a starving bear after fish, had darted down, in case, in case. Why? She knew exactly why, and knowing, she crossed into a new dimension. She was in here, and it was by no means, by no means whatsoever, certain how or when she was going to get out.

She remained sitting on the floor, her head on her hand, leaning lightly on the hamper. She thought again of Maury. She had not, in the chaos of the last ten minutes, thought of him at all, but now it was of his phone call that she thought, a transatlantic phone call that would save her.

They had agreed that he would not call. She needed her unhampered trips—no mail, no phone calls across all those wastes of ocean, plugging in the always complex past to the sunny, simple present. *She* would call, when and if she felt like it.

But now, in her blue and lavender cell, as the brightness through the small window softened and muted itself, she was convinced that Maury would call. He had called her—last year—in Yugoslavia to repeat to her something a little girl had said behind him on the crosstown Forty-ninth-Street bus. He would call her again, at the Regina this time, and staring over the swollen hydrangeas in the lobby, the desk-clerk would say politely but pointedly, no, no, the Signora had not taken up her reservation for the day before yesterday; he would say that, in Maury's terminology, she had not showed. And then (she went step by step) came the phone, pealing in her bedroom, hour after hour, and finally, worried Maury turning the key in her front door lock, his shocked gaze taking in her open suitcase on the bed, her weak shout; the screwdriver. She and Maury would sit on her sofa, Maury's fingers on the back of her neck, and drink draughts of bourbon, without water, very icy. She pushed herself up from the tub's edge and went to his photo on the clipboard. Backlit by the summer sun, he smiled at her, posed in front of a low-hung fringy tree. She looked at his arms, bare to rolled-up sleeves, with their veins and tendons and furry down, familiar by sight in the sun, by touch in the reassuring dark. It was strange that, never having needed Maury with any violence, her present need of him, violent enough, should be so grotesquely limited.

The lines of the clipping just to the right of Maury's picture read, ". . . and the good people of Boonesville know how they feel about Gerald Ford. It is gas, and gas alone . . ." It was the only thing in the room which placed her in time. At once she remembered a quotation she had used in her last article, not yet out, which she had embedded in a paragraph about proportion: "It is by dried cornflowers that we know that Tutankhamen died in April."

Definitely, the room was darker. She stood in the tub, so that she more directly faced the little window, and peered out. Everything was exactly the same, except that the wind, which had gotten higher, made the trees ride heavily, and small flocks of leaves sailed and skittered over the cinder path, beginning to heap themselves up against the wire fence. She thought that there were perhaps twenty more minutes in which someone might walk by.

She propped her elbows on the tiny sill, which was always a little sooty. The wind blew in gusts, and traffic vibrated in the distance. She whirled round, stepped out of the tub and picked up the little transistor; then, for fear that someone might pass the window at a run, she scrambled back. She switched on the tiny bevelled wheel, and immediately from the black leather case a babel burst out around her: contending voices, a scratch of music, a high-pitched blatting. A hair's breadth turn, and a voice right in her hands said clearly ". . . by seven out of eight doctors." "Seven out of *eight?*" repeated a small delighted feminine voice. Her finger moved a fraction and someone said loudly ". . . and is bringing with it a low-pressure Canadian front. In the extreme northwest, snow is a possib—" merging a thousandth of an inch further with the hard, quick beats of a tango. She switched it off and put the small black object down hastily on the edge of the basin. Its outrageous magic struck her as inexplicable, as though the transistor had never been invented. What was, actually, going on in the stillness of this room? How could that babel, over silent lakes, and mountains and turnpikes, withhold itself? What else might be in the room? What was distance? What, above all, was closeness? She looked at the small black rectangle in horror, appalled by the naiveté of habit.

She stepped back to the window, and there, in the distance, on the short, visible section of sidewalk, were two women, walking slowly. One was short, both were bareheaded, and the taller had a poodle, straining against a leash.

At once Mrs. Glessner gave a mighty shout; the wind caught it up, whipping it about with a new cloud of leaves. The women disappeared, though the poodle, its muzzle poking at something, held back for a second, still in view. The sun, contracted and reddened, sent diagonal shafts through the tallest trees. The phone rang.

It rang seven or eight times—Mrs. Glessner was not sure which, she was listening so ferociously; and hearing it repeatedly shrill, she knew this was how it sounded in the empty apartment, in the dark of many evenings, echoing over the motionless objects. It stopped; and in the immediate silence, Mrs. Glessner noticed that she was hungry. This was really unlikely. She was used to little or no lunch, and she seldom had dinner before eight. It couldn't be six o'clock yet. Why was she hungry?

Two small boys came into view on the cinder path, directly below her, heads bent together, lingering. As though a switch had been thrown, a wave of heat went through Mrs. Glessner. Her throat felt raw: "now," she said, "this is it," and thrusting herself as far as she could manage through the window, "Help! Help! Help! Help me!" she shouted into the wind. The boys moved slowly ahead. Mrs. Glessner seized the radio and, on tip-toe, flung it with all her strength out of the window to strike and shatter eleven stories below. Instead it disappeared into a heap of leaves behind the children. She saw it land. The boys rounded the corner, were lost, as the radio, the day, the room, the world were lost, as the planet plunged willfully away from light.

Like a monk adjusting to his coffin, Mrs. Glessner sat down in the tub. A conflict raged in her, the sense of remoteness, of isolation, of the gulf of galaxies between her and the woman with the poodle, the lingering boys, the stellar space; and the sense of sly immanence, the unknown tumult in this tiny room, boiling with voices, music, the uproar of contesting action, all utterly silent. The women were blocks away now, the boys, nearer. Georgia, Montreal, Havana raged in the bathroom. Mute now, buried in the colored leaves, the tiny box could not change or stop them; it could only deceive her. Perhaps Maury was in the room; perhaps she was in the sky, like her plane; over the dark ocean.

She got up heavily, stepped over the edge of the tub, took the toothbrush mug and drank some water. It was fresh and belovedly real. In the mirror, her face was so dim that she hastily switched on the light; all the porcelain glared and gleamed at her.

She picked up the dictionary. (What book would you choose to take with you . . . ?)

aback	*all'indietro*
abandon	*abbandonare*
abbess	*badessa*
absurd	*assurdo*
abuse	*cativo abuso*
barbarous	*barbaro*
barley	(as in late summer) *orzo* (base, base; how, base?) vile

beemaster	*Mischino alveare?*
	(a fringy tree, struck by the sun
	over her shoulder, July, July.)
congeal	*congelare*
congenial	(what curious sequences)
	degli stressi gusti?
devotion	*devozione*
devour	(root cousin; or so she had always believed,
	wise she, wise, most wise, Maury) *divorare*
dearth	*carestia*
death	*morte*
debar	*escludere*
debase	*abbassare*

In the back of the dictionary was a series of situations helpful to the student: *A la spiagia: Piace a lei la mia vestita? Al viaggio: Ho perduto la mia borsa.* Localities: *La sala da pranza: la tavola,* the table; *la credenza,* the sideboard. Ah, here she was. *Nel bagno:* the basin, *il bacino;* the toilet, *la toletta;* the bathtub, *il bagno.* These letters were—or were they?—her terrible porcelain companions. But what was the actual connection between the letters and the porcelain objects close upon her? The translation from English to Italian was nothing to the other translation, from letters to matter.

She sat on the toilet lid. I am a writer, she said. For the first time, ever, she became conscious of what she knew. In her non-fiction, she never described things truly; not even as truly as she could. She gave the article its shape, its stance. Whatever weakened, whatever altered the neatness of that shape, that form, lost its rights, was changed, was moulded, disappeared in a quiet wink between writer and reader. That was what gave her prose persuasiveness, its dazzling quality, even. It was as though intruders, whose identity might wreck the prefectly constructed plot, were introduced by another name: the basin, *la tavola,* the tub, *lo speccio.* "Jane Glessner," she said aloud, twice. "Jane Glessner." What had been the name of Woman With Poodle? Of Two Boys? If she had called their names, would they have heard? She had read somewhere that tests showed that one's own name

carried uniquely to one's ear, could pierce a crowd, or carry an unlikely distance. Maury was a name defined as lover. Lover: *il
telefono*.

She raised her eyes to look uneasily around. The hamper with
yesterday's clothes heaped like discarded costumes. The cabinet,
holding possibilities behind the world's most ambiguous object, a
waiting mirror. The purple fish, dry and motionless. Over the fish
hung the Haitian painting, a small rectangular canvas, a woman's
head, skin the purple of a ripe plum, long, judging eyes, thick firm
lips. A yellow bandana. When Mrs. Glessner had chosen it, the
Haitian artist said in her impeccable French that she was a bad
woman, that one. Fantastic bones. "A tough one?" Mrs. Glessner
had echoed. *"Elle faisait des anges,"* the artist said simply. Unfa-
miliar with the phrase, Mrs. Glessner had at once understood the
succinct cynicism. Now, far from the hot, green light of Haiti, the
abortionist's long eyes stared patiently over Mrs. Glessner's shoulder.

It was quite dark outside. "What shall I do next?" said Mrs.
Glessner. "I could take a bath," she said. This struck her as a bit
of gallows humor, and she actually began to undress, hanging the
navy-blue jacket of her now-rumpled suit on a hook, where it
covered the empty knob-hole. "The shroud: *il jacqueto*," she said
brashly, stepping out of her slip and peeling off her pants.

The sound of the stopper dropping down was thunderous, but
when the hot water fell in its own steam, the gentle familiar vapor
brought tears of self-pity to her eyes. Never did she say in her
mind, *starvation . . . death*. She was saved by the low comedy of
the situation. Men in Arctic crevasses, in their four minutes of
consciousness, could think of a great single phrase; men in
disabled submarines could write, with their last, weak gesture a
message. But a message, in lipstick, on toilet paper . . . She knew
this night had its special message, but she could not translate it.

"This is a bath," she said. "When I have finished, I will open
the door and walk out. Or I will leave behind me silence. Because
of the difficulties of translation." She knew it was the silence she
could not direct. It all led up to the quality of the silence.

Naked, extended in the tub, she looked down at her body, still
so useful, cut off from motion, from food, from love. The cell, she
thought, what are the letters for that? Tonight a hundred thou-

sand lived that word, but what were its letters? c-e-l-l meant nothing. She reached out a dripping hand, but *cell* was not there; the little dictionary's uses anticipated neither biology nor crime. She replaced it on the hamper.

It was time to get out of the tub, but as this bath was obviously going to be the night's one activity, she lingered. Drops fell, from the tap at intervals; somewhere a dog barked, barked, barked. Perhaps it was the poodle. Or Barnie's dog. Barnie had a bony charmless mélange of setter and several other breeds, with caved-in looking sides, and a ratty plume of a tail. Tendentiously scrupulous where the tenants' cleanliness was concerned, Barnie showed an appalling indulgence to the dog's less attractive habits. Constantly, it soiled the sidewalk and deposited feces on the pachysandra by the door. Perhaps this was Barnie's revenge. Mrs. Glessner loathed the dog; it always looked starved, though she knew Barnie gorged it. But she disliked even more the organized hostility of the tenants. There was a move afoot to force Barnie to do away with it.

The water was cooling. She shuddered a little and stood up, wrapping herself in a thick, blue towel; the water sucked and whirled away. It reminded her of something, and she looked at the little yellow capsule, now dry and stuck to a Kleenex. Much help that would be.

Well, she thought, with this awful sort of mirth which kept rising in her, I shall have it for supper. Was this the rumor of hysteria?

The little radiator poured out heat; it was always too hot. Mrs. Glessner did not dress. "That is sensible," she said; "nothing, absolutely nothing, can happen tonight." She discarded her blue towel, and gradually the heat in the room made small beads of sweat appear on the face of the Haitian woman, on Maury's forehead. The two syllables of Maury's name, that name by which she identified him, formed and then escaped in a clutter of images: ticket stubs, restaurant checks, a pair of trousers over a chair. She tried to visualize his body, then his eyes, his nose; but they had gotten translated into wavery lines, into foggy shifts. Deliberately, she tried to remember his entry into her body; but it was less real to her than the silent clamor around her. *Il amante: the silence.*

Once, hours later, the phone rang again. Eight times.

The quarter moon, pitted-looking and incomplete, appeared in the narrow window. Mrs. Glessner had heard conversations from it. People had talked, back and forth, calling each other by name. It stayed in the casement space a long time, apparently without moving, and then it was gone.

Rewrapped in her blue towel, Mrs. Glessner lay in the tub. She put a small lavender towel behind her head and got down on her spine, propping her feet against the waste-end of the tub. She had swallowed the yellow capsule, scraping off the fuzz of the Kleenex, and drunk a glass of water; she did not expect to sleep at all. But in some sort of perverse exhaustion, she fell asleep at once. She woke in a misery of discomfort, and shifting, lay flat on the bottom of the tub, her knees crooked, her head on the little purple towel.

When she woke up for the second time, the light in the bathroom was a curious dilution of street light and pre-dawn thinning of the dark. For an instant, utterly bewildered, she knew only the awful sinking sensation with which the waker, knower of intolerable news, resists focus.

She sat up in an agony of stiffness, the full, ludicrous, unbelievable, locked misery drowning her. She clambered to her feet, turning around to look out over the ragged, hanging screen. The wind had died. The faintest lemon light stained the treetops.

A great gust of furious hope and rage rocked her. She took a breath, held it, let it go. Though she was quite dry, she began to rub herself hard with the big blue towel. She stepped out of the tub, switched on the light and put on her underclothes. There was a comb in the cabinet, and she combed her hair, dragging the tines savagely across her scalp until it tingled. She chose a lipstick and colored her parted lips. For a moment, a stomach cramp seized her and made her bend over the basin; then she splashed toilet water over her neck and arms and pushed her feet into the black pumps. She hesitated before her suit. Should that be an event for later? But impelled by a pressing haste, she buttoned the blouse, stepped into the skirt. She switched out the light, and the room was filled with a watery visibility of the palest gold. Preternaturally strong, she sat in an attitude of expectancy on the tub's edge.

Beyond her preparations was a sheer cliff. She could see its rim, but she sat there with her stomach cold and contracted and her eyes bright with knowledge. She knew the names of things. Perhaps she would never write another word, but she knew which words to write and which illusory silences to allow for. She would not see Maury again, perhaps, but she knew what a lover was, and was not. She would not see Italy, perhaps, but she knew what distance was.

The traffic sound had swelled. A point of very thin sunlight struck a cluster of purple undersea foliage.

A short, broad man with a dog on a leash came into view from the right, and moved below her on the path. She stared at him, as at a grounded flying-saucer, shocked by the apparition. The dog paused by the wire fence, lifting its leg as the squat man patiently stood waiting. Mrs. Glessner put her head, softly, softly, like a bird-watcher, out of the window.

"Help, Barnie! Barnie!" she cried in the thinnest voice. The dog lowered his leg. "Barnie!" she cried.

Uncertainly, the man looked around.

"Barnie! Your name is Barnie!" she cried.

He pivoted slowly, his head tilted. Suddenly he saw her. He called something, some amazed inquiry.

But her throat froze, and no sound came. He gave the leash a little tug, still staring up; they disappeared from view the way they had come, the dog hanging crossly back.

Mrs. Glessner stood just where she was, an awful tearing sensation in her stomach. It was as though she were being split directly into halves. Something was rushing away, rushing away, and in came the other flood—the rooms beyond the door, the elevator, the streets, the misnamed objects of her life. She stayed perfectly still.

The bell rang, her front door bell, this time; rang again. Barnie was not very bright.

It must have been ten minutes that she stood there without moving at all. Finally she heard the front door slam and heavy steps creaking in the little hall. "Barnie!" she called, and amazingly, tears began to pour down her cheeks.

"Mis' Glessner?" asked Barnie's voice, baffled.

"The handle's off!" she sang out. "I'm locked in! I've been here all night!"

"My goodness," said Barnie with distaste. After a little pause he said coldly, "You got a screwdriver?"

"Yes, yes," she said. "In the kitchen, in the tool-box. In the broom closet."

One half of her mind said, Barnie walked the dog there because of the tenants. Barnie heard me because the wind had dropped. The other half said, These are steps I hear. That hush-hush is the swing door to the kitchen. When I think of this, it will be the way it was. I will not change it. Barnie heard his name.

Trudge, came Barnie back. Metal scratched on metal, the door shook. There was a sucking click, and it swung in, Barnie with it, the screwdriver still in place. He looked at her, displeased.

"How you do that?" he asked.

She neither flung her arms around him, nor told him the secret. That was the first modification. She stepped, very slowly, over the threshold, past him. Everything waited, noncommittal, balanced.

Watch it, she said to herself. What actually happened? You got locked in the slapstick bathroom. But what would happen now?

The suitable spoke the first words for her, after all.

"Just wait a second, Barnie, let me get my purse," she said, and she crossed another threshold, Barnie stooping with a martyred sigh to pluck the glass knob from the hamper.

DUST

PATRICIA GRIFFITH

PATRICIA GRIFFITH grew up in the northeast corner of
Texas near the Red River. She is the author of a novel,
The Future Is Not What It Used to Be, and other short
stories. This is her second appearance in the O. Henry
Prize Stories. She lives in Washington, D.C., where she
is an editor of the new *Washington Review of the Arts*.

A SEVEN YEAR DROUTH plagued East Texas in the '50's.
The rich, black, river bottom land crusted and cracked like a near-
emptied paint can. Boll weevils scourged the cotton fields year
after year and the farmers grew dry and tired and hopeless with
the land.

One spring day a county agent strolled through the long rows
of new cotton plants fresh green and not half way to his knees.
He squatted between the dusty rows counting insects on random
groups of twelve plants, then he raised his young face to the glum,
sun tempered farmers around him and recommended a crop
duster. The farmers nodded and went their ways to borrow
money.

The duster appeared three weeks later on one warm Friday afternoon buzzing over the two commercial streets of town in a red
Stearman bi-plane, flying low over the flat topped one story buildings and not far above the telephone poles. People ran from the
stores and stopped their cars to gaze. Sally Bills at cheerleader
practice raised her orange crepe paper pom-pom against the blue
sky and saw the plane buzzing around beyond the gym, then
with the other cheerleaders she hopped into a '51 Studebaker and
followed the plane out Farm-to-Market 319.

Sally Bills was sixteen. Her eyes were blue, her lips were pink from just a brush of Tangee liptsick. Her eyebrows were unplucked and her hair curled naturally. Her steady boyfriend, Billy Hutchinson, could encircle her waist with his hands. The only thing wrong with Sally Bills was a chipped eyetooth from falling off a horse onto a pig trough when she was twelve.

Sally Bills had never dated anyone but Billy Hutchinson. They started church dating when she was thirteen. They'd sit on the back row of the Baptist church and touch hands. He was a country boy, big and solemn. There was talk that he'd make the all-State football team that year. She felt clever with him and easy. She would marry him after graduation and then her father, Texas A&M '30, would send them both to college. She would major in elementary ed, he, agriculture. She would teach school a year before her children began to come. Billy would join the National Guard and eventually take over her father's farm, two thousand acres, the site of the county agent's stroll three weeks before.

The cheerleaders sang as they sped out the highway . . .

"If you lov-v-v-ed me half as much as I loved you . . ."

The red Stearman bi-plane stopped in front of a scattering of poor whites' shacks outside the city limits. A skinny yellow dog pulled himself out from under the underpinnings of a shack and barked hoarsely at the plane and the green pickup and the cars and the cheerleaders piling out of the Studebaker with their orange pom-poms. The dirty red plane looked old-fashioned and flimsy as a kite. Along the side was inscribed in neat, black letters, "THE PEARLY THOMAS."

The pilot removed his goggles, drew out an Australian soldier's hat pinned up on one side and plopped it on his balding head. He hopped down from the plane light as a grasshopper and not much over five feet even in his hat and yellow cowboy boots. He smiled . . . a cavalier, with worndown yellow teeth coated with tobacco stain, thin, greasy tufts of rusty colored hair poking from the sides of the hat. His skin was deeply tanned and creased. Strutting up and down, ignoring the kids crawling on his plane, shaking hands as he went, he announced himself: Weedy Revenall. The crop duster to solve their problems. His shrill voice spit words like a carnival barker.

"Before long there won't be an insect in the county," he

droned. Then his eyes fell on smiling Sally Bills. He turned away toward the shacks semi-circled by pine trees, the naked ground sloping down from the highway, the tar papered out-houses, bulging as though inflated.

He was born in Hall County he said turning back, but he'd been raised mostly in Bangkok, Thailand where his father was a Baptist missionary.

Shaking hands with Sally Bills he said he'd served his country in World War II.

His hand was rough and cool and he held on. His lips looked soft and moist like a woman's.

Meanwhile Homer Bills, a large man with faded blue eyes left his pickup, hitched up his khakis and started across the road. Sally's face reddened and Weedy let her hand go throwing his arms open saying this country reminded him of the area around Sydney, Australia.

Homer Bills introduced himself. Weedy smiled showing his small yellow teeth. His small, dark eyes flicked from Homer to Sally and back again. He told Mr. Bills he was looking forward to working with him and solving his problems. Homer Bills rubbed his head. He was not a man of easy conversation. He gave the duster directions to his house where he could park his plane and sleep in the room beside the garage.

Sally said goodbye to her friends. She slid into her father's pickup beside Charlie Willard who worked for her father and who looked as weathered and lean as an old barn. His vocal chords had been damaged at an early age by bad sweet milk he claimed. "The Pearly Thomas," he read in his squeaky voice as they drove away. The pickup gathered speed passing the stunted pines, the scrub oaks. The great tangle of Sally's orange pom-pom spilled over them like a shredded pumpkin.

"I reckon," Charlie Willard said, "just from looking at that runty feller, we'll be lucky to have a tractor amongst us by the time he leaves town. . . .

"I hear them's always drinkers. That poison gets into their systems, near drives em crazy."

"Isn't that sad?" Sally sighed.

Homer Bills said all he was interested in was getting rid of some of those bugs. If the man could do that he'd be satisfied.

The plane appeared, circled. Homer Bills and Charlie Willard flagged from either end of the pasture. The Pearly Thomas bumped in for a landing. Beside the stocktank two jersey cows watched calmly like a reception committee.

That night in the Bills' house the farmers gathered. They deposited their straw hats on the bed in the sitting room and sat in their khakis and overalls sipping iced tea. Weedy Revenall watched Sally's small bottom as she side-stepped in the circle of men pouring tea.

"Had a white face heifer give birth to twin calves this spring," a farmer said.

"Heard some feller across the river made a hundred bushels of sweet potatoes on a non-irrigated acre last year."

After awhile they told Weedy Revenall about their bad times.

Weedy smoked one Lucky Strike after another. Sometimes he held them between his teeth and sometimes a slight tic in the right side of his face would flicker for an instant like a short in a neon light. His yellow boots hung over a rung of straight backed chair and he rocked dangerously back and forth on two legs. After listening awhile he settled the chair on four legs and leaned forward.

"Well," he said. "There ain't nobody in Las Vegas, Nevada that's as big a gambler as a man who puts his back forty in cotton."

The farmers shifted.

"It's the truth, God help me," he said.

Weedy Revenall looked down at his hand that held the cigarette and there was a flicker on the side of his face. "But there's something beautiful about a cotton field. Something like a miracle about little sprouts of cotton pushing outta them bolls. . . . But nowadays a man gotta experiment . . . try new ideas. Don't nothing come easy as it used to. I guarantee you men you'll bless the day you started dusting. . . ."

Then Weedy Revenall explained that it would take him a few days to prepare. He'd dust once, then he'd wait a week or two for the next hatch of insects and dust again.

The farmers were holding their hats, about to leave when Charlie Willard spoke in his creaky voice. He said his wife was a preacher's daughter and she thought all this dusting with chemicals was putting nature out of balance. The farmers scowled at him but Weedy took the charge seriously.

"Land ain't intended to produce so much of one crop," he explained. "A man plants 500 acres of cotton and weevils live off cotton, he's raising a crop of weevils, too. I figure dusting's important cause it's *restoring* the balance."

The farmers left feeling a surprised respect for Weedy Revenall despite his peculiar looks and in the next room Sally had listened respectfully to every word.

The next morning when she backed her yellow Henry Jay out of the garage Weedy Revenall appeared from the side door stretching his arms up, palms out, a thin buddha worshiping the fresh, blue sky.

He leaned on the opposite car door. "You look bright as a morning glory," he said. "Don't reckon you're going to town."

He wore a kelly green western shirt with mother-of-pearl buttons, fresh Levis no bigger than a boy's, and a beaded Indian belt that spelled "WEEDY" on the back. He looked newly scrubbed. His tooled yellow boots shone. At the road they met her father and Charlie Willard in the pickup, a cloud of dust trailing them.

"Where you going?" her father asked. His brow was wrinkled below his hat.

"To town," she said. She always went to town on Saturdays.

"Morning, Mr. Bills," Weedy Revenall ducked his head and smiled up at Homer Bills in the pickup. Then he leaned back resting his left arm on the back of the front seat.

"You going into town, Mr. Revenall?"

"Thought I'd take a look around," Weedy said, ducking his head and smiling.

Charlie Willard made a stripping sound in his throat and spat out the window.

"Be glad to give you a lift later on myself," Homer said.

Weedy took his time lighting a cigarette and flipping the match out the window. This time he didn't bother to duck his head.

"Much obliged, Mr. Bills. Guess I'll just go on here with your daughter."

Mr. Bills lifted his eyebrows at his daughter and raising his hand goodbye drove on.

Sally heard a new rattle in her car. All the pleasure of the day was drained by her father's disapproval. She wondered how he could be suspicious of a missionary's son.

"You're welcome to ride into church with us in the morning, Mr. Revenall, I guess you being a missionary's son you're regular as clock work on going to church."

Weedy stared glumly. The minutes passed. She was reaching out to turn on the radio and break the uncomfortable silence when he spoke.

"You seem like a nice girl," he said. "You'll soon learn what it's like on this earth. I ain't a handsome man. I ain't got a lot of money. . . . And I got a different way of making my living. I can't do nothing about them things. But your father thinks I don't have the right to sit in a car next to his daughter."

She glanced out the window as they passed a clearing in the woods where a mound of sawdust rose like a giant ant hill.

"He didn't mean anything like that," she protested. "Goodness, he'd never say anything like that, Mr. Revenall. My father is a good man."

"They's all good men," he said. "It's always good men that do the damage in the world. That's why I don't go to church, 'cause of all them good men. It's only plants and animals that's got any honor in this world and they don't count."

She pushed the accelerator down further so that the wind whipping through the car made talking difficult.

He raised his voice. "You won't find any god in churches."

He waited for her to ask, "Why not, Mr. Revenall?"

"If there's a god he's up there in them clouds," he said, "and I'll be obliged if you'll call me Weedy." His voice grew wistful and the wind carried some of it away. ". . . up there in them clouds . . . everybody . . . little insects . . . the sky fresh . . . all alone . . . pure. . . ."

He turned and spoke more loudly. "Always thought if I could live where everybody's flown . . . had the same kind of purifying experiences in the sky . . . might find some good people. . . ."

Sally told him she believed there were good people everywhere. Even in Russia there were good people and bad people. It was simply a matter of finding the good ones and being tolerant of the bad.

"It ain't a simple matter at all," he said. "People you gotta try out . . . like motors."

Near the Population 1,946 sign Sally exchanged honks with two cars. She slowed to see who was parked at the drive-in restaurant, waved at the manager as she passed the Chevrolet place, and stopped on the corner by the drugstore. As soon as she saw the WEEDY belt recede she felt once more happy with the day, and headed back toward the drive-in cafe to look for friends.

Post Office Cafe: Weedy Revenall devours two eggs sunny side up, fried ham, home cooked biscuits. Addresses local men, waitress Gracie Evans. Re: Flying big game hunters in Africa, meeting Ernest Hemingway.

Ned's Barber Shop: Gets a haircut. Addresses barbers, fellow customers. Re: Barnstorming through the South, Southwest, California doing batman jumps (mid-air acrobatics before opening of parachute); designing formations for Blue Angels.

Chevrolet Used Car Lot: Kicks tires, tries motors. Addresses acquaintances from Post Office Cafe and Ned's Barber Shop, two mechanics, three salesmen. Re: Flying Thunderbolt during World War II, shooting down fourteen (14) Messerschmidts. Bailing out over the Brenner Pass. Survival by a., disguise as a Turkish monk, b., employment by the French underground. Demonstration of French language ability—a few words ending in "Anglais."

At four o'clock Weedy was waiting on the drugstore corner. Five minutes later Sally arrived smiling, groceries stacked in a box in the backseat, hair tied back with a blue ribbon. She spoke excitedly: Her third closest girl friend, Marsha Nell Adams had eloped the night before with a boy from DeWitt, Arkansas she'd known only two weeks.

Sally started out the highway. Weedy Revenall said it seemed like a nice little town. Sally said it *really* was. She turned on a radio request program and began singing along on "Don't Rob Another Man's Castle."

When they approached the place where Weedy had landed the day before he asked her to pull over. Sally hesitated, but because it would have seemed discourteous to do otherwise, she pulled over onto the gravel shoulder leaving the motor running.

Weedy flipped off the radio. It was quiet except for the humming of the motor. He looked out the open window toward the shacks beside the road. Three Rhode Island Reds and a white Leghorn were scratching at the bare ground. There were four large shacks and three small outhouse size buildings behind with a well and a pump off to the side. A utility wire ran from the road to the biggest shack. There the door was open though it looked simply like a hole in the middle. A tow-haired boy of five or six came to the door and stared at them.

"You see them shacks?" Weedy asked her. "That's where I growed up. It wasn't here, but it was like that out in Hall County, up in the panhandle."

He talked with only his head turned toward the shacks as though trying to separate as much of himself from the scene as possible.

"It's cold in them shacks in the wintertime. You can see daylight through some of them cracks in the wall. Nights we wore coats to bed."

The tow-haired boy jumped down from the opening of the shack and began kicking a rock toward them. He wore only a girl's pink panties too big for him pulled up to his thin chest. As soon as he'd hopped down, the yellow dog crawled out from under the shack and gave a few half hearted yelps.

"My mama made glue by cooking flour and water. She'd try to cover the holes in the wall with canned goods labels. . . . And them kerosene stoves, they smoke something awful. . . ."

Weedy put a cigarette in his mouth, crumpled the pack and tossed it out the window. It made a glittering arc and caught the attention of the boy who'd worked his way near the car by kicking the rock. He ran up and squatted beside it, resting his chin on his dirty knees.

"In the night when it was freezing cold the animals come up from the woods and crowded under the house. I'd wake up nights hearing them move underneath. At school I'd look at them clean washed kids and I'd think I had more in common with them animals than them kids."

A cloud of smoke spread against the windshield of the Henry Jay then drifted outward enveloping Sally.

"At Christmas church ladies would bring them snotty kids out to leave a bundle of food on the steps. They'd run back to the car and look, hoping we'd come out 'fore they drove off. We wouldn't though; we'd hide. . . . That's why I don't go to no church. I always see them women driving up the aisles carrying Christmas food bundles."

The little boy stood beside the car picking his nose and staring at them from narrow brown eyes. He had a straight strip of a nose and a round scaly ringworm patch on the side of his forehead.

Weedy reached in his pocket, pulled out a quarter, and flipped it toward the kid. The boy picked it up, wiped the dirt off it carefully, and moved back toward the car. He stuck out a tentative, dirty finger and touched the door handle, watching Weedy uncertainly.

"Git away, kid," Weedy Revenall muttered, "you ain't nothing." He motioned for Sally to drive on.

That night after Billy Hutchinson brought her home from a movie starring Roy Rogers and Dale Evans at Double R-Bar Ranch, cokes at the drive-in, and necking on the river, Sally told her father what Weedy Revenall had said that day. She paused in the door of the bedroom in the shadows hoping he wouldn't notice smudged lipstick or wrinkled clothes.

"I wouldn't pay much attention to what he has to say," her father said. He'd been waiting up for her, sitting in the big chair by the bed reading a farm magazine. His feet in white work socks were propped on a round plastic hammock. His face was two-tone red and white where his straw hat cut across his upper forehead. He looked tired.

"But that was interesting," she said, slipping off her sandals. "I've been passing those shacks all my life. I've even taken Christmas bundles there. But I never thought about it much. . . ."

Her father sighed and rubbed his forehead. She'd noticed that their conversations often embarrassed him and he would inject a mannerism between them.

"There's always been poor people, Sally. Always will be. You divide up all the money in the world, in six weeks it'll be back the same."

His voice sounded old and dried out. She'd heard that justification many times. It was always there; without turning any mental knobs it flowed out.

"Well, goodnight," she said and picked up her sandals.

In her own room she draped her cotton skirt and blouse over a chair, leaned over the dresser, resting her face in her hands, and stared into the mirror. Gritting her teeth she looked at the chipped eye tooth waiting there broken and ugly.

Sunday. After church Sally delivered a tray of food to Weedy Revenall. He opened the door in his stocking feet and she stepped back from the alcohol fumes that sailed out the door. Smiling moonily he thanked her, his eyes frayed with tiny red threads.

The next morning he supervised the building of a shed for his plane. Sitting under the wing of the plane, shaded from the sun, he talked to the three black men as they worked. He'd organized a farm cooperative outside of Baton Rouge he told them. Why, they should have land of their own! Organize cooperatives! Not spend their lives working other peoples' land!

That evening Charlie Willard reported.

"Why, Mr. Bills, we've hired us a commie sure as the world. Fomenting revolution amongst the niggers right out there in your pasture. We may not have our lands by the time this feller leaves."

Sally dropped a dollop of mayonnaise into her waldorf salad and said she thought co-ops were a good idea. Mr. Bills said he didn't think that necessarily meant Weedy Revenall was a communist. He turned back to the newspaper. Charlie Willard said he sure thought somebody oughta keep an eye out on that runty feller.

Tuesday. Weedy Revenall borrowed the pickup and drove to Texarkana to buy chemicals.

Wednesday. He worked on his plane, crawling around on it like a slug, Charlie Willard said, adding that he was beginning to think he could stomp out all those insects with his heels before Weedy Revenall would ever get airborne.

Thursday. Weedy in a rubber jump suit and mask mixed chemicals. Also put a windsock on the garage though he told Sally the best windsock in the world was the tail end of a cow.

Friday morning. The sky a gray lake in the east. The engine of the Pearly Thomas buzzing. Weedy loaded the drums from either wing. The dew, he said, would hold the dust to the plants.

The plane loaded, Weedy climbed into the cockpit and waved to the group watching. The Pearly Thomas taxied up the pasture and turned once before gathering speed for the takeoff. The plane rose with difficulty like a heavy tired old woman.

Sally looked toward the long horizon and thought how much

sky was there and how seldom she noticed it. The plane crossed
her vision, banking gracefully and then straightening and passing
over the sun which was only an orange buoy on the east horizon.
It cast an iridescent sheen over the red wings of the plane.

From the house she watched the plane descend to thirty feet
over the field, a real wheel roller Weedy called it. Suddenly a
mountain of dust erupted from the plane leaving a wide swath of
gray fields behind it. The plane dipped and glided over the fields,
then rose, turned, and dipped again. By mid morning the dew was
gone and Weedy rested, waiting for late afternoon to dust again.
Another morning and evening's work and the cotton fields were
flocked as Christmas trees. There was nothing to do then but wait
for the next hatch.

Anthonomus grandis, of the family Curculionidae; snout beetle.
Commonly known as the boll weevil. About one-fourth inch long,
snout one-half length of body. Ugly! Both adults and larvae feed
on the bolls, eggs deposited in cavities formed by eating into buds
and fruit of plant. Usually requires two to three weeks for weevil
to develop from egg to adult. Combated by dusting with chemi-
cals, early planting, and destroying infected plants in the autumn.

The week after dusting Weedy finagled himself a second hand
Ford convertible. Afternoons he'd drive into town and hang out
at the cafes and talk about flying. One night in the Post Office
Cafe Leo Pinkham suggested Weedy do some stunt flying for the
grand opening of his new John Deere tractor dealership. Weedy
had been talking about being inspired as a child by Marble Cody's
Flying Circus. He seemed surprised at Leo Pinkham's suggestion.
He slicked his thin rusty colored hair back and there was a flicker
on the side of his face.

"I'll pay you decent," Leo Pinkham said. "Whatever you think
is fair." He cocked his red haired, round head waiting for an answer.

Weedy pulled a paper napkin out of the metal holder in the
center of the table. He raised his coffee cup and folded the napkin
into the saucer to sop up the spilled coffee and set his cup back
down.

"You ain't yeller, are ya?" Charlie Willard asked, chewing on a
matchstick.

Weedy looked beyond him at the jukebox in the corner. It was swirling bright colors and playing, "*I'll Walk the Line. . . .*" "It ain't nothing like that," he said.

By the end of the evening they all took it as decided.

It grew hot, sweltering, unremittingly hot by July. There was no rain. The roads grew dustier, the fields drier. Each day before going to town Weedy would check a cotton field studying the rising green plants.

"They're not ready," he told Homer Bills the day before the tractor opening. He wiped the dust from off his yellow boots and shook his head. "Maybe two or three more days," he said.

AIR SHOW!

Dare Devil WEEDY REVENALL, Flying Ace

at

GRAND OPENING CELEBRATION

Leo K. Pinkham's Tractor Implement Co.
(Authorized John Deere Dealership)

Sat. July 12, beginning 12 noon
(in case of rain the next Saturday)

Highway 74, Next to the old gin

Entertainment by the ARKANSAS GENTLEMEN!!

Free Door Prizes: brand new John Deere tractor
'14 inch Muntz TV
electric ice cream freezer

Y'all Come!

Sally had an ominous gray feeling before she even opened her eyes that Saturday morning. Her body felt sticky against the bed clothes. The day before Weedy had removed the chemical tanks from the Pearly Thomas. There was talk of all sorts of dangerous tricks.

"Gonna break his scrawny neck right there in front of the ladies," Charlie Willard had predicted.

Leo Pinkham had decorated the tractor shed with plastic streamers on wires like the used car lot down the road. The crowd began drifting in before noon commenting that there wasn't a breeze or a cloud to hide anything Weedy Revenall wanted to do up there. Many of them would stay all day and the men go straight to the stag fish fry on the river that night.

At one o'clock the Arkansas Gentlemen climbed onto a little platform between two tractors and started playing. Charlie Willard's wife said didn't a one of them look like a gentleman to her. Long sideburns! Glittery western shirts! Matching initial rings! People milled around the tractors listening.

In twenty minutes the glittery western shirts of the Arkansas Gentlemen were soaked.

> "I'm throwing rice at the girl that I love . . .
> After she just said I do . . ."

a blond Arkansas Gentleman twanged, sweat rolling down his tall forehead and trickling across his eyebrows and down his concave cheeks.

Two o'clock. The air show. The sheriff cruised up and down the road with his siren swirling and roadblocks were set up to allow the Pearly Thomas to land after the show. The crowd flowed outside and began looking for Weedy's plane.

The people waited. They stared up over the gravel, over the patch of johnson grass, the barbed wire fence across the road, across the field, and the field beyond that, and on and on to a nearly endless horizon, all of it as crisp and intractable as a beetle. They waited for thirty minutes, ladies cupping their hands over their eyes, children kicking up dust until they were all standing in a cloud. But all they saw across the road and the fields and the burning pearl sky was a flock of blackbirds that scattered from one fence to another.

Sally stood at the edge of the crowd twisting her car keys. In her mind she'd seen herself rushing Weedy Revenall's broken

body twenty miles to the nearest hospital to save his life. But now
the idea was preposterous. It seemed impossible for that thin,
cloudless sky to hold a plane at all.

". . . be surprised if that little man ever did any stunt flying in
his life!" a man said.

"I never seen a man could lie hour after hour like that little
bastard."

When Leo Pinkham invited the crowd back inside to hear
more from the Arkansas Gentlemen Sally slipped away. She ran
down the hot asphalt past the line of cars parked along the highway and slid onto the hot plastic seat of the Henry Jay. She made
a U-turn and floorboarded it . . . past the O'Donnell Hardware sign . . . the Lions Club Welcomes You . . . Population
1,946. . . .

The plane sat in the shed, the convertible beside it. The windsock drooped. She turned off the motor and heard only the lonely
sound of a rooster crowing in the distance. The sun seemed to
have baked the life out of everything within sight and left the
earth stunned and colorless.

"Mr. Revenall?"

The door was cracked. She pushed it open and stepped into the
semi-dark room. The shade to the one window was pulled down.
After the glare of the sun she could see nothing for a minute only
smell . . . stale smoke . . . liquor . . . dirty socks. . . .

When her eyes adjusted she could see him sitting in the corner
of the bed, leaning against a soiled, slipless pillow, his body bare
above his levis, his short legs spread out before him on the bare
mattress, the sheet in a heap at the bottom of the bed. His head
leaned against the cheap knotty pine wall. He held a bottle in his
hands. On the floor his yellow boots lay on their sides. He looked
at her with no surprise or curiosity.

"People are waiting on you," she said. Her voice sounded loud
and childish and frightened. "I just came to tell you that everybody in town is about to get sun stroke waiting on you."

He rocked forward. "That right?" he said. His voice had a sput-
ter in it. There was a small triangle of hair in the middle of his
chest. He looked miniature and repulsive to her and suddenly she
wished she'd never come. She wished she'd stayed at the tractor
shed and maybe she'd have won the Muntz TV.

"What they waiting on, reckon?"

"They're waiting on you to put on your air show like you've been talking about for weeks."

He dropped a cigarette into a coffee can on the floor beside the bed. A stream of smoke rose beside him slowly like a charmed snake.

"Some folks would think it was a sin for me to go out there and risk my neck for a bunch of white trash and niggers' Saturday entertainment. . . ."

He's drunk and crazy she told herself. You don't have to talk to him.

". . . just wanting me to break my neck . . . ," he said petulantly.

She began to feel sorry for herself coming all the way out there to help him and receiving such an ungrateful reception.

He took a drink from the bottle.

"My plane's broke down," he said, ". . . have to order a part from Shreveport."

"Well, why didn't you tell people that. Why don't you drive in and explain what happened!"

He laughed suddenly holding the bottle with both hands against his stomach and letting his head roll back but his laugh was phony and humorless.

She wanted to leave but she felt trapped in her pleading. "If you heard what they're saying. . . ."

He snorted. "I been hearing it all my life."

She glanced through the open door beyond him to the little bathroom where the lid and seat to the john were raised and then quickly away to his face and then settled on the bottle he was holding and stared at it for a moment waiting for him to speak. But he said nothing.

"You're not coming?"

He took a drink from the bottle and set it on the floor, swung his legs over the side of the bed, and fumbled for his boots. One of them slid toward her and she picked it up and stepped forward to hand it to him. As soon as she was within reach he grabbed her arm and pulled her toward him. She could feel his arm cool and hard and sinewy like a rope, and smell his sour breath in her face.

"You know . . . some countries a man comes into another

man's house . . . he's offered whatever woman's available be it wife or daughter . . . it's the polite thing to do."

Up close his eyes were dull and uneven as though there were droplets of glue in them.

When she pulled away he released her easily. The boot fell between them making a loud "clop" as it hit the floor and Weedy started. He reached for the bottle and propped himself back up on the bed.

"You're just like all of them crackers. You don't care if I break my neck long as I put on my little show . . . hillbillies . . . ," he muttered.

No one had ever said such things to her. She felt her face hot and stinging and her hands trembling. *You can't talk like that to me*, she wanted to scream. She could feel the fury bringing tears and knew she had to say something quickly.

"Your daddy wasn't any missionary in Bangkok, Thailand," she charged shrilly and unexpectedly.

He stared up at her. There was a flick on the side of his face and when he laughed it was real.

The laugh followed her outside the door, through the bright afternoon and into the house where for the first time in her life she locked the door behind herself. In her bedroom she threw herself on the bed and cried hating Weedy Revenall, wishing mayhem would befall him. She cried and cried until the reason she was crying was no longer clear to her but she was crying for her whole, young uneventful life.

When the tears stopped she daydreamed. She lay on her back on the now rumpled bed and daydreamed of stealing the Pearly Thomas and flying to another country. Of becoming famous and rich and receiving an apology from Weedy Revenall. She daydreamed until all that remained of the day itself was night.

Saturday night. Billy Hutchinson at the stag fish fry. Sally at home; washing her hair, pressing a dress for church. There was no sound from Weedy Revenall's room. At 10:30 Sally went to bed.

It was after midnight when she woke hearing the cars stopping along the road. She lay in bed afraid, her heart thumping. The room was dark cubes of varying grays. Car doors slammed. Laughter, raucous, drunken, muffled. She stood beside the window looking beyond the light in their drive to the figures moving toward the plane shed. The plane waited in the darkness like a chained prisoner.

The men gathered around it and after a short while there was a great burst of flame that sounded like a mighty yawn. It rose from the tail of the plane and spread up the length of it and across the wings. The flames lapped at the body. There were spits of fire where the chemical tanks had been and soon the shed was burning. When small streamers of fire broke outward toward the pasture the men moved quickly stomping them out.

Sally heard her father move in the next room. She pictured the two of them standing at their respective windows in their bare feet watching.

It was strangely quiet. She could sometimes make out a figure standing back from the fire. She saw Charlie Willard, waving Weedy Revenall's goggles, move to the convertible and soon the rag top was burning. The men moved back enlarging their circle around the fires. When they moved she saw a man laughing at Billy Hutchinson who was bent vomiting beside the stock tank.

The smell of the burning plane slowly filled her room. She watched the figures familiar to her; watched them move around the fires, talk to one another, laugh. Some seemed serious, intent, committed to restoring their own balance. And she had known them, she thought; had believed them as predictable as her broken eye tooth, had believed them singular, not thoughtless bodies capable of generating destruction in the dark. She felt a calm contempt for them as she watched, and she watched until the fires died and they left, backing away from the glowing mound and turning, fading away into the darkness together.

When the doors were slammed and the cars gone she looked out toward the cotton field beyond the pasture and waited. She could see the line of the plants, like a black fence against the sky. She imagined the stirring of all those new brown snouted bodies. In the darkness, as though lightning flashed, she pictured all the green leaves falling to the earth at once. She saw the field as barren and colorless as the burned plane.

The men had been gone for nearly an hour when Weedy emerged. Carrying his duffel bag and a bottle he walked unsteadily across the back lot and out to the pasture. The shed had collapsed on top of the plane so that what remained was only a blackened hulk like a burned out chicken house. Now and then a breeze would cross it and generate a flicker of light.

Weedy paced around the plane bending once to pick up his goggles. Carefully he knocked the broken glass from the frames and adjusted the empty metal rims around his eyes. After that he moved quickly to the car, threw the duffel bag into the backseat and climbed in under the skeleton of his rag top. The engine was slow to start and then he raced it a minute before backing out the gate. He circled around behind the house stopping long enough to take a long drink. When he finished he flung the brown bottle against their concrete steps. It shattered into a million brown glittery pieces.

Suddenly the car started down the drive and passed under the light beside the house. The empty eyed goggles turned toward her as it passed. Sally leaned forward, raised her hand in a wave, which motionless became a salute. The car inched forward as though he were waiting. She pushed the latch of the screen letting it fall away and leaned far out into the dark. The car accelerated then and she watched it move down the drive and rattle over the cattleguard. It turned onto the road and fairly flew toward the highway.

THE ACTES AND MONUMENTS

JOHN WILLIAM CORRINGTON

JOHN WILLIAM CORRINGTON has published three novels, a collection of short stories, and four volumes of poetry. His work received a National Endowment for the Arts fiction award in 1967. He is a lawyer and lives in Shreveport, Louisiana.

AFTER THE CORONARY, I quit. I could have slowed down, let things go easier, taken some of the jobs where little more than appearance was required. But I didn't do that. I like to believe that I cared too much for the law. No, I *do* believe that. Because if I had cared nothing for the law, I would have played at being an attorney—or else simply stopped being involved with law at all. But I did neither.

Rather, I let go my partnership and began looking for some way to use all I knew, all I was coming to know. It wasn't that I couldn't stand pressure; I could. I could stand quite a bit of pressure. What I could not stand was the tension that never lets up, the sort of thing generated by corporation cases that might take four and five years without resolution. Brief peaks followed by relaxation: those, the doctor said, would be all right.

So I was thirty-eight, a good lawyer by any standard—including the money I had let collect in stocks. A bachelor, and a one-time loser on the coronary circuit. What do you do? Maybe you settle down in Manhattan and have fun? Maybe you don't. There is no room in Manhattan for fun—not in the crowd I knew, anyhow. You are either in it or out of it; that was the rule, and everybody understood and accepted. Poor Harry wasn't in it. So Harry had to walk out of it. Who needs to be pushed?

But Harry is no loser. Not since Harry climbed out of Brooklyn Heights and into Yale Law School. No, Harry has to find himself a blast he can live with. Out of New York. So, where? London? Not really. We don't function well in other places. Rio, Athens, Caracas, Tokyo. Any one of them is easy with my contacts. But they are imitations of what I am having to leave.

So Harry comes on very strong. Much stronger than anyone can credit, believe. Who knows where I caught the idiot virus that took me down there? Maybe it was *Absalom, Absalom*, which once I read, not understanding a word of it, but living in every crevice of time and space that the laureate of the cracker world created.

It is no overstatement to say that my friends paled when they received postcards from Vicksburg. It was much too much. They were old postcards. Pictures in mezzotint of the Pennsylvania memorial, of the grass-covered works outside the town. Postcards that must have been printed at the latest in the early 1920s, and which had been in the old; flyblown rack, waiting for my hand, almost half a century. I cannot remember what I wrote on the cards, but it must have been wonderful. I can say it was wonderful, because outside one slightly drunken phone call from Manhattan late at night about a week after I arrived, I got no answers to those cards at all. Perhaps they never arrived. Perhaps they slipped back into the time warp from which I had plucked them at the little clapboard store outside town, where there was a single gas pump with a glass container at the top, which the proprietor had to pump full before it would run down into the tank of my XKE.

Should I tell you about that man? Who sold me gas, counted out my change, made no move at my hood or windshield, and told me in guarded tones that he had seen a car like mine once long ago. A Mercer runabout, as he remembered. Never mind.

I rented a place—leased it. Almost bought it right off, but had not quite that kind of guts. It was old, enormous, with a yard of nearly an acre's expanse. I came that first day to recognize what an acre meant in actual extent. I stood in my yard near an arbor strung with veiny ropes of scuppernong, looked back at the house through the branches of pear trees, past the trunks of pecan and oak strung with heavy coils of that moss that makes every tree venerable that bears it. My house, on my property. Inside, I had placed my books, my records, my liquor, what little furniture I had collected in the brownstone I had left behind.

My first conclusion was that the coronary had affected my mind. I could have committed myself to Bellevue with my doctor's blessing. Or, secondly, had I found in some deep of my psyche a degree of masochism unparalleled in the history of modern man? Is it true that Jewishness is simply a pathology, not a race or a religion? Perhaps I had, in the depths of my pain and the confusion attendant on my attack, weighed myself in the balance and found life and its slender probings at purpose wanting utterly. Could it be that a man who, in the very embrace of probable death can find no reason for his living except the sweating grab of life itself housed in a body, looks at all things and condemns himself to Mississippi?

Or finally, grossest of all, was there an insight in my delirium whereby I saw Mississippi not as exile, not as condemnation, but as a place of salvations? Must we somehow search out the very pits and crannies of our secret terrors in order to find what for us will be paradise? Consider, as I did in retrospect, that no man of normal responses raised in Manhattan is going to look for himself in the deep South. And yet, how many of those men of normal responses are happy? How many die at the first thrust of coronary, dreaming as life ebbs of a handful of dusty, dark-green grapes, a sprig of verbena, the soft, weathered marble of an old Confederate monument within the shadow of which might have lain the meaning of their lives? I offer this possibility only because we are, most of us, so very miserable living out the lives that sense and opportunity provide. I wondered afterward, when I came to understand at least the meaning of my own choice, if we do not usually fail ourselves of happiness—of satisfaction, anyhow—by ignoring the possibilities of perversity. Not perversion. Those, we invariably attempt in some form. No, perversity: how few of us walk into the darkness if that is what we fear. How few of us step into a situation that both terrifies and attracts us. If we fear water, we avoid it rather than forcing ourselves to swim. If we fear heights, we refuse to make that single sky dive that might simultaneously free and captivate us. If we cannot bear cats, we push them away, settling for a world of dogs. You see how gross my insights had become.

In order to live, I thought, standing there staring at the strange, alien house that was now my legal residence and the place where I was determined to create, as in a crucible, the substance of my new life, it may be essential to force, to invade, to overwhelm those shadowed places we fear, and fearing, learn to ignore as real possibilities even when we know them to be real, to be standing erect against a hot sky windless and blind to their own beauties, realizable only to those of us who come from distant places.

A simpler explanation was offered me later by one of Vicksburg's most elegant anti-Semites, a dealer in cotton futures who, loathing my nation and my region, my presumed religion and my race, became a close friend. He suggested that Jews, for their perfidy, are condemned to have no place, to strike no roots.

—Don't you live always out of a moral and spiritual suitcase? he asked slyly. Isn't it notable that there has never been any great architecture of the synagogue? How many of you speak the language of your great-grandfathers? Isn't placelessness a curse?

—Yes, I told him in answer to his last question. Indisputably yes. But think of the hungers of a placeless man. Can you even begin to conceive the mind of a man who has suffered a failure of the heart once, who has fled all ordinary lives and come to Mississippi? No, he said, no longer joking or arch. No, I can't conceive that mind. But I expect there must be riches in it. You'll be using your talents, he half asked, half stated. You'll be going to help niggers with the law, won't you?

—Yes, I told him. That, certainly. Not that it will mean a great deal. Only the reflex of the retired gunfighter who no longer hopes either to purge the world of good or evil but whose hand moves, claws at his side when pressed, out of a nervous reaction so vast and profound that the very prohibition of God himself could not stop it.

—Good, he said. Not about the niggers. Everybody in the country wants a try at that sack of cats. But not your way. We've never had a man who came loving, needing, down here to do that kind of thing. I want a chance to see this. It has got to be rich.

—What? I asked. What will be so rich?

—Why, seeing Yankee Jew fighting in the South because he

needs her, because he loves her. Did you ever in your life hear the
like of that?

How could I help loving? Where else could I come across such
a man? But he was the least of it. There was, at the garage that
saw to my car, an avowed member of the Klan who asked me why
I had come so far to die. My answer satisfied him. Because, if you
have got to die, it is stupid to die just anywhere and by an accident of some valve in your heart. If it comes here, I will know
why and maybe even when.

He looked at me and scratched his head. My Christ, he said. I
never heard nothing like that in all my life. You are a fucking nut.
How do you like it? I asked him over the hood of my Jaguar, now
dusty and hot with April sun. Why, pretty well, he said, grinning,
putting out his hand without volition or even, I suspect, the
knowledge he had extended it. I took it firmly, and he looked surprised. As if the last thing on earth he had ever expected to do
was shake hands with some skulking Yankee kike determined to
stir up his coloreds.

By this time you have dismissed me as a lunatic or a liar or
both. Very well. You only prove that the most profound impulses
of your spirit can find their fulfillment in Fairlawn, New Jersey.
Good luck.

But if your possibilities are . . . what? . . . more exotic, then I
want to tell you the proving of what I found here in Vicksburg,
Mississippi. I want to tell you about Mr. Grierson, and the cases
we worked on together—cases which, whatever else, have found me
for myself. So saying, I have to retreat to my first conclusion. The
coronary affected my mind. This, I'm sure of. Because, satisfied
beyond any hope I brought from Manhattan with me, I am still
enough of a rationalist to see that my satisfaction, my new life,
and what Mr. Grierson and I do—have done—is beyond even the
most liberally construed limits of ordinary sanity. I am not a mys-
tic, thus able to excuse any deviation in myself, blessing the lunacy
as a certain portent. I am a sensible man who, so cast, must admit
that he has found sense nonsense and empty, and that a tract of
lunacy laid out before him has bloomed like the distant desert
glimmering before Moses as he lay down at last, his final massive
coronary denying him the power to cross over Jordan and dwell

some last loving days or months or years amid the plenty that his lip-chewing endurance had reared up out of the sands.

I was handling now and again the smallest of cases for certain black people who had heard that an eccentric Yankee lawyer had come to town and would do a workmanlike job of defending chicken thieves, wife beaters, small-time hustlers, whores, and even pigeon droppers. This alone would have drawn me little enough custom, but it was said, further, and experience proved it true, that the Yankee did his work for free, a very ancient mariner of Yankee lawyers doomed to work out his penance for bird mangling or beast thumping by giving away his services to whatever Negro showed up with a likely story. It was said that if you had no likely story, he would help you make one up—not inciting to perjury, you realize. Only fooling with the facts in such a way as to produce a story diverting enough to keep the judge from adding a month or so to your sentence for the boredom you caused him in addition to the inconvenience of having to keep court for the likes of you. All that aside, I seduced by asking no fee. It was at first amazing to me how a Negro was willing often to take a chance of six months or a year in prison to avoid a fifty-dollar fee, even when he had it. For some reason I could not at first grasp, my own logic had no purchase with them. Think: suppose a man offered you free legal service. Wouldn't you, like me, presume that the service would be about worth the price? Yes, you would. But how do you suppose the Blacks reasoned? One of my chicken —actually, a pig—thieves explained why he trusted me. You got a nice house, ain't you? Yes, I said. You out of jail yourself, ain't you? Yes. You look like you eats pretty good. I do, I eat very well. Except no pork. No saturated fats. Huh? Never mind. Oh, religion, huh? All right. Anyhow, if you got a good house, if you look like eating regular, and if the judge let you stand up there, you got as much going for you as any jackleg courthouse chaser I seen.

It was that very pig robber who carried me down to town one day in search of a law book. Something to do with the statute of limitations on pig thievery. It seems that my man was charged with having stolen a pig in 1959, the loss or proof of it having come to light only in the past few days. I wanted to make absolutely sure that there was not some awful exception to ordinary prescription in Mississippi law when the subject was pigs. There

are some oddities in Texas law having to do with horses. I had
never had much practice connected with livestock in Manhattan.
I thought I had better make sure.

So I was directed by a deputy, who was everlastingly amused by
the nature and style of my practice, to the offices of Mr. Grierson.

They were on a side street just beyond the business district.
Among some run-down houses that must have been neat and even
prime in the 1920s but which had lost paint and heft and hope in
the 1950s at the latest, there was a huddle of small stores. A
place that sold seed and fertilizer and cast-iron pots and glazed
clay crocks that they used to make pickles in. Just past the pots
and crocks, there was a flat-roofed place with whitewashed doors
and one large window, heavy curtains behind it, across which was
painted

FREE CHURCH OF THE OPEN BIBLE

There was a hasp on the door with a large combination lock hanging through it. I wondered what might be the combination to the
Open Bible.

Just past the church, there was another store-front building
standing a little to itself. There was a runway of tall weeds and
grass between it and the church, and it was set back a little from
the sidewalk with a patch of tree lawn in front. On either side of
the door was a huge fig tree, green and leafy and beginning to
bear. Through the heavy foliage, I could see that there were windows behind the trees. They seemed to have been painted over
crudely, so that they looked like giant blinkered eyes that had no
wish to see out into the street. Above the door itself was a sign
made of natural wood hanging from a wrought-iron support. On
it was graved in faded gold letters cut down into the wood

W. C. GRIERSON
Atty. at Law

The door itself was recessed fairly deeply and I got the notion
that it was not the original door, that it had nothing really to do
with the building, which was, like those nearby, simply a long
frame affair, what they—we—call a shotgun building, although
much wider and longer. I stood there in the early-summer sun
looking at that door as if it were the entrance to another place.

Why? I rubbed my chin and thought, and then I found, back in the fine debris of my old life, back behind the sword edge of my coronary, the recollection of another summer afternoon spent with a lovely woman at some gallery, some wealthy home—somewhere. We had gone to see paintings, and there had been one among all the others that I could not put out of mind. It had been by the Albrights, those strange brothers. Of a door massive and ancient, buffed and scarred, the very deepest symbol both of life and of the passage through which life itself must pass. On its weatherbeaten panels hung a black wreath, each dark leaf pointed as a spike, shimmering in the mist of its own surreality. My God, I remembered thinking, is death like that? Is it, finally, a door with a wreath standing isolated from air and grass—even from the materials that are supposed to surround the fabric of a door? And then I thought, the lovely woman beside me talking still about a Fragonard she had spotted nearby, of Rilke's words: "Der grosse Tod . . . The great Death each has in himself, that is the fruit round which all revolves. . . ." But the title of the painting was "That Which I Should Have Done, I Did Not Do," and I could find neither sweetness or rest in that.

Later, when I had done with the lovely woman, I remember somehow managing to go back to see the painting again. It was evening then, winter I think, and whether in a museum or a private home (I could remember such things with perfect clarity before my heart failed me), I was alone, standing before it with the light soft and nothing but loneliness stalking the roofless windowless doorless wall-less room there with me.

I had come back looking for some release from it, I think now. I had gone back not for appreciation—any more than one goes back to see Grünewald's Isenheim altarpiece for reasons of art. I wanted to find the key to that door—the flaw, the crack in its reality. To be free of the Albrights and their loathsome portal, I had to find, somewhere in the canvas, a false note, a tiny piece of sentimentality or stupidity. But there was nothing. The weather of the painting was unfathomable. It did not change. Even with the summer brightness purged from the room, it was the same—as if the door, the wreath, the very canvas had the power to absorb or reject exterior light so as to keep the painting always within that awful twilight that flowed like sidereal influence out of the door's dead center, the wreath hanging against it like a demonic target or some emblem of absolutism linked with the imperturbable power of death itself.

Yes, I am standing still in front of that frame building in my town of Vicksburg and, yes, looking inward past the great figtrees at the shadowed door, which now after all looks only the least bit like that other one, the weather, the light, the substantiality of all things about being so much less dense. Reality spares us; we do not have to know what else there is very frequently, do we? A colored boy, no more than twelve, walked by in a polo shirt and worn corduroy pants. He exchanged a quick glance with me and stepped on past, a transistor radio hanging from his neck, a tiny tinny thing which crooned:

> . . . looks like the end, my friend,
> got to get in the wind, my friend. . . .
>
> These are not my people, no, no,
> these are not my people. . . .

Surely he had his radio aimed at me. How could he tell? And was the announcer a friend of his? He an agent of the station, which had discovered me, an alien, waxing in their midst? All of this I thought in jest, putting sudden flash cuts of the Isenheim crucifixion out of mind, reaching for the doorknob, and stepping inside.

I do not know why I was not prepared. I should have been. No reason for me to suppose that a lawyer's office here, in an old frame building, would have the sort of Byzantine formality I remembered from New York. Receptionist, secretary, inner office —with possibly a young clerk interposed somewhere between. But the mind is stamped inalterably with such impressions when we have done business a certain way for a very long time.

So I was not prepared when Mr. Grierson turned in his chair and smiled at me and said:

—Well, this is nice. Mighty nice. I don't know as I expected it.

—I beg—I began. Then I tried again. Best not beg. —I'm sorry. Have we met? Is it better to be sorry than to beg? I thought instantly. Too late.

—You'd be the lawyer just come down. Got you a house and everything.

My God, I thought, even a B movie would tell you that things travel like lightning here. He probably saw the deed, the note of transfer on the title. Knows what you paid for the lease, what you owe on the house if you pick up the option. Knows your last address, your last place of employ. Knows about your little chicken-thief cases, your car . . . I almost thought, about your coronary.

—Yes, I said, putting out my hand as he rose and offered his

—I'm Harry Cohen.

He motioned me to a chair near his desk and I sat down, trying as I did to begin the task of seeing him, of seeing this place in which he worked. Trying at the same time to put out of mind the impressions I had created, had begun to suppose from the moment the deputy had told me where to come. If we could only stay free of our own guesses, what would ever make us wrong in advance?

He walked over to a large safe against the wall to the left of the door. It was taller than he was, and the door opened slowly as he turned the handle. He stood reaching into its dark recesses, his back to me. I wondered what he was looking for as his voice came to me, small talk like a magician's patter, over his shoulder.

—Yes, Mr. Cohen. It's kind of you to pay a courtesy call. A custom languishing. Not dead, but in a bad way. A fine custom. Men who stand to the law shouldn't meet for the first time arguing a motion before Basil Plimsoll or one of the other boys on the circuit here . . .

I scanned the room as he spoke. I would deal with him later. It was a bright room—almost the opposite of what the door suggested. Or was it only the opposite of what the Albrights' door suggested?

On the wall over his flat desk, the shape and design of which, I suspected, had vanished long before, beneath a welter of papers and books, there were three old tintype portraits. Only, they were not tintypes. They were fresh, modern reproductions of tintypes. In the center, in a military uniform I almost recognized, was that stern, beautiful face one recognizes without ever even having seen it. It was Lee. To his right, left profile toward me, hung that other one, that crafty rebel whose religion had almost severed the continent, Jackson. I did not know the third. He had a Tartar's face, long, bony, richly harsh—as if only in that uniform, only involved in that calling of arms had his life meant anything to him at all. His eyes were straightforward and overpowering even at a hundred years' remove. And yet they were somehow at ease, their intensity more a matter of something evoked in the viewer than something essential to the eyes themselves. He had a high forehead, hair long, black, brushed back. His beard was a careless Vandyke and the effect was that of seeing the man had last closed the Albrights' door, nailed the wreath on it, and walked away, hands in uniform pockets. Whistling.

The rest of the room was austere and predictable. Near a long window there was a rocking chair done in some kind of chintz. Another table covered with papers. A third table in a corner with a coffeepot on it, a wine bottle or two, half a loaf of bread, and a plate upon which rested, glowing faintly, a large wedge of cheese. It looked like cheddar from where I sat. It was a room without quality—except for the portraits, which were, I thought, a ritual observance no more meaningful to this man whose life had been lived in another country than washing his face in the morning, spitting at noon, closing his eyes at night.

Mr. Grierson turned from the safe, hands filled with two tumblers and a dark-brown bottle without a label. It had no cap. There seemed to be a cork stuck in it. He set all of it down on the edge of his desk and pulled the bottle's stopper with his teeth. The liquor was the lightest possible amber, a cataract of white gold as it twinkled into the glasses.

He smiled up at me. —You'll like it, he said. —Maybe not this time. But you let me send you a couple bottles. You'll come to like it.

—Corn, I said.

—Surely. Comes from upstate. Costs more than it used to. Bribes are just like the cost of living.

I sat back and sipped a little. It was peculiar, nothing like whiskey, really. It was a shock in the mouth, vanished as you swallowed. Then it hit the pit of your stomach and paralyzed you for the briefest moment. Then great warmth, a happiness that spoke of cells receiving gifts, of veins moving to a new rhythm, muscles swaying like grain in a breeze-swept field. It was lovely.

Nothing like whiskey. More like sipping the past, something in-
tangible that could yet make you feel glad that it had been there.

Mr. Grierson sat watching me now. As I took another swallow,
deeper this time, I watched him back. A man of middle height,
aged now but hale. Steel-rimmed glasses revealing large, innocent, blue eyes that seemed never to have encountered guile. He
had that almost cherubic look that one associates with country
doctors—or, in certain cases, with southern politicians. He wore
an old suede coat, cut for hunting. I had never seen anything like
it. It was a soft umber and fit as if it were his own original pelt.

—Your jacket, I couldn't help saying, feeling the whiskey lift
me and waft me toward him, toward his smile. —Could I get one
. . .

—At Lilywhite's, he said.

—Here?

—London, he said apologetically. —And even there back in
1949. I wouldn't reckon they make 'em like this any more.

He wasn't putting me on, I could tell. But I could tell, too, that
he enjoyed that level of conversation. It pleased him to please
with pleasantries. One moves from a series of set exchanges to another. An infinite series. And when the last series is exhausted, it
is either time to go, or you have lived out your life and death
clears its throat, almost loath to interrupt, and says that it is time.
I thought I would not want to go on like that.

Did I tell you that, on the far side of the coronary (Oh, God,
how that word has come to press me with its softness, its multiple
implications! Corona. Carnal. Corot. Coronary. A place, a name,
the vaguest warm exhalation glimmering from an eclipsed sun.
Shivering golden and eternal around the glyph of a saint. Called
then a glory. I lay for weeks thinking Coronary, wondering when
it would reach into my chest once more and squeeze ever so
gently and bring out with its tenderness my soul, toss that gauzy
essence upward like a freed dove to fly outward, past morning,
past evening, past the blue sky into the glistening midnight blue
of deep space, and past that even to the place where souls fly,
shaking great flakes of its own hoarded meaning outward, downward on all suns and the worlds thereunder.) I had had a certain
gift with exceptionally sharp teeth. Yes, I had been cruel. I had
enjoyed finding certain lawyers in the opposition, men I had

known who were blessed with a kind of unwillingness to go for blood. They worked within the confines of their dignity, their gentleness, their inadequacy. But I worked elsewhere and won invariably. But such work tightens the viscera. One cannot play bloodster without gradually coming to possess the metabolism of a jaguar, a predator. Was it imagination, or did I come to see better in the dark as I aged in my profession? Was I a little mad, or did I move more smoothly? Did my walk take on a certain ease, a bit of stealth? Did I smile with that humorless, lynx-eyed expression that flows from the second sight of the killer? If it had not been for my success, I would have gone to a psychiatrist saying, Doctor, there is in me a germ and I fear it grows. Watch your throat, Doctor. What? Yes, I invent metaphors for killing. I am not psychopathic. Never that. Not at all. No, I must kill without killing. I am a child of the century. Do you understand?

But Coronary came upon me, slackened the knotted nerves, the plaited muscles. I cannot say if I look younger or older now. But I am much different. I do not—no, will not—want to pursue and strike and rend. I am more peaceful. I want to do my part. And what is my portion will come to me. It is chess after professional football. But even so, not Mr. Grierson's gambit, not at his tempo. Though even as I looked at his pink, uncreased face and considered the folds and inlets of the world behind him, I wondered if his pleasantries, his kindliness were not analogous to mine. What if one has, in passion or confusion, or from habit, taken men of another hue out and strung them to a near tree? What if that is how, or a small age, we have shaken from ourselves that rage that can tear a whole society to pieces? Suppose, from outside, something like Coronary should come? What might we do in the shadow of knowing that we cannot ever lynch again on pain of dying? Chess, after all, is a pleasantry profoundly complicated, Byzantine in its intricacies. Is there something in this?

—Another little drink, Mr. Grierson suggested. —I believe you've already found something in it.

—I was thinking . . . of martinis.

—No comparison. Next step from corn would be . . . perhaps a pipe of opium.

I did not even wonder if he spoke from experience or from

some book by Saxe Rohmer. I wanted to go on. —Mr. Grierson, I wonder if you have the Southwest Reporter fro—

He poured each of us another glass. —I have it all, he said. —I think my . . . library will fill your . . .

I looked around. There was a single bookcase across the room, and only a handful of books in it. I must have looked doubtful. He gave me the oddest of small glances, and I took refuge in my whiskey.

—Maybe we should go on into the library, he said, rising and walking toward a door at the back of the room that I had not even noticed until now. It was painted the same dull color as the rest of the office. There was a hook nailed badly to it with coats and jackets and what looked like an old fishing hat hanging from the hook.

I followed him and stepped ahead of him as he opened the door.

What shall I say? I have to tell you that Coronary fluttered not far away and I stepped in and turned in the new room slowly, slowly, taking it in, feeling, thinking in a simultaneity resembling that first moment of the attack.

So this is what lies behind them Southerners. There is always that front room, the epitome of the ordinary, a haven for bumpkins. And behind, in one way, one sense or another, there is always this. No wonder even the most ignorant of them is more complex, more intricate than I have ever been. They stand upon this. This is behind them, within them. My God, what does that make . . . us?

Because it was, properly speaking, not a room. No, many rooms. It went on, back at least four more rooms, and perhaps side rooms off each of the main rooms toward the back. And I knew without even entering the others that they were all more or less like this one I was standing in:

Filled from floor to ceiling with books. Thousands upon thousands of books. Books in leather and buckram, old, new, burnished bindings and drab old cloth. Behind and around the shelves the walls were paneled in deepest cherry wood. Before me was a beautiful nineteenth-century library table surrounded by chairs. It was like the rare-book room of a great private library. I moved spellbound toward the nearest shelf. It was . . . religion. What was not there? Josephus. The Fathers in hundreds of volumes. The Paris edition of Aquinas. Was this a first of the Complutensian Polyglot? Scrolls in ivory cases. Swedenborg, Charles Fort. A dissolving Latin text from the early-seventeenth century. The *Exercises* of Ignatius. Marcion, Tertullian. And I could see that the rest of the room was of a kind with those I was looking at.

—I had a house once, Mr. Grierson was saying. —But even then it didn't seem fitting to have all this stuff out where my clients could see it. Folks here can abide a lot of peculiarity, but you ought not to flaunt it. You want to keep your appetites kind of to yourself.

This is a depreciating voice, as if possession of books, especially in great number, was somehow a vice—no, not a vice, distinctly not a vice, but an eccentricity that must disturb the chicken thief or the roughneck with a ruptured disc. Was it a kindness to spare them this?

—I think you'll find 'most anything you'll need here, Mr. Grierson said softly. —Except for science. Not much science. Darwin, Huxley, Newton—all the giants. I kind of gave up when they went to the journals. They stopped doing books, you know.

—Yes, I said. Still thinking, this is where the Southerners have stored it all. You ask, how could Faulkner . . . how could Dickey . . . down here, in this . . . place . . . ? This is how.

I knew that this was madness. I did not question that. This time, had there been a psychiatrist close by, I would have gone to him at once without a doubt. Because, after all, this was not what I thought, but worse: what I felt. I *knew* it was not so, and still I *believed* it.

—This is where I do . . . my work, Mr. Grierson was saying.

—Work, I repeated as we entered another room, filled with literature. All of it. My hand fell on a shelf filled with French. Huysmans, Daudet, De Musset, Mérimée—and a large set of portfolios. They were labeled simply Proust. I took one out. It was bound in a gray cloth patterned in diamond-shaped wreaths, each filled with starlike snowflakes, smaller wreaths, featherlike bursts gathered at the bottom, nine sprays flaring at the top.

—It was the wallpaper, Mr. Grierson was saying. —That pattern . . .

I opened the portfolio. In it were printed sheets covered with scrawling script, almost every line of print scratched out or added to.

—Proofs. Of *Du Côté de chez Swann*. I was in Paris . . . in 1922. Gide . . . anyhow, I came across . . .

—Of course. You've studied them?

—Oh, yes. The Pléiade text isn't . . . quite right.

We went on for a long time, shelf by shelf. But we did not finish. We never finished. It could have taken weeks, months, so rich was his treasure.

I left at dusk with Grierson seeing me to the door, inviting me back soon, offering me the freedom of his library. I was back home sitting under my arbor with whiskey and a carafe of water on a small table beside me before I recalled that I had never gotten around to checking the Mississippi law as to its position on pigs and those who made off with them.

The pig had prescribed, sure enough. But on the way out of court, I found myself involved in another case, dealing, if you will, with similar matters.

They were bringing in a young man in blue jeans, wearing a peculiar shirt made of fragments, rags—like a patchwork quilt. He had very long hair, like Prince Valiant, except not so neat. He was cuffed between two deputies. One, large with a face the color of a rare steak, kept his club between the young man's wrists, twisting it from time to time. There seemed somehow to be an understanding between them: the deputy would twist his club viciously; the young man would shriek briefly. Neither changed his expression during this operation.

—What did he do? I asked the other deputy, who looked much like a young Barry Fitzgerald.

—That sonofabitch *cussed* us, he told me with that crinkly simian smile I had seen in *Going My Way.* —We should of killed him.

—Local boy? I asked.

You got to be shitting me, he answered, watching his partner doing the twist once more. —He's some goddamned Yankee. Michigan or New York, I don't know. We should of killed him.

—Did you find anything in his car?

—Car, your ass. He was hitching out on U.S. 80. We better not of found anything on him. I know I'd of killed him for sure. I can't stand it, nobody smoking dope.

—What's the charge?

—Reviling, he said, eyes almost vanishing in that attenuated annealed Mississippi version of an Irish grin. —Two counts.

—Two?

—We was both there. He was vile to Bobby Ralph and me both.

—What did he say?

—Wow, Barry Fitzgerald's nephew crinkled at me. —We should of killed him and dumped him in Crawfish Creek.

—What?

—Pigs.

—Sorry?

You heard. Called us—Bobby Ralph and me—pigs. My God, how do you reckon we kept off of killing him?

I think it was a question of free association. Pigs. I had had luck with pigs so far. Maybe this Yankee sonofabitch—pardon me —was sent for my special care. God knows the care he would get otherwise. Just then Barry's partner gave the young man a final supreme wrench. He came up off the floor of the courthouse hall-way at least three feet. He squealed and looked at me with pro-found disgust.

—You old bastard, he drawled, hunching his shoulders, —would you let 'em book me so I can get these things off?

—I'm a lawyer, I said.

—You're fucking bad news, the young man said wearily.

—See, Barry said, as his partner shoved the young man down the hall toward the booking room. —Reckon we ought to take him back out an' lose him?

—No, I said. —You don't want to do that.

—No, Barry said, walking after his partner and their day's bag. —No, you lose him and the feds shake all the feathers out of your pallet looking for him. Christ, all you have to do to make him im-portant is lose him. Or paint him black.

—You leave the ninety-nine lambs and seek the one that's lost, I said, striving for his idiom.

—Anyone does that is a goddamned fool, Barry said over his shoulder. —And he's going to be out of the sheep business before he knows it. Lost is lost.

Later—you guessed it—he sent for me. On the theory that I seemed to be the only one in the town able to speak English as he knew it, as opposed to lower Mississippian. We talked in a corner of his cell. There was a sad Mexican and a local drunk in the cell with him. The three had reached a kind of stand-off between them. None could understand the others. Each seemed weird to the others. Since they had no weapons and were roughly the same size, an accommodation had been arranged. No one would begin a fight that could not be handicapped.

His name was Rand McNally. He might have been a nice-looking young man if he had wanted to be. But he was not. His eyes were circled, his skin dry and flaked. I could not tell precisely what color his hair was. He had a small transistor radio the size of a cigarette pack stuck in the pocket of his shirt. It was tuned to a local rock-music station:

> She's got everything she needs,
> She's an artist,
> She don't look back . . .

—The spic stinks and the redneck keeps puking over there in the corner, Rand McNally told me. —But that's all right. I've got it coming. I deserve it. Jesus, I wish I'd kept my mouth shut.

—Or stayed out of Mississippi.

—It was an accident, Mississippi.

—Some say that, I told him.

—Oh, shit. I mean being here. I was running away from a . . . girl. It came up Mississippi.

—Where are you from?

He sat back and fingered his essay at a beard. It was long and a kind of dark red. I supposed his hair was probably the same color if it was washed. The beard was sparse, oriental. Above it, he had large, green eyes that somehow gave me a start each time I looked squarely into them. I am not used to being put off by a physical characteristic, but those eyes, deeply circled, seemed to demand a concentration and attention I had no wish to muster. They seemed, too, to require the truth. Not knowing the truth, I evaded such demands whenever possible. I wished I had let him pass on with Barry Fitzgerald's kinsman and his partner. No I didn't.

—I don't know, Rand McNally said. —From one place after another. I just remember serial motels and rooming houses. The old man was an automobile mechanic. I never had the idea it started anywhere. I mean, it had to start somewhere. I got born, didn't I? But I remember it being one dump after another forever. Al's Garage, Bo-Beep Motel; Fixit Tire Company, Millard's Auto Court; Willie's Car Repair, Big Town Motor Hotel. Somewhere the old man had a woman and she had me—told him I was his— and then on to the next place. She dropped off somewhere. I think he whipped up on her. I seem to remember something. About money? Sure, probably. I don't remember her.

I saw his father, a great, tall harried man with grease worked permanently into the skin of his knuckles, under his fingernails, with the soul of Alice's white rabbit, an ancient Elgin running fast in his pocket and a notebook listing all the small towns, garages, and motels he was obliged to move through before it was done. One entry said: *Get Son.* Another said: *Son Grown. Leaves.* There were faded, smeared pencil checks beside each entry. Life lived between Marvin Gardens and Reading Railroad.

—How do you want to plead? I asked him.

He shrugged. —Make it easy on yourself. I've got a couple of months to do here. Price of pork.

I had not thought him intelligent enough to have a sense of humor. We smiled at each other then. The transistor was quacking another of its vast repertoire of current tunes:

> These are not my people,
> No, no, these are not my people.
> Looks like the end, my friend,
> Got to get in the wind, my friend . . .

—I'm going to plead you innocent. No malice.

He tossed his hair back and smiled up at me. His green eyes seemed to hang on mine for a long while. It surprised me that someone so worn, so ground off by the endless procession of new people in his life could reach across to the latest in that anonymous parade with even the appearance of interest.

—No malice, he said. —That's true.

It was late that evening when the phone rang. At the other end was Billy Phipps, one of the county attorney's assistants. His voice was lazy with an undertone of something like amusement or exultation. I did not like him. He was provincial as a Bronx delivery man and took pleasure in the webbing of paltry law as it snared those who had not the slightest idea of its working. His own ignorance made him delight in that of others.

—Well, what do you think of your boy Rand McNally? he asked.

—Not a lot, I said, wondering why he would bother with a call on such a matter. —It seems silly to put him on the county for a little mild name calling. Hadn't you ought to leave room for rape-murderers?

At the other end of the line, I could hear Phipps draw in his breath.

I pause only to say that I neither believe nor disbelieve in magic, precognition, spiritualism, and so on. I am not prejudiced. But I have come to feel that all we do in the four dimensions of our world is like the action of water beetles skating on the surface of a still lake, turning our tricks between water and air, resident truly, fully, in neither, committed vaguely to both. Are we material—or other? I receive hints from varied sources. If you have loitered at the gates of Coronary, you must wonder. Is a massive heart seizure only a statistically predictable failure of meat mechanism? Could it be counted a spiritual experience? Who, what seizes the heart? Who, what attacks the heart? Could it be an entrance into the indices of those currents that play above and below the beetle, in the great eternal world where there are neither serials, sequences, nor statistics? Where forever, possibly, dear God and his precious Adversary choose to disagree as to the purpose of their copulation? At my worst—or best?—moments, I seem to hear, like a radio signal from the most remote reaches of time and space, the voices of the entities making their cases over and over, yet never the same, because each permutation is a case unto itself. Is it the voice of God one hears, arguing point by

point, A to B to C, coolly, without rancor or regret—like Herman
Kahn? Is it Satan who cries and exults, demands, entreats, laughs,
chides, tears a passion, and mutters sullenly? Or are those voices
reversed? Maybe I am gulled believing in polarities. Why not?
Could not God howl and sob the Natural Order of normal occa-
sions? While Satan urges quietly the Stewing Urgencies of
Madness? Why not? And why should we not in one way or another receive darts and splinters from those age-long and intricate
arguments?

So much to explain my mind as I heard Phipps draw in his
breath. *Jesus*, I thought, *a message.*

—What did he tell you? Phipps asked quietly, his normal sneer-
ing country manner gone altogether.

—Nothing, I said. —What do you mean?

—Counselor, we got a telegram from Shreveport. They want to
talk to Pig Boy. About a rape-murder.

—Ah, I said, and felt those faintest stirrings in my chest. Not
even a warning, only the dimmest—can I say, sweetest—touch of
recollection, of terrible nostalgia, from the distant geographies of
Coronary. Like the negative of a photograph of a memory, saying:
this twinge, this whisper, is what you felt without noticing before
you came that day for the first time upon the passage to Coronary. Be warned and decide. Is it a landscape you wish to visit
again? Is it, pulsing once more, a place where gain outmeasured
loss? Stroke the contingencies and wonder your way to a decision.
You have been once across the bourn from which few travelers
return. Do you have it for another trip? And will that trip, too, be
round?

—Ah, I said again to Phipps. —Let me get back to you, all
right?

It was all right. Spatially, Rand McNally was fixed. This allowed certain latitude with time. Tomorrow would be just fine.
Since the rape-murder, evocation of a nameless victim cooling
after life's fitful fever three hundred and fifty miles away, in
northern Louisiana, was fixed irrevocably in time and there could
be, for those to whom its being was announced, no moving from
it even as it receded backward and away now, one more permutation in the patterns spoken of in that bower where God and His
Son ramble on to no probable conclusion.

Is it strange to say that, after the call from Phipps, I found myself thinking less of the long-haired boy than before? Before, I had been searching for a way to free him from, at most, a three-month term in jail. Now, when he might stand within the shadow of death or a lifetime in prison, he seemed somehow less a point of urgency. Perhaps because I believed not only that he had committed that rape-murder in another place and time, but that he had, in passage from one serial point called Shreveport to another called Vicksburg—both noted as mandatory in a book like the one his father had been slave to—placed upon that act, called rape-murder by authorities who have the legal right to give comings together names and sanctions, his own ineradicable mark: a fingerprint, a lost cap, one unforgettable smile caught by a barmaid in a cafe as he passed toward or from the fusion with another—presumably female—in that timetable inherited from his father, and for all either I or he could say, from the very Adam of his blood. However that might be, there was no hurry now. Ninety days in the county jail, so implacable only a little while before, no longer mattered. Which called to my mind, making me laugh inordinately, that on the day of Coronary I had developed a painful hangnail, had given it much thought. Until it vanished in the wilderness of my new world. Had it healed in the hospital? One presumed. I could not recall it after I had stepped out of that world in which one nags for the sake of a hangnail. It is a question of magnitudes. When Coronary came, I was transformed into one who, having disliked mosquito bites, now used the Washington Monument for a toothpick. Mosquitoes, landing, would fall to their deaths in the vastness of a single pore. And later, drinking off my bourbon and water and sugar, I slept without dreams. Or, as I am told, dreaming constantly but remembering none when it came time to awaken.

—I hear you reached in for a kitty and caught yourself a puma, my telephone was saying.

It was Mr. Grierson calling. He wanted to know if he could be of assistance.

—Seeing you hadn't figured on anything quite like this, he said blandly.

Yes, I told him. Hell yes. Only small boys and large fools stand alone when they might have allies. Anyhow, I thought, McNally will barely have representation anyhow: a heart patient obsessed with the exotica of his complaint; an old man gone bibliophile from sheer loneliness. We would see.

We did. It was noon when we got in. Rand McNally stared out at the jailer, in whose eyes he had obviously gained status. When he opened the cell, he loosened the strap on his ancient pistol. *This here bastard is a killer,* I could almost hear him thinking.

Mr. Grierson hitched up his pants, passed his hand over his thin hair, and sat down on a chair the jailer had provided for him. I made do with the seat of the toilet. Mr. Grierson studied the boy for a moment, then looked at me expectantly, as if protocol required that I begin. I nodded, returning the compliment to my elder. I had divined already how such things would move in Mississippi. Mr. Grierson returned my nod and cleared his throat.

—Well, sir, it appears that clandestine hog-calling is the least of your problems.

Rand McNally stared at him in astonishment. Then he laughed, looked at me, saw me smile despite myself. He went on laughing while Mr. Grierson sat quietly, an expression bemused and pleasant on his face.

—I'm glad you got such a fine spirit, son. You're gonna need it.

Rand McNally took the earplug of his transistor out and hung it through the spring of the empty bunk above his. The Mexican and the farmer were gone now. Perhaps released to the terrors and punishment of sobriety; perhaps simply transferred to other cells in honor of Rand McNally's new status.

—Huh, McNally said to Mr. Grierson.

—If you did to that lady in Shreveport what they say you did, you're gonna have a chance to stand pat whilst they strap you in the electric chair. Shave your head, I believe, before you go.

Rand McNally shuddered. Whether it was the standing pat, the chair, or the head-shaving, I could not tell.

—Well, Mr. Grierson asked him. —What about it?

Yes. Well, he told us. He was glad it was over, was tired of running. ("Son of a bitch only did what he did three days ago," Mr. Grierson observed later. "What do you reckon? Think he's been reading *Crime and Punishment?*") He had gone to work for an elderly widow in Shreveport, had cut the yard for a meal, had hung a shelf for a dollar, and come back the next day to whitewash a fence for two dollars. Had whitewashed most of the day with her looking on from her kitchen window past the blooming wisteria and lazy bees. Near sundown, covered with sweat and whitewash, he had gone inside to get a glass of ice water and his two dollars. As he drank, the woman squinted out at the fence, saying, "It'll take another coat." "Huh," Rand McNally said. "Another coat. Then I'll pay you," she said softly, smirking at him, some last wilted, pressed, and dried wisp of her ancient femininity peeking through. At the very worst time.

She said something else that he could not remember, and he picked up a knife with which she had been dicing peaches and pushed it into her throat. Then he pushed her over on the kitchen table, pulled off her clothes and down his pants, made with that agonized and astonished crone the beast with two backs, blood, coughing, and great silence between them. In retrospect, he was mildly surprised by it all. It was not, he told us, a planned happening. He was curious that, following the knife, he had discovered himself erect. Why he pressed on with it, distasteful and grotesque as it was, he could not say. But when he was done—he did get done, by the way—he found that she was still very much alive, admonishing him with one long, bony, liver-spotted finger.

So he got the remainder of the whitewash, dragged it back into the house in a huge wallpaper-paste bucket while he held up his pants with one hand. While she lay there mute, violated, bleeding, he whitewashed the kitchen: the walls, floor, cabinets, stove, icebox, calender, and four-color lithograph of Jesus suffering the little children. Chairs, hangers, spice rack, coffee, tea, sugar, and flour bins, breadbox, and cookiejar. All white. At last he rolled her off onto the floor, whitewashed the table, and put her back in the middle of it. After studying it all for a moment, he decided and whitewashed her too. Which, so far as he could remember, was all he could remember.

—Ummm, Mr. Grierson said. —So she was alive when you were done with your fooling?

—Alive and kicking, Rand McNally said without smiling. —You see I got to die, don't you?

—Well, Mr. Grierson said, looking at me, —you ain't done much by way of making a case against that. Do you want to die?

—Everybody wants to die, Rand McNally said. He was picking

his toes, disengaged now, considering certain vastnesses he had talked himself to the edge of.

—Right. At the proper place and time. How do you like the chair?

—Ride the lightning? What a gas! Rand McNally almost smiled —Anybody'd do that to an old lady has got to pay the price. You know that's so. The price is lightning in this state.

—Well, Mr. Grierson said, getting up stiffly. Let me study on it, son. I'll see you.

As we left, Rand McNally was screwing the transistor's plug into his ear. —Christ, he said, —a sonofabitch would do that has *got* to die.

Outside, we passed Billy Phipps talking to a couple of police we didn't know. Phipps nodded to us. I supposed they were from Shreveport.

—Do you smell Rand McNally . . .

— . . . sneaking up on an insanity plea? Mr. Grierson finished my sentence. —Indeed I do.

—It looks good. From slimy start to filthy finish, doesn't it?

—Ummmm, Mr. Grierson hummed, smiling. —All he's got to do is convince a jury he's Tom Sawyer . . .

— . . . and she was Becky Sharp . . . ?

He looked at me sorrowfully and shook his head as if only a Yankee would have pressed it that awful extra inch. —Thatcher, he said. —But there is a question still . . .

— . . . ?

—If he *is* trying to get himself decked out with an insanity plea, the question is, why *did* he kill the old lady, and then do that to her? If he hadn't, he wouldn't need any kind of plea at all, would he?

That afternoon under the scuppernongs, I felt as if I were waiting for some final word, some conclusive disposition of my own case. There was a dread in me, an anxiety without an object. I thought ceaselessly of Rand McNally and his insane erection in the midst of an act of violence. I thought of his surprise at it. I thought of my own prophecy over the phone to Phipps. What had brought him to this place, this conclusion? He had stepped from life into process: extradition, arraignment, indictment, trial, sentencing. I came to feel that he had ceased to exist, to be a human being owed and owing. He was no longer a proper object of feeling. Now one only *thought* about him. One took him into account along with Dr. Crippen, Charles Starkwether, Bruno Hauptmann, Richard Speck, and the others of that terrible brotherhood whose reality is at once absolute and yet moldering day by month by year in antique police archives or grinning dustily in the tensionless shadows of wax museums.

It was just after supper when Mr. Grierson appeared. He pulled into the drive in a 1941 Ford Super DeLuxe coupe. It was jet black and looked as if it had been minted—not built, minted—an hour or so before. He wore a white linen suit and a peculiar tie: simply two struts of black mohair which lay beneath and outlined the white points of his narrow shirt collar. It was not that his car and clothes were old-fashioned; it was that while they were dated, they were not quaint or superannuated or amusing. As if by some shift, Mr. Grierson had managed the trick of avoiding the lapse of time, of nullifying it so that what had been, remained, continued unchanged. Could one pile up the past densely enough around himself so as to forbid its dwindling? And what would happen if the rest of us shared that fierce subterranean determination to drag down the velocity at which today became yesterday? It would fail, of course. You cannot disintegrate the fabric of physics. But what would happen?

We spoke of the weather, hot and dry, the bane of planters hereabouts. No sweet June rain. Only scorching sun, the river lying like a brown serpent between us and those like us in Louisiana. It was the mention of Louisiana that Mr. Grierson chose as his pathway past the amenities.

—He's crossing the big river tomorrow. Waived extradition.

—Oh? Did you . . . ?

—Talk to him again? Oh yes. Surely.

He smiled at me, knowing what thoughts had crossed my mind and instantly been dropped as I asked my question.

—He was forcefully apprised of his rights. Not once, but several times. And he repudiated every one of them in obscene terms.

—What? I don't . . .

—He said it was a goddamned piss-poor legal system that gave all these rights to a . . . fucking pervert.

Mr. Grierson looked embarrassed for the sake of the quotation.

—Jesus, I said, almost dropping the bottle of sour-mash from which I was pouring our drinks. —Christ, he *is* crazy. He *must* have been reading Dostoyevski.

—I don't know, Mr. Grierson said. —He gave me this. Said it was your fee.

He handed me a greasy fragment of oiled paper—the kind they wrap hamburgers in. There was what looked like a quatrain scrawled on it in No. 1 pencil:

> It's bitter knowledge one learns from travel,
> The world so small from day to day,
> The horror of our image will unravel,
> A pool of dread in deserts of dismay.

—What's that? I asked Mr. Grierson. He smiled and sipped his whiskey.

—You can come over to my place and look it up, he said.

—The idea is interesting. Wine don't travel well.

—". . . The horror of our image . . ."

—Seems what broke him up was that business after he stabbed the old lady. He didn't seem much concerned about the stabbing, you know. It was . . . the other.

—And the finale . . . ?

—The whitewashing? Oh no, he liked that fine. You can't make up for it, he told me. But you do the best you can. That boy is a caution . . .

We sat drinking for a while. I shook my head and said, not so much to Mr. Grierson as to myself: —It's . . . as if Rand McNally was a . . . historical figure.

—Well, yes. That's so. But, then, we all are.

—Yes . . .

—But history ain't like grace, is it? It has different rules. Which is to say, no rules at all.

I stared at him. Grace? What might that be? Luck? Fortune? I had heard the word. I simply attached no meaning to it. Now this old man set it before me as an alternative to history. I felt that dread again, some low order of clairvoyance wherein I imagined that Coronary might open once more: at first like the tiny entrance to Alice's garden, then like the colossal gates of ancient

Babylon. It struck me at that instant with ghastly irrationality that grace was the emanation of vaginal purpose and womb's rest. Is grace death?

—Is grace death? I heard myself asking aloud.

—It could be, Mr. Grierson answered. —I can imagine in a few years I might ask for that grace. But not altogether. History is the law. Grace is the prophets. History comes upon us. I reckon we have to find grace for ourselves. The law works wrath rather than grace, Luther said.

—That line ". . . The horror of our image . . ."

—Yes. Well, that's what brought grace to my mind. I think that boy has just broke into and out of history.

— . . . ?

—Something else I remember from Luther: certain it is that man must completely despair of himself in order to become fit to receive the grace of Christ. . . .

—I didn't know you were a Lutheran.

—Hell, I'm not. Never could be. Most often, I quote Calvin. But you always go for water out of the sweetest well, don't you?

—You mean Rand McNally doesn't care any more? He's done with the motels, the garages?

—No and yes. He cares, all right. He wants to get on with it, don't you see? He's sick of problems. But no, there won't be any more motor courts and repair shops for old Rand McNally.

—Problems . . .

—What happened to him that evening in that old woman's kitchen? Do you know? How is it that killing moved to something like what they call an act of love? Neither fit the hour's need. What happened? That's the problem.

I felt very warm, my face flushed, my hands wet as if I had just climbed out of the river. Believe me, I was afraid. I thought it was another attack. They call the coming of Coronary an attack. Tryst might be better. Liaison, assignation.

—You feeling bad? Mr. Grierson asked, pouring us both a little more whiskey.

—No, I lied. —I'm fine. Just thinking. Was it grace that came on Rand McNally? Is that what you want to say?

—Lord no! Mr. Grierson smiled depreciatingly. —That'd be

crazy. Grace to kill and rape an old woman? Naw, I never said
that. I wasn't speaking *for* grace, you know.

—He's insane. They'll find him insane.

—Sure. So was Joan of Arc. So was Raymond of Toulouse . . .

—Raymond . . . ?

—A hobby of mine. He spread his hands. —I take on old cases
sometimes. Not Joan. She's all right, taken care of. But Raymond
. . .

Who was an Albigensian—or at least no less than their
defender in his province. Tormented by orthodox authorities most
of his life, he died outside that grace which Rome claimed to pur-
vey exclusively, and lay unburied in the Charterhouse of the
Hospitalers for four hundred years. Mr. Grierson told me much
more—told me that he had written a three hundred-page brief in
Latin defending the acts and character of Raymond of Toulouse
as those of a most Christian prince. But that was, he said with a
perfectly straight face, ancient history. He was working now on
the defense of Anne Albright, a young girl burned during the
Marian persecutions at Smithfield in 1556. It was to be a class action, aimed at overturning the convictions of all those Protestants
burned under Mary Tudor.

—What about the Catholics? I asked sardonically, draining my
whiskey.

—Fisher, Southwell, Campion? No need. The world's good
opinion justifies them. As well waste time on More or Beckett.
No, I go for those lost to history, done to death with no posthu-
mous justification.

—That's a mad hobby, I told him. Somehow his pastime made
me angry. At first I supposed my anger came from the waste of
legal talent that so many people needed—like Rand McNally. But
no, it was deeper than that. Could it be that I, a child of history,
descendant of those whom history had dragged to America,
resented Grierson's tampering with the past? How many of yesterday's innocents, perjured to their graves, can we bear to have
thrust before us? Isn't the evil in our midst sufficient unto the
day? —The past is past, I said almost shortly.

Mr. Grierson looked disgusted. —My Christ! he said. I had
never heard him speak profanely before. —You sit under an arbor

in Vicksburg, Mississippi, and say that? You better get hold of history before you go to probing grace.

We were quiet for a long while then, Grierson's breach of manners resting on us both. At last he left, walking slowly, stiffly out to that bright ancient automobile, which came alive with the first press of the starter. I stood in the yard and watched him go, and found when I went into the house again that it was much later than I had thought.

I found myself gripped by a strange malaise the next day, and for weeks following I did no work. I walked amid the grassy parkland of the old battlefields. I touched stone markers and tried to reach through the granite and marble to touch the flesh of that pain, to find what those thousands of deaths had said and meant. It was not the northern soldiers I sought: history had trapped them in their statement. It had to do with the union, one and indivisible, with equality and an end to chattel slavery. That was what they had said, whether they said it or not. But the Southerners, those aliens, outsiders, dying for slavery, owning no slaves; dying for the rights of states that had no great care for their rights. In the name of Death, which had engulfed them all, why?

But I could find nothing there. It was history, certainly: the moments, acts frozen in monuments, but it told me nothing. I could find nothing in it at all. One evening as the last light faded, I sat on a slope near the Temple of Illinois and wept. What did I lack? What sacred capacity for imagining had been denied me? Could I ever come to understand the meaning of law, of life itself, if all history was closed to me?

Or was it not a lack but a possession which kept me from grasping the past as it presented itself, history as it laid down skein after skein of consuming time about us all? I imagined then that it was Coronary. That I had been drawn out of history, out of an intimacy with it by that assault. What was time or space to an anchorite who stared forever into forever? How could sequence matter to one who had touched All at Once? When I tried to concern myself with practical matters, I would remember Coronary and smile and withdraw into myself, forget to pay the net electric bill on time, suffering afterward the gross. Surely, I thought, I cannot care within history because I am beyond it, a vestal of Coronary, graced with a large probable knowledge of how I will die. Knowing too that superflux of certain action can even pre-empt the day of that dying. I know too much, have been too deeply touched to succumb to history. I have no past, no particulars, no accidents. I am substance of flesh tenderly holding for an instant essence of spirit. I am escaping even as I think of it. Surely, I thought, a vision of one's dying must be grace. Yes, I am in grace, whatever that means.

Toward the end of some months of such odd consideration, I saw a small notice in a New Orleans paper that announced, purported to announce, the judgment of Louisiana on Rand McNally. He had been found incompetent to stand trial. Yes. The People had adjudged him insane. Not culpable. Simply a biological misstep within history. To be confined until the end of biology corrected the error of its beginning.

I found that I was sweating. As if in the presence of something immutable, and preternaturally awful. It had no name. And I could give it no shape. I began to reduce the feeling to an idea. Was I sorry? How is that possible? Capital punishment is a ghastly relic from past barbarism. To place a man in such a state that he knows almost to the moment the time of his death is . . .

Is what? The blessing of Coronary? My God, is it punishment or grace? I sat with my face in my hands, feeling my own doomed flesh between my fingers, trying to plumb this thing and yet trying not to let the juices of my body rise stormlike within, carrying me toward that dark port once more.

One evening a few weeks later, I drove downtown and bought two dozen tamales from a cart on a street corner. It was an indulgence, the smallest of sneers behind the back of Coronary. It was possible to go on with bland food and a rare glass of wine, so long as the notion dangled there ahead that one day I would buy tamales and beer and risk all for a mouthful of pretended health.

I carried home my tamales, opened a beer, and began to eat with my fingers. The grease, the spices, the rough cornmeal, the harsh surface of the cheap beer. Before the attack, in New York, I would never have dreamed of eating such stuff. But to live in grace is to dare all things. Then I looked down at the faded, stained palimpsest of the old newspaper. Above Captain Easy, next to the crossword puzzle, was a short article. It told of a suicide, that of a mad rapist-killer about to be sent to the state hospital, how he had managed to fashion a noose of guitar strings and elevate himself by a steel support in the skylight.

It was Rand McNally, of course. No doubt enraged by a system so blind and feckless as to suffer his kind to live, a self-created lynch mob determined to do justice to himself. My hand trembled, spilling beer. A rapist-murderer will lead them, I think I thought. A little later that evening, my second cardiac arrest took place.

Dr. Freud, with the most fulsome humility I say you should have been in there. You would have forgotten physiology: it was not the smooth, agonized tissue of my heart that sent tearful chemicals upward to trek the barren steppes of my brain. No, in there, within the futureless glow of Coronary, I was constructing my soul. What, precisely, transpired there? Why should I not smile like Lazarus and suggest that the price of such knowledge is the sedulous management and encouragement of your own coronary involvement? Because I need to tell it. That is why we do things always, isn't it? Because we must. Not because we should. Which is what Rand McNally came to know, isn't it? And why he came to want death, demand punishment for himself, because he was no longer able to count on himself: what he did was outside any notion of *should*, was wholly given to *must*. Isn't that the way it is with animals?

But never mind. I am not guessing. That is part of what I have to tell you. I saw Rand McNally in there, and Joan of Lorraine, Raymond of Toulouse, and Anne Albright. All in Coronary, yes, Dr. Freud. Being a man dead, there is no reason one must honor time or space, chronology or sequence, in his hallucinations.

It was the Happy Isles where I was, looking much like the country around Sausalito. There was worship and diversion, of course, and the smoky odor of terror. Two Mississippi deputies dragged Raymond before the Inquisition. Anne Albright was condemned once more for having denied the doctrine of Transubsegregation. They claimed that Joan had stolen something: Cauchon, pig? A Smithfield ham? Mary Tudor curtseyed to Lester Maddox as they sat in high mahogany bleachers in Rouen's town square. Agnew preached against the foul heresies of all spiritual mediums, while shrouded Klansmen tied Rand McNally to a stake, doused him with whitewash, and set him afire.

I think I saw Jesus, now only an elderly Jew, in a sidestreet

weeping, blowing his nose, shaking his head as the Grand Inquisi-
tor passed in triumphant procession, giving us both a piercing
stare, blowing us kisses. Behind him in chains marched Giordano
Bruno and John Hus, Mac Parker and Emmett Till. Savonarola
was handcuffed to Malcolm X, and Michael Servetus walked painfully, side by side with Bobby Hutton. The line went on forever, I
thought, filled with faces I did not know: those who had blessed
us with their pain, those suffering now, those yet to come. I wondered why I was not among them, but old Jesus, who was kind
and whom they ignored, said that there were those who must act
and those who must see. It was given, God help me, that I should
see.

There were other visions, which I have forgotten or which I
must not reveal. I saw, in the ecstasy of Coronary, the end of all
things, and was satisfied. It was only important that nothing be
lost on my account. What does that mean?

—What does that mean? I asked Mr. Grierson when he came
to the hospital to visit me, as soon as they allowed anyone to
come at all.

—Ah, he said, his pink scalp glistening in the weak light above
my bed. —Economy. You got to note all transmutations. Correct
all falsehoods. Don't you see that? Lies, falsehoods, perversions of
reality—those are man's sovereign capabilities. Only man can rend
the fabric of things as they are. Nothing else in the universe is
confused, uncertain, able to lie, except man. And through those
lies, those rifts in reality, is where all things are wasted. But . . .

—But what . . . ?

—Well . . . Mr. Grierson smiled. —That's what my hobby is
about.

—Your . . . cases . . . Anne Albright . . . ?

—Sure. No lie survives so long as the truth is stated. Those are
the terms of the game.

—I don't see . . . what if people *believe* the lie . . . ?

—It doesn't matter. Tell the truth. Sooner or later, that mere
unprovable, undefended assertion of the truth will prevail.

—How can you believe . . . ?

Mr. Grierson shrugged. —How not? We got all the time in the
world. When the profit goes out of a lie, nobody wants to bother
defending it any longer. That's where grace joins history, you see?

I did. I *did* see. He was right. A lie *couldn't* stand forever. Because there is no history so old, so impervious to revision, that the simple truth doesn't establish itself sooner or later. Like gravity, the consequences of truth can be avoided for a while. Sometime a little while; sometime a great while. But in the end, that which is false crumbles, falls away, and only the truth is left. So long as that truth has been once stated, no matter how feebly, under whatever pain.

—Yes, Mr. Grierson said quietly, taking a sheaf of yellowed papers out of his briefcase. —What with all the time you've got on your hands just now, I reckoned you just as well get started . . .

—Started . . . ?

He handed me the file. —In southern Texas, summer of 1892, there was this Mexican woman . . . they gave her something like a trial, then they went ahead and lynched her, which was what they had in mind all along. It was the late summer of 1892. There was a panic that year, a depression, some trouble in Pullman Town . . .

I lay back, eyes closed, veteran of trances. Why not tell you of one part of my final vision? Why not? Yes, I saw, larger than the sky, what they call the Sacred Heart, burning with love for all the universe. I saw its veins and arteries, how we every one moved through it and away again, the sludge of lies and torture and deceit choking its flow like cholesterol. I saw that heart shudder, pulse erratically. I saw the fibrillation of God's own motive center, and I cried out that I should share his pain and rise to the dignity of sacrifice.

Yes, I came then to realize why Rand McNally had gone out of himself. In order to find himself. To tell the truth. Time matters only to liars, and they are, at last, worse than murderers, even rapists of old ladies. Because, caught in the grid of His truth, they yet try to evade, even as they see time vanishing before them. Grace is history transcendant, made true at last. And faith is the act of embracing all time, assured of renewing it.

—It's an easy one, Mr. Grierson told me. —They did Rosa Gonzales wrong. You won't have any trouble . . .

I smiled and reached for the file.

—I don't think I'll ever have any real trouble again, I told him.

THE THEFT

HELEN HUDSON

HELEN HUDSON is the author of three novels, *Tell the Time to None*, *Meyer Meyer*, and *Farnsbee South*, and a collection of short stories, *The Listener*. She was born in New York and now lives in New Haven.

T HE BOX ARRIVED ON A RAINY MONDAY MORNING looking slightly sinister, she thought, all blotchy and wrinkled with the string falling off one end. Or was it just that the front doorbell sounded so eerie? She had not heard it for months. A sound from the other world, the world from which she had been ejected, from which people came to live a bit of their lives in her house, filling her rooms with their voices, putting their lips to her cups and their rumps to her chairs. Even letting their words spill out all over her rug, to be left there for good, ground into the nap. When she walked, she imagined them oozing up between her feet. And when her guests went, they left their cigarettes in her ashtrays and their ice melting slowly in her glasses. And their breath mixed with hers. But such intimacy on the part of Alice and Harry and Charlotte and Mel seemed inconceivable to her now.

For that was before—before her husband moved out forever, taking only an overnight bag in which he packed her entire future and twenty years of her past rolled up in a pair of socks. As if to say that nothing he had acquired in his life with her was suitable for his new apartment and his new wife. For he had become his *real* self, he told her, thanks to Miss Parkhurst, and his old shirts would never fit his new dimensions. Tess had been living, it seemed, with a fraud. But Miss Parkhurst, a girl of perception and compassion, had found the real Paul, buried for twenty years by his wife beneath the domestic debris of Mondays and Tuesdays. The real Paul said cruel things in the old Paul's quiet voice. Miss Parkhurst would bring him peace and understanding at last, he said. It would be like living in heaven instead of a supermarket with the canned goods piled on the open shelves and the crowds shoving and grabbing and the steady ring of the cash register in his ears.

"You can be in complete control now," he had said. "Which you've always wanted. Only not over me." Over the cooking and the cleaning and the carpool. He had left her in the town where he worked, in the house he could afford, with the friends he had sifted from among his colleagues. Where she had, for twenty years, been told to control her emotions. What else, she wondered, had she ever tried to control?

He's got me mixed up with someone else, she thought. His mother no doubt. But she was nothing like his mother, a large woman with a firm mouth, who had maintained a terrible authority over her family by crying steadily into the sink. It had shrivelled her body and eroded Paul's will, he said. And made a peninsula of his father, surrounded on three sides by silence. Linked to his family by the monthly check.

But Tess was nothing like that. She was small and dark and energetic and cried only on Mondays when the washing machine broke down. The rest of the week she was out, tutoring in the ghetto and serving on the school board, waiting to begin her real career with Chaucer and the *Legend of Good Women*. Unless Paul had a manuscript to be typed. While the boys lounged around the house, their hair getting longer and their music louder. When Paul came home, the living room floor was covered with guitars and records and teenagers. Making up for the early years when his sons had been confined to the sandbox and the playroom, a generation away from the closed study door. Dinner was hamburgers and telephones and a rush to a meeting or a lecture. Conversation was the leak in the furnace and college tuitions coming up and who was going where. Tess saw Paul's head sink lower and lower into his plate. But what could she do? Johnnie was late for rehearsal right now. "Anyone seen my car keys?" she shouted.

"Our life is sordid and dull and disheveled," Paul had said in the tone of Miss Melissa Parkhurst.

He was right, Tess thought, cleaning out the drain in the bathroom sink. The hair came out in damp wads or long strands, covered with muck. She looked up and saw her face in the mirror. She was getting old. And dragging Paul along with her. That was what he saw when he looked at her: the last twenty years scrawled all over her face and settled in lumps on her body. And felt himself being pulled, inexorably, into old age. Tied to her and the children, there was no escape. No wonder he had bolted. Cut the knot, leaving her to drift on alone. While he hitched on to Miss Parkhurst. Who would pull him back into the twenties with her. And keep him there forever.

The ashtrays and the glasses were always empty now. She used nothing but a coffee mug stamped "Yellowstone National Park," acquired on their honeymoon, and the seashell from Ipswich, Mass., bought on their last camping trip when the old, phony Paul had pretended to have such a good time, sleeping in the sun and swimming with the boys and steaming clams under the stars. And talking of their next vacation, which would be out of the country, for once, a quick survey of the new republics of the Caribbean, for future study. Just the two of them. They would stay in hotels instead of sleeping bags and dress for dinner. A second honeymoon with the children happy somewhere else. He was right there now, she thought. On a honeymoon indeed. Only not with her. With Miss Melissa Parkhurst and the new Paul. If only they had left the old Paul for her, complete with moods and melancholy and bouts of self-doubt. But Miss Parkhurst, who had no husband of her own, had been greedy and taken both of Tess's. The old Paul had disappeared completely, too, even from the past.

Looking back, Tess could not find him anywhere. Only a strange man with a careful mouth, waiting, his face sealed up tight as an envelope with the future folded up inside. He even dressed differently. He no longer wore jeans and the old sweaters she had knitted with holes in the elbows and the sleeves permanently bunched. Instead, she imagined him in the smart new turtlenecks of the new Paul and corduroy pants and jaunty little caps for driving the new Mrs. Paul in the new Porsche. He no longer, even in memory, laughed or slouched or rumpled his hair; or fed her beer from his can and bits of Plessy vs. Fergusson from his Constitutional Law.

Instead, he was always, even in memory, as she had last seen him with the stamp of Miss Parkhurst upon him: his face stern and his hair combed down straight and slightly longer, as if he had been going to a "hairdresser" instead of a barber, and his big body stiff, moving carefully, protecting his "real self" zipped up inside. Until the moment when he stripped off the old Paul, releasing the other. "I'm leaving," he had said so calmly, so casually, hanging the old Paul and the old life away like the old winter coat he would no longer be needing. From now on he would be living in perpetual spring.

She carried the seashell around the house with her for her ashes and used the coffee mug for almost everything else: brushing her teeth and taking her pills and swilling her Scotch. Which she tried to limit to certain definite periods, nothing before noon and as little as she could tolerate. And nothing again until after dinner, unless the raging of the slipcover on Paul's old armchair drove her wild. Sometimes she sat on it to shut it up. But mostly she tried to postpone her real drinking until after 10:00 P.M. Because of the children. Until they were completely grown. Which should be soon now except that they stretched it out so. Unlike most children, they dawdled. As if something were still owed them from childhood and they were waiting to be paid off. They still slowed down and dropped their voices before Paul's closed study door. Three boys of varying temperaments, they were all shuffling their way through adolescence and kicking the dust in her face. Almost adults, they seemed to linger maddeningly as they neared the exit. As if reluctant to make the turn which would leave her free. For what? With whom? Sometimes she wanted to stop them completely, restrain them forcibly, prevent them from moving on through the month or the week. Or even another half-hour. "Don't get any older, my darlings. Please. Dig in your heels. Stay where you are." For time would only pull them away from her. As it had Paul. Which was like telling them to stand still on the surface of the sea. For there was no solid ground anywhere for planting a foot. Only air and water, on which one could only drift. So she floated, an island unto herself. "No man is an island." But every woman is. Surrounded by time.

She sat staring at the package. It was quite wet and the ink on the address had run. Did it say *Mr.* or *Mrs.* Paul? And if *Mrs.*,

which Mrs.? It was obscene. Like being a second head. Except
that she had been cut off. To roll in the dust.

She had just finished breakfast, a pot of coffee and a half a pack
of mentholated Trues. The children were off at school and her
stomach was off on its own, jumping with nausea, threatening to
jump out of her mouth. She yanked it back and poured herself
two fingers of Scotch. Though it was only ten-thirty. And tightened the belt of her robe. Paul's robe really. She had never owned
one of her own. Had never needed one. When she got up, she was
dressed. She undressed only to go to bed. She never lounged. But
she was lounging now, all day, every day, in Paul's robe with his
sleeves around her. He certainly had a new one for his new wife
and his new self which would certainly do much lounging. There
would be no children, no job to interfere. A year-long honeymoon
paid for by the university. And by the old Paul who had worked,
white-faced, sixteen hours a day with a typewriter beside his bed
all night, preparing the good life for the new Paul. Paid for by
the children who had accepted the closed study door and had
learned to read "Do Not Disturb" before they could read their
own names. Paid for by Tess, scrubbing and saving and resigned
to neglect with her eye always on the clock and the calendar, waiting for the next semester and the next year and the next leave;
waiting for this degree and that promotion and the eternal haven
of tenure. He had them all now. And a new wife to give them to.
There was nothing more to wait for now except another Wisconsin winter and the picture of Paul, lounging with Miss Parkhurst,
beside a salad-green sea.

The belt of Paul's robe went around her twice. She had lost
twenty pounds. He had divorced far less than he'd married. And
she was losing still. As if her body were deserting her too, to join
Paul and Miss Parkhurst in the warmth of that perpetual sun. She
shivered. Even his robe did not warm. She wore it like a hair shirt
over her remaining flesh. But there was nothing of him left inside
it except the pain he could inflict, pinned like a lining to her skin.
Nothing else. Not even a whiff of him. He had never used lotions
or deodorants of any kind. What self-assurance, she had thought.
What indifference, she thought now. Was he using them now,
now that he had his arms around Miss P? Who had appeared so
sweetly, so complacently, just as he was lingering on the threshold

of middle-age, staring in horror at his hairy sons and his harassed, bitter wife, employing her Ph.D. for reading recipes and the instructions on the can opener. Staring in horror at himself, moving from one semester to another while the female students sneered slightly at his thinning hair and thickening glasses, and the boys flaunted their "chicks" and their new research methods. And, all over town, Mike and Alec and Roy and Bill were slamming doors on their old lives and their old families. Now that they had long since acquired the third child and the second car and the full professorship with tenure, where else was there to go but out? With Kristi and Neena from the department office. There were new, young Mrs. Roys and Alecs and Mikes all over town. All over America. But there had been nothing new for Paul except, perhaps, a new chairmanship and a new committee on student-faculty relations.

Until Miss Parkhurst arrived showing him that he could shut the door, too, could wander farther than any of them, all the way to the land of sun and rum and dinner on the terrace. To be himself at last. Leaving Tess to be *herself* a statistic, a cliché, an embarrassment. Another deserted wife. Teenage kids were dropping out of school and middle-aged men were dropping out of marriage all over America. So what else is new? But her old friends backed away. As if she exuded pain, a pain to which they were especially susceptible. For Paul was not like Mike and Alec and Roy. Or so they had thought. Paul was like their own husbands, Harry and Mel, dependable and loyal. To whom they had given their whole lives with the promise only to love and honor and cherish. Not to remain "forever fair," keeping him "forever young." They were not Grecian urns, for God's sake. So they did not want to see Tess with her face gathered at the corners as if it had been sliced off and basted back on again. It might force them to look too carefully at Harry and Mel, carving up the roast. And recognize that they had the power to cut up their own wives too. And even the desire, perhaps, the next time the door opened on the next student or the next secretary or the next research assistant. They did not want to see Tess. The sight of her made them feel the knife in their own faces.

But, of course, these things were never one-sided, they would say. Tess was too bossy, too old, too tight. Her skirts were too long, her shoes too pointy, and her comments too sharp. And her face too familiar, exciting as the kitchen clock. She was the aging wife of an aging man, discovered at last. And sentenced like the others. She must learn to behave like the others, keeping her face properly stitched up and her stomach tacked down. For the sake of the children. And think of her future when the children were gone, when she could have a little apartment of her own and a little job of her own and a season ticket to the symphony. Like all the other obsolete wives who found themselves walking, in redundant pairs, up the steps of Community Hall. But she was too tired to do anything but sit still, drinking Scotch and leafing through her mind for the appropriate quotations:

> ". . . There's no art
> To find the mind's construction in the face.
> He was a gentleman in whom I put
> An absolute trust."

Words she thought long since forgotten came rolling toward her day after day, while the bottles collected on the floor beneath the sink. Almost everything else had been put away when Paul left. Except the dishes needed for the boys, and the shell and mug for her. "And that sustenance, Despair." She wanted no *things* to trip over, tumbling her back into the past. She had always hated things anyway: assertive, demanding, carrying, all of them now, Paul's prints. She turned gratefully back to words which she had neglected for so long, eyeing them, sounding them, rubbing them against her pain:

> "Never seek to tell thy Love
> Love which never can be told."

> "I measure every grief I meet
> With narrow, probing eyes"

Words to stick like adhesive tape over the wounds, to ease the throbbing and bind her to the hurts of others.

The house was terribly quiet. The clocks were all electric and the typewriters all closed. It was always quiet now, even when the boys were home. But they stayed away as much as possible. They played their instruments and their records and the television some place else. But watched her secretly out of the corners of their eyes. And jumped to answer the phone. To save her from saying that Paul doesn't live here any more. She should have sent out announcements. The public should be informed of a divorce as well as a wedding. "What ceremony else?" For death of a heart, a marriage, a family? But she hardly saw her sons. She was living in a padded cell in which she heard nothing, saw nothing, felt nothing, except the monstrous pain that had come to live with her, to live *in* her, occupying her from the bottom of her stomach to the top of her head, with its tail beating against her temples. As if she had swallowed a cat that stretched and scratched and filled her mouth with fur. She could taste nothing else. Except the metallic flavor of the Scotch, like nails on her tongue.

She began to unwrap the package. It had been sent from the St. James Hotel, San Francisco, California. For the *other* Mrs. Paul, clearly. Tess knew no one at the St. James Hotel. Or in San Francisco, California. Though she had been there once, last year, with Paul, for the Law Professors' annual meeting. Explicitly invited to the President's dinner as the wife of the Program Chairman. The only time she had ever gone. Wives were not expected. They stayed home—long after the children were grown—to pick up the groceries and the cleaning and the phone for their husbands' messages. So their husbands could take their research assistants.

"You don't want to go," Paul had said. "It's a mess and a bore. Too hot and too crowded and too god-damned noisy."

"I don't care. I've never been. I'd be interested. Make a nice change. I've never been to California. *Or* a convention."

"What about the kids?" That jagged, twisted question. Used to skewer her to the wall whenever convenient.

They compromised. He went for a week. She joined him for two days; free drinks and the President's dinner. And one night in a first class hotel.

It came back clearly, now, that big luxurious room with the two double-beds—why *two* or why *double?*—and the stall shower *plus* bath. And the wide, brilliantly lighted dressing table, for women who have time to dress sitting down. The largess of the state of California, home of movie stars and conventions and husbands away from home. It had assaulted her, the housewife from

Madison, Wisconsin, in her shy little beige suit which dared not
be either mini or midi but hung diffidently half-way between, just
brushing her knees, the jacket too short and the seat slightly
baggy. She arrived late and was tired and confused by the change
in time and temperature and decor. And the lack of Paul.

She saw him first at the cocktail party, saw his face above the
back of a tall woman with long blonde hair to her waist and
naked arms, predatory arms, ready to reach for a drink or a man.
Taller and blonder and younger than Tess and with her skirt
frankly mini. A woman, clearly, who dared to be herself. Tess
could not see her face, only Paul's floating above her and smiling
down at her beneath lowered lids. A smile Tess had not seen for
years. But which she remembered so well. It had always, till now,
been directed at *her*, making her want to drop to her knees before
it. But the blonde woman continued to stand up straight and tall
while Paul's face went on smiling and floating around her, closer
and closer to that blonde head. It will come to rest on her shoulder, Tess thought, and the long naked arm will reach out and tie
it to her with the bands of her long blonde hair. Tess's stomach
began to bob and float away like a balloon on a string. She made
her way to the bar, feeling hot. I smell, she thought, groping for
her perfume.

She drank four martinis while men she vaguely remembered
drifted around her. "It's one in the morning in Madison, Wisconsin," she said. She had had no dinner. She felt her neck go rubbery
and her head begin to wobble. She felt hot and weak. She must
find Paul. But Paul must not be disturbed. He was busy with a
head of long blonde hair and no face at all. She put her cheek on
a nearby shoulder and passed out.

When she awoke she was alone in bed, fully dressed. It was
morning and Paul was coming out of the shower. "I'm so sorry
and ashamed about last night," she said. "I guess I was tired and I
hadn't eaten all day. And I was worried at not finding you."

"It's O.K.," he said. "I've got a meeting in three minutes. See
you later."

"When?"

"I don't know. I can't possibly know. This thing could go on
for hours. And there might be a press conference afterward. Or a
last minute Council meeting to deal with some last minute crisis."

"Well . . . roughly. When? and where?"

"I'm telling you, I don't know. Jesus Christ. I can't give you a minute by minute agenda."

She began to cry.

"I told you a conference is no place for a wife."

Not *your* wife, at any rate, she thought. The sides of her head were trying to meet in the center, and her stomach was hopping around, feeling for a way out. She dared not get up. "Would you hand me my purse, please. I think I've got some aspirin. . . ."

"Where is it?"

"Where did you put it when you brought me up last night?"

"Christ, how can I remember? Yes I do. Janice Marcus brought it up. She said she put it on the bureau. But it's not there."

Well, you can't miss it. It's big and black with a long . . ."

"I don't see it and I haven't time to look. You'll have to find it yourself. I've got to go. Where's my wallet?"

Where are my clean shirts and my winter gloves and my brilliant promise? Where is my thick hair and· my seminal work and my other sock? Where in hell did you put my glittering youth?

"How do I know?" she said weakly. In the bottom drawer, perhaps on top of mine.

"Jesus Christ," he said slowly. "I think we've been robbed."

"Robbed? *Here?*"

"Robbed. Your purse and my wallet. Where else could they be?"

He began to look frantically for a moment, tossing blankets and pillows and shirts about. Suddenly he stopped. "That's it, of course," he said. "We've been robbed." There was no other possible explanation. Someone had come during the night, while they were asleep, silently, skillfully, and taken his wallet and her purse. But nothing else. Everything else was still there, Paul's watch on the bureau and her Woolworth earrings. He began to collect his papers.

"What time did you come in?" she asked. He was on his way to the door.

"God, I don't know. Besides, what difference does it make?"

"Did you lock the door?"

"Of course. Call the police if you want. I've got to go." He hurried out, slamming the door behind him.

But, in spite of the lock, they had been completely unprotected, as the city detective showed her later. Anyone with a plastic card could slip it between the doorjamb and the lock and open it. As if they had left it unlatched and invited him in. She thought of him, the thief, entering so quietly, standing over them while they slept, knowing just where to go and how to move so that no footfall would, in any way, make a rip in their sleep. Thank God Paul had been there when it happened. Thank God she had not been all alone, so completely and degradingly vulnerable while some stranger, crafty and cruel, stood over her and fitted his breathing to hers. She had not been all alone. She had had her husband beside her, sharing the humiliation. She was grateful, at least for that.

She lay in bed after Paul had gone, remembering what was in her purse—everything: wallet and sunglasses and reading glasses and license and library card and make-up and perfume and comb and pills. She would be cruelly handicapped without it, unable to drive or read; unable, even to appear in public, with her mouth and eyes completely naked and her hair a mess. And no perfume to cover the peculiar odor that had settled over her at the cocktail party: the smell of shame. She lay in bed paralyzed by her need for trivia. As she lay there, she felt a sudden violent trembling of the floor and bed beneath her. But she remained perfectly still, nailed to the mattress. It was only a minor tremor, she learned later. California was used to much worse.

That was over nine months ago. The insurance company, after her fifth letter, had finally refunded the money. The credit companies sent duplicate cards. In the end, everything had been replaced. But she could still remember her feeling of helplessness and humiliation. She had spent that whole day in bed. For how could she be seen in the hotel without her face? And her face was in her purse which had been stolen. By an arrogant, anonymous thief who had dared to come in the night while they were right there. Even Paul, to her amazement, had allowed himself to be robbed.

She stood up to open the package. And knew, suddenly, what it contained. Sure enough, inside the box lay her huge black bag, a shoulder-strap bag big enough to carry a weekend supply of sandwiches for the family or paperback books for her. And her face, ready to be reassembled. She opened it slowly and there, among wads of crumpled Kleenex, was everything: wallet and license and glasses and cosmetics. Everything except the money. She had a sudden sense of well-being, as if the whole episode that night in the hotel had never happened. Nor the terrible months that followed, when her marriage itself was stolen right out from under her unseeing eyes. As if that slight tremor in San Francisco had thrown everything out of perspective.

Except that, she realized slowly, there was still something missing. The feeling of well-being slipped away, slipped out between the cracks of the door as the thief had made his way in. For Paul's wallet was not there. Strange, that everything else should be returned, and not that. And then, suddenly, she knew why.

Because it had never been stolen at all. It had not been there to be stolen. And she knew, too, exactly where it was that morning when she lay in bed while her head and her stomach came unhinged, watching her husband, angry and irritated, not at the thief but at *her*. For being there. And being his wife. He had not, after all, been beside her in the dark when the thief came. He had not been robbed at all. She had been all alone. He had left her all alone while someone, someone with no face and no scruples, someone who knew exactly when to come and what to take, walked in and stole away everything she needed to live her life.

She sat down slowly and stared at her belongings, spread out on the kitchen table. And realized she no longer needed any of them. They had all been replaced months ago. They had been returned too late.

BRIDGE OF MUSIC,
RIVER OF SAND

WILLIAM GOYEN

WILLIAM GOYEN is a novelist, short-story writer, and play-wright. A native of Texas, he now lives in Los Angeles. His most recent novel, *Come the Restorer*, was published in 1974; his *Collected Stories*, in 1975.

D O YOU REMEMBER THE BRIDGE that we crossed over the river to get to Riverside? And if you looked over yonder you saw the railroad trestle? High and narrow? Well that's what he jumped off of. Into a nothing river. "River"! I could laugh. I can spit more than runs in that dry bed. In some places it's just a little damp, but that's it. That's your grand and rolling river: a damp spot. That's your remains of the grand old Trinity. Where can so much water go? I at least wish they'd do something about it. But what can they do? What can anybody do? You can't replace a river.

Anyway, if there'd been water, maybe he'd have made it, the naked diver. As it was, diving into the river as though there were water in it, he went head first into moist sand and drove into it like an arrow into flesh and was found in a position of somebody on his knees, headless, bent over looking for something. Looking for where the river vanished to? I was driving across the old river bridge when I said to myself, wait a minute, I believe I see something. I almost ran into the bridge railing. I felt a chill come over me.

What I did when I got off the bridge was to draw my car to the side of the road and get out and run down the riverbank around a rattlesnake that seemed to be placed there as a deterrent (the banks are crawling with them in July), and down; and what I came upon was a kind of avenue that the river had made and paved with gleaming white sand, wide and grand and empty. I crossed this ghostly thoroughfare of the river halfway, and when I got closer, my Lord Jesus God Almighty damn if I didn't see that it was half a naked human body in what would have been midstream were there water. I was scared to death. What ought I to do? Try to pull it out? I was scared to touch it. It was a heatstunned afternoon. The July heat throbbed. The blue, steaming air waved like a veil. The feeling of something missing haunted me: it was the lost life of the river—something so powerful that it had haunted the countryside for miles around; you could feel it a long time before you came to it. In a landscape that was unnatural—flowing water was missing—everything else seemed unnatural. The river's vegetation was thin and starved-looking; it lived on the edge of sand instead of water; it seemed out of place.

If only I hadn't taken the old bridge. I was already open to a fine of five thousand dollars for driving across it, according to the sign, and I understood why. (Over yonder arched the shining new bridge. There was no traffic on it.) The flapping of loose boards and the quaking of the iron beams was terrifying. I almost panicked in the middle when the whole construction swayed and made such a sound of crackling and clanking. I was surprised the feeble structure hadn't more than a sign to prohibit passage over it—it should have been barricaded. At any rate, it was when I was in the middle of this rocking vehicle that seemed like some mad carnival ride that I saw the naked figure diving from the old railroad trestle. I dared not stop my car and so I maneuvered my way on, mechanical with terror, enchanted by the melodies that rose from the instruments of the bridge that played like some orchestra of xylophones and drums and cellos as I moved over it. Who would have known that the dead bridge, condemned and closed away from human touch, had such music in it? I was on the other side now. Behind me the music was quieter, lowering into something like chime sounds and harness sounds and wagons; it shook like bells and tolled like soft, deep gongs.

His hands must have cut through the wet sand, carving a path for his head and shoulders. He was sunk to his waist: a figure with

its head buried in the sand, as if it had decided not to look at the
world anymore. And then, as I watched, the figure began to sink,
as if someone was pulling it under. Slowly the stomach, lean and
hairy, vanished; then the loins, thighs. The river, which had
swallowed half this body, now seemed to be eating the rest of it.
For a while the feet lay, soles up, on the sand. And then they
went down, arched like a dancer's.

Who was the man drowned in a dry river? eaten by a dry river?
devoured by sand? How would I explain, describe what had happened? I'd be judged to be out of my senses. And why would I tell
somebody—the police or—anybody? There was nothing to be
done, the diver was gone, the naked leaper was swallowed up. Unless somebody had pushed him over the bridge and he'd assumed
a diving position to try to save himself. But what evidence was
there? Well, I *had* to report what I'd seen, what I'd witnessed.
Witness? To what? Would anybody believe me? There was no evidence anywhere. Well, I'd look, I'd search for evidence. I'd go up
on the railroad trestle.

I climbed up. The trestle was perilously narrow and high. I
could see a long ways out over Texas, green and steaming in July.
I could see the scar of the river, I could see the healed-looking
patches that were the orphaned bottomlands. I could see the tor-
nado-shaped funnel of bilious smoke that twisted out of the mill
in Riverside, enriching the owner and poisoning him, his family,
and his neighbors. And I could see the old bridge which I'd just
passed over and still trembling under my touch, arching perfect
and precious, golden in the sunlight. The music I had wrought
out of it was now stilled, except, it seemed, for a low, deep hum
that rose from it. It seemed impossible that a train could move on
these narrow tracks now grown over with weeds. As I walked,
grasshoppers flared up in the dry heat.

I saw no footprints in the weeds, no sign of anybody having
walked on the trestle—unless they walked on the rails or the ties.
Where were the man's clothes? Unless he'd left them on the bank
and run out naked onto the trestle. This meant searching on both
sides of the trestle—Christ, what was I caught up in? It could also
mean that he was a suicide, my mind went on dogging me; or insane; it could also mean that nobody else was involved. Or was I
suffering a kind of bridge madness, the vision that sometimes

comes from going home again, of going back to places haunted by deep feeling? Had anyone ever told me the story of a man jumping into the river from the trestle? Could this be some tormented spirit doomed forever to re-enact his suicide? And if so, must he continue it, now that the river was gone? This thought struck me as rather pitiful.

How high the trestle was! It made me giddy to look down at the riverbed. I tried to find the spot where the diver had hit the dry river. There was absolutely no sign. The mouth of sand that had sucked him down before my very eyes had closed and sealed itself. The story was over, so far as I was concerned. Whatever had happened would be my secret. I had to give it up, let it go. You can understand that I had no choice, that that was the only thing I could do.

That was the summer I was making a sentimental trip through home regions, after fifteen years away. The bridge over the beloved old river had been one of my most touching memories—an object that hung in my memory of childhood like a precious toy. It was a fragile creation, of iron and wood, and so poetically arched, so slender, half a bracelet through which the green river ran. The superstructure was made more for a minaret than a bridge. From a distance it looked like an ornate pier, in Brighton or early Santa Monica; or, in the summer heat haze, a palace tower, a creation of gold. Closer, of course, it was an iron and wooden bridge of unusual beauty, shape, and design. It had always been an imperfect bridge, awry from the start. It had been built wrong—an engineering mistake: the ascent was too steep and the descent too sharp. But its beauty endured. And despite its irregularity, traffic had used the bridge at Riverside, without serious mishap, for many years. It was just an uncomfortable trip, and always somewhat disturbing, this awkward, surprising, and somehow mysterious crossing.

Some real things happened on this practical, if magical, device for crossing water. For one thing, since it swayed, my mother, in our childhood days, would refuse to ride across it. She would remove herself from the auto and walk across, holding on to the railing, while my father, cursing, drove the rest of us across. My sister and I peered back at the small figure of our mother laboring darkly and utterly alone on the infernal contraption which was her torment. I remember my father getting out of the car on the other side, waiting at the side of the road, looking toward the bridge, watching my mother's creeping progress. When she arrived, pale, she declared, as she did each time, "I vow to the Lord if my sister Sarah didn't live in Riverside I'd never to my soul come near this place." "Well you could lie down in the back seat, put the cotton in your ears that you always bring, and never know it, as I keep telling you," said my father. "I'd still know it," my mother came back. "I'd still know we was on this infernal bridge." "Well, then, take the goddamn train from Palestine. Train trestle's flat." And, getting in the car and slamming the door, "Or stay home and just *write* to your damned sister Sarah. Married to a horse's ass, anyway . . ."

"Mama," said my sister, trying to pacify the situation. "Tell us about the time you almost drowned in the river and Daddy had to jump in and pull you out."

"Well, it was just right over yonder. We'd been fishing all morning, and . . ."

"Aw, for Christ's sake," my father said.

On the other side of the bridge, after a crossing of hazards and challenges, there was nothing more than a plain little town of mud streets and weather-faded shacks. The town of poor people lived around an ugly mill that puffed out like talcum something called Fuller's Earth. This substance lay on rooftops, on the ground, and in lungs. It smelled sour, and bit the eyes.

As I drove away toward that town, haunted by the vision of the leaping man, and now so shaken in my very spirit, lost to fact but brought to some odd truth which I could not yet clear for myself, I saw in the mirror the still image of the river bridge that had such hidden music in it, girdling the ghost of what it had been created for, that lost river that held in its bosom of sand the diving figure of the trestle that I was sure I had seen. I was coming in to Riverside, and already the stinging fumes of the mill brought tears to my eyes.

AN ENEMY OF THE PEOPLE

IRA SADOFF

IRA SADOFF has published short stories in *The American Review*, *The Paris Review*, and *Transatlantic Review*. His volume of poetry *Settling Down*, was published in 1975. He now lives in Yellow Springs, Ohio, and teaches at Antioch College.

I OFFICIALLY QUIT MY ACTING JOB on AS THE WORLD TURNS three weeks ago, but my director tells me I'll have to wait until he turns me into an alcoholic and gets me to volunteer for the Army before he can let me go. He keeps assuring me I should be getting my enlistment papers any day now, but I think he's dragging this thing out to get even with me for all my muffed lines and unrestrained laughter during crucial love scenes.

One of the worst problems I've had with the job is what my wife would call "overflow." Lately I'll come home, and in all seriousness tell her, "Nothing means anything to me anymore, Lorraine," and she'll tell me to do Shakespeare in the Park for a couple of weeks to purify my soul. One thing I've noticed is that the longer we are married the more reluctant my wife is to put up with all my little neuroses.

Last night when I got home Gerry and Ellen Farber were sitting on our couch trying to convince Lorraine to go bowling with them. "How else are you going to meet the *people?*" Gerry asks her. "You lead such a sheltered life, Lorraine," Ellen adds. "There's an ugly world out there you owe it to yourself to know. How long can you go on living in a vacuum, for god's sake?"

Gerry teaches Economics at the City College and his wife works part-time as a counsellor for the Welfare Department. Gerry's in the middle of a scholarly book constructing a revolutionary model for a planned economy in the United States, and Ellen is trying to overthrow the bureaucratic City government by bankrupting it with all her clients. She is very serious about it. I wish her luck and then tell them to leave my apartment. "If the people want to meet me," I tell them, "they can set up an appointment. Besides, I have a sore thumb and couldn't even break a hundred tonight." "It's great to be cynical," Gerry says as he walks out the door, "it excuses you from everything."

Today my television wife is going to have a nervous breakdown. She has had enough of my drinking, she says, and the thought of bearing my child is driving her crazy. I tell her to get off my back, that if she doesn't stop nagging me I'll leave her and join the Army. I wasn't supposed to say anything like that until they found a love interest to take my place, but I'm getting very tired of this job. I tell the director it was only a "foreshadowing," something I had learned in acting school.

I got out of acting school nearly twelve years ago and used to get really good parts in off-off-broadway plays before there was an off-broadway. And I really did do two Shakespeare in the Parks: I played the Earl of Gloucester in *Lear* and a weird fairy in *Midsummer Night's Dream*. I was actually pretty bored.

I met Lorraine in the Figaro Cafe ten years ago. She always came into the city on weekends to meet interesting people, and when I told her I was a serious actor she thought I was pretty interesting. She went to college in Montclair, New Jersey and lived at home with her parents, which was not too interesting, but at the time I was not very choosy, and besides, I thought she was smarter and less full of herself than all the actresses I knew. I still feel that way, I guess, but by now we're both pretty bored.

The Farbers brought one of the *people* over to our apartment today. It's Saturday, a day I usually like to relax with a book of Eastern Philosophy so I can find The Truth—I'm afraid I'm even cynical about myself. It's a product of growing up in the Fifties, Gerry tells me, although he's only two years older than I am and not nearly as cynical. Anyway, the people's name is Jeffrey Wilbur and he cleans up dishes at Horn and Hardart. Ellen picked him up during her lunch hour, and as soon as they sat down Gerry pumped him with questions about his Union, the wage differential between him and the manager who sits on his butt changing nickels all day. Jeffrey agreed. "Yeah, that's awful," while his eyes were darting all around our apartment, our modern furniture, the expensive stereo, making me blush—I wanted to tell him it was all my wife's idea, I would have been perfectly happy with a couple of orange crates and a mattress, like I had in college. When the Farbers left to pick up their little boy at the Day Care Center they left Jeffrey at my place so I could feed him dinner. Lorraine was very accommodating and said nothing throughout the entire meal. It was a very odd meal with each of us staring off at the pictures on the wall, resigned to living out this mistake rather than admitting the whole thing was incredibly stupid. I asked Jeffrey why he went along with a complete stranger and he blushed; then, turning away from my wife, he said, "That Mrs. Farber is a very nice looking woman but she has some strange ideas. When she said she wanted me to meet somebody, I couldn't believe she really meant it."

When I asked him did he like to bowl, he said, no, that it was boring and it hurt his back, I began to think that maybe the people weren't so bad after all, even though I could not imagine spending a lot of time with Jeffrey. There was one embarrassing moment when he was about to leave; he thanked us for the meal and I thought it might have crossed his mind to say anytime you're in the neighborhood of a Hundred and Eighth Street you're welcome to stop by, but he must have thought better of it. I got the feeling by what he didn't say that he understood us pretty well.

Today my television wife, whose name is Elaine (both on and off the screen) refuses to talk on the show. The director is pulling his hair out. She writes a note on the script that says she has to audition to sing for a commercial and she doesn't want to take a

chance on ruining her voice. As a P.S. she adds, "You could say I
went into shock and the nervous breakdown has begun."

And that is exactly what we do. One thing we have in common
is that we all hate the show, and we will do almost anything to
make it easier for us to go through it, especially if it upsets the
people who run it.

After the show is over the director tells Elaine that she'd better
do well in her audition, because right now he's thinking of either
sending her overseas with me or having her institutionalized.

Elaine used to be a prostitute. Our director, who is the most
Hollywood of all of us, dreams of winning Emmies and likes to
make finds on the streets of New York, picked her up at Chuck's,
a bar on Fifty-third Street which usually caters to airline steward-
esses and models. Once I asked him why he picked her, and he
told me he thought she would make a good wife. When I asked
him why, he said, "She's a prostitute." That was all he said. She's
still a prostitute, actually, but we don't get along as well as we used
to.

There was a time, though, when she first joined the show, that
we were pretty close. Once after a very intimate confession scene,
when she admitted that she had been having an affair with Doctor Milford but promised she wasn't going to see him anymore,
we made love right after the show. It was a tremendous emotional
release. I didn't pay her a nickel. And we talked for hours afterwards, about the show, about how I had hoped to get out of it
someday, how wonderful it would be if I could find a real acting
job, and then she told me I was just like every other man she had
to make love to, they always told her what they were going to do
because they knew their wives wouldn't believe them. She didn't
say this with any bitterness, but just as a matter of fact. When I
got home that night I felt guilty. After I left Elaine I felt I had
shared something with her; but looking back now I think it was
boredom.

The Farbers came over again. They are having marital difficulties, they admitted to us for the first time. Gerry says that it is an
ideological conflict, that he's much more Centralist than Elaine.

"Centralist?" she says. "You mean Stalinoid, that's what you mean."

I tell them, "Look, if you really believe in the breakdown of the nuclear family this shouldn't be all that much of a problem for you two."

Gerry gives me one of those wide smiles that say, "Aren't you funny?" or "I don't know why I bother talking to you at all," or something in that genre. I am offended and want to protect my own seriousness. "I just don't believe people get into trouble over 'ideological conflicts,' that's all." It's not a belief that I hold with very much conviction, but when you talk to Gerry you have to have some kind of a position, so this was the one I chose.

"That's a luxury you have when you operate in some imaginary bourgeois world where your conflicts are so hyperbolic you couldn't believe anything could be a source of conflict."

As usual there is an ounce of truth in what Gerry says, and it rubs me the wrong way. "That's not true. Your personality is definitely a source of conflict for me."

He smiles at me again and Ellen looks at him like a comrade and tells him she thinks it's time for them to go. Lorraine is very apologetic for my behavior, but I feel as if I have helped unite them against a common enemy.

After they leave Lorraine does not lecture me as she might have earlier in our marriage; she is probably a little more fatalistic about my personality now so a lot of things just go unsaid. They are things we both know in advance, but since they go unsaid we can dismiss them a little more easily. I think she wants to tell me that I feel threatened by the way they take themselves so seriously; I'm not sure that's true, but if she's thinking that I haven't lost any faith in her. We go to bed and make love with the lights on and the TV blaring in the background.

We watch very little television (only late at night to help Lorraine unwind a little)—I know too much about what's going on behind the camera to really enjoy it even as an escape. Strangely Lorraine never watches me on TV anymore. It used to bother me and once I came home and said, "What's the matter, can't you stand to see what I've become?"

She shook her head. "Overflow again, huh?" she said. "No, it's just a lousy show and I have better things to do with my time."

What she does with her time is work afternoons for Zero Population Growth. Gerry tells her ZPG is a kind of genocide against Third World People and I tell her it is a kind of mahjong, but she is not easily discouraged.

Given the fact that I hate my job I suppose quitting is a positive act; but given the fact that I haven't the slightest idea what I want to do next or how I'm going to support myself or my wife I suppose it is a very nihilistic act. There are two sides to every issue.

That is if my director ever decided to let me go. This morning I saw him audition two ex-tv doctors and a school-teacher-type, but he said they all looked too distinguished to play my part. He wanted someone, he said, who always looked as if he were on the verge of laughter, or someone who had droopy eyelids and walked around in a trance. Someone down on his luck. Housewives like that, he said. I think I am just not going to come to work tomorrow, to make it easier for him to find a replacement for me.

Since I haven't shown up for work for a couple of days I've been walking around the city a lot. I have passed by appliance stores and seen the show on the air without me. It is a strange sensation watching people make excuses for me, about my going to the hospital for tests on my liver, or going on a drinking spree. It almost sounds exciting. Last night I called up Elaine and asked her if she would sleep with me again. Not for less than fifty bucks, she said. I talk too much.

The Farbers finally got us to go bowling with them, under the guise of helping them save their marriage. I told them that things would never happen this way on AS THE WORLD TURNS. First of all there would be a scene in front of the neighbors, and there always has to be another woman. After Gerry converted a difficult spare he sat down and said, "There is another woman."

"You picked up a cleaning woman, right Gerry?" I said. "Out of total empathy with her oppression."

This was the closest Gerry ever came to hitting me; I'm glad we

were in a public place—I'm not very good at defending my honor.
I suppose there was an ounce of truth to what I said.

"No such thing," he said. "It's one of my students. It's too
bourgeois to be believed. She's not half as sharp as Ellen; in fact,
she makes Hubert Humphrey look like a raving Wobblie."

"Then why?" Lorraine asked.

"She likes me," Gerry said meekly. "I know it's stupid, but she
likes me."

After that I could not get the ball out of the gutter. I looked
over at Ellen every once in a while but she could not look me in
the eye. For some reason she was very attractive when she was
upset, and she knew I was looking at her.

All and all I had a miserable time, and the only *people* I got to
talk to was the cocktail waitress who overcharged me a dollar fifty
on the drinks. Gerry told me to pay it, that she probably didn't
make five thousand a year.

In some of my walks crosstown I seem to gravitate toward the
nearest Horn and Hardarts. It gives me some kind of goal in an
otherwise directionless day. I wonder if I will run into Jeffrey Wilbur. I don't have any idea what I would say to him if I did run
into him, but that doesn't seem to concern me.

Lorraine and I used to go on long walks when we were first
going out together. I would recite my lines to her and she would
give me my cues; it was all very romantic. Up until recently we
still went through my lines every once in a while, whenever my
lines weren't too awful to recite. "It's what the people want to
hear," the director used to tell me, but I know he doesn't have the
slightest idea about what the people want to hear; he just knows
they'll put up with almost anything on the screen that moves.
And if there are tears, sexual secrets and marital disasters, so
much the better.

Elaine must not have gotten her job doing commercials. As I
passed by a Motorola dealer I happened to see her playing up to a
man named Wilson Geary, an up and coming doctor who just
moved into town. He seems to be taking his lines very seriously;
he must be hoping someone will see him and sign him up for the
movies. I give him another two months before he'll be fluffing

lines with the best of us. Frankly I'm a little upset with Elaine's taste; Geary is incredibly ugly and she can only be after comfort and security. Actually there are four or five other men on the show who are more interesting, and three of them are married and could have brought some interesting complications to the plot.

Lately I've been very irritable when I get home from my walks. I'm not in the house two minutes before I snap at my wife, "What have you been doing all day?"

"Kneeling in front of the door waiting for you," she says.

"I don't think my cynicism wears very well on you, Lorraine. Why don't you go out and get a job instead of wasting away in the house?"

"I'd like nothing better," she says and walks away into the kitchen. She has learned to stay out of my way when I'm out of control and this is my way of telling her not to ask me, "Now that you've quit your job, now what are you going to do?"

I think I've just been through my first encounter session. The Farbers called up tonight and *asked* if they could come over, that they had something important to say to us. As soon as she got off the phone Lorraine said to me, "I'll bet they're splitting up."

"I don't believe it," I said, and I turned out to be right. They sat down on the couch and before I had time to offer anyone a drink Gerry said, "I don't exactly know how to say this, but I don't think we're going to be coming over to see you two anymore."

"Oh really?" I said. "What's the cause of this little melodrama?"

"Ellen and I have talked this over very seriously and we both agree that you're having a detrimental effect on our relationship."

"So now you're trying to blame your relationship, little Lolita and all, on the two of us? Well I can't hack it, Gerry; I've got enough problems of my own without taking responsibility for someone else's mistakes."

"Actually, Lorraine," Ellen turns to my wife, "we've got nothing against you. It's just that your husband refuses to engage in a serious relationship with anyone."

Most of all I resent being talked about in the third person.

"And what makes you say that, Ellen, because I don't think Trotsky was an anarchist? Because some of the things I say hit home a little too hard?"

"We're all vulnerable," she said, "that is everyone but you. And we can't satirize you because nothing would bother you. We thought you'd be better after you quit that awful job, but now you're only worse."

Lorraine turned pale; she tried to move her lips but nothing came out. At first I thought she was going to defend me but instead of looking at them she turned toward me. I felt like a War Criminal in Israel. "I suppose you were going to say, 'That's what I've been trying to tell you but you wouldn't listen to me,' right?"

"I wasn't going to say that," Lorraine said. "I wasn't going to say anything."

I became furious and started talking as fast as I could, telling Gerry what a hypocrite he was, how all his grand theories about man and the state didn't have a thing to do with his everyday life, that Ellen became a Marxist to win Gerry's approval and because it was so fashionably compassionate. The three of them were intolerably tolerant of me, and though there was truth to everything I said, everything rang hollow. Everybody knew I was fighting for my life.

After four or five hours Ellen and I went into the kitchen to make drinks for everyone. I felt as if I had been up for five nights straight. We tried hard not to look directly at each other, and I think we both felt that if we touched each other we would fall apart. Her dark features looked very attractive to me again, and there was a complexity in her face I had not really seen before. I began to fantasize her separation from Gerry, what a wonderful person she could be if she got out on her own. Once before we left the kitchen she smiled at me and held on to my wrist with her hand. "I'm sorry," she said. It was very unsteadying. I think if we were to meet accidently on the street the next day we would have found a hotel room and made love, not because we felt anything in particular about each other, but because we were both wandering, and under those circumstances distraction is the easiest way to live your life.

When they left the house I felt certain their marriage would not break up, not because Gerry had promised not to see his student anymore, because I didn't believe him, and not because I thought much of Ellen's power of resistance. It did just not seem possible for them to leave each other. Their last words were, "I hope you two get straightened out soon; we'll be thinking about you a lot." If I hadn't been so tired or if I hadn't been through the mill for the last six hours, I think I might have laughed.

I found Jeffrey Wilbur; actually it was not all that difficult. All I had to do was look for a Horn and Hardarts near where Ellen works in City Hall. He was in the second place I looked. The first time I only watched him, just to see what he did all day. He cleared the dishes off of the tables, carried clean glasses out of the dishwasher, cleaned out ashtrays, mopped the floors and made sure the napkin holders were always full. He always walks around in a kind of trance, a half-sleep. In spite of myself I could not help but think of all Gerry's lectures on alienated labor; and here was Jeffrey, a first-class example. No wonder the Farbers were drawn to him.

When I came back the next day I waited for him to clear my table before I said, "Do you know who I am?" The sound of my voice startled him and he dropped his dishrag. He stared at me for a moment and said, "Oh yeah, now I recognize you, I've seen you on television, on one of those soap operas. Wait Till Tomorrow or something. I used to watch you all the time when I worked the late shift."

I was a little embarrassed, both that he had seen me on television and that I felt good about it. "No, I didn't mean that," I said. "You had dinner at my house once. A Mrs. Farber brought you over."

"You mean you're the same guy? No kidding. Boy was that weird, I'll tell you." He moved on to the next table when he thought his boss was watching him. I waited until he was finished, giving some thought to the fact that I make a better impression as an alcoholic on a fourteen-inch screen than I do in my own living room. It was very disconcerting.

I offered to take him out for a beer when he got off work.

"Nah," he said, "I owe you a dinner already. I'd buy a couple of rounds but my wife's waiting for me to get home."

"I think we've got a lot to talk about," I told him.

"We do?" he said, giving me a strange look.

"Sure. Like your job, for example. You won't believe this, but my job was just as bad as yours. Worse in some ways. And we both have the Farbers in common. We both think they're weird."

"Go on. You're going to tell me that being on television is awful?"

"No, really, it was horrible. It was so bad I had to quit, and I didn't even have another job lined up. I mean it."

"And what about your family? What about your wife, is she independently wealthy or something?"

"No."

"Well I might not have a right to tell you this, but I don't think that's right."

I began to realize I should not have come uptown to see him, and had I known how I was going to behave, I know I wouldn't have. I was thinking that I wanted to ask him what kind of a wife did he have, did she appreciate the degradation he had to go through at work, but instead I listened to him talking about sure his job is bad, but it could be worse, that he gets to meet interesting people, that he doesn't have to do any heavy lifting, which is important because on his last job he permanently injured his back. It was all very depressing. I would like to imagine that Gerry could not have come any closer to talking to Jeffrey, but I don't know that for sure.

"And I suppose now I'm supposed to admit that you were right about everything else, right?"

Lorraine walks into the kitchen as she always does when I make an AS THE WORLD TURNS remark. It is a difficult habit to break, and only now do I realize the full impact that show has had on my life. I begin to weep, but they are soap opera tears for Lorraine, to let her know I am sorry I was so edgy.

Recently my fantasy life has become very rich. On the subway I think I am going to be approached by the Puerto Rican woman sitting next to me, I am afraid that when I open the door to my apartment I will find my wife with another man, or I will not find her there at all; it is as if I were afraid Gerry and Ellen had revealed something to her that she might not have known already.

But when I get home and find her there as usual, I am a little disappointed. But I am not irritable—I can feel the humility in my voice. She kisses me at the door. "Guess what," she says, "I got a part-time job with the Welfare Department, thanks to Ellen. It'll help us get through this thing without too much trouble, and besides, it'll give me something to do with my time. You were right about that."

Today I stopped by the William Morris Agency to fill out my unemployment forms and let them know I was available for work. I looked through the listings just for laughs and noticed there were two parts opening up on THE SECRET STORM: one middle-aged professional-looking male with experience on daytime TV, and one younger man as a recent college graduate-type. I could imagine Gerry's reaction right off, the whole upward mobility fantasy played out for the leisure class. I wondered for a moment what Gerry's Lolita would look like, what kind of clothes she wore, and I also wondered how long Ellen would be able to put up with her and him. I felt reasonably certain I would not find out. I wondered too whether I ought to think seriously about auditioning for THE SECRET STORM. I would make a good professional-type.

There is a TV set that they turn on at William Morris whenever one of their featured actors is on an important show. I turned it on to see what was happening on AS THE WORLD TURNS, and there was the ugly doctor proposing to Elaine. Elaine looked about ten years older since I left the show; I don't know how much more she will be able to take. She hesitated for a moment, mentioning my name, wondering if I would ever come back, and if I did what would I think about her, falling in love so soon afterwards. It was discomforting to hear me being talked about in such a way. She did not answer him right away, but I knew eventually she would say yes, and that there was no way of preventing her from making this horrible mistake. It occurred to me that in a couple of weeks I would not even be missed.

When I got back to my apartment it was quiet and empty; Lorraine had not yet gotten home from work. And I could not quite shake the feeling I would not be missed, that if Lorraine came home from work and I were not here, she would not be all that concerned. I was tempted to call Elaine and tell her not to marry that idiotic doctor, that if she could only persevere for a little while longer I'd be back; but I resisted the temptation. Instead I turned on the television to see what was going on with THE SE-CRET STORM, to see if they might really have a part for me, if they needed someone down on his luck, weary of love, someone who walked around in a trance.

LEAVING THE CHURCH

MARK HELPRIN

MARK HELPRIN was born in 1947 and grew up in New
York City, the Hudson River Valley, and the British
West Indies. He holds degrees from Harvard College and
Harvard's Center for Middle Eastern Studies, and has
seen service in the British merchant navy, the Israeli in-
fantry, and the Israeli air force. He is the author of *A
Dove of the East and Other Stories.*

I HAVE NEVER BEEN AS CALM IN MY LIFE," said Father
Trelew. "No, not ever." He was speaking to Helen, his
housekeeper, but she was not much in his mind, even though she
had been with him for several years—he could not remember exactly how many. He looked at the sky. "Soon I will be on the
plane to New York, and then to Rome."

"Have you been to Rome before, Father?"

"Yes, I have, in 1925 when Mussolini was in power. You know
what I think of him, don't you, don't you, Helen."

"I most certainly do."

It was hot where they stood, but his clothes were clean and
white and his thick hair was white, so he had no discomfort.
There was a black spot of oil on the drive. A shimmering desert
stretched beyond—his parish. He could smell the hot sand and
see waves of heat rising from it, distorting the mountains.

The driver put the bags in the car, and after bidding goodbye to
Helen and shaking her hand Father Trelew got in the back and
clicked the door shut. The car was air-conditioned. It was taking
him to Phoenix for the plane. He was going to Vatican II.

It was years since he had left his parish. In New York before his parents died, they had called him sometimes "The Indian Priest," but he never heard them, they thought. They were ashamed of him. They wanted him to be an archbishop. Instead he spoke to deep-brown faces in a dark church with no lighting, while the sand blew outside. He could see it through the window sometimes —perfectly white against the blue sky and billowing like foam on the ocean, and yet it was cool and dry. His mother and father thought he would come back from Arizona as if from some foreign campaign, distinguished and likely to advance. The bishops would appreciate his sacrifice. He knew he was not coming back, but he never told his parents. They died in the Depression, sure that at the end of the Depression he would be called back from Arizona.

If he thought about being an archbishop, he clenched his fist and banged it on the table. When he had too much to drink, he thought wild thoughts about seeing God, about golden staircases and whitened plumes rising from the wide floor of Heaven, about places where it was so bright you couldn't see anything at all. He had such prideful dreams only after wine or whiskey, so he drank rarely.

He arrived in Rome early in the morning. He felt young, for he had slept on the plane and Rome seemed to him not to have changed since 1925, when he was thirty and had been there for two months as a student. Now there were few carriages, but the streets were the same. In Piazza Navona, the old colors still stood; the fountains had been going for almost forty years since he first saw them. He wondered if they ever stopped, for even a moment. Perhaps each time the city died—after the March, or when the Germans were there—the fountains stopped. He thought to ask an old man, but realized that no one man would have watched constantly, and besides, he thought, I am an old man and could tell no one if ever in Arizona the mountains turned pure white or the sky the color of gold, because I have not watched them the whole time. At least, the fountains appear never to stop; at least, I have seen them while they were going.

His budget for this trip was delightfully large. The Vatican paid much of it, his diocese another great part, and his savings the rest.

He thought he would live for this short time in a fashion unlike that of his small frame house on the reservation. There the wind came in a steady stream through an unputtied crack of the window. In the morning gold light glinted off his porcelain shaving basin. At these times there was only silence and cold. After he shaved, he opened the window, and after he opened the window he dressed and prayed—but not in Rome. He would pray, yes, but in Rome he would pray in his own good time. There would be no kneeling on hard wooden floors, no fasting, and no cold.

He checked in at the Grand Hotel, which was full of priests and extremely elegant—marble, rich Oriental rugs, chandeliers, and in his room French doors with a view of a piazza and its enormous fountain shooting a hundred feet upward. As the weeks passed, he habitually ate his breakfast on the balcony. With high winds, he felt slight droplets of spray from the fountain. His bed was large, with a satin quilt. As always when he stayed in hotels—even in Phoenix—he wondered what people had made love in the bed, and then laughed good-naturedly at himself. He had learned to live with *that* a long time ago.

Father Trelew's role at the Council was not very exciting; indeed, the Council itself was not very exciting. He was just a priest. From where he sat near the entrance of St. Peter's, the Pope was only a white spot and the Dove of the Holy Ghost a needlepoint of light—a ray. When he removed his glasses, the sea of cardinals before the Pope was a mass of red, and when they stood their motion made them look like red waves. They were seated on both sides of the aisle. It was as if Moses had spread them back into the galleries. But whom would Father Trelew tell? Helen? Helen thought only of her child, who broke windows and stayed alone in the hills at night even when it was cold. Perhaps Father Wohlen from Los Angeles, who was Father Trelew's friend simply because they were both at the Grand Hotel; Father Wohlen had an idea that anyone from west of the Mississippi was somehow a loving brother. But Father Trelew did not like Father Wohlen, for he ate too much and had an unconvincing laugh. There was no one to tell. "There is no one to tell," he said. "Maybe I will sketch it." He had not sketched since he had last been in Rome. He was in a drawing class then. He was mainly interested in architectural form; Rome offered him that, while the desert did not. He had tried to paint the Indians and the things they did, but there was not much left of them by that time, and he suspected not much left of him—or, rather, of his talent to draw.

Did he dare begin again? "I must," he said, the blood coursing to his face. The hair at his temples was silver. When his face lit up, he looked like giltwork. I am the only priest in the world, he thought, who looks like a church. He would have to buy a pad and charcoal.

One day, he left the council early and began the walk back to his hotel. He passed through Piazza Navona, and somewhere off it on a side street he found an art store. "Could I have," he began but found that he was not able to speak the words. "Could I have . . ." and then, like a madman, he rushed from the shop.

He was disturbed by this, knowing precisely what it was. He tried not to think, flooding his mind with words that formed in silence on his lips, like the cries of men in dreams of sinking ships. "Flood it with good cheer. Fill it up, fill it up, for life is short." If he could somehow get supplies, he could sit by the fountain and sketch.

What is the power of a priest's life? It is that he need not fear. "Father Wohlen," he said next day, too nervously, "do you think that on the way back from the Cathedral tomorrow you could stop in an art shop and get me a large pad and some charcoal?" He gasped for breath. "Because I must stay late for chapel vespers. I don't mean to trouble you . . ."

"No trouble, no trouble," said Father Wohlen. "I'll do it. You just give me the money, tell me where to go, and I'll do it."

Father Trelew did not go to vespers; he did not even go to the Council that day. It was an important day, too. He stayed in his room, and it seemed to him that God was working wonders with his body. If he had been a proud man, he might have presumed that he was undergoing Divine revelation, that he was receiving saintly visions. Only once in his life, only once, had the rest of his body responded to his mind and made him tremble. No, it was the body responding to the *heart* which caused trembling.

He sat on the edge of his bed, with his glasses off, and the blur of outside sunlight made him feel the enlivened world. "Oh my

God, my dear God," he prayed, "I am not having visions, am I?"
He said this to a shaft of sunlight in his room at his feet, and the
golden dust danced in center beam.

When Father Wohlen gave him his materials, Father Wohlen
thought Trelew was sick. Something was wrong with the man.

Father Trelew ran his hands over the pad, took the charcoal out
of its box, and felt the smooth rectangular blocks. The cool of the
blocks reminded him of the desert at evening, their blackness of
the night, but the night was full of white stars. That was an advantage he would not have had as an archbishop—seeing the
Milky Way stretched as a shimmering band over the great dome
of his little life. The power of a priest's life is that he is unafraid.
All is concelebration. "I am beginning to realize this," said Father
Trelew. "That all is concelebration—all of the city, all of the
stars. The Church is for me. A man need not fear his loneliness.
He need not fear his loneliness, for God is strong and all is
concelebration. The power of a priest's life is that he need not
fear."

The next day he was up very early. He read most of *La Stampa*.
A bus took him to the Vatican.

It would not be right for him to sketch in the Cathedral. His
idea was to study a particular scene and commit it to memory for
drawing. Back in Arizona, he would paint it. Somehow he got
very close to the Pope. Though it was thrilling to see him, it was
not the Pope he chose to study but the under-secretaries close to
the Papal Throne, seated at a table next to the balustrade of the
Confessio.

Another priest from America was determined to guide him.
"That is Bishop Wilhelm Kempf of Limburg," he said, "and
Archbishop Villot of Lyons, Archbishop Krol of Philadelphia, and
the archbishop of Madrid—I do not know his name."

"Thank you, thank you," said Father Trelew to the other priest,
who wanted to say more, and then to escape he stepped much
closer to the scene than he would ordinarily have dared. He was
the foremost of observers; between him and the under-secretaries
was only a slight and terrible plain of marble. The Pope was not
far. I am so near greatness, he thought. Princes! He studied the
scene. He had always had a good architectural memory. He was

fine on detail, but here he was impressed by grandeur, which was glowing, descript, calling out to any man.

Entrenched in the blackness of distant high walls, the red table of the under-secretaries glowed scarlet; ringed with gold and tasselled, its colors moved in front of the eyes. The under-secretaries, in pure white with upswinging conical hats of flattened design, did not rest upon their red ribbons banded about them in curves and sweeps like water falling. They worked at papers, and they were in different positions, so that the tall conical hats pointed together in a smooth indication, like a crest of ocean foam, to the Pope. And beyond them was a swirling black column edged with a rotating blade of gold. It was so bright it made Father Trelew shudder. He stood for a good half hour, intent upon the secretaries. His gaze was powerful. He was having the time of his life, for he knew he would soon begin to draw.

One of the Papal secretaries noticed Father Trelew when he first came, and then again after half an hour. He thought perhaps he was wanted and crossed the forbidden marble at a glide. His robes were such that his feet did not seem to move. "Is there anything I can do for you, Father?" he said curiously.

Father Trelew, who had tried and failed to escape when he saw the bishop coming, could not answer. His steadfastness had provoked the great man, but he could not answer. His mouth hung open.

"Are you all right?" the bishop asked. He laughed pleasantly and touched Father Trelew, who felt again like sinking ships, and whose mouth was still open while the bishop returned to his table, silent and smiling.

Father Trelew managed to close his mouth as he walked back into the crowd. Everyone looked at him as if he were in some way connected to the Pope. He might have enjoyed that had he been able to answer the bishop, but he was expressionless and numb. And yet he did not panic. He wanted to get back to the hotel to draw, and then the next day to Piazza Navona, with his pad, to sketch the central fountain. He could use his material freely there. He was marvellously excited. He quickly forgot the incident with the bishop, bent down to tie his shoe, and strode like a master through St. Peter's to home in the hotel. He did not think, Oh, I am such a little man, until he arrived in his room and could not draw what he had remembered.

Father Trelew had many times told weeping Indian women that sleep helped the troubled. He had many times watched tears travel down a face like wind-cut brown granite—sparkling black eyes in the church's dimness—and thought how deeply the woman would sleep. Always the next day he saw her going about her business, which is precisely what *he* did the next day.

Late in the afternoon, he found himself in Piazza Navona. He thought to draw the fountain and the buildings vanishing in perspective, to test his draftsmanship. He planned to have dinner at one of the restaurants there so popular with Roman families (fairly well-to-do, he assumed) and clerics, and perhaps find an acquaintance with whom to chat as it got dark.

He took a seat at one of the smaller fountains and put his legs up on the stone wall. In his freshly pressed white suit he looked as if he might have been a missionary from the Congo or Asia. "Perhaps they think I am a jungle priest," he said happily. "But I am not a jungle priest, I am a desert priest—and how many of those are there? Very few in the Sahara, none, as far as I know, in the Gobi, and none in the Nafud. That leaves me, and a few others. I should find out who they are, write to them, perhaps start a journal."

He was a good priest, and did his job well. He thought of photographers he had seen on the reservation, who paid people small sums to be photographed and recorded their humiliation and discomfort only to pass it off to the world as the pathos of humankind. In the operations of caring for his flock, Father Trelew tried to avoid the photographers' fallacy. Only rarely did tragedy face them. There were complaints and sorrows, but not much passionate loss. He had to accept that. It was a small population, and not a battlefield—he was *truly* needed once in a great while, but he refused to buy the illusion that when they came to him aching from life in the world he was doing great service. In that way, when he did great service he felt he could vault over mountains. In other words, he was a lean man.

He thought, My dreams can be dreamed in forty-five minutes, and then I become either tired or empty and stop dreaming—

again, leanness. In the weakening sun he began to sketch Piazza Navona, and his hand moved rapidly, surprising him with what it had remembered. He included cars and carriages, and the horses, drawn well. After several hours, when it was dark, he closed his pad and put a little piece of charcoal into the box, which he then put in his pocket. Putting the box in his pocket was like the sheriff putting his gun back in his holster after a shoot-out. When he swung his legs back to the ground it was as if they had boots and spurs. He had drawn the Piazza, and it was therefore his.

With dinner, he ordered a bottle of white wine. He was not used to it; it was a mistake, he told himself halfway through, but drank it anyway. Then everything began to fall into place as he watched the lights of Rome in the heat of September and wandered about like a young drunk.

He was a good-natured man, had always been a good-natured man. His father, who was ambitious for him to the point of hating him, said once, "Michael, what have you got, what the hell have you got?" Father Trelew had wanted to reply that he was a good man, could draw, and loved God. But he wept instead, and only later, half weeping, did he say to his mother, "Tell him, by my honor, that I am just a man," and left for the train to the West.

He was good-looking. He had a wonderful face. Even at his age, and he was almost seventy, women were not unmoved by his glance. When he was younger they had frequently fallen in love with him, especially the troubled ones, who always fall for priests of one sort or another. There had been one in Rome in 1925, when he was thirty and had rebuffed already a good many trouble-seekers and those testing their power. A priest is familiar with that. He can handle that. It is the guileless ones, the ones who really love, who make things difficult.

In 1925, the library of the old Accademia was farmed with sea-green reader's lamps, which glowed in the day. The walls were so old one might have been sorry for them had they not been painted with angels, gardens, and bursting suns.

Father Trelew was not merely appreciative but ecstatic. He often stayed in the library all day and well into the evening. He was writing a paper on Oderisi da Gubbio, a miniaturist of the thirteenth century. When he left the library he saw only the colors he had seen all day in illuminated manuscripts. It seemed to him that he sailed home without a word, simply gliding and brimming.

One was assigned a seat, and results were not always pleasing. Harvard undergraduates dying for the sunburnt girl in purple who sometimes wore black were placed across the room from her facing the other way into a bunch of nuns. Father Trelew could hardly breathe for two weeks; he was the only man at a table for Radcliffe girls. One of them fell in love with him, just by looking.

"What is your name . . . Father?" she asked, since there was no one else at the table.

"Michael Trelew," he said, frightenedly.

"And where are you from?"

"From. From. I'm from Ossining, New York. Perhaps you have heard of us—I mean it, as it is the home of Sing Sing Prison. Where are you from?"

"Forty-nine East Eighty-sixth Street," she said, waiting.

His fear was beginning to bore him, and in anger he wanted to be reckless, if only not to be dull. But he could only stare at her. She was thin, and blond. He could not decide if she looked like the Madonna. She was very brown and her dress was white.

She said, and with her green eyes, "Can we eat together tonight?" It was for her a difficult request, and she blushed. She felt like what she thought of popular music—brash but finally very beautiful. She was embarrassed by her own directness, expectant, and altogether very open and tender.

Father Trelew was taken. Yet he answered as if from a prepared hollowness, "I have no money. I am a priest . . ." He hesitated, because he was no longer interested in what he was saying. Instead, visions of neutral Switzerland flashed at him and he entertained the profoundly impossible notion of running away with this girl.

The weeks that followed were very sad for both of them. They were both gaining, but they were also losing, and perhaps what united them so strongly at first was that they felt they knew what the other was relinquishing. And then they had that particular camaraderie which exists among schoolboys, soldiers, and outlaws.

It did not take long before they were speeding to Switzerland in a touring car he had rented with the remainder of his grant for study in Rome. He told her the speedometer's thin red needle reminded him of a hummingbird's tongue. They stopped at a dam in a valley of the Alps. Across the spillway was an automobile bridge that led nowhere, and fog from the rushing water cascaded in a convection arch over the bridge, over the two of them.

The time together in Rome had made the priest and the girl heady. She was young, and he not so young but it was new to him. When he removed his collar he sighed in relief and walked out into the warm sun where she was waiting in the open car in a hat and heavy coat ready to head north. There was singing all the way. In one inn, Father Trelew, having had too much wine, told the porter that he was a priest. The porter raised his arms as if to say, "That is very serious, but so what?"

They stayed in Switzerland for more than a month. He was going to give up the Church, when she left him. There was no comfort. Everything had failed. He had not written his paper and could show nothing for his summer in Italy. The bishops at home would have his head for that. There would be nothing he could say; he could see himself gaping at them.

It would not be the first time he had found himself mute. The first was the time he and the girl had been unable to resolve an argument and it grew wider and wider, until she was on a platform waiting for a train and nothing he could say made anything better. He felt untrained for that sort of thing. The argument had started while they were drawing by a lake, and he threw his picture to the ground. He was angry. She had too many plans for him. She had him in the White House when he was not yet even just a defrocked priest. He threw his picture on the ground because he realized that she was young and nothing could be done about it. When the train came, she was crying, for she did love him, and perhaps because she was crying and she was young she struck a blow she had not meant to strike. She was not even Catholic but Episcopalian. She said through the steam and rain which soaked them both and was warm and very much like their tears— she said on that hot misty August day so uncommon for Switzerland, "And you are such a little man." It was then that his mouth dropped open and he could say nothing. She cried and cried, and as the train left he ran after it halfheartedly with his

mouth still open and tears streaming down his cheeks and the
steam from the gaskets making his suit smell as if it had been just
pressed.

He looked at the high white mountains, and his smallness
choked him. He boarded the next train to Rome after waiting in
the station for seventeen hours. He did not eat, nor did he return
for his belongings. It stayed misty and warm until he left.

They sent him to Arizona. They would have thrown him out,
but they needed someone there. He was perfect for the job. He
could have left on his own. They offered him that, but he was
afraid. The archbishop made him afraid. Offices made him afraid.
Even cathedrals now made him afraid.

The only thing that calmed him was the desert and its silent,
dry heat. In the desert he started to seek God as he had not ever
sought him. In some ways he stayed weak, and in others he became very strong.

He watched the blue mountains and the billowing sand, which
was like the foam on the ocean when he came home from Italy,
but cool and dry.

A man from the desert is not a dry man, but he keeps what is
wet inside him, like a cactus, so that visitors to him wonder how
in such a world he can be alive and have enough. Father Trelew
had not been born in the desert, but his forty years there taught
him much. Although there will be some who might deny that a
man may be taught such a thing, it is a fact that Father Trelew
was calm, quiet, and gracious during his first heart attack. It occurred while he dined with several other American priests near
the hotel in a restaurant they had all frequented during the first
weeks of the Council, and then abandoned, then remembered and
rushed to, as Father Trelew had done with his drawing. He ate
prosciutto and melon, *scaloppine alla zingara*, and drank gaseous
mineral water and cold white wine. He was contemplating dessert
and had his wine-glass raised to his lips when he felt the first pain.
It seemed as if the entire restaurant had been jolted by an
earthquake, and the electricity somehow savagely unleashed to attack the assembled priests. At first he thought there *had* been an
earthquake. He kept his glass to his lips, afraid to move. He would
put it down, slowly. He would go without dessert, excuse himself,

and walk to see a doctor. He did not want to trouble his companions, because they were younger and he felt they did not like him; he had said hardly a thing in the course of the meal while they burned with the politics of Council.

But he could not move his arm to put his glass down. It was there for a full minute and no one noticed until he fell to the ground, for he could not stand the second wave. He fell to the ground still with the glass in his hand, apologizing and begging the pardon of the assembled priests, who were younger and who had ignored him.

When he awakened in his hospital room, he was grateful that the walls were not white. Rome is a yellow color, an old saffron-powdered sun color which seems always rising upward. His room was a comforting beige, the color of a lightly done roll in the oven.

He was happy to be alive and would not move his head until later, when a nun told him it was safe. He saw by turning his eyes the tops of pine trees and green hills in the not so far distance. He judged himself to be on a mountaintop. "Splendid," he said. "I'm on a mountaintop." He could hear birds and the clicking of crutches in the garden. After a few weeks he was up and about. He could see most of Rome from the garden and some of Rome came up to meet him, although that part of Rome which travelled up the hillside to him was not people but houses and streets.

When he had been a priest in Arizona and visited parishioners in the hospital he thought because of its bustle and crowded corridors that a hospital was a social place. He had often thought of going to a hospital on some physical excuse to cure his loneliness, but in Rome (and he assumed that hospitals were spiritually the same everywhere) he discovered himself more alone than he had ever been. The face of his nurse was constantly changing, and there were eight doctors who cared for him in varying degree, none with particular intensity. He was alone during the day, and in the night. He did not dare draw. He was afraid to look in the mirror. No one paid him any attention, because he was old.

There was a man dying of some unknown disease, a violinist in a symphony orchestra in the North of Italy. He looked as if he were made of old loops and patches. He smelled of death. It came from inside him—from his bowels, from his throat, even from his legs and fingers. Father Trelew had smelled the same smell in Arizona when some boys cut open a deer they had shot in the mountains several days before. Every day the violinist sat in the garden and played. He was particularly fond of the Andante of Prokofieff's Second Violin Concerto, and he played it again and again. The officials allowed it because it helped those who recovered recover, those who were dying to die, and those in the middle of the road to pass the time. Father Trelew wanted to talk to the man whose music was so beautiful; he had never before heard any Prokofieff. When he went to him in the garden, he found the old man unable to speak. But the patterns of the music were so strongly ingrained, and his hands so powerful, that he played, he played, until the day of his death—not always correctly, often out of time, but always with much passion.

Father Trelew was not afraid of dying. He was afraid of what he might be before he died. When he first realized that he was dying he stayed in his chair—an old man in a chair—and tried frantically to remember all the parts of his life. He thought that when a man dies a man reviews what he has seen. He expected memories to jolt his frame, and visions to seek him and turn him, and shower the room with light.

But it just didn't happen as he expected, which he might have expected but did not. He became whimsical, prided himself suddenly on his sense of humor, and found the truth in sayings. He would say, "Love makes the world go round," and laugh. He was generally good-natured. Every four hours a nurse, never the same one, came to ask him if he had moved his bowels. He thought this was hilarious.

"Father Trelew."

"Yes, Sister."

"Have you moved your bowels in the last four hours?"

"Moved them where?" he said, and burst out laughing.

He was happy for no particular reason, and for that reason he adjudged himself particularly happy. One would have thought he was getting better. He said, "I want to have a good time on earth while I can," and spent the days in the garden, in the sun, watching flowers and delighting in the smell of rich grass, which was green as if on a riverbank. At night, he looked from his window at Rome, and because he remembered his memories so well he did not think of them, or need to. One look at Rome from a moderate distance was to see his life, but it was past and he had no need for that.

A week after the death of the violinist who could not speak, Father Trelew died. The bishops in New York sent a militant priest who had been embarrassing them to fill his place in Arizona. He died in late afternoon. It had been raining. He knew from years before in his student days that there is a special name for raindrops in Rome because they are often so big, but he could not remember it. He was admiring the light coming off the wet buildings, and he was calm, listening to the wash of the rain. The bushes in the garden glistened with drops, and when someone went by and hit them the water flew off like water off a vibrating dog. Streams of warm water coursed down the gray stone streets of the mountain—or hill—of the hospital. All across Rome flocks of pigeons were seeking the rays of sun, which came from holes in the clouds, and they flew in great masses, looking for light that quickly vanished with new configurations of the dark sky. Father Trelew listened to the work of the rain, to the wash of the rain, and to a car going through a puddle. The water is warm, the blood of the earth. He was a man resting for the afternoon in his chair. Warm breezes thick with invisible mist moved his white gauze curtains, and he faced the wind. He turned his head to it and breathed it in.

Then it seemed again as if there were an earthquake. For an instant he imagined that lightning had hit him, for his vision had flashed white at first, but then he knew, and when the bolts kept on coming he knew he was dying and he became very excited.

He tried to think of the girl he had once loved—of her face, of the heat and their well-being—but could not do it. He had not enough time. He realized that dying takes away time, and that is all, and he was dying when fear gripped him and his mouth dropped open in its customary manner. He had planned to die with a vision, but there was no vision. The rain had stopped, and the water ceased to flow as rapidly inside the gutters. He noticed that. The walls seemed to him a very dark olive-green instead of tan. His mouth hung open, but he raised himself in his chair of a sudden and said, "Damn you, shut, damn it!" and it did shut and he was so surprised that he smiled and his eyes came alive. It seemed to him that he was a new man, that he was no longer a priest, no longer Michael Trelew. He was only sorry that they would bury him as Michael Trelew, Priest. He had gone out of those doors.

He lived that way for the short span of time between the lighting of his eyes and the entrance of a priest who was rushing in the door to administer last rites. Father Trelew saw the priest through the corner of his eye, but by the time he would have had full view he was dead. The last thing he thought was how beautiful the summer rain in Rome—and he died, and he died with great courage.

BLOOD-SWOLLEN LANDSCAPE

JOYCE CAROL OATES

JOYCE CAROL OATES is the author most recently of *The Assassins*. She makes her home in Windsor, Ontario, and teaches at Windsor University. In 1970 she was the first recipient of this series' special award for continuing achievement.

APPROACHING HIM was a person he hated: he wished dead.

In and out of his eyesight floated that thought. *Die. Be dead.* It was weightless, it couldn't be stopped. Couldn't be unsaid. It was a wish that sprang to life somehow in his vision, in his eyes; as soon as he saw that man the thought wished itself to completion and. . . .

And so he was a murderer in his heart.

But look: reimagine. Return and start again.

Martin was coming out of the Science Building, hurrying, upset about some news he had just received, news of a friend's wife, and so his control was shaky, he really was not himself—Martin Hershfield, twenty-six, an instructor in the Physics Department of this comfortable little college—and perhaps not to blame. He happened to glance up and saw, approaching him, one of his enemies: also a young man of twenty-six, with a bony, grim, harassed face, wearing a suit that looked cheaper than Martin's, bought off the rack probably at the Norban's Discount Store at the shopping mall. He and Martin were moving like missiles in a head-on collision course. Would they collide? No. Martin stared at him and a thought flashed into his head that terrified him: He wished that young man dead.

Martin veered guiltily off to the right and crossed a patch of soil—walked right through a fragile barricade of white string, which twisted around his ankles, oh, damn it, oh, my God, surely other people had noticed, and not just his enemy?—but it was too late, he had to keep walking right through the new-planted grass. In a daze he kept on walking. He regained the sidewalk and made his way deftly through the packs and swarms of students, staring past them, over their heads and shoulders, trying not to register the effect of their smiles and grins and occasional bright hellos— *Hello, Dr. Hershfield!* If he didn't make eye contact with them they would not exist and he would not exist.

His beige wool-and-dacron suit was too warm for this mild day. Too warm. And his face was too warm; he was afraid he would burst into tears. He was a young man six feet two inches tall, carrying a valise stuffed with books and examination papers and mail and the paper bag he had brought his lunch in, and was taking back home so it could be used again, and his height and appearance and position and age made it necessary for him to get to a private place, so that he could cry. Otherwise, shame.

He took a short-cut behind the library, not a sidewalk but only a dirt-and-gravel path, not much used. This would take him away from the center of the campus. If Merrill, back there, was also wishing him dead, it would take him away from Merrill as well; he detested, dreaded Merrill and the others, he was overcome by the snaky uncanny confidence of his enemies, which looked, on the surface, like his own nervousness, but which was really a deathly strength he could not comprehend. . . . Yet he did not wish anyone dead, not really. Not dead. Dead. Absent but not dead . . . "dead" but not dying-dead, the state of being that comes after the throes of active dying. . . . No. It wasn't in Martin's heart to wish anyone dead, not even his deadly enemies.

And yet. . . .

But wait, return and start again. Return quickly and start again:

Martin reached in the pigeonhole assigned to him ("Hershfield") in the row of instructors' mailboxes, the row nearest the floor, and pulled out a handful of letters. He pawed through them, hoping as always for good news. Hoping. Hoping for something. But the important letters—the Confidential Letters—the letters that might, might mean he had a future, he wasn't going to be finished at twenty-six, would be at home, waiting for him, and at school he usually received advertising brochures and other impersonal professional mail, envelopes with his name stamped on them. Occasionally he received a real letter, from a friend: but the friends' letters had become dangerous, since if they contained bad news they would depress him and if they contained good news they would depress him also. Good news meant, now, that someone had a job for next year or a post-doctoral grant or a fellowship, and since Martin had been tentatively scheduled for "nonrenewal" of his contract here at Tull College, he dreaded hearing about his friends' good/bad luck. So, when he found Marie McGahern's letter he should not have opened it, but taken it home to his wife, and opened it with her, or in front of her, or handed it wordlessly over to her to be opened. . . . But he had torn it open anyway, recklessly. He had read:

. . . feel very out of touch . . . floating-free, detached . . . not really concerned with my own feelings, it's strange. . . . Wanted to call you one night, just to talk. But your wife would not understand. So. Wondered about you & her. Is she precious-sacred to you? does she allow you to touch her? or? Or do you allow her to touch you? We all got married too young. . . . Haven't been in contact with Bob for 4.5 weeks now. Over with? It dies hard. He kept saying to me & maybe wrote you heartbreaking letters on the subject, kept saying "You do what is best for you. . . ." And: "You do what is best for you . . . for you . . ." So I did. So I arranged it. The method used on me has a very illustrative name your wife would know . . . since she is a scientist, like you & Bob & others . . . but I have forgotten the name (suppressed it?) . . . a kind of suction, vacuum-suction. . . . I recommend it. It all shoots out, dense clotted blood, in five minutes it just comes out . . . which saves a lot time, you must admit: five minutes vs. the usual five days. . . . And you don't know if you're really pregnant or not. You think well maybe I am . . . but . . . but maybe I'm not . . . you're terrified & think yes maybe . . . but the doctor himself doesn't know (doc-

tor=intern on duty) & you don't, of course . . . & there's no
mess & you walk home after 30 min. in the usual way, not
dizzy or stumbling or hemorrhaging & if anyone glances at
you on the street that person does not see a vicious murderer
or even a panicked blood-drained woman or. . . .

He had stopped reading. He had stuffed this letter into his
shabby valise and walked away.

Walking out of the building he had thought of Marie, his
friend's wife, and of his own wife, and of himself and others, and
in a queer panicked instant he had felt himself drained of blood,
wobbling, unwell, doomed—wondering where he was—so far
from Boston, from home. He stared in front of him. Confused.
His suit was too warm for this surprise of a day, a pre-spring day.
Very far from Boston and his eight years of advanced schooling,
very far. In fact he was in a town called Mason, Ohio. *Mason,
Ohio.* He always had to force himself to remember it, it was not a
place anyone knew; but Tull College was located here, founded
1850, a liberal arts college with a small enrollment and a fine solid
reputation. . . . Mason, Ohio, was Martin's home, temporarily.
Therefore he should acknowledge it, not dread it. He should acknowledge all facets of reality, benign and evil, so as to order it,
and out of order would come clarity and happiness. Clarity and
happiness. So he walked out of the handsome brick-and-aluminum
Science Building (built 1966) and saw his enemy—one of his several enemies—and fled from that enemy and from everyone else,
cutting across a plot of fragile green grass, quarter-inch grass, getting string entangled in his shoes, making a fool of himself, perhaps destroying what remained of his future, all in an effort to get
away somewhere so that he could cry. . . .

Mid-April sunshine. A morning of forsythia and opened windows in classrooms and bare-armed students swarming everywhere, a tide of smiles Martin could not handle, even when he
was in a normal state; he fled blindly. He thought: *Oh Jesus,
we're being punished . . . it's starting . . . but why?*

As soon as he got out back in a field, and then in a sparse
woods, he began to cry. He had not cried for ten or twelve years.

Martin's wife, Rosalind, forty miles away in Columbus, took
down notes as one of the professors dictated to her, strolling be-

tween the rows of caged white rats. The experiment—"Aggression-Inducing Factors in White Rats"—was similar to one Rosalind had helped with back at Harvard, the year before, but of course said nothing about this.

"Okay," the professor said, "have one of the girls type it up. But be sure she can read your handwriting—otherwise it will be a mess. They're all moronic, they can't spell."

"Yes," Rosalind said.

She changed out of the lab coat and handed the papers in to one of the secretaries, helped the girl read through the statistics and notes, and paused before going home; wanting somehow to talk with the girl, to exchange simple, trivial news, to laugh about something. The typist was about twenty years old and Rosalind was a few years older. But the girl smiled only courteously, shyly, at Rosalind, and would not venture anything further. So Rosalind gave up.

. . . *might as well go home.*

She was a laboratory assistant in the Psychology Department here, not officially admitted into the doctoral program—as the chairman of the Graduate Committee had explained to her, bitterly, their doctoral studies program had been cut back by the university, the university budget had been cut back by the state, and — Her credentials were excellent, of course. She had a B+ average from Harvard, a Master's Degree in experimental psychology. Excellent. But the doctoral program here was being cut back, severely, and no new candidates could be admitted at present; of course, as soon as the budget was restored, they would be delighted to accept her as a candidate. . . .

Rosalind had told the chairman of the committee that this was fine; she would be happy to wait.

She understood.

The chairman had smiled, relieved. "You understand, Mrs. Hershfield?"

Yes, she understood.

And so she had smiled that day, and she smiled most days. She knew the value of a smile, unlike her husband, whose smile had turned jagged and ironic. . . . In high school all the popular girls had smiled, at everyone; perhaps they smiled because they were popular, or were popular because they smiled.

So she smiled. And the department had hired her, over countless other applicants, as a laboratory assistant on the part-time salary scale. Martin had been shocked at the salary and had said, "Is
this a misprint?" And Rosalind had said cheerfully, "Honey, this
is just a phase in our life together, a temporary phase."

Martin's mouth shaped itself into that jagged smile. "Everything is temporary," he said.

She dreaded driving back to Mason, returning to the duplex
they rented, unlocking the door, looking down to see what mail
had come. . . . She dreaded it, but it was the next thing she must
do.

You spend your life walking in straight lines, turn sharply
left/right, following the direction of sidewalks and other necessary
guides. In this way you create certain human routes. The natural
human route, in civilization, is straight, sharp-angled, perpendicu-
lar to its goal. This does create tensions in civilization. *Tensions
are possible. Probable.* So one morning in Ohio a young man
felt the containment of his former life begin to shift out of shape.

He crossed through the faculty parking lot, walked along the
edge of the bulldozed hill, on muddy planks, and on, out, until he
was in a field and safe and his face shifted into a face of anguish,
a boy's face. He wiped at his eyes angrily. Then he was in a woods
and crying and at the same time shamefully aware of himself crying, angry at himself, not yet frightened at what was happening to
him. He felt very warm and itchy; this suit was a mistake. It was
his only good suit. In Massachusetts April would not be so warm,
not even on a freakish spring day. He could not always remember
where he was but he knew he wasn't home.

He stopped crying. It had lasted only a minute. It was over.

From this hill he could look back down toward the campus. In
the foreground was the partly excavated hill. He couldn't remember what had been planned for this side of the campus, but he
knew it had come to an abrupt end, just as the "Expansion Program" itself had ended abruptly. A financial disaster of secret proportions had struck Tull College; everyone used that expression,
saying that disaster had "struck." Like lightning, something had
rushed in from the outside. Don't ask from where. Don't ask why.
Don't.

And therefore Martin had four enemies, three of them young men and one a woman of about thirty. They were all on the lower faculty, they did not have tenure, they had all received the same letters informing them of "nonrenewal" of contract. . . . But it was not such a simple matter. Their letters had been waiting for them on the first Monday after the official start of the fall semester; a shock from which Martin had yet to recover, but he had performed his duties this year as if he had recovered; after all, he was an adult and he had a degree from M.I.T. Weeks passed. Then, on October 20, Martin had been called into the chairman's office and was told that the nonrenewals were the result of tragic financial setbacks, *not* meant to be personal, not personal at all. But there was hope, the chairman said. The faculty association was engaged in a struggle with the college senate, and with the Chancellor himself, in an effort to regain ten percent of the budget, and if this struggle were won, the Physics Department would, or might, or would like, to rehire one of them.

Martin had stared. "One of us?" he asked.

"We hope very, very much to rehire one of you," the chairman said, smiling his nervous smile. He was a pleasant man in his fifties, from M.I.T. also, but unfortunately too old to have known Martin's advisor.

"That's. . . ." But Martin had fallen silent, staring at the older man's face. It was a peculiar, difficult moment. He had wanted very much to say *that's good*, but he could not quite say it. So the moment passed, awkwardly.

The winter had passed and now it was April and Martin knew no more; no one knew any more. He had four enemies, four rivals. One of them was the gaunt-faced Merrill, whom he had just avoided—neurotic, brilliant, with his degree from Stanford. He was unmarried, though. That might count against him. He was also very shaky, he smoked a great deal, he dressed badly. The most serious rival was a big red-headed kid from the University of Wisconsin, with his ex-football player's manliness and stamina and a reputed I.Q. of 190, married, and with a pregnant young wife; he was an assistant professor, however, which meant his salary was higher than Martin's, and would cost the department more to rehire. Another assistant professor, a blond woman Martin especially disliked, had come here from M.I.T. five years before, but no one seemed to like her very much, or to defend her, and Martin had heard rumors about her missing classes. So perhaps she was out of the running. His fourth rival was an instructor who had been hired along with him, new to Tull, a sweet-faced young man who suffered from asthma and whose family was reputed to be wealthy—he even had a last name which was a famous brand name in the United States, though this might have been simply a coincidence—and whom Martin for some reason did not take seriously, always forgetting to worry about him. *Don't forget Daryl,* part of his brain would shout.

He wished them all dead.

He had walked into a clearing and he began to hear noises somewhere. His head was heavy, leaden, as if there were something inside it he could not get clear. The sound of someone walking nearby irritated him; but it distracted him. So he thought: A *simultaneous phenomenon.* He followed a path slick with mud and saw someone ahead of him, a figure moving slowly. The person seemed to be trudging. It wore boots and slacks and its arms were bare.

It was a woman: but her body was not womanly. Martin paused for a moment, watching her. She looked familiar. She stopped to reach inside her boot, clumsily, as if she were trying to pull up a sock that had ridden down inside it. Her boots were made of a shiny synthetic material and were splotched with mud. Martin saw that she had gotten mud on her hand and seemed not to know what to do . . . then she wiped it, carefully, on the back of her thighs, out of her own range of vision.

A quick hot flash of a thought entered Martin's brain, through his eyes—

But he did not allow himself to think it.

A sudden knocking in the car made Rosalind accelerate. The car was a five-year-old Pontiac, bought second hand, and each drive to and back from Columbus she considered a risk, then an accomplishment; the car had lasted the winter and might last out their term in Mason. Now she was entering Mason, passing a denuded strip of land advertised as *Parkway Estates: A Planned Residential Community.* None of the foundations for the houses had yet been laid, though the land had been stripped for as long as she had lived here.

Mason was a small city, with a downtown of typical midwestern stores, grim and old-fashioned, a single movie house which was open only on weekends, and one large AAA-approved hotel; Rosalind avoided it, and did her shopping at the mall outside town, where the new, fluorescent-lit stores sometimes cheered her up. Now she thought suddenly of the duplex apartment, the unlocking of the door, the mail lying inside, and she did not want to go home. Not yet. So she parked at the mall and ran into the drugstore to buy a few things—she did not want to go home—instead she would walk through this enormous store and take notice of the wide, clean aisles, the merchandise displayed—terrace tables with fringed, green plastic tops, lawn chairs, inflatable rubber rafts, a Diet-Counter that displayed bottles and boxes and foot-long candy bars made of "Chokolate"—and the cosmetics counter, with a wide accusing mirror behind it in which Rosalind always happened to catch sight of herself, guiltily, seeing that small, unstriking, unsurprising face of hers, and realizing once again that it wasn't a face that belonged in that mirror.

She stared at the magazines on display, her eye drifting without effort from cover to cover, from the face of one beautiful woman to another, moving on . . . skipping the sports and detective magazines . . . coming to a stop on another face: that of an Asian child, whose features were twisted with pain. Rosalind stared. She saw that his lips were edged with sores, reddened and angry as boils. . . . She touched her own lips, involuntarily.

In that instant she felt a terrible premonition: *We are all going to be punished.*

Martin walked through things that resisted him. Bushes, limbs that were elastic, healthy, with the greening of this April day. . . . He did not pay attention to them. Sharp little hooks caught at his trousers but he ignored them. Spongy, springy, wet earth, his shoes would be muddy, muddy as that woman's boots, but he did not think about it. *Dear Sir: I am inquiring about a possible position in your department, beginning in September of this year. At present I am an instructor in. . . . My Ph.D. degree is from. . . . I studied with Dr. A. G. Cordoba and. . . . If you are interested, my credentials and transcripts (undergraduate and graduate) and letters of recommendation are on file at the Place-*

ment Bureau. . . . *If you are interested in my application.* . . . *If you are.* . . . His wife had typed that letter and its variants out 240 separate times, but Martin was not thinking of her either; he was thinking of possibility-probability factors. Genes. The barometer. A too-warm suit. The pattern of clouds in the sky if you bothered to look (like a quilt, various shades of white and gray and darker gray). Healthy instincts of blood and muscle and eyes, directing the scene. Staring at the woman ahead of him Martin thought freely of all these factors, feeling himself a machine programmed in infinite patterns of complexities. He recalled Cordoba stating in a lecture, "What we know is likely to happen, but what we don't know is also likely to happen—" Martin had not understood. Now he thought he might understand.

"Hello?" he called to the woman. "Hello—?"

She stopped and looked back at him, cringing. Her face was broad, pale, doughy. Her eyes had a dead-dull luster to them and were slightly bulging . . . her lips were parted in a silent astonished scream. . . . Martin saw at once that there was something wrong with her. He stared, he stumbled against something. He brushed out of his way a branch covered with small white bell-shaped blossoms. He said again, softly, "Hello."

The woman might have been any age—twenty-nine, forty. He had seen her a few times around town, always dressed in slacks, always with her hair cropped short and curly, the curls stiff with grease. Her body was slightly misshapen, especially ungainly in the shoulders and torso; but her face, apart from the staring eyes and the working, shapeless mouth, was almost attractive. Dull-thoughtful, dull-meditative. Brain damaged. Martin was staring into the eyes and into the brain of a damaged person.

Rosalind tore open the first of the letters. Her heart pounded sickeningly. She saw the extremely smooth sheet folded inside the envelope, recognized it as the kind of paper used for mimeographing, and, yes, when she unfolded the letter it was another mimeographed reply: *We are very sorry to inform you that.* . . . She crumpled it and threw it aside, it bounced off the kitchen table and onto the floor, she opened the next letter, more carefully, and noted that there were the impressions made of typing on this piece of paper, she could feel them beneath her fingers, unmistakable, and for a long moment she held herself back from unfolding it. . . . It was so important, a typed-out letter on authentic stationery! Finally she unfolded it and her eye, practiced and cynical, skimmed the paragraph for crucial phrases: *we are interested in your application, we hope to, our budget has not yet, if, if you are still, following year.* . . . She put this letter down and opened the third, which was from a college she hardly remembered writing to, somewhere in Alabama. *We regret that.* . . . She threw it down. Then she snatched it up again, trembling. Something had thrown her off: yes, the letter was a form letter, but her husband's name and address had been typed in, as well as the date, and there was a salutation: *Dear Dr. Herchfeild.* . . .

"Dear Dr. Herchfeild," she laughed. "Go to hell, Dr. Herchfeild."

She threw away an advertisement and came upon the last of the letters, from friends they had known in Boston. The return address said just McGahern. Rosalind believed it was the wife's handwriting. She opened the letter and began to read it, with that helpless, flinching, cringing antihope, the hope not to read good news, her eye skimming the close-packed handwritten paragraphs. Then she began to read:

> . . . something is happening like rashes or bumps on the face . . . that are mysterious patterns . . . things trying to get said by the blood? the corpuscles in the blood? . . . Well you & Martin & Bob are the scientists & make the statistics. . . . I don't hate you. I don't even hate Bob. We're out of touch since 4.5 weeks ago . . . did he write you? . . . how I got rid of the baby . . . ? Try Martin & see what he will do . . . he will make you do the same . . . it's a vacuum suction method very safe & efficient & not very painful so they say . . . I was out of my head anyway & couldn't feel or focus & I might have missed important parts of the scientific procedure. . . .

Rosalind dropped the letter. Her fingers had gone cold. She picked it up again, walked quickly into the bedroom with it, as if to read it in secret. She read it through twice, then a third time . . . then she put it in a drawer, beneath some things, so that Martin would not find it. She stood for a while, staring at the rented bureau, the rented bed with its slick-pine headboard, the bedspread she had pulled hurriedly up that morning to cover the rumpled bedclothes. . . . She lifted the bedspread, drew it back; looked at the bedclothes; did not focus upon anything; drew the bedspread back up again and tucked it in. . . . They did not make love any longer. That seemed to be over. That was not a risk, not a danger. . . . *I couldn't feel or focus & I might have missed important parts of the procedure.* . . .

The woman walked away from him, her head bent.

Martin followed her. "What's wrong? Why are you leaving? Why are you afraid of me? Is something wrong? What do you know? Do you know something I don't know?"

She hurried. Her shoulders were hunched. Martin saw dizzily the quivering flesh of her upper arms, very pale, dough-like, the loose flabby flesh. It was ugly. It irritated him. He dropped what he had been carrying so that he wasn't weighed down, and he said, irritably, "Where are you going? Why are you running away? Wait—" He was willing. Watchful, heated, cautious. His body was drenched with heat. *Wait.* It was his body that remembered, not Martin himself, how he had once been in love . . . *in love* . . . how he had told his friends excitedly that he was in love and now he realized . . . oh, God, he realized what it was, what it was to be *in love* . . . he had never guessed at it before. . . . Had never guessed at it. Had never guessed. There were things you could not guess at. They existed, but in a dimension not yet opened to you. Like a book you can't read because its printed words are in a language you don't know, or because your eyes are filmed over with something opaque, blood-tinted, a throbbing membrane like the membrane that covers the soul. . . .

"Don't run. Don't do it. Don't run, please, don't," Martin said. He grabbed at the woman's arm. His fingers closed around her forearm, she jerked violently away from him, his fingers slid down around her wrist and held. Out of his body came a strength, concentrated in those fingers, that he had not noticed before.

She cringed away from him, her body bent. Her eyes were narrowed now, the lids nearly closed, as if she were staring into a bright light. She was breathing laboriously. Panic. He too felt it: the mucous-like coating of panic on the tongue. His own breathing was audible. It was a dense ungainly rhythm—her breath, his breath—a pumping of lungs and hearts, the two of them standing in a strange equilibrium, Martin holding her body straining and yet balanced perfectly against his own, the bulk and weight of a body that belonged to him. . . .

Then her face twisted violently and she began to cry. She sobbed. Her eyes narrowed to cracks and he saw in terror the way the tears came out of them: liquid springing out of those ugly eyes, streaming down that coarse-skinned face. . . . It was something too ugly to experience. He said, "Don't—" But the word was choked off, his throat felt paralyzed. He felt his own eyes narrowing and the hot pressure of tears behind the lids, stinging like salt. Like salt rubbed against a flimsy membrane. *Don't. Wait. Please.*

He saw a man's face lunging at his, and he saw the length of his own arm dragged out hard, he saw the bulk of his body out of the blinded lower half of his eyes. He heard the man cry, "Don't—"

The visible and invisible world was swollen tight with blood.

He felt his body hunch, grow taut and stiffened with terror, he felt the man's hard fingers closed about his wrist—

He felt the rhythm of their gasping for breath—

He felt the man's terror, the salt-stinging of tears against that man's eyes—

Then the fingers released the wrist: the fingers let go, the wrist and the arm and the springing, panicked body jerked free. It was free. The pulsation in his head, concentrated in his eyes, drew back into his own head now, released her, drew back sharp and delicate as a gesture, flowed back into his own being and released her. . . .

The woman ran from him. He half heard the crashing of her flight. Then he heard nothing, he was not hearing any sounds, anything; he stood, still, in that posture of balance, his arm outstretched, his fingers outstretched, as if for a long frozen moment he were still holding the woman.

It had been a balance, an equilibrium.

He had seen himself.

He saw.

At four-thirty Rosalind called her husband's office. The telephone was answered on the first ring, by another instructor—Merrill, who shared Martin's office—who told her, brusquely, that he did not know where Martin was. No. He had not seen Martin all day. In fact, Martin had not showed up for his three o'clock freshman class and students had been milling around for fifteen minutes or more, causing a commotion, and it had been very irresponsible of Martin, to say the least—

"He didn't teach his class?" Rosalind asked, shocked.

"I just told you," he said.

"But—but—Haven't you seen him all day?"

"I really don't remember," Merrill said.

He hung up.

Rosalind hurried out of the house, out the front walk. She did not know what to do. For a while she stood on the sidewalk, staring down the road. It was a paved road but its shoulders were wide, made of gravel that had been partly washed away, and the dark-hued mud gave a peculiar countrified look to the area. The newsboy appeared on his bicycle; that meant it was late in the afternoon.

He handed her the paper, hand to hand. He must have said hello, or "here's your paper," some phrase that also involved her name, *Mrs. Hershfield,* but she could not quite comprehend it.

He rode by. She turned slowly and walked into the house. She was observing herself now, almost against her own desire, as she had observed the behavior and often the death agonies of experimental animals—rats, guinea pigs, cats, even a few dogs. All these creatures had lived and had lived out certain procedures, within her range of observation. And now she herself was living out a certain procedure.

He came home some time later. It must have been after six. She went to the door and he stepped inside, staring at her; his face was Martin's face, and yet it was altered. She was going to say, "Where were—" but she only stared at him.

"There's nothing to be afraid of," Martin said.

She saw that he was trying to smile. His lips looked dry and awkward. It was not his own smile, but something else; she saw the queer straining of his facial muscles, and the straining of his eyes to get in focus.

"Why—what— What happened to you?" Rosalind whispered.

"Nothing. Nothing to be afraid of," he said.

He walked past her like a sleepwalker. He seemed to be favoring one side of his body, as if he were in pain. Rosalind followed him but did not touch him. His hair was uncombed, there were burrs and streaks of mud on his clothes, his shoes were muddy and wet—he was empty-handed—

"What happened? What happened to you?" Rosalind cried.

He went into the bedroom. Slowly, lowering himself with great effort, he lay on top of the wrinkled bedspread; the way he moved, so timidly, so carefully, made Rosalind realize that this was a man she no longer knew. But she forced herself to call him by name: "Martin—" She forced herself to ask what was wrong, what had happened, something of course had happened at the college and she had a right to know, she was his wife, he must explain all this to her—

Martin interrupted. "Let's sleep," he said softly. "Sleep. Sleep with me. Help me. Hold me. Sleep with me, please."

She stared at him. "What—?"

"Everything is refuted," Martin said. He closed his eyes and lay very still. "So help me, sleep with me. I'm so sleepy . . . help me. . . ."

"What do you mean? *Everything is refuted*—what does that mean?" Rosalind asked. He lay still, his eyes shut. His face seemed nearly abstract with exhaustion. The skin on his nose and forehead was slightly sunburned; his lips were partly open, motionless. She wanted to scream at him—*What does that mean? What have you done to yourself?* But she was too frightened to speak.

He lay on his back, his arms and legs flung out as if with exhaustion, his face strange to her, unreadable. Without opening his eyes he said hoarsely, "There's nothing to be afraid of. . . ."

She walked quickly out of the bedroom.

THE IDOLS OF AFTERNOON

JERRY BUMPUS

JERRY BUMPUS was born in Mount Vernon, Illinois. He has published over seventy short stories in literary magazines, and a collection of his short fiction, *Things in Place*, was published in 1975. He lives in South California with his wife and two daughters, and teaches at San Diego University.

O<small>N DIFFERENT DAYS OF THE MONTH</small> the West Frankfort Rotary, Elks, and Moose met at the Downtowner Hotel, where they had lunch and, over coffee and cigars, listened to speakers tell of their travels, or their acquaintance with famous people, or their power of memory.

With the dour vagueness of old hotels, the Buckner stared across the town square at the doings at the Downtowner. In better days Abraham Lincoln stopped over at the Buckner, or so it was said, and a week after his death he began roaming the halls and rattling doorknobs. You weren't a regular at the Buckner until you heard his heavy tread or woke to his fumbling at your door—though if you were a regular you knew the footsteps were likely those of two widows who lived on the second floor. Square-shouldered and tall, they looked like old men in big gingham dresses, for life had duped them at the end, thickened them, solidified them, and led the poor things off into a muddled, shadowy sort of manhood. The two old widows were heard but seldom seen about the hotel, and when seen they would be fading down a hall or turning a corner.

When Miss Eula Kirk's heart gave out, she retired, left St.

Louis, and came home to West Frankfort. She stayed at the Buckner, planning to find a room in a private home; surely a nice widow lady or an older couple wouldn't mind taking in a quiet roomer who sewed. But the window in Eula's room at the Buckner looked down on a side street that was never busy, and the hotel's comfortable brown silence, as if it were always late afternoon, held Eula. She felt peculiarly content at the hotel. One night she woke and heard the floor creak outside her door. The next day as she went down to the lobby she stopped and, staring through the still air, suddenly expected to see her father, long dead, walk through the front door and head for the cigar counter.

When Eula met Miss Smight, the matter was settled; she would stay on at the Buckner.

Miss Smight had a two-room suite, and each afternoon she and Eula talked in the sitting room, a small, hexagonal room with walls slanting to a ceiling smaller than the floor, and tending to lean the ladies forward and make them whisper. Eula's favorite place was a love seat facing Miss Smight's large chair by the window, where early afternoons framed Miss Smight with white that sank gradually to yellow.

Miss Smight loved dark blue organdy; it rustled eagerly as she leaned to the side, her chair straining, and crossed her legs. Though not fat, Miss Smight was certainly stately and wore on her amazingly large face—the largest Eula had ever seen, and the most beautiful—white powder, very much of it, and bright red lipstick.

As they talked Miss Smight sometimes assumed a rather plangent expression and, tilting, paused as an intriguing murmur came from within the organdy. At first this mystified Eula, but she caught on and if she happened to be speaking as Miss Smight began to tilt, Eula would stop so the muffled comment could be heard.

Many nights Eula lay awake in her own narrow room, going over their conversations, her eyes wide in the darkness and seeing her friend's big face which seemed always to be smiling in a special way just beyond what was being said and just beyond Eula's grasp. Once Eula was still awake when the slow, suspicious gray of

dawn entered the hotel and stirred the two old widows onto a
prowl—or maybe it was Lincoln, for the footsteps were heavy and
urgent. As if she had been waiting for him to come, Eula slipped
off to sleep, where she went running barefooted down a dirt road.
Suddenly there came a fog and then she saw Miss Smight at the
side of the road. She had been waiting for Eula!

In their afternoon conversations Eula didn't mention the
sounds, but once she and Miss Smight were interrupted by muttering in the hall. And the door jarred, but didn't open. "Who is
that?" Eula whispered to Miss Smight.

She smiled. "Them."

"Oh." Eula assumed she meant the widows, for one evening
Eula had seen them in the distance looking at her over their
shoulders. "Have they always been here at the hotel?"

"They came after me."

"It's nice they have each other."

Miss Smight took a handkerchief from her sleeve and putting it
to her lips whispered through it: "If people knew what goes on,
there would be a scandal. People would say it's naughty." Miss
Smight laughed, her voice quite deep. "Would you?"

"It would depend."

"Indeed." Lowering the handkerchief, Miss Smight fanned herself and said softly, "It would depend on whether you like a little
naughtiness now and then."

Eula felt herself blushing, and again Miss Smight laughed.

That Saturday they strolled around the square. Tuesday, Eula
and Miss Smight listened to the band in the pavilion. Later in the
week they drove in Miss Smight's Hudson to a shopping center at
the edge of town, returning to the hotel exhausted but excited.
And Eula sat down and without knowing she was going to, talked
at great length about her bosses and the seamstresses in the shop
where she had worked for forty-three years—the squibble-squab-
bles and fights, the time Earline Griggs was gone two weeks and
came back without saying a word as if she hadn't missed a day,
and the time they found a dead bum in the alley behind the shop
. . .

Eula talked faster and faster. She remembered when Mr.
McShane fired Mavis Coy for putting a dead mouse in his lunch

pail, though he hired her back the next day. And she remembered
when little Eula Kirk, just a girl, started work. During her first
week in the shop she happened to be in the toilet when Mr.
McShane, who had been working two days trying to fix a sewing
machine, came in carrying it over his head, his face red and his
eyes bulging. "Out of the way!" he roared. Eula hopped up and
Mr. McShane slammed the sewing machine into the commode.

Eula talked all afternoon and the next day. But when she went
to Miss Smight's the third day and they were seated, nothing
came. "Well," Eula said. She gave a little laugh. "Well, I guess
. . ." Suddenly burning as if she would cry, she took a deep
breath and held it.

Miss Smight said, "While you were there, I stayed in West
Frankfort." Miss Smight's face was expressionless under all its
powder. "I could go, and you could stay here . . ." She lifted a
hand and turned it palm-up as if it would be equally easy, a gesture of air, to unlive lives and set forth again.

Oh no, Eula almost said. For she already felt she had lost everything—and, even worse, Eula heard crass little voices laughing inside herself, and, like a naked boy dancing around her, the
thought taunted her that she had lost nothing, that not a day, not
one minute of it, had been worth keeping.

Miss Smight took Eula's arm and led her from the room and
the hotel. She walked Eula around the town square, pausing before store windows, and Eula saw her own and Miss Smight's
reflections and beyond them the mannequins, and beyond them,
very far away, like tumbling mounds of shadow, people shopping
in the stores.

They returned to the hotel and in the sitting room, with the
window yellow behind her, Miss Smight began a story about
something that happened to her. Eula cried as soon as Miss
Smight started and kept saying, "You poor thing. You poor, poor
thing," and as she cried harder, everything swam together in that
vague air which seems to prevail—and Eula saw herself and Miss
Smight looking in store windows, their faces blank and owly.
Then people came by and looked in at Eula and Miss Smight
who sat motionless inside a window.

When Eula stopped crying she was startled to see that Miss

Smight hadn't also cried. Her great white face was as placid as ever; moreover, her lips were lifted in a rather sly smile.

The next day Eula knocked and Miss Smight called out for her to enter, but she wasn't in the sitting room when Eula went in and sat down. She waited, staring at the door to the other room. Then it opened and Miss Smight made her entrance. She wasn't wearing organdy, but a tight-fitting silk dress, dark green and shiny like the skin of some great sleek beast. She stood before Eula, an imperiously bland expression on her face.

Eula sat with her mouth open, her face burning. She turned and looked up, as if for a way to the ceiling.

"Well?" Miss Smight said softly. "How do you like it?"

"I don't."

Miss Smight sat in her chair before the window, and they were silent, Eula refusing to look at her. Then Eula heard a steady, dulcet clicking. And though she tried to resist, she looked . . .

Smiling, Miss Smight fingered a strand of big black beads around her neck. She spoke.

Eula refused to listen. But in spite of herself—maybe it was those beads, clicking cozily—Eula listened as Miss Smight talked about Jasper Satin of Wichita Falls, Texas. "So manly," Miss Smight said. "And frisky."

Eula stared into the beads and, not intending to, said in a petulant, helpless whisper, "Why? . . ." She couldn't say the rest, couldn't ask why of all words Miss Smight had turned loose those, for inside Eula they jiggled forth the awesome concept of manly friskiness!—and Eula realized she had been ignorant of something vast. It was as if she had lived all these years without knowing there was yet another state in the Union, one where there was always a lot happening, and which people only talked about in secret.

Miss Smight was silent. "Well?" Eula said, her teeth clenched.

"Well, my goodness," Miss Smight said and, looking down, succeeded in smiling shyly.

"Did you and this Jasper Satin fall in love?"

"Did we fall in love?" Miss Smight fairly crowed with laughter, and tilting to the side, crossed her legs and beneath the smooth slide of silk there stirred a mirthful and rather loud murmur. "Love barely describes it."

The next day there was Owen Wiggler of Duquoin, Illinois, a horseman . . .

And that—*horseman*—had odd force, stunning Eula as if air had grabbed itself into a fist and socked her into a float across the bottomlands of Southern Illinois, where horses splashed through creeks and up muddy banks . . .

"Owen Wiggler was a small man—." Miss Smight paused, smiling in that sly, special way, "I never knew what to expect." Of course! Eula realized all at once how fascinating small men were. Quick—and unpredictable! "Owen Wiggler took me to the horse shows," Miss Smight said.

Eula sank back and put her cheek to her shoulder. Owen Wiggler, small and rigidly straight, walks arm in arm with Miss Smight, taking her to a horse show . . . "Those at night were best," Miss Smight said. Of course they were, because they were under torchlight. Eula sees torchlight glinting on sleek horses like fire under water, as they are led by small men with muscular arms and cunning hands. The horses stride smoothly, their heads nodding in that elegant agreement of walking horses . . .

Whispering, Miss Smight described the prizes, and though Eula listened intently, everything receded, falling into her like stars from a black sky. Alone, Eula Kirk whispers *Prizes* and is off to distant fairgrounds, *Prizes* lifting her lips as she whispers it again, kissing air.

The next afternoon when Eula was in her chair and ready, Miss Smight said, "Keg Jamaket hurt me."

"Oh," Eula breathed levelly once, twice. "What happened?"

Miss Smight lifted a hand. "My thumb." The thumb pointed to the ceiling. "And he hurt me here—" Smiling archly, she turned in the chair, reached under her arm, and ran her hand down her ribs. "And here—" She tapped her thumb on one breast, then the other. "And here—" as Eula closed her eyes. "And here . . ."

Eula sees a woods sunk in watery grayness, and then a young woman, tall and straight, in a white dress, pauses astride a log, then steps over it and walks swiftly, almost defiantly, through the woods, and a little woman hurries after her. The girl stops, and the little woman too, and Eula listens with them. Nothing. Then the wan, complex song of birds. And beneath that a distant mutter, like the first vague voice of intention, a burring sigh, that as the girl and the little woman move on, becomes distinguishable as the rasping of a saw. The girl runs . . .

"He was in a thicket," Miss Smight said. "He jumped out and grabbed me. 'Keg Jamaket, you leave me alone,' I told him. But he held me and kissed me and pushed me down . . ."

Eula can't see them. She again hears the saw grinning its vicious glee through wood. It slows; the sound fades. A wind moves through the woods like a great animal leaning from the sky, bending the trees as it lies down. The wind dies and the sitting room is tight with silence. Eula sees them, and it is not as Miss Smight said, not at all.

Keg Jamaket in overalls stands against a tree. Slowly a long arm swings up, with a very large hand at the end of it, and the girl in white steps forward and with both hands she takes it, one hand grasping his big thumb.

Squinting, Eula squeezes the gray woods tight and turns it on end: Miss Smight's words sink, clopping deep into the woods, a garble of stones dropped in an empty well. Eula listens to her own breathing, stentorian, monstrous.

But she is with them again, standing against the girl's back, her chin dug into the girl's shoulder and looking with her into Keg Jamaket's flat face. His eyes are big and perfectly round and set far apart. His ears tuck neatly against his head. "His cheeks were so smooth," Eula hears. And Eula sees they are. Then everything is gone.

After a long wait Eula opened her eyes. The yellow window framed Miss Smight, and Eula couldn't see her face. Perhaps a corona was drawing Miss Smight out the window and into the sky. Or Miss Smight was drawing the sky down onto her, bringing it on the huge wings of surprise into the room to lay on Eula's lap.

That night dogs came loping out of ravines in the walls, and Eula kept talking—it was her only hope. She talked faster and faster, not hearing a word, and then woke as she was tiptoeing down the hall. At the stairs she stared into the lobby. The old, high-backed chairs gaped at the lobby reflected in the smooth black front windows, beyond which was framed the street and town square, an old gray picture. Eula turned and calmly followed herself down the hall to Miss Smight's door, which was locked, of course. On the other side was the sun shining, and did Miss Smight sit by the window, whispering to the room? Then Eula was again in her own bed, suddenly awake and hearing *her* door rattling, followed by those familiar hurried footsteps passing as dawn shrank her room still narrower.

She refused to go to Miss Smight's that afternoon, and the next day Eula left the hotel and walked down a tree-lined street to a house where several little women came to the windows and looked out. She went up to the door and was admitted. Eula was at the Eastern Star. The ladies sat in a circle in the living room and talked four hours. When Eula left, she walked up the street and, reaching the town square, stared across at the Buckner, its windows blazing red in the late afternoon sun.

"It was so nice," Eula said, "and they're all just wonderful. I know you'll love it. We will go every afternoon . . ."

Looking into the light, Eula couldn't clearly see Miss Smight's face, but it seemed even larger than before, as if time, alone with her, had pressed especially hard against her face, pushing her deeper into herself. And Miss Smight sat with her eyes closed. Had she fallen asleep? Or . . . No—for at that moment she nodded and spoke.

But not to Eula. She spoke over her shoulder to the window, the sky. "You just wouldn't believe it."

"I'll believe it," Eula quickly said. "I'm sure I will."

"Charlie?" Miss Smight said as she turned to the room.

Eula glanced at the door to the other room, then along the walls to the hall door. Eula whispered, "Who is he?"

Miss Smight closed her eyes. "Why, he is Charlie Leonard. Men come miles to see him. He . . ." She opened her eyes and turned, whispering, "Charlie?" and as she looked out the window, Eula said, "I see them." Eula sees two men walking down a dirt

street—and, walking the other direction, a little woman who stops
as they pass, and turns and follows them. They come to a large
house where several men sit on the front porch smoking their
pipes. A man stands before them, his hands on his hips, talking.
"There's Charlie," Miss Smight says. But the house, the street,
slipped into a wall.

Eula waited, but it wouldn't return. Miss Smight sat with her
head cocked to the side. Eula said, "How long did? . . ."

Miss Smight laughed and sat back. "I have no idea." Of course
not. Eula understood perfectly—for now when she tried to think
of things that happened a month ago, or a week, or even yesterday, a turn in the corridor brought her to a wall without a door.
"You had Charlie Leonard for years and years, didn't you?" Eula
said. "Even when you were old."

Miss Smight's expression grew pensive. She nodded carefully.

Eula crosses the porch and steps through the front door into
the living room, as big as the Buckner's lobby, with a wide stair-
case like the Buckner's, and she knows there are just as many
rooms upstairs, if not more, all with little ceilings, and through
each room winds the same faded carpet with its subtle, purple
vine which Eula has traced so often, deciphering its loops and
convolutions.

Miss Smight and Eula sit on the sofa in the living room, and a
door opens. Charlie Leonard enters wearing a black coat and a big
hat. Taking off his hat, he speaks to Miss Smight, though Eula
can't hear. As they talk, a pale young man steps from behind
Charlie Leonard. And then another, who isn't wearing a shirt—
his chest pale and bony—and then another young man steps
forth, and another.

Charlie Leonard crosses the room, shaking the floor, to the sofa
and stands squarely before Miss Smight. Eula sees his face: a
coarse chin, bent nose, and heavy-lidded eyes that are certain and
bright. Eula is afraid Charlie Leonard will strike Miss Smight, for
he stands looking down at her cruelly. Then Miss Smight amazes
Eula. She glances at Eula, winks, then turns and, reaching out,
Miss Smight sews a big gold button on Charlie Leonard's trousers.

The young men, all of them shirtless now, crowd around.
"What about all the young men?" Eula says.

Miss Smight laughs. "Oh my, yes. The boys. We can't forget

the boys." In a yellow room Eula sees Miss Smight slowly lying down, her great white body rolling on itself like cumulus clouds, and a young man springs forward, a javelin, and is lost in her. "The old men," Eula says.

Miss Smight moans. "My oh my, how they loved it, coming home to mama." Miss Smight, large and wearing pale blue organdy, kneels before an old man who sits on the side of a bed, his hands on his knees, looking down at her and talking. He lifts a hand, dark and huge, a wedge, and puts it on Miss Smight's shoulder as she pulls off one of his shoes.

A young man, then another, playing chasing through the hotel, burst into the sitting room and out the other door. Another runs in and stops. With his eyes big, intent, he takes off his clothes. "Touch him and you burn your hand," Miss Smight whispers. Eula feels his blood pouring through him like fire. Eula runs her hand along the shoulder of an old man, smooth and cool. Eula goes down the hall to the open door of another room and sees a skinny boy, big-eyed and almost scared, drop his overalls and glide across Miss Smight. Far down the hall Eula hears Miss Smight laugh. Then she hears Miss Smight whispering, her head beside hers on the pillow in Eula's bed: "Sweet. So sweet." Eula licks the boy's shoulder, a big warm apple, the sun burning deep inside it. His stomach is flat and smooth.

Eula turns on her side and he isn't there. By the special, dense darkness in the window she knows this is that long moment in which night ends, and as she knew she would she heard the boards groan under the carpet in the hall and as her window and the room lift in the stern opacity of dawn, he stops at her door and finds it wide open. Without hesitating, he enters, and he is taller than Charlie Leonard, taller than any man Eula has ever seen. He goes to the window and stands with his back to Eula. At last he turns and walks to her bed. He leans down, his chest and shoulders and head becoming larger and larger, a huge tree, its limbs widening to all the sky, and she wonders if he will ever reach her—and thinking that, she loses wondering and becomes the night left behind, smoothly and easily a part of his descending. She takes a deep breath as she realizes his falling will take forever.

NIGHT MARCH

TIM O'BRIEN

TIM O'BRIEN is a native of Minnesota and a former reporter for the Washington *Post*. His stories and articles have appeared in *Playboy, Redbook, The New Republic, Penthouse,* and *Ploughshares.* He is the author of a novel, *Northern Lights,* published in August 1975.

THE PLATOON OF TWENTY-SIX SOLDIERS moved slowly in the dark, single file, not talking. One by one, like sheep in a dream, they passed through the hedgerow, crossed quietly over a meadow and came down to the rice paddy. There they stopped. Their leader knelt down, motioning with his hand, and one by one the others squatted or knelt or sat. For a long time they did not move. Except for the sounds of their breathing, and once a soft, fluid trickle as one of them urinated, the twenty-six men were silent: some of them excited by the adventure, some of them afraid, some of them exhausted from the long night march, some of them looking forward to reaching the sea, where they would be safe. At the rear of the column, Private First Class Paul Berlin lay quietly with his forehead pressed against the black plastic stock of his rifle, his eyes closed. He was pretending. He was pretending he was not in the war, pretending he had not watched Billy Boy Watkins die of a heart attack that afternoon. He was pretending he was a boy again, camping with his father in the midnight summer along the Des Moines River. In the dark, with his eyes pinched shut, he pretended. He pretended that when he opened his eyes, his father would be there by the campfire and they would talk softly about whatever came to mind and then roll into their sleeping bags, and that later they'd wake up and it would be morning and there would not be a war, and that Billy Boy Watkins had not died of a heart attack that afternoon. He pretended he was not a soldier.

In the morning, when they reached the sea, it would be better. The hot afternoon would be forgotten, would not have happened; he would bathe in the sea, and he would forget how frightened he had been on his first day at the war. The second day would be better. He would learn.

There was a sound beside him, a movement, and then a breathed "Hey!" The shadow whispered, "Hey!" and Paul Berlin opened his eyes, shivering, and the shadow whispered, "Hey! We're *moving*, for Chrissake. Get up."

"Okay."

"You sleeping or something?"

"No." He could not make out the soldier's face. With clumsy, concrete hands he clawed for his rifle, found it, found his helmet.

The soldier-shadow grunted. "You got a very lot to learn, buddy. I'd shoot you if I thought you was sleeping. Let's go."

Private First Class Paul Berlin blinked.

Ahead of him, silhouetted against the sky, he saw the string of soldiers beginning to wade into the flat paddy waters, the black outline of their shoulders and weapons and packs. He was comfortable. He did not want to move. But he was afraid, for it was his first night at the war, and he hurried to catch up, stumbling once, scraping his knee and groping; his boots sank into the thick paddy and he smelled it all around him, the fear, and the war. He would tell his mother how it smelled. Of mud and algae, he would tell her, of cattle manure and chlorophyll, decay, breeding mosquitoes and leeches as big as mice, the rich warmth of the waters rising up to his cut knee. He would tell her this, but not how frightened he had been in the afternoon, when Billy Boy died of a heart attack.

Once they reached the sea, things would be better. Their rear would be guarded by five thousand miles of open ocean, and they would swim and dive into the breakers and hunt crayfish and smell the salt, and they would be safe.

Private First Class Paul Berlin followed the shadow of the man

in front of him. It was a clear night. Already the Southern Cross
was out. And other stars he could not yet name—soon, he
thought, soon he would learn their names. And puffy night
clouds. There was not yet a moon. Wading through the paddy,
his boots made sleepy, sloshing sounds, like a lullaby, and he tried
not to think. Though he was afraid, he now knew that fear comes
in many degrees and types and peculiar categories, and he knew
that his fear now was not so bad as it had been in the hot afternoon, when poor Billy Boy Watkins got killed by a heart attack.
His fear now was diffuse and unfocused—ghosts in the tree line,
nighttime fears of a child, a boogieman in the closet that his father would open to show empty, saying, "See? Nothing there,
champ. Now you can sleep." In the afternoon it had been
different. The fear had been bundled and tight, and he'd been on
his hands and knees, crawling like an insect, an ant escaping a giant's footsteps, thinking nothing, brain flopping like wet cement
in a mixer, not thinking at all, watching while Billy Boy died.

Now, as he stepped out of the paddy onto a narrow dirt path,
now the fear was mostly the fear of being so terribly afraid again.

He tried not to think.

There were tricks he'd learned to keep from thinking. Counting: he counted his steps, concentrating on the numbers, pretending that the steps were dollar bills and that each step through the
night made him richer and richer, so that soon he would become
a wealthy man, and he kept counting and considered the ways he
might spend the money after the war, what he would do, what he
would say if asked. He would look his father in the eye and shrug
and say, "It was pretty bad at first, but I learned a lot and I got
used to it." Then he would tell his father the story of Billy Boy
Watkins. A good war story, a story to be passed on. Yes, he would
tell the story, but he would never let on how frightened he had
been. "Not so bad," he would say instead, making his father
proud.

Songs, another trick to stop the thinking: *Where have you
gone, Billy Boy, Billy Boy, oh, where have you gone, charming
Billy? I have gone to seek a wife, she's the joy of my life, but she's
a young thing and cannot leave her mother*, and other songs that
he sang in his thoughts as he walked toward the sea. And when he
reached the sea he would dig a deep hole in the sand and he

would sleep like the high clouds, and he would not be afraid again.

The moon came out. Pale and shrunken to the size of a dime.

The helmet was heavy on his head. In the morning he would adjust the leather binding. He would clean his rifle, too. Though he had been unable to fire it during the hot afternoon, he would carefully clean the breech and barrel and muzzle so that next time he would be ready and not so afraid. In the morning, when they reached the sea, he would begin to make friends among the other soldiers. He would learn their names and laugh at their jokes. Then when the war ended he would have war buddies, and he would write to them now and then to exchange memories.

Walking, sleeping in his walking, he felt better. He watched the moon come higher.

Once they skirted a sleeping village. The smells again—straw, cattle, mildew. The men were quiet. On the far side of the village, deep in the dark smells, a dog barked. The column stopped until the barking died away; then they marched fast away from the village, through a graveyard waxed with conical-shaped burial mounds and tiny altars of clay and stone. The graveyard had a perfumy smell. A nice place to spend the night. The mounds would make fine battlements, and the smells were good and the place was quiet. But they went on, passing through a hedgerow and through another paddy and east toward the sea.

He walked carefully. He remembered what he'd been taught: stay off the center of the path, for that's where the land mines will be planted, where stupid and lazy soldiers like to walk. Stay alert, he'd been taught. Better alert than inert. Ag-ile, mo-bile, hos-tile. Walking, step on step, he wished he'd paid better attention to the training. He could not remember what they'd said about the awful fear, how to stop it, what to say to it. They'd forgotten the lessons in courage, and they hadn't mentioned how Billy Boy Watkins would die of a heart attack, his face turning pale and the veins popping out.

Private First Class Paul Berlin walked carefully.

Stretching ahead like dark beads on a chain, the string of soldiers whose names he did not yet know moved with the silence and slow grace of smoke. Now and again, moonlight reflected off a machine gun or a wristwatch. But mostly the soldiers were quiet and hidden and faraway-seeming in a peaceful night, strangers on a long street, and he felt quite separate from them, as if trailing behind like the caboose on a night train, pulled along by inertia, sleepwalking, and afterthought to the war.

So he walked carefully, counting his steps. When he had counted to three thousand four hundred and fifty, the column stopped.

One by one, the soldiers squatted or knelt down.

The grass along the path was wet. Private First Class Paul Berlin lay back and turned his head so he could lick at the dew with his eyes closed, another trick to forget the war. He might have slept. "I *wasn't* afraid," he was saying, or dreaming, facing his father's stern eyes. "I wasn't afraid," he was saying, coming up on his elbows. A soldier beside him, quietly chewing mint-smelling gum.

"Sleeping again?" the soldier whispered.

"No," said Private First Class Paul Berlin. "Hell no."

The soldier grunted, twisted the cap off his canteen, swallowed, and handed it through the dark. "Take some."

"Thanks."

"You're the new guy."

"Yes." He did not want to admit it, but he said it again. "Yes."

The soldier handed him a stick of gum. "Chew it quiet, okay? Don't blow no bubbles or nothing."

"Thanks. I won't." He could not make out the boy's face in the shadows.

They sat still, and Private First Class Paul Berlin chewed the gum until all the sugars were gone; then the soldier said, "Bad day today, buddy."

Paul Berlin nodded wisely, but he did not speak.

"Don't think it's always so bad," the soldier whispered. "I don't want to scare you. You'll get used to it soon enough, I guess—they been fighting wars a long time, and you get used to it."

"Sure."

"You will."

They were quiet awhile. And the night was quiet, no crickets or birds, and it was hard to imagine it was truly a war. He searched for the soldier's face but could not find it. It did not matter much. Even if he saw the boy's face he would not know the name, and even if he knew the name it would not matter.

"Haven't got the time?" the soldier whispered.

"No."

"Rats . . . Don't matter, really. Goes faster if you don't know the time, anyhow."

"I suppose."

"What's your name, buddy?"

"Paul."

"Nice to meet and greet ya," he said, and in the dark beside the path they shook hands. "Mine's Tony. Everybody calls me Buffalo, though." The soldier's hand was strangely warm and soft, but it was a very big hand. "Sometimes they just call me Buff," he said.

And again they were quiet. They lay in the grass and waited. The moon was very high now and very bright, and they were waiting for cloud cover.

The soldier suddenly snorted.

"What is it?"

"Nothing," he said, but then he snorted again. "A lousy heart attack! A *heart* attack! Can't get over it—old Billy Boy croaking from a lousy heart attack, pow, down he goes. A heart attack—can you believe it?"

It made Private First Class Paul Berlin smile. He couldn't help it.

"Ever hear of such a thing?"

"Not till now," said Paul Berlin, still smiling.

"Me neither," said the soldier in the dark. "Gawd, dying of a heart attack. Didn't know him, did you?"

"No."

"Tough as nails."

"Yeah."

"And what happens? A heart attack. Can you imagine it?"

"Yes," said Private First Class Paul Berlin. "I can imagine it." And he imagined it clearly. He giggled—he couldn't help it. He imagined Billy's father opening the telegram: SORRY TO INFORM YOU THAT YOUR SON BILLY BOY WAS YESTERDAY SCARED TO DEATH IN ACTION IN THE REPUBLIC OF VIETNAM, VALIANTLY SUCCUMBING TO

A HEART ATTACK SUFFERED WHILE UNDER ENOR-
MOUS STRESS, AND IT IS WITH GREATEST SYM-
PATHY THAT . . . He giggled again. He rolled onto his belly,
pressed his face into his arms. He was shaking with the giggles.

The big soldier hissed at him to shut up, but he could not stop
giggling and remembering the hot afternoon, and poor Billy Boy,
and how they'd been drinking Coke from bright-red aluminum
cans, and how they'd started on the day's march, and how a little
while later poor Billy Boy stepped on the mine, and how it made
a tiny little sound—*poof*—and how Billy Boy just stood there
with his mouth wide open, looking down, then shaking his head,
surprised-looking, and how finally Billy Boy sat down very casually,
not saying a word, his foot lying behind him with most of it still in
the boot.

Paul Berlin giggled louder—he could not stop.

He bit his arm, trying to stifle it, but remembering: "War's
over, Billy," the man had said in consolation, but Billy Boy got
scared and started crying and said it was over. "It's all over," he
kept saying, scaring himself. "Nonsense," the medic said, Doc
Peret, but Billy Boy kept bawling, tightening up, his face going
pale and transparent and his veins popping out. Scared stiff. Even
when Doc struck him with morphine, Billy Boy kept crying.

"Shut up!" the big soldier hissed, but Private First Class Paul
Berlin could not stop. Giggling and remembering, he covered his
mouth. His eyes stung, remembering how it was when Billy Boy
died of fright.

"Quiet!"

But he could not stop giggling, the same way Billy Boy could
not stop bawling that afternoon.

Afterward Doc Peret had explained: "You see, Billy Boy really
died of a heart attack. He was scared he was ready to die—so
scared he had himself a heart attack, and that's what really killed
him. I seen it before."

So they wrapped Billy Boy in a plastic poncho, his eyes still
wide open and scared stiff, and they carried him over the meadow
to the paddy; then, when the medevac helicopter arrived, they
carried him through the paddy and shoved him aboard; then
things were exploding everywhere, people yelling, the heat, and
the chopper pulled up and jerked and Billy Boy came tumbling

out, falling slowly and then faster, and the paddy water sprayed
up as if Billy Boy had just executed a long and dangerous dive, or
as if Billy had been killed by a heart attack.

"Shut up, for Chrissake!" the big soldier hissed, but Paul Berlin
could not stop giggling, remembering: scared to death.

Later they had waded in after him, probing for Billy with their
rifle butts, elegantly and delicately probing for him through the
thick waters, singing—some of them—*Where have you gone,
Billy Boy, Billy Boy, oh, where have you gone, charming Billy?*
They found him. Green and clothed in algae, his eyes open and
still scared, dead of a heart attack.

"Quiet!" the soldier screamed, shaking him.

But Private First Class Paul Berlin could not stop. The giggles
came from that place deep in his groin, the place that secreted the
purple chemicals of fear, and he could not stop. Giggling, lying on
his back, he saw the moon move, or the clouds moving across the
moon. Wounded in action, dead of fright. A fine war story. He
would tell it to his father, how Billy Boy Watkins had been
scared to death, never letting on . . . He could not stop. He was
afraid, and he could not stop.

The soldier smothered him. He tried to fight back, but he was
weak from the giggles, wet in the eyes.

Then the moon was under clouds. The column was moving. He
was tired. The soldier helped him up. "Okay now, buddy?"

"Sure."

"You can get killed, laughing that way."

"I know. I know that."

"You got to stay calm, buddy. It's the whole trick, staying
calm." The soldier handed him his rifle. "Half the battle, at least,
just staying calm. You'll get better at it. Come on, now."

He turned away, and Private First Class Paul Berlin hurried
after him. He was still shivering.

He fell into the pace of the march, began counting again, each
step, one and the next. Lightheaded, blank-eyed in the great
dark, he lost track of the numbers, which came without sequence,
randomly, a jumbled and tumbling and chaotic rush of numbers
that ran like fluid through his head. Ahead of him, quiet, the column of soldiers plodded through the ongoing nighttime. He felt
better. He would never be so afraid again. It would become a part

of history, it would become a funny and sad tale to tell to his father and his friends, who would either believe or not believe, and there would be other stories later. He walked fast. In the morning he would do better. A war story, a good joke. He closed his eyes and walked, and he smelled many things, He smelled the grass and the trees and the clouds of low fog, and soon he could even smell the sea, but he could not stop being afraid.

PAST THE ISLAND, DRIFTING

ANITA SHREVE

ANITA SHREVE was born in Dedham, Massachusetts, and attended Jackson College in Boston. She has published short stories in numerous literary magazines and is a contributing editor to *Viva Magazine*. For the past year, she has lived in Africa with her husband.

We are what we pretend to be, so we had better be careful about what we pretend to be.
Kurt Vonnegut, Jr.

C HLOE DRIFTED. Other people call themselves drifters—poets parked quietly beside milky pernods and future-shocked lemmings migrating to New Athens or Sacramento—but Chloe had a special talent for whizzing through her life like a fat bee. She drifted from house to house, friend to friend, from airport to harbor, from gynecologist to ophthalmologist, but more important, from garage to garage, where she stored the pickings of her past like dead Chevys in an automobile graveyard.

Behind the weathered shingles of her sister's Cape Cod garage, she kept a cardboard box of wooden wedding presents: bowls, wine racks, ice buckets, and candlesticks. They changed their shape impressively in the damp creek fog that slithered through the window casing. Her sister, who visited her garage as little as possible, insisted that she come and fix the box that sagged from sitting on wet concrete. Chloe wanted to feed it to the muskrats.

On top of the rafters in the red brick garage in Duxbury, her mother kept a wicker basket, painted white, full of old letters for

First appeared in the *Ball State University Forum*, XVI, I (Winter 1975). Used by permission.

her. There were scented letters from her grandmother who died on lavender satin sheets in Newburyport, and gaudy cut-out cards addressed to "My Favorite Niece On Her Birthday." She could not throw anything away, and like memories, these ribboned piles of paper were a burden to her.

Her T.V., stereo, and toaster gobbled watts in Portland, and the ferns and ivies that she could no longer care for rested on window sills in Wellesley, where her friend watered them like stepchildren.

And when she boarded the sleepy, rocking bus in Boston, she abandoned in the garage of her sloughed-off husband, her books, her passive dreams, and her diamond ring. Chloe watched through the dirty windows of the bus, the drifting vistas of her past. She thought about that ring.

Chloe met Jack at a party in Cambridge. Ice clinked and smiles twinkled. Chloe sat off in a corner, aloof, yet central to the circulating currents that meandered around that dormitory room. Fresh from Europe, she still inhabited her continental personality. Jack walked directly to her. He later confessed that her healthy glow had attracted him.

"Who are you?"

"I'm a drifter," Chloe introduced herself.

"Why do you drift?"

"I like to please people, but not get too close."

"I'll change that," he forewarned.

His granite Mormon jaws distracted her from the bittersweet aftertaste of a love in Paris. It had died, mid-sail across the Atlantic, but she didn't know it then. She had been drifting almost all her life, culling personality from real life characters as well as from the fictional ones in the books that overflowed her suitcase. At that particular time, she sat there in her pink silk shirt, she thought her spirit combined in equal parts the wrath of Eugene O'Neill, the bravado of Antigone, and the loneliness of her father, an airline pilot, in constant flight. She was hoping to find an anchor someday.

They lied voluminously that first evening together, and later did not reproach each other as the truths popped out, one by one, in contradictions and confessions.

"I thought you said you'd never been in love before."

"I did?"

He wore, that night, a scratchy woolen shirt and a navy jacket; he hitched his belt a lot while he talked. She smoked Players and spoke in cadences. She regarded him with care. He reminded her of a cyclist, tilted toward the center, riding furiously in ever tightening circles, racing, racing, wide-eyed toward a future that would be another set of circles. Later, she tried to toe-down with him, but couldn't absorb the pace; on a particularly hard pedal, she spun off like a particle, a fragment of his racing self, and drifted . . . but that was much later. Immediately she could see that he had never drifted.

After that evening, they saw each other every day.

In a concrete dorm, they made love and plans. Both made up in spirit what they lacked in skill. He read his crystal ball, which told him happily he would be a great doctor, but when she looked into hers, it changed colors like a chameleon.

"I want to learn to be a great surgeon, the best there is. If I didn't think I could be the best someday, I wouldn't try at all."

"And what will I be?"

"You will be my wife."

"Do you think that's enough?"

"I'll read Matthew Arnold to you, and Ben Jonson."

"Ben Jonson?"

"And we'll ride the rapids and go camping in the wilderness regions of Utah."

"I've never done that before."

"We'll be tough, together."

Their conversations spiraled and twisted in that cinder block and ashen room. Behind the standard issue box of a bed, a bold red Navaho rug hung from the molding, a comely backdrop for Jack, who sat tipped back in his black college chair, feet on the equally standard issue desk, and talked. To Chloe, he looked like the man in the Marlborough cigarette ads—the one with the sheepskin jacket. One year, for his birthday, she bought him a jacket like that to complete the almost perfect portrait. In Cambridge, he tried to preserve, in conversations and gestures, his democratic, western, Jacksonian virtues, and then when transported to Utah, to savor the elitist tidbits she had given him.

Chloe grew up in a small town outside of Boston, and inherited from the Methodists and the high school cheerleaders a kind of energetic passivity. The eldest of three daughters, she experimented with independence in the form of lying to her parents and writing poems which she sent to *Jack and Jill* magazine. Her lies were exposed, and the poems rejected; she learned to cry bitterly, but silently, in her bedroom closet.

In high school, she grew into a thin, blond, athletically sound young woman and stopped writing poems. She drifted from one friend to the other, and from one imitation love affair to the next, in search of the unfathomable glory of popularity. She became the person she was with—tough, cigarette smoking with her group of girl friends—rational and scholarly with her teachers—and bitchy with her parents. Her adolescent mind never contemplated the existence of a true submerged Chloe. She was happy when she could attach herself to the lives of others.

In college, her illusive nature flourished. Professors doted on her for returning to them their thoughts intact, without a blemish. Attractive boys sought her out, because she kept her mouth shut. She knew she had very little to say. She had drifted too carelessly to ever absorb anything substantial. Jack enjoyed her vacillating moods, so different from his own, and Chloe found herself drawn to this man who could make decisions by listening to an interior voice, who could commit himself to an idea or a person, and stay committed in spite of the odds.

Because of her admiration for him she felt occasional doubts about how they would survive together. She felt that she would prefer not to drift, but couldn't prevent it. Sometimes she felt like a milkweed fluff, less substantial than the wind, spending her entire time in flight looking for something to stick to. During her solitary walks in Cambridge, she searched out eyes that were stronger than her own. In her best fantasy, she dreamed of following internal vectors, like Antigone; but she knew that she had become so thin that she must follow external currents instead, plummeting into treacherous air pockets. Had the currents led her to Jack? And was he the anchor she had been looking for? She didn't know then that just as the sea skate couldn't exist on the mountain, neither could the plays of O'Neill be written in the Zionist Temple.

They drank bourbon and cider after football games on Saturday; and on Sunday they drove in the green Volvo to the tidy brick church where the Mormons never drank. Matching his contradictions, tit for tat, she sang the hymns but ignored the prayers. She knew that the glow, the flush, that lighted on the faces there, that made them all (even the men) look like exhilarated brides, was not for her. For Chloe slipped in and out of philosophies as easily as Tolstoy's Pierre, but she doubted she would ever meet the peasant who would tell her that life is the mere living of it. They ate hamburgers in Hazen's and lobsters in Gloucester. Jack's fixed opinion on all subjects worried her a little, but in the end they appealed to Chloe, because she had none. Vietnam was bad. Kennedy had been bad. Harvard was good. Classic English poets were good. J. D. Watson's egotism was bad, but his theories were good. Again, chameleon-like, she tried to be him. A friend observed that they looked alike, and this observation pleased her. A totally new disposition she had never tried before was hers for the taking.

One day in June, the Japanese beetles hunched in clumps on the glistening leaves on the roses; he walked her down to the river which stank with its own clogged residue. Shells of matured freshmen rowed along the flattened, bleached surface of the Charles, and they sat on the grass patches, watching and waiting for the right moment to pledge themselves to each other. His clear brown eyes stared straight ahead while he made pronouncements, and she wept for his belief in them.

"I will be a doctor, and you will be my wife."

"Yes."

"I will teach you to love the mountains and the cultural depravity of Salt Lake City."

"Yes."

"I will help you not to drift."

"Yes. Thank you."

"I love you very much."

"I love *you* very much."

A hint of worry flickered over his eyes.

"I'm not an island that you're drifting by?"

"No, no. I love you. I said that."

She gave herself for the mountains and the roots and the diamond ring he promised to give her in August.

When Jack left to work in Salt Lake City for the summer, Chloe hung like a pendulum between two threads: one attached to the bristly bank of the Charles in June, and the other fixed to a jet flight in August. Suspended, she rocked, back and forth, and refused to think about her life. She wrote letters about concerts and cook-outs that she attended loyally single. She read books and woke up early to walk the hot city blocks. Jack wrote letters in a prematurely cramped professional scrawl that gave reports, like the United Fund, about the financial progress toward the diamond ring. He worked hard loading heavy boxes on trucks; Chloe never worked less.

"Dear Jack,
   I miss you. I think about you nearly all of the time. Today I went to visit my parents and told them about our plans. They were glad."

"Dear Chloe,
   The mountains are majestic today. I cannot wait for you to come, so that I can share this beauty with you. You will love it as I do."

"Dear Jack,
   I think of nothing but you. . . ."

"Dear Chloe,
   Soon you will be happy. . . ."

That summer everyone around Chloe talked about Cambodia, Kent State, smashed windows from Harvard Square to the Orson Welles, and the stand-off of the ROTC Building. In August, Janis Joplin gave the last public concert of her life in Harvard Stadium and shouted to the crowd that she made music to fuck by, not fight by. Chloe sensed these things as if from very far away, items she read in the paper that wouldn't sink in. She spent the summer, ashamed that she could not feel the shards of the utterly jagged world she lived in. She had been insulated by Jack and by herself.

During this summer also, her Paris suitor came to fetch her, and Chloe resisted him nobly, foolishly, like some medieval maiden, accosted by a visiting knight. She passed the shabby test, trying out new promises. He evaporated, after a fair battle.

The house that Chloe lived in that summer had once belonged
to William James. Its current owner, a Harvard potentate, used to
conjure up for her the famous image, seancing in the old parlor,
or entertaining his literary brother, who had lived next door. Like
an old barn, the massive gray-brown structure had been transformed into small apartments, one of which she occupied. She
loved that apartment. One large fireplaced room, with a closet
kitchen and a Victorian bathroom, it filled with light on good
days. In her soporific state, she did not make very good use of that
apartment, but it sheltered her remoteness.

Occasionally, but only very seldom, when she awoke in her bed
alone on damp summer mornings, and tried to remember who she
was that day, she wondered where, in all of this, was the self who
could say "I want" or "I don't want." Where was the woman who
should have emerged from the injured cocoon, blighted or no, to
use her own senses for a change?

When August came, Chloe packed her suitcase. She flew to the
West with only the vaguest thoughts and remembered bits of letters. The simulated drifting of this flight pleased her like a secret
indulgence. She emerged happily from the plane; and at once the
hot dry air closed in on her. The rigid mountains, the desert, the
salt flats, the sterile salt sea loomed monstrous. Salt Lake City
terrified her. Without the jet or the car, she felt that she would
die there. In Boston, the ocean gave her space, false freedom. In
the desert, she had no illusions.

Jack met her at the airport. They hugged wildly.

"Chloe, you're here! Really here! You look great."

"Let's sit down for a second. I feel funny."

"Well, come sit out in the car. I want to show you this place."

She clung to him, scared out of her wits. If she had been docile
in Cambridge, she was prostrate here. The only familiar touch in
a fearful land, Jack led Chloe; and she followed him, obediently,
gratefully. She got into the old Volvo. He sat beside her, proud,
confident; he started the car.

"We'll go right to my house, so you can meet my mother. She's
dying to meet you. I haven't told her yet. I thought you should be
there with me when I told her."

"Do you think that's wise?" Chloe wiped her face with a Kleenex. "I mean, don't you think we should give her a little time to

get used to me first?" The flat-roofed houses flickered by the windows of the car.

"Don't be so worried." He held her knee. "She'll love you. I know she will. Hey, come sit where I can feel you."

He stirred the old memories, and Chloe began to focus a little more clearly. Very tanned, very attractive, he helped her view the mountains objectively. For one moment Chloe believed the complex, inclining fragments would straighten out after all. Cut off by haze from the ground, they hung suspended in the hot, shimmering blue sky.

When they walked into his house, a suburban ranch just on the city limits, his mother sat throne-like on the gold French provincial sofa. The room seemed sheathed in a Las Vegas gold lamé, and his mother, her tight beauty-parlored curls adorning pale blue-speckled glasses, seemed a perpetual visitor in her own living room. Good manners and expectations produced smiles all around, and Chloe sat primly in her new dress answering questions about a plane ride she could barely remember.

"Well Mother," Jack began. Only a slight nervousness seeped through his confident voice. "I think it's time you should know. Chloe and I. . . ." He turned here and smiled at Chloe, who returned an imperfect imitation of his face. ". . . are going to get married." He looked back at his mother, and beamed.

The silence numbed them all. His mother's face cracked and fell. She cried, sobbed, keened. Between dainty noseblows, just on the verge of a mounting panic, she sputtered, "You are betraying the Church, and your father. You are betraying me. . . . How could you do this? How could you?"

Mortified and heartsick, Chloe watched Jack's face clench and unclench. She sat there, the crux of the messy display. She dared not touch him, although she felt that she should. He had hoped so intently for this encounter to be perfect, for everyone to be happy. He had forgotten (how could he have forgotten?) that Chloe was a heathen.

"It doesn't matter," Jack said. "She doesn't know what she's saying. For Christ's sake, Mother. Can't you apologize?"

His mother cried and wouldn't look at them.

Jack grabbed Chloe's hand, and he stormed out, frayed, fringed, undone. She followed, again obedient and mute, but secretly relieved. If a mother rejected you, didn't that mean that you were free to go? She didn't know it then, but she began that day a ledger in her mind, where she kept a subconscious record of excuses that would finally let her drift away from her commitments. Chloe later remembered this entry only because it was the first.

The week progressed from one blunder to the next. In spite of her attempts, Chloe could not scrub the spot of herself from their home. As if she had peed on that gold upholstered sofa, the stain mocked her wherever she went. If she met his mother in the kitchen, she had to reveal that she couldn't cook. Mealtimes, alarmingly regular in that house, became labyrinthine tests of diplomatic skill. At a church supper, his mother's friends watched her coldly. She sensed she ought to say good-by and quickly vanish; but duty to Jack, fear of losing him, and the blind stubborn belief that backgrounds and pasts were superfluous baggage for sturdy lovers kept them going, kept them planning, kept them climbing mountains together. Cozily tucked into the laurel on a mountainside, Jack gave Chloe the diamond ring, simple, sparkling, beautiful. But the topmost tingling of joy that should have been there, wasn't. That day, when she looked at that ring, she wondered if the brilliance of their promises could ever match the brilliance of that stone. In September, in the rain in Cambridge, as they had promised to do, they married.

While Chloe taught school and Jack developed fat black notebooks with stickon titles that said Bio-Chem and Physiology, they set out to fulfill prophecies and she kept adding notes to her secret ledger, secret then, even to herself. In the beginning, she tried to be what she had promised to be: a good wife, who worked hard to smooth over the contradictions of their marriage, in the same way that she smoothed over the wrinkles of their bed each morning. The list of selfless feats grew: the calibrated emotions timed perfectly so as not to alarm or intrude; the all-purpose sexuality, ready at a moment's notice; the new cookbooks swelling shelves that used to house a Proust or a Didion; the unscrupulously dishonest, but genteel letters to his mother; the fondue dinner parties for self-controlled physicians; the virtuous shield warding off all other human relationships. She tried.

But as she learned, old habits die hard. Her black ledger grew so full, it began to seep into her consciousness, trickling out here and there, when she least expected it. When he said, "Let's spend Christmas in the West," she said, "No, we'll go to Maine." When he was waiting for his dinner, she joined a theater group and came home late. These tiny protests popped out tentatively at first, but gradually grew in strength. Eventually she stopped being mute and obedient, and chafed at invisible chains.

Chloe knew that drifters cannot get too close. Perhaps they lose out in the end, but it can't be helped. She felt again the old restlessness, the desire for flight that would not perish.

Jack feared the new Chloe. "What's happening to you?"

"I don't know."

She didn't fit into his preconceptions. "What have I done wrong?" he would ask, over and over again, as they sat, staring straight ahead, watching television.

"It's not you, Jack. It's me. I need my freedom."

"But I will give you your freedom."

"You can't give freedom. Can't you see that?"

He didn't, though he tried. Life for Jack was a series of patterns that you chiseled into the mountains. He didn't see how they could change.

"Chloe, it just doesn't have to be this complicated."

She was silent. Flight was simple, wasn't it? Or was it that drifters simply cannot learn to love? She watched him hurt; and she knew that when the inevitable moment of flight came, she'd be sorry for dragging him through her mistakes.

Baffled, Jack withdrew into black textbooks. His inexhaustible frustration surfaced in reckless driving. He made louder pronouncements, trying to drown out her louder protests. He learned to fight, and to be sad, for he was learning that his will alone could not hold her to him.

Finally she traded the strains of pretense for the exorbitant price of pain. She realized that their promises had become a jumble of broken rocks. One clear, cold morning, she tucked the ring and their memories into his hand for safekeeping, and they kissed each other. Both cried.

"I was an island, wasn't I?" he said.

Jack settled in the West, Chloe drifted, in the rolling bus, off to Montreal.

From the windows, she watched the landscapes shift and change.

WASH FAR AWAY

JOHN BERRYMAN

JOHN BERRYMAN (1914–72) was educated at Columbia and at Clare College, Cambridge. He taught at Harvard and Princeton and was Regents' Professor at the University of Minnesota at the time of his death. He was awarded the Pulitzer Prize in 1965 and the National Book Award for Poetry in 1968. His poetry volumes include, *Dream Songs, Love and Fame, Delusions,* and *Homage to Mistress Bradstreet.*

L ONG AFTER THE PROFESSOR had come to doubt whether lives held crucial points as often as the men conducting or undergoing them imagined, he still considered that one day in early spring had made a difference for him. The day began his deeper—deepest—acquaintance with "Lycidas," now for him the chief poem of the world, to which he owed, he thought, as much as anything else, his survival of his wife's death. The day had humbled him and tossed him confidence. One decision had come out of it—to give up research. He had gone back, of course, two or three times, but briefly, guiltily, without commitment and without result, abandoning it again each time more firmly; now he had not touched it for years. He knew that his appointment with tenure, four years later, must have been opposed on this ground, and barely managed through by his department chairman. The sense of stepping up on Alice's body came bitterly back—she had just died, and he had even at the time seen clearly what silenced the opposition. Not that he had cared for promotion, for anything, then. And that day seemed to him the last day of his youth, though he

was already a year over 30 and had not for a long time thought of
himself as young.

He sighed and smiled awry: he *had* been young. He closed his
eyes.

This is not exactly what he remembered.

He stepped down into the brilliant light, blinked, sweating, and
set out. My god, away. The small leaves of the maple on the
corner shook smartly as he passed. Alice's fierce voice echoed. Sunlight plunged to the pavement and ran everywhere like water,
vivid, palpable. I am a Professor, he reflected, moving rapidly, or a
sort of professor; there is a breeze, a wild sun. As he leveled his
palm sailing along the even hedge, it tingled. He felt his toes in
his shoes. The hedge danced faintly.

My life is in ruins, he thought. She begins the quarrels, but
they are my fault. Here is this weather and we are desperate.
Hugh and Penny never quarreled. I'm no further on than when
we started—*I* started.

He groped back seven years to the brimming fear that had
choked him while he waited in the hallway before entering his
very first class. He had handled it, empty, irrecoverable. But the
students had been friendly. What passion that year called out!
Hugh and he had been worked like Percherons, and they had
stood it and done more than anyone wanted, half the night up
with papers, all day with students, planning coups in class, coax-
ing, worrying, praising, ransacking like a bookshop the formless
minds in front of them for something to be used for understanding, levering rich in alternatives, roaming the real world for
analogies to cram into the boys' world for truth. He saw the facts
strained, awed, full, at the hour's end. I must do it again.

He had been teaching for seven years and he felt quietly that
he had been dead for the last five. The Dostals' garden,
anemones, snapdragons, crimson, yellow, rose-pink; colors swimming, the air sweetened, he went by. He thought: I enjoy myself,
I quarrel, but I am really dead.

What could change? Hugh, it seemed to him with the first re-
sentment he had felt for his friend, kept steadily with him like a
deadweight he could never live up to. He had once thought of
himself as going-to-be-a-writer; but he had never actually written

anything except his dissertation, some unfinished stories, three articles. Hugh *had* been a writer. They had been going to revolutionize scholarship too. The Professor acknowledged that he had no such wish now. He was just a teacher (word he didn't like—assistant professor was better); not a very good one, and stale.

Of the class that was meeting this afternoon, he really knew what? Nelen was dark, from Philadelphia, lazy. Warner was articulate and disconcerting; the blond fashion plate who sat by the door, Stone, was not so dull as he looked; Landes, who was always carefully prepared, always grinned; Holson twitched and could not keep to the issue; Rush was a wit. The others were dimmer, except Smith, who took in every point made, a likable boy. He liked them all, and he was aware that they liked him (he wondered why), but he didn't know them. Yet he could still write out, he supposed, half the troubles and strengths of his students of that first year of teaching.

He was doomed to the past or an unalterable present. What could change his hopeless relation with Alice?—quarrel and reconciliation; quarrel and reconciliation. Another emotion mounted new to the history of his memory of Hugh: he felt that Hugh was lucky—if he had lived, he and Penny might have quarreled. They had had two years only; that was lucky.

The bell rang slowly down from the campus.

He could determine to teach today as he hadn't for a long time, to swing the whole class to a fresh, active relation, an insight grave and light. Well, he did determine. What must it come to, under the inescapable routine? Since the first year, the boys repeated each other. He repeated himself. Teaching was worthy, and indispensable; but it was dull. No riskiness lived in it—not after the beginning. Perhaps when one came to organize one's own courses; but he doubted that. It was no use pretending: what had truly counted—the reciprocal learning—who older could set up again? He thought he was a man modest enough, but greater modesty than his was wanted to hope to learn from Landes or Stone.

Yet he was glad of his resolution. It seemed to bring forward for possible settlement some issue that he could hardly define but knew should be at stake. He glowed, unsmiling, and strode faster, confident.

The Professor paused for traffic and experienced a disappointment. "Lycidas." He was teaching "Lycidas." He crawled across the street.

There was no poem he liked better. In his junior year he had written a defense of Dr. Johnson's supercilious remarks about it, then had his position swept away by his experience of the poem when reading it next. But he knew the boys would find it formidable, egotistical, frozen, their hatred of Milton developed to a fine pitch in the schools. A burden fell on him—that unpleasant majesty, cold grandeur of Milton. And the poem was about Death and Poetry; what did they care for either? He could substitute some attractive poem of the period in their anthology. The boys not having been assigned any other, time would be wasted; he cast about all the same, dawdling, magnolias gleaming on the wall ahead. He would have to do "Lycidas."

If he shirked the greatest poem in English—he turned into the gate—what could his resolution be worth, or his teaching? Nothing, and his confidence returned in the sunlight. "A dreamy and passionate flux," he remembered Robert Bridges's phrase, though none from his own essay, and entering the high doorway of his building smiled at himself for the comparison, half-pleased nevertheless with himself and remembering that at any rate Bridges hadn't known Milton borrowed his river-god Camus from Fletcher, not made him up. Except for one student and a committee meeting—no, called off—he would have the whole morning for preparation. Which Fletcher? He had forgotten (not John, anyway); and he found two students waiting to see him.

One rose and stood forward, diffidently holding a paper while he unlocked the door of his office. Sperry, dull and willing. Don't know the other, do I? "Good morning, come in."

The Professor was no scholar, though he had wearied through several Elizabethan authors to find a degree; but he had once noticed Camus, he had a memory, and it vexed him to forget. Settled at his desk in the low bright room, he answered questions and helped the boy normalize a small bibliography, feeling attentive, virtuous, competent. Phineas, I expect, but where? ". . . and remember that the authors' names are *not* inverted in the footnotes; only for alphabetizing. Good luck with it."

Sperry closed the door. In a moment there would be a knock.

The sun lay level across his blotter, photographing the dust on a dust jacket. Abruptly he saw it in a line-end, "old *Chamus* from his cell," guarded by a hundred nymphs or something—some short piece of Phineas's. "Come in!" he called, radiant.

This was a young man with a high forehead and a nervous smile who wanted advice about majoring in English, his adviser having given him less than satisfaction. He explained that the Professor had had his brother several years before, so that he—Oh yes: what was his brother doing now? His brother was lost in Italy.

The Professor's mind as well as his brow clouded.

He remembered Sutton: a broad brow like this boy's and large eyes, a yellow sweater, smoking. Once they had had an argument about *Volpone* in conference, and he had an impression later that Sutton was right. He remembered it all. Indeed—he thought with a vacant grin—do I do anything ever but remember? Does anything *happen*? Why yes . . . yes . . . students in yellow sweaters die. "Camus, reverend sire, came footing slow." As the line sounded heavily in his ear, its movement was terrifying, as if Camus were Death. It would be good to say "Sutton, you were quite right about *Volpone*, I hadn't considered it deeply enough." A ranging mind, original. "Sutton, Wade" on a course- or casualty-list, the name forever reversed. With the most serious effort he had required for some time, the Professor wrenched himself to expectancy, muttering, "I'm sorry. . . ."

Sutton's brother kept him nearly half an hour. After the first ten minutes, urgent for the afternoon, he itched to come at "Lycidas," but he couldn't bring himself to hurry the boy, and the record, the possibilities, dragged on. The portrait of Hugh, with its living depthless eyes and indefinable unease, watched them from the low shelf over the books at the back of the desk. The sunlight died, returned, died. He spun an ashtray, talking. At last the boy stood up, effusively grateful, knocking a book on the floor, effusively contrite, and, undecided, departed.

Instead of plunging into Milton, the Professor went to his window with a fresh cigarette and looked down a little into the bright, sunless lawn. The rememberer. Teaching is memory. If it came to that, he could remember enough. How proudly he had begun at some point to say, "I haven't read that for ten years." Hugh's golden stories the summer in Canada. Tunes that summer. This was the superiority of aging one waited for: just to remember. True or false, evil or gay, never mind. The Nobel Prize for Memory. Recipient a suicide en route to Stockholm, having remembered all his sins at once, sitting in a deck chair, sharpening a pencil.

Now the sun moved out from a cloud, and forsythia blazed by the walk. ". . . think to burst out into sudden . . ." Hugh lay on a couch in the August sun, his short beard glinting, saying, "It's just as well. I could never have got done what I wanted to." Later, when he had got very weak and was chiefly teeth and eyes, his wandering mind wanted pathetically to live, certain he would. But the Professor clung still to the resignation, the judgment on the couch; he himself had done nothing he wanted, and he had come to believe that Hugh was right. He had come to believe this after his grief had dimmed. When he took over Hugh's classes he had felt, perhaps, as a tree would, growing into a dry riverbed grieving still for water—good, but unexpected, trembling, and wholly inadequate. He stared at the forsythia beyond the flat green. "Came footing slow . . ." Came footing fast. But it was "*went* footing slow," and recalling this he exorcised suddenly the ominous in the line. He felt unaccountably relieved, normal; he enjoyed an instant the luminous scene, and turned back to his desk under the torn beloved print of the "Anatomy Lesson."

The Professor was a systematic man. He opened his Milton and read the poem thoughtfully, twice, before he laid out side by side two other Miltons got from the library early in the week and began to work his way through the editors' notes. The Professor was also honest. Though he'd not looked at the poem for months, he felt very little as he read, except admiration for the poet's language and minute flirts of emotions he had probably experienced in previous readings, and he did not pretend to feel more. Consistently Lycidas was Hugh—even was Sutton—but without pressure. What were teachers if not shepherds? "Henceforth thou art the Genius of the shore," he whispered reverently to the brown portrait, thinking of his class, ". . . and shalt be good To all that wander in that perilous flood." The second time through he was uncomfortable with the sterile complaint, "What boots it with

incessant care To tend the homely slighted Shepherd's trade?"
Both times he was gently moved by the exquisite melancholy of a
semi-couplet at the end of the flower-passage:

> For so to interpose a little ease,
> Let our frail thoughts dally with false surmise;

He wrote "exquisite melancholy" in the margin the second time.

The editors he read closely, he read long, and he was astonished
when he learnt that "flashy" meant insipid. What were the
"songs"? Preaching . . . teaching. Insipid teaching, like his. Was
all this preparation a mistake? His teaching during the first years
had been very disorderly, quick, dialectical, free. He and Hugh had
hated elaborate plans—sometimes too they hadn't a moment to
prepare but for reading the assignment—but they had learnt and
worked things out *with* the students, and that made the difference.
Today he would be as free as he could. He wanted still to learn,
he didn't feel superior to the students (Smith, Sutton) more now
than then. But his experience was what it was. Who would know
"flashy" unless he told them? He went eagerly on.

A student knocked, went off with a book.

As Milton's imitations and telescopings multiplied, he com-
menced to feel restless, distant, smaller. What one editor
neglected, another observed, and he began to have a sense of the
great mind like a whirring, sleepless refinery—its windows glittering far out across the landscape of night—through which poured
and was transformed the whole elegiac poetry of Greece and Italy
and England, receiving an impress new and absolute. *Mine!* it
seemed to call, seizing one brightness, another, another, locking
them in place, while their features took on the rigidity and beauty
of masks. Through the echoing halls they posed at intervals, large,
impassive, splendid; a special light moved on their helms, far up,
and shadows fell deep between them. The Professor collected
himself and glanced at the time.

Naturally he wouldn't finish. It would take fortnights to weigh
all the notes. And questions marked for further study would have
to go—not that they were likely to come up. Making a late lunch,
he ought to be able to do everything else. He stretched, luxurious,
warm. When had he felt so thoroughly and profitably occupied?
Throwing the window wider, he went rapidly, speculationless,

through the notes to the end of the poem. This done, he closed
the books except one, put them aside, pulled his ear, and stared at
"Lycidas."

Now came the part he called "penetration." Although he knew
very well what the subject of the poem was, he pretended he
didn't, and pondered it pencil in hand, to find out. Elegy by an
ambitious, powerful, obscure man of 28 for a successful junior of
25, drowned. Academic status: Non-Fellow (grand poet) for
Fellow (little poet). Probably commissioned or at least requested.

> Invocation, or *complaint*.
> Elegy proper: another invocation
> > (his own death)
> > their friendship
> > Nature's lament
> > Nymphs, where?
> > (Fame: Apollo)
> > the cause? Triton, Aeolus
> > University mourns: Camus
> > (Clergy: St. Peter)
> > flowers for hearse
> > where now? Nature godless
> Consolation, by metamorphosis (Christian, pagan)
> Ottava rima "Thus sang . . ." & so an end.

Four sections, with three personal digressions. And the opening
was really another personal digression, this unpleasing insistence
on his being compelled to write. No one *made* you, after all. The
Milton-passages came to less than a third of the poem—but where
the power was. Reasonable enough; Milton may never have
spoken to Edward King, except to ask for the salt. The Professor
studied the text and his notes, waving his pencil slowly by his ear.
Cunning. He saw that. The testimony of Triton and Aeolus, and
the speeches of Camus and Peter, actually made up a sort of trial
—so that the poet's diverse materials would be given an air of
unity. What on earth made Milton think of a trial? . . . *Oh.* His
own inquisition of the nymphs above! They had deserted Lycidas,
when he needed them: who then *had* been with him, for evil? Let
a court find out.

The Professor leaned back in his chair with surprise. All this revealed only in the word "plea" and the sense of the passages. And one meaning of "felon." His vision of the refining plant recurred to him, but he grimaced impatiently at it. Better say Vatican. Only the "privy paw." A Puritan Vatican then, with catacombs.

Bending to the poem again, after a new cigarette and a dozen notes made compactly on a small yellow pad, he approached almost warily, as if toward an animal long familiar suddenly displaying resources unsuspected, even dangerous. But in the first moment he saw that his discovery made the Fame passage more obviously than ever an excrescence, and with a touch of indignation he relaxed. It split the trial. Milton's mounting sense must have worked strongly indeed if he was willing to do this; and then that fantasy of arrogance wherein Phoebus singles him out by touching his ears! The Professor, no poet, pulled his own ear.

He drew up a schedule for the discussion. How many hours, he wondered, would it take to teach "Lycidas" properly? I might give a course (first semester) English 193: "Lycidas" I-84. He stretched again, smiling, crinkling his eyes toward the lightstream.

And finally—it was very late—the "lesson." He wouldn't have admitted to anyone, of course, that this was what he called it, but call it this he did, had for years. He remembered a time when he hadn't used the "lesson," when in fact he had detested above all things a "message" (his derisive tone he heard still) of any sort. So had Hugh. His face shadowed, and he shifted his eyes to the portrait, which the sun reached. Have I betrayed you? Here in the sun? Feeling melodramatic, he set his mind uneasily to the "lesson."

Then all at once he felt hopeless. What could a one-hour class do to change what he had become? He had been a fool. One class, he raged, and the new man leaps from the old skin. With his schedule and his "penetration" and his "lesson." He stops catering to the boys' shiftlessness, he develops tongues of fire. A marriage like a tiger lies down and purrs. Dark in his office at one-thirty, he sat clamped in despair. And the despair threw him onward. No, he *had* been a fool, but he was a fool still, a worse one. You have to start. You have nothing to lose. Jump overboard now, you might as well try. At least you can become serious, and let the rhetoric take care of itself. If you fail, you fail anyway. He would finish his preparation and do everything he could do this afternoon, and see. Even the "lesson." Why not? It was only a joke with himself. Hating "teacher," he pretended to submit to "lesson"—merely the general moral truth, or some general moral truth (God knows he wasn't dogmatic) arising out of whatever they were doing. Nothing pretentious, nor original, but if you didn't make a form for it you might pass it by altogether. Hastily he wrote at the bottom of the schedule, cramping his hand, his "lesson" for today, and as he wrote an image sprang up of Milton rapt forward unconscious at a window-table in the twilight, his drastic mind and dull eyes on the shade of King, his pen and the swirling threshold-forces on himself: "Whatever we do and think we are doing, however objective or selfless our design, our souls each instant are enacting *our own* destinies." Moral enough! Did the boys even believe in souls?—they didn't give a hoot for immortality. But this was the point of teaching.

He arranged his notes and ideas with returning satisfaction. Hat, window. But after these hours he was tired, very tired, and the breeze and the blade brightened him less than he would have liked as he hurried toward the Club, deciding to have—how rare for him, how usual for others—a cocktail before lunch.

The bar was nearly empty, the Martini firm and immediate.

Through lunch he resisted the silly recurring desire to say aloud what he heard again and again in his head, "Nor yet where Deva spreads her wizard stream," a line that gave him intense pleasure; for example to his speechless neighbor at the round table, a dry short man, very hungry, evidently, in Classics. The verb seemed as brilliant as the epithet. King sailed from Chester-on-Dee. Deva, the Dee, like Wordsworth's Winander. Charles Diodati lived on the Dee; maybe he and Milton (Milton the diva of Christ's— beaten, disappointed genius) had sat on the bank the summer before and traded legends of the sacred stream . . . "youthful poets dream on summer eves by haunted stream." "What do you think of Edward King?" a soft voice. "I doubt he deserves a Fellowship," a stern one from the incredibly youthful face, "and it came to him too soon." Behind the slight body, clenched grass. "Your luck, John, wait, will change." The late afternoon airs, the dappled water. There was more in that line than the fatal sailing.

He didn't even mention King in his letters to Diodati between the death and "Lycidas." However. Had he written to anyone of Hugh? None ever: how? Diodati had a year to live. Who did Milton write to then? God-given, God-withdrawn. The Dio stoops to the Dee; twice. And stoops no more.

He drank his coffee slowly. He hoped the boys had prepared well; he had told them to use the stacks. The dining room had emptied, a waiter hovered, still he lingered. He was remembering a lunch he and Hugh had had together once on a day as bright as this one—Friday too—in a restaurant neither could afford. Italian bread. Something had gone very wrong for him, and Hugh was consoling and sympathizing with him in the merriest, gentlest way imaginable. They had told jokes, and were free together as two old friends can be in a strange, agreeable setting. He was leaving next day, he recalled; so that the occasion had urgency forward as well as back. But what was odd? He couldn't hear their voices. He could see the glints and sheen from the table, his own arms on the table, hand on a wineglass, he saw Hugh's face and the white wall, he saw the whole scene, but he heard nothing. It was completely silent. The Professor struck his palm on his table, and rose, his heart beating, and left.

The breeze had died away, leaving the campus placid, almost hot. Crossing, however, he looked forward eagerly like a defendant facing the last day of a suit that had so far gone well: anxious and confident, pacing out the final hour of his imputed, fantastic guilt. He went by his office for a book and notes, opened the window, touched the frame of the portrait, and arrived in his classroom just before the bell.

Where were the others? The high, dark-brown, sun-filled room, too large for a class of 14 anyway, seemed all but deserted, and he looked around it annoyed while the bell rang. Who were missing? Only Cotton, it appeared, in the infirmary ("A good place for Cotton," said somebody), and Fremd. He smiled, throwing his Milton on the table, and felt better, although where was Fremd?

"Well, gentlemen," he went over to the windows—well known for roaming and for picking up chairs, he knew, but he had long ceased trying to refrain, "how do you like it? I assume you acquired an unholy aversion to it in school, as also to *Macbeth*

and some other works not perfectly uninteresting. But what do
you think of it this time, Mr. Rush?"

"Marvelous," the young man said mildly.

"Your diction is rich, but your tone is slack," the Professor
smiled, "as applied to the most celebrated poem in our language.
What precisely is marvelous about it?"

Rush grinned above his olive tie and thought. "There is a marvelous lack of emotion."

"Oh?" Crossing for the book, he read the opening lines aloud.
"Unemotional? Did the rest of you feel the same way?"

No, they didn't.

"I meant emotion about his friend," Rush amended.

"Well, what about these?" Refusing to be hurried into his the-
sis, he read aloud some other lines:

> But O the heavy change, now thou art gone,
> Now thou art gone, and never must return!

Their languid gloom oppressed him. "Those are about King
straight enough."

"Well . . . all those nymphs and flowers and wood-gods . . ."

"Such properties needn't be inconsistent with strong emotion,
as we'll see presently. But let's find out what Milton's subject is.
What's the poem *about*, gentlemen? What lay essentially in his
mind as he set about it? We have a poem in the form of a pasto-
ral elegy, heavy in certain parts with passion. What about?"

"It's about his friend's death, isn't it?" Wright duly said.

"No!" Landes's high confident voice broke out. "It's about Milton himself. In other words, it has a subject he felt very strongly
about, and it's very emotional whenever it comes to him or things
that interested him. King was just the occasion. If his cat had
died instead, the poem might have been just as good."

"Hardly his cat," said the Professor, "though Gray did well
enough. But I agree with you that the poem is not on the whole
passionate about King. . . ." He talked easily and warmly, striding about the room with restless sudden turns, his ideas throng-
ing. As he sat down lightly on the table edge, the sun streamed in
afresh, glowing on the rim of Warner's glasses and white collar.

". . . In his crisis of discontent with hard long solitary study
and protracted obscurity, *doubt* of the poetic priesthood he'd en-

tered, *scorn* for the worthless pastors of the priesthood he had refused to enter," he caught Hale's eye back in the corner and realized with vexation that the tall, bland youth was engaged on some
very different speculation of his own, "in this crisis all his passions
and anxieties welled up at sight of a young man, dedicated as he
was himself, though hardly in the same degree, *cut off*. Ah! To
what end, then: self-denial, labor, patience, wisdom even? King's
had simply vanished, and so might his."

"I don't see why he was worried about dying," said Nelen's
good-natured, empty face.

A real young man's remark. "Two things. One I just indicated—
a colleague five years younger suddenly being killed. The other
is that there was some actual danger. The plague was fierce. People had died even in the little place where Milton was, Horton.
And he planned to go to Italy the next year. As you sit here, a
voyage from England to Italy seems safe enough, but travel was
risky three hundred years ago. If King had drowned going just to
Ireland, why couldn't he, going farther?"

"But there are only four lines about his own death," Smith
drawled, in the voice that made everything he said sound like a
man dreaming.

A hand moved, Nelen's again. "Sir, who *is* King?"

Ugh. "Edward King," the Professor explained with Oriental re-
straint, "was the *friend* of John Milton about whose death the
poem we are discussing ostensibly is." Or rival.

"It seems to me the poem is about King," Stone said doubtfully, uncrossing his legs.

"Critics pretty much agree—Legouis and the rest—that Milton's feelings about himself are the real subject."

"Could they be wrong?"

Warner's simple, uninflected question somehow moved the Professor very much. The trust, the measureless respect both for them
and for *his* judgment of them, entered him so deeply that he
couldn't answer for a moment, but merely looked at the dark boy
tilted back in his chair smoking. Perhaps it *was* after all an honor
to be a critic, or even a teacher. But how deserve such confidence,
this privilege?

"They certainly could. I've told you all year not to take anybody's word for anything if you feel competent to judge it your-self and can bring evidence forward. Sometimes, it's true, in mat-ters of *feeling* there isn't much evidence. But here there is a good deal. Take the last line: 'To-morrow to fresh woods, and pastures new.' What do you make of that? Anybody."

Smith sat forward. "He doesn't want to be any more where his friend was with him, and all the things he sees will remind him of his loss."

Dumbfounded he looked down at the page. Smith's rapid intel-ligence working through the incantation of his voice had often affected the Professor, but this time he felt as if an oracle had spoken.

. . . Why not? "Yes, it seems possible. It's simpler . . . What I was going to say was that the line is usually taken as a reference to Milton's plans either for moving to London or traveling to Italy. Of course, there might be an allusion to this anyway. But your contemporary meaning is better—after all his readers knew noth-ing and cared less about Milton's plans."

"Sir? Did people like this poem when it came out?" asked Hol-son, crawling about on his seat.

Did they? "No, they didn't, so far as we know. In fact, at least a century passed before any attention was paid to it at all, before any of his minor poems were recognized."

Curiously, from Rush, "Who recognized them?"

The Professor, puzzling still over Smith's point, felt cornered. He cast back. "I think Warton was the first important critic on their side, but Pope and Gray knew them well. It was really the beginnings of Romantic taste that rescued them." Or so I say.

"Classics don't like them?" Landes wondered.

"Well, Milton is a classical poet but he is also a Romantic. The word is difficult, as you probably know. . . ."

He described its ambiguity, called Johnson's *Life of Milton* a model of respectful churlishness and vindictive merriment (he remembered his undergraduate phrases, after all), and glanced at the Pound-Eliot campaign against *Paradise Lost*, abbreviating, anxious to get on.

". . . But let me ask *you* some questions. Who are the 'rout'? In fact what does 'rout' mean? It's in line sixty-one."

"The Maenads," said Warner.

"No doubt. And who were they?"

Nobody knew, or nobody answered: he explained; and nobody knew that "rout" had any but its modern sense. Holson, indeed, thought the modern sense would be better. Briefly, and without expressing the asperity he felt, the Professor laid down precepts of submission to a poem and fidelity to an author's sense. He was aware of some resistance in the class. He should have been fuller. What was "welter"? Nobody knew exactly. He read a few lines aloud, farsing. For five minutes he probed their familiarity with the meaning of details.

"You've got to look these things up, gentlemen. It's not only the matter of intellectual responsibility" (who would ever have taught them that? the major thing?), "it's a matter of enjoyment. We miss quite enough anyway, inevitably. How many of you know jessamine, crowtoe, woodbine—have visual images when you see the words or hear them?"

One hand hesitated.

He went off to the windows. "I don't myself," he said looking out. Forsythia, daffodils, snapdragons. "Now it's true the passage has literary sources and a symbolic intention, but if the flowers are nothing more than words for us, we miss a good deal. Jammed in cities, we have to. The whole country experience is disappearing. Not only the country. Do you know the old rhyme about London bells? I can't remember it all, most of it though, but each couplet rings the bells of some church, at first senselessly, and then a frightening continuity commences to emerge.

> Brickbats and targets
> Say the bells of St. Marg'rets,
> Brickbats and tiles—it was *Bulls'-eyes* and targets—
> Say the Bells of St. Giles, and so on.

It's violent and beautiful still, for a modern reader. It sometimes stands my hair on end. But how dim must the effect be, compared to its effect on its first hearers, accustomed all day to hear the ringing of the peals, high and low, now here, now there, from the hundreds of churches all over London, pealing like friends and warnings across the otherwise more or less silent city. No traffic or machinery, only the voice of the militant Church, the bells. The poem must have been a nightmare of reality. From this point of view, in fact, our prolific, active cities, with all their noise, have become in truth absolutely still—stiller than that," he gestured to a print of the Roman Forum high on the sidewall. "You lose out of literature some experience every year, and you need all the knowledge you can get." Hugh would have liked that. How quiet the room feels. Here comes Warner, here comes a chopper.

"What's the knowledge *for?*" said Warner in a loud voice bristling like his hair. "Poetry is supposed to be dreamy and vague, like Keats. Why pick it apart? I'd like to know how a super-jet works, that's useful knowledge, but I don't care how a poem works. This poem makes me feel half-asleep. I like the feeling. I don't think a poem *does* work, I think it loafs, and teachers pretend to—no offense, Sir—pretend to know all sorts of things about it that don't really exist."

The Professor picked up his chair. A true feeling, though lazy enough; "dreamy and passionate flux"—and then all the claptrap.

"Tell me, Mr. Warner, would you admit that there are conventions in 'Lycidas'?"

"Sure," the boy stretched. "They're not real shepherds, they're Milton and his friend. The nymphs are fanciful, and so on. But that's all obvious."

"We might be more definite than that, and fuller. . . ." He elaborated a little, dangling his chair, on the artificial character of the properties. The poem seemed Watteau-*ish* as he talked—he did not like Watteau—and he felt abruptly that he was tired. Was he doing as well as he wanted to? What had happened to his excitement?

". . . So. Now: who is the 'blind Fury,' Mr. Warner? Line seventy-five."

"What's-her-name. Atropos. The one who slices."

"Very accurate." (The yellow sweater smoked on, faceless.) "Except that she isn't a Fury."

"She's not? The fellow I read said she was."

"I doubt if he did. Atropos is a Fate. The poet in his rage against her *calls* her a Fury." He put the chair down.

Warner was decided, superior: "What's the difference?"

The Professor suffered a flick of rage. The cold self-assurance in the voice cambered as from endless metallic contempt for these subjects, these feathers.

> Thy age, like ours, O soul of Sir John Cheke,
> Hated not learning worse than toad or asp.

"The difference is between understanding a world-poet, Mr. Warner, and not. Or between cultivation, and Ignorance trucu-lent." Warner sat straighter. (Fatuous, and then unjust?—as to Alice.) "Of course I don't mean yours, but the difference is frankly as great as if one of your friends referred to your mother as an aging woman—say she is one—and another called her a witch, an evil witch." Frank, indeed. "The point is that the anger and horror of the line will be wholly felt only by a reader who already knows that Atropos is not properly a Fury but a Fate. As most readers I suppose do, or did." He didn't look at Warner, then made his voice general, "Let me give you an analogy. Some time ago, a century and a quarter, say, an audience assembled to hear a new piano concerto in Vienna. Piano, orchestra, conductor, a large aristocratic uncomfortable room, ladies, gentlemen. Now there is nothing very striking about the concerto's opening phrase but, as the piano began it, every nerve in the audience tightened." He stopped.

Silence, curiosity.

Doubtfully, at last, from Holson, "Did you say the *piano* began . . . ?"

"Yes. why not?"

"The piano played the introduction? But the orchestra always does," the boy said nervously.

"That's the point. It's the orchestra, gentlemen, in a piano con-certo, that begins and prepares for the entrance of the piano, which is the star of the occasion. That night, for the first time in history, a piano concerto began *not* in the orchestra but with the piano. It was Beethoven's Fourth. What sort of position is a lis-tener to it in who simply does not know that concerti begin in the orchestra? He won't even hear the most important thing about the opening phrase. This is an affair, isn't it, of pure knowledge? No quantity of attention or insight will assist your ignorance, if you happen to be ignorant."

Hale wanted something! "Yes?" That admirable courtesy.

"Is there a good recording of that, Sir?"

"What it comes to—just a minute—is that what the artist does is sometimes even more interesting in its negative aspect, that is, in the alternative or other-possibility that it displaces, than in what it is itself. So in 'Lycidas.' The fact that Milton couldn't keep to his subject, or his nominal subject, shows that he had powerfully other matter on his mind. The digressions are in a way the poem's best testimony to his complete seriousness. But the reader observes them precisely in the sudden disappointment of expectation; that is, the poem ceases to be about King. Mr. Hale, I think there is a recording by Schnabel, if not there is one by somebody else, and a question more remote from the drowning of King I haven't heard for fifteen minutes." He looked at his watch, "Sixteen minutes."

Several boys laughed.

The Professor had looked at his watch, however, to see what time it was, having lost during the Warner moment his usual sense of what piece of the 50 minutes had lapsed and what remained. More remained than he had feared, but it wasn't much.

"Sir," Smith spoke just before he hurried on, "what do you mean, that the poem ceases to be about King?"

Surprised, he explained: the two long, intense passages on Fame and the corruption of the clergy were obvious excrescences.

"But Milton qualifies their differences from the rest, doesn't he?"

"He does? Where?"

The slow-voiced, serious boy bent, scanning. Motes waltzed in a sunbeam across Hale.

"Here, eighty-six. He says *that strain* 'was a higher mood.' From a god, that is. And one thirty-two, 'the dread voice is past.' At the end of each."

The Professor studied the lines. He felt, uneasily, as if he had never seen them before.

"Maybe '*various* quills' at the very end is more of the same explanation," the boy went on.

"I don't quite see how these *explain* them. It would be easy to invent transitions at the ends after you had left your theme—or come to it, rather, nakedly, since Milton is his own theme."

"But they grow naturally out of the situation," Smith argued. "Each of King's masters gets a word in: Apollo, Cambridge, St. Peter. Orpheus perished horribly, like Lycidas; therefore why break your neck to be a poet? Then the Church mourns, right after the University—promising son lost. What's out of order about that?"

"It's not so much that they're out of order, as that they're about Milton, not King," the Professor repeated.

"Well, Milton felt them hard. It might be his own situation. It *is* King's though, isn't it? The only things I know about him are that he was a scholar and poet and was going to be a clergyman." The boy considered. The others were listening to him with interest. "It's King's life that got slit, and then Apollo consoles Milton by saying that his lost friend, after all, will be judged in Heaven, not here. So will Milton, but that doesn't keep it from being about King."

"But it's Milton Apollo singles out by touching his ear," exclaimed the Professor, resisting a weak sense that the discussion was getting—how?—past him, dragging him.

"Only to defend him," Stone said unexpectedly. The blond, handsome boy lifted his book. "My editor said if your ear trembles, you're being talked about, that is, people would be saying Milton had his own fame in mind, so Apollo reproved them—for him. Fame is only Heaven's judgment, where King is."

"But the genuine rage is in the other passage," drawled Smith. "It seems to me King's death is awful to Milton, especially, because the Church needed good men."

"Why didn't Milton go in then?" Rush asked.

"How do I know?" Smith tilted his chair to see past Holson. "You don't have to do something yourself to want other people to do it well. Milton was a damned serious man. Maybe he thought poetry was more important."

"He quit it for politics for years. He probably was too aggressive to be a clergyman," Stone said from his corner.

The Professor found his voice. The storm that had seemed to be gathering round him, from Smith, had somehow not descended. But was the boy right? What do I think? He wished the hour were over. Milton or King, he wondered wearily, what mat-

ter? He smiled at "aggressive" to raise his spirits; Stone it was who
had remarked admiringly that Shakespeare's Cleopatra "had *id*."

Pacing the front of the classroom again, he told them his discovery of the morning, the Trial that linked Triton-Aeolus-
Camus-Peter. "What brought into Milton's imagination, do you
suppose, the notion of a trial?" he asked, sitting on the warm sill
and lighting a cigarette. "Mr. Nelen, any ideas?" Mr. Nelen had
no ideas, he revealed. "Mr. Holson?"

While Holson was reflecting, the Professor made a short excur-
sion. He climbed, dripping, under a blinding sun, up and up a
sand dune, one of the vast dunes hanging over Lake Superior,
panting. He was laughing and calling up. Once he looked back,
fearful. Hugh helped him at the top, and as he stood up a wind
caressed all his skin. The miles of blue lake gleamed. No other
dune so white as this. The sky was full of the sun. He wanted to
stay. But he knew Hugh was saying, "It's wonderful," running
back toward the edge, "just step as far as you can with each foot,"
then disappeared over it. Now he had to? Yes. He shuddered,
cold, came toward the edge, shrank. Feet moved by strong love
on. Fought. He leaned erect off the world's edge, toppling, and
stept! Through empty air straight down, terror of the first, the
bounce and astonishment of the second. Pure joy the third, his
eyes cleared. He rushed through the sunlight wild with delight in
deep jumps, foot far to foot, touching the earth, down and down
toward Hugh, bounding far below. Far off, another world.

"Himself," Holson said.

"I'm sorry?" said the Professor, getting up.

"Did he want to show what a trial it had been for himself?"

"Hardly. The trial, I think, gentlemen, continues the dramatic
method of Milton's own inquisition of the nymphs, earlier. It's a
unity."

"Why the inquisition in the first place?" Stone's voice, after the
pause, was thoughtful.

"Why not?" he smiled.

"Well," the young man in the corner went on deliberately,
"but if the unity or the meaning isn't real, is just an illusion, how
can the poem be good or true?"

The Professor reached for his book, but a light came on in his
brain. *Why!* He heard his voice sudden and tense: "Why the in-

quisition! What does a man think when a friend dies, what does he do? He *asks questions*—'not loud, but deep.' *Why? Where now? Why? Where?*" He saw the class again, and realized he was trembling. "But you can't just ask these questions over and over again in a poem, as you do in life. You have to have something to ask them about. What situation will let you ask the most questions? A trial. An inquiry, a trial. It doesn't matter what the questions pretend to be about. Where the nymphs were on Tuesday, which wind blew. What matters is that there *be* questions. Behind all the beauty we haven't had a chance to discuss, the versification, the imagery, behind the foliage, there is this urgency and reality."

His difficult, morning sense of the poem as a breathing, weird, great, incalculable animal was strong on him again. He returned to the table excited, constrained, for the book.

"That's like what I meant," Smith hastened his drawl, "he really asks the questions about King. They're his questions, but he kept himself out of the poem as much as he *could*."

His questions. Did he? The Professor as he opened the book felt that all things were possible, and seeing the flower passage he imagined a rustling, as if his metaphor were true, and under the passage moved the animal, the massive insight of the grieving poet.

"Yet the flowers are to satisfy himself, not King. Of course, the whole elegy is in King's honor, but I mean their pathos is less than their beauty. The melancholy is all Milton's. Listen.

> Bid amaranthus all his beauty shed,
> And daffadillies fill their cups with tears,
> To strew the laureate hearse where Lycid lies.
> For so to interpose a little ease,
> Let our frail thoughts . . ."

At this point, an extraordinary thing happened. The Professor saw the word "false" coming FALSE. He felt as if snatched up by the throat and wrung. "False" threw its iron backward through the poem. The room shook. Then the unutterable verse mastered his voice and took it off like a tempest:

> "dally with false surmise;
Ay me!"

The cry rang hopeless through his mind

> "whilst THEE the shores, and sounding seas
> Wash far away, where'er thy bones are hurled,
> Whether beyond the stormy Hebrides,
> Where THOU perhaps under the whelming tide
> Visit'st the bottom of the monstrous world—"

A bell sounded, and the Professor was able to dismiss the class a moment later—remembering that he had forgotten after all the "lesson." But whether he could have read a line more he wondered, as he closed the strange book and held it in both hands. The students made for the door. The sun shone steadily in at the windows. The class was over.

The Professor sat a long time in his office, not thinking of anything and perhaps not unhappy, before he went home. Once he read over the transfiguration of Lycidas, and was troubled by the trembling of light on the page; his eyes had filled with tears. He heard the portrait's voice. At last he rose, closed the window and took his hat. Shutting the door as he left, in the still-bright hall he looked at the name engraved on his card on the door. He felt older than he had in the morning, but he had moved into the exacting conviction that he was . . . something . . . not dead.

THE SISTERHOOD

ANNE HALLEY

ANNE HALLEY was born in Bremerhaven, Germany, in 1928 and came to the United States in 1938. Educated at Wellesley and the University of Minnesota, she is the author of *Between Wars and Other Poems*. She is the poetry editor of *The Massachusetts Review* and lives, with her three sons, in Amherst, Massachusetts.

THESE AFFAIRS, though I am about to give them away, are not what you think. At thirteen, Janice wore a belted, red coat. Seen from behind—in motion—the high, squared-off slope of her backside, covered by red fleece, moves hardly at all. She holds her arms well away from her body and bent outward at the elbow: her fingers are curled. She swings the arms back and forth in a stiff parody of grace. Her legs are swinging too—out from the knee, a little more sideways than forward. Janice is running in a slow, peculiar careful way, seeming to shelter fragile innards. As if she concealed a thin piece of china *there*. She is also showing-off. Girl running is already girl caught: I hate her most bitterly at this moment.

And hate us all, poor bitches, ten twenty thirty years gone, still fluffed-out and strapped-in, swinging a sideways leg and proffering a breast, glancing confusedly at boss or co-worker or stray, flathead stranger. Our rushing voices pleading beneath the flow of words: I work my ass off all right, but oh, never mind that. It's still pretty; I'm nice.

Age thirteen and a half, Janice began to go out with the young trainees stationed at the college. To church functions, to dances: she would have an orchid wilting on her sweater Mondays at school. She had a way of laughing, then, that was as simply affirmative as a baby's. The sound would well out of her, partly a gurgle—pure pleasure. She was nice. Her mother loved buying her the formals, the bunny wraps and silver slippers—loved dressing her up. I'm almost certain that Janice didn't get taken advantage of by those boys who wrote her love letters, and proposed marriage from distant army posts, nor by her later fraternity swains. But the wonderful laughter went, as virginity was preserved and pretty clothes multiplied. When Janice was twenty she had a mother and a fiance who loved her in sheared beaver; she had a solitaire on her ringfinger. She married a year or two later—a man her mother liked no better than the others. He likes Janice thin and in fluffy dresses, fifteen years younger and not quite so tall.

Advantage was taken, as well as had, though I—left behind somewhere holding the Camp Fire Girl's manual and the skate key—will not point a finger. Running, I'll hold my head down, bend my back and pump with my arms. Try to land on the balls of my feet. And since it is a spiritual exercise only, close my eyes tight. It is, after all, only that recalcitrant muscle under the ribs that still pumps away, runner and world-beater after the long-gone. Our present—as you know—is different.

It is in our present that I propose we now watch two women meet. They have stayed the course and caught their breath. In our present, in a lobby: any kind of ante-room or minor public set for small, temporary dramas. There is resilient rubbery tough substance under their sandaled or platform-booted, their clog-cumbered feet; a breeze, a change of air, ruffles their garments as a tufted padded door swings noiselessly back and forth. On one side, a plateglass rectangle brings up the shadowy blue-black sky, festooned with its random, significant groupings of white and yellow lights, whirring, faint twittering noises come from somewhere: the other wall is full of elevators.

They move towards each other: two women, tottering or gliding over expensive green carpets. Their bare, their softly-sheathed, arms extended. Light-catching bits of stone and metal move and dangle about their persons. They utter small, name-like sounds. Pause, embrace, do something with their heads that is kissing or sniffing, even as they seem to hold each other, tightly enveloped, at arm's length. And behind each of them—in this emblematic public set-piece—a blockier, square shape covered in tough hairy, harsh-to-the-touch layerings, and sprouting flaps, buttons, and knots: a pillar shape with pockets, with linings, pads, interfacings and seams, all protective of money, advances more slowly, draws up to wait some paces behind.

At the most ordinary, Saturday night out to dinner level of performance, the husband in the scene will have an embarrassed, mildly pleased but waiting to move on, look: Nanny and the dog walker in the park have something of this. It is made up of suspended possessiveness and appreciative evaluation, and the threatening loneliness of a separate species, with other ways. And the women hold each other as they hold each other off. You know I have no people, one says in the blue-greased droop of eyelids. I've got my own ass to peddle. But kiss me, please.

I know. You look it too. But hold me a little—I wouldn't say it aloud. Yes, that's good. And I've got one of my own—not quite a god maybe—if you ever paid attention.

When the husbands shake hands—reach out those small squares of flesh weighted by starched cuffs, metal links, a double layer of woolly outer casings—it is all over. Ruth and Naomi have said, in spite of fabled precedent and at the moment of recognition: Goodbye.

That's the way it goes, but some of us—the other kind of runners—cannot leave off following after, inside. I still follow Rosalie: when I walked her home from the high school, it took an hour. All down Main Street hill and across the tracks, we dawdled past the darkness of bars and rummage sales, the A&P feed bags lined up on the sidewalk, to the island of Morton's Pharmacy. I had a coke and Rosalie a birch beer. Then around the bend, away from Polack town, out to the new, neat houses beyond the Country Club. Rosalie was the only person I knew who lived in a new house with a curved decorative chimney, and an initial—a slanted S—on the storm door.

Walking all that way, we kept bumping into each other; we are so involved in talk, we almost trip each other up. Sometimes our hands meet and our fingers interlock, surprised and fitting as if by accident. Rosalie wants me to marry her older brother. His framed photograph is all I know: he is in uniform and mostly visored cap. But sometimes I can almost imagine us: four faceless grown-ups at a card table. Shadowed by bridge lamps.

Rosalie ties on an apron when we get inside. We feed the cat again, take things out of the refrigerator, fool around with the spray-hose on the sink. She decides to make cole slaw with pineapple and raisins. I lean against the counter while Rosalie cuts and bustles; she pushes me to sit down on the step-stool and hangs over me—her hair in my face. Stay. Call your house and stay. You have to. That night, in Richard's freshly made-up double bed, we tussle and bounce so much that her mother calls to us angrily, Girls! I could not, could not sleep, though I had nothing to think about.

I was Rosalie's Maid of Honor when she married the returned soldier, the boy from next door. At the Lake Cottage we swam naked and her legs and arms, glimmering green under the water, were all intertwined with his. He ran after her, wet giggly and squealing, and the springs in the curtained cubbyhole screamed. But she had wanted me there. Come, come out. You have to come. You have to, she sang over the phone. Rosalie had four children, so close together that her mother quarrelled with her. Rosalie had red—almost pink—hair, and golden unfreckled skin; we used to sit close together in the early show on Friday nights. I watched her eyes move pale and restless with reflected light. Until that sudden seizure, she never liked boys.

I will not pretend that I never learned to run like my sister Janice, like Rosalie. Or in any case, never learned movements as careful and of like significance. In the fall of 1942 I dressed in green corduroy pants with nailhead trim, a white dickey under my sweater. I put a velvet bow on top of my head, bristly with bobby pins. Carried my Chicago Rollers in a square fiberboard case and walked—alone—the ten blocks to the skating rink. Full of hope and terrible apprehension: paid my quarter and looked at no one until I had my skates laced up. I wished that my mother had not let me come; that she would stop thinking of skating as healthy, with children screaming, falling down. She should have taken in the meaning of the whirling lights and heard the organist, noticed the eagle tattoos on the forearms of the chinless man who blew the whistle. Or at least have recognized the sharp look of the boys, the round-calved neat girls, like serious dolls, on bell-trimmed skates.

Couples floated by me with their arms about each other under the dimming, whirling spots of colored light: their faces dedicated, rapt. I meant to meet a boy. A conscious hustler, I knew what I needed. Which again, may not be quite what you think. Curt taught me a flashy, low-swooping glide and dip in which our clasped hands first rode high up into the air, then nearly swept the floor; his hand on my hip was our rudder. But under the Exit light, waiting for me, he looked pale, snotty. When he put the plaid winter cap with earflaps on his head, a ragged line of hair showed against the back of his neck. I saw what he was—off the floor: a poor kid, a bologna-eater, one of those no one remembers.

We walked home in a group of other, nondescript, even younger kids: rabbity, already winter-faded faces. Last year we would have played kick-the-can in the empty lots by the tracks. I edged away from Curtis and kept my face carefully blank whenever he spoke. By the time we got to my corner, he was walking with someone else.

But Darrell, whom I also met at the skating rink, lasted through winter and spring. And though I was not nice, the years I practiced to be a nice girl, I think we must have been friends. About the third time we went skating together, he had his father's car. I never met his parents, but that evening he took me to his house. A grocery and candy store behind a gas pump on the highway. It was a low building, more like sheds strung together. We went in through a back kitchen to sit on a brightly-patterned, stiff sofa in front of the space heater. I looked at a magazine. Darrell's smell was something like spearmint, or arrow-root, so he must have gotten close to me, but just then we heard the backdoor slam. A girl in a white unifrom stood in the kitchen, grinning at us. She had her hands at her temples: just lifting a hairnet and carefully loosening the elastic. Which is what you do when you need to make it last. Ohhohh! Oh oh Daaaarrell! She backed out quickly and started water running, clattering dishes. That's Esther-Jean, Darrell said. She was just a girl who stayed with them. We went out through the front, unlocking and locking again the dark little store. Darrell picked a bag of potato chips from the rack behind the counter on the way out.

Darrell and I broke up in an undramatic confusion of sex and class. The months we roamed together through the skating rinks, diners, movie theaters, of Salamanca, New York, we were both—I suppose now—making do. For reasons of our own, not making-out. I was pleased to have a tall, soft-spoken boyfriend, and he must have been putting in time, waiting until Sampson Navy Base would transform all present unrealities. That would be in early summer. For now, he called me names: Minnie M. and Maggie and Ermintrude, and sometimes Cap. He would punch my arm, very gently: Come on, Skipper. I would fall into a daze as—shoulder to shoulder—we drifted out of Pick-Up's for Good Food into the delicately cutting, frosty air; a mustard smear and crumbly meat clogging the tongue always part of our equation. I did not recognize myself in the names he gave me. But they made me feel that someone I had mysteriously missed, not known until that moment, now walked down the emptied small town street, and leaned slightly, meaningfully, against the boy who knew her name and history. Perhaps her future.

From which paint-flaked two-family frame house, down narrow porch steps, had Skipper come? And from what days of taking care of kids, putting up her hair, doing dishes? To the sound of what flat-vowelled imperatives, what hanging phrases with un-voiced consonants? Jane Darwell, her arms and stomach damp-ened by soap suds, is at the sink. She is saying something. It sounds like, Listen here, Sis . . . And Skipper stands in the kitchen, under the dangling lightbulb, ironing her brother's work pants. The roots of her hair are darkened with sweat: she sets her face, hard and passive, against the other. As daughter will. It is her I love.

From Sampson, Darrell sent me a final name. An object, an ar-tifact, that—had I had the fortitude to preserve it—might now be something to marvel at, sigh over, and display with a small laugh at all our former simplicities. A golden object, bright and openly cheap: a fringed satin pillow case with a verse printed on it in solid navy blue. To My Sweetheart. It rhymed—more than you can guess—with, your tenderness. When I took it out of its enve-lope I felt physical shame, and panic. There was no girl in my mother's house, no attic bedroom even, to which such an object could find relation. I wadded up the stiff cloth and hid it, far behind and under the paper dolls and coloring books I had never remembered to throw away. When Darrell came home on leave we went out on a double-date with one of his buddies. A sailor's suit makes him look able-bodied. When we parked, the others— an authentic couple—rolled magnificently on the back seat. We knew that we would not see each other again.

I still see Skipper sometimes, though. She is a young grand-mother now: sometimes stock-clerk, sometimes a shopper, at the Discount Department Store, and wearing—not aprons—but a pastel-pink pants suit. The suit was made on Taiwan, or in Korea, perhaps by other women whose fingerings, whose turnings of the head, ways of leaning weight on a hip, none of us know. Or I meet her in an office; she sometimes types or files, her ankles only slightly swollen, and she will answer the phone when Janice calls her husband. When Rosalie and her youngest daughter, again un-fashionably pregnant, pause during an afternoon of errands, Skip-per takes their order in the tea-room. In my office, which is low-pressure, all five of them take their coffee-break together at ten-fifteen. That's when I come in, some mornings, and I find them in the lounge: a circle of teased heads and girdled, substan-tial bottoms—a recipe exchange, a living newspaper of deaths and taxes. A catalogue of misguided medical aids and children's names and stuffs that do up nice and all the minutiae of women's flesh and bone. I stand outside and admire their solidarity, which ex-cludes me for good reasons. But I start to run again, to pound out my anger, when I see them twitch and wiggle in their chairs, crane necks and smile—giggle as we did together at fourteen. Himself has walked by and thrown them a liberal, Hello Dears!

And that, Naomi, old woman old wrack and wreckage, is why I think I shall come home to you. Or how I come, having run down, through something like beginnings. I never told you about the marriage. When I was young you always had husband or lover: you showed me what to do. And whenever you had slipped your bonds, or been escaped from, I was just tied. You sent me into the world to seek my fortune, as women (we thought) must; and sometimes—with luck—we met in lobbies with our fortunes in tow. Statistically, we met more often in kitchens, and one of us would lower her eyes, back down to the table, to follow the hand's scrubbing. We had our moments, too, in classrooms, in hospital wards, in backyards before everyone comes home. You helped fit me out—with clothes and advice, ideas and chamois buffers and much other outmoded, moonstruck lore, certificates of learning as well as Wasserman and Papp and frog tests. I came to learn footnotes and eye-liner, Kama-Sutra, the Skater's Waltz, how to use iamb and diaphragm. While you found me an abortionist, I thought of finding you a new lover. And believe me, it has all been useful. You always listened; gave me lodging for the night when I needed it; offered money and sent me on my way. And, growing older, I did the same for you. Yet we were always busy in our own lives, and you always took your hand away after a minute or two. I mean, you are not to blame.

I don't even know why you lie there, propped on three pillows and wheezing for breath, a bloated sweating, evasive-eyed commentary, an elaboration, on all our former selves. Nor will you want to tell me why you take pills, or drink, or did whatever it was you did that has landed you here. Probably you will tell me a fairy-tale, something about a tragic love. I will pretend that I believe your brave lies. Then you will be ready to listen, as you always have, and you will tell me with all your old fierce wrong-headed conviction, where I went wrong.

What I will tell you is that it happened in a taxi. Began in a taxi and lasted years. A good man whom you know and have treated as a friend. An adult male, a boss, of some learning and position, and whatever else one might ask. Well yes, we were grown-up and in the world, no barriers of taste or class to come between us, and he just the right distance ahead. He put his arms around me, naturally, and he said, You're tired, Darling. Whenever you're tired, Darling, your voice fades. Then I can't hear what you're saying. And naturally, he kissed me and I was quieted. It was the name, Naomi old friend, that quieted me. I thought that if he used it—with that authority and in that deep, so beautifully modulated voice—it must be mine. And he was right about the other thing. I was tired. Close to thirty and still lugging my little skate-case from pleasure dome to pleasure dome after a day of gainful employment. Still in fear and hope.

But he never found out my other name, and never needed to

ask. It grew harder and harder to imagine Darling, or where she
had come from, what she ate and where she grew. She lay in a
daisy-meadow, under a cow's sweet breath—she sprang, full grown
and all loins, from a bed of oysters. An islander, and another's island, cut off now from running. In what name was she to bless
the daughters coming up? How increase their inheritance? She
took to asking the mirror on the wall all kinds of counter-produc-
tive questions. You will tell me, Naomi, that I have failed: that it
is selfish to refuse the names the world has waiting for us: that I
have not been willing to love enough. And as usual, my wise
mother, you are right. I have loved neither you, nor Rosalie nor
Janice, not Esther-Jean or Skipper or the others in you, enough.
But let us begin. I am called Ruth. Entreat me not to leave you.

WHY I QUIT
THE GOWANUS
LIBERATION FRONT

ROSELLEN BROWN

This is the third time that ROSELLEN BROWN has been
included in the O. Henry Prize Stories. She has published
a book of poems, *Some Deaths in the Delta,* and a volume of short stories, *Street Games.* Her first novel, *The
Autobiography of My Mother,* had just been published
by Doubleday.

AND AT THE SAME TIME LEFT MY WIFE AND KIDS
AND FLUNG MY WHOLE LIFE IN A CARDBOARD SUIT-
CASE WHICH, IF I EVER PUT IT DOWN IN THE RAIN,
WILL DISINTEGRATE AND LEAVE ME WITH APPROX-
IMATELY NOTHING, GIVE OR TAKE A COUPLE OF
SUBWAY TOKENS:

Because on the morning of the George Street Fair, or the
George Street Street Fair, or whatever the hell it was, I woke up
with a headache that said, Take nothing for granted. There are
two kinds of people, my old friend Henry James once told me—
those who take things hard and those who take them easy. You
know. Beware hot dog venders who give the wrong change and
neighbor ladies who work for *Time* magazine and want your sig-
nature. Go back to sleep is what I also said, but I was supposed to
help erect a giant spider between Fontaine's and Rosenberg's opposed—oh how opposed—houses, and so I swung out of the
choppy surf of those sheets and summer blankets and began the
morning.

I went downstairs. What is this? I asked my wife, aflap in her red and pink kimono giving Tang to my children, who, male and liberated female, aspire to be astronauts.

What is what? she answered. The twenty-third of July? Saturday morning? A hot day even before the sun came up? The Borough of Brooklyn? Kix and Cheerios? What is *what*?

I don't like her to talk that way to me, it truly cuts me. But she is a sassy girl, I assure myself, the way you like her. She makes some worth-while trouble for you, pal. And is nearly black, just barely inescapably black and vivid and has given me these two maybe black and vivid children here, Sebastian and Nineveh.

Vivid they are indeed, now that I recall, and that was the beginning of this headache I'm holding in my hands: This very Sebastian appearing in our doorway at about two this morning when I was quite involved with his mother in ways not enhanced by conversation with a six-year-old. Can I get in between you, he asked with an innocence that knocked the breathless breath out of me (for we were fortunately and purely by chance modestly under a sheet in the street-lamp brightness of that room). But just to check I asked, Why do you want to get in between us, sport? All of a goddamn sudden?

And it was the usual sort of answer—either it was sharks or skates or sting rays, or something in that category of exotic predator that sounds like a sports car but is really an invading army in a technicolor nightmare perhaps the result of a wet bed, or then again brought on, poor child, by our indiscreet though wholly legal languors down the hall.

No you may not, I told him. Go back to your own bed where a big boy belongs. I was, mind you, disappearing fast from the warm clutches of his mother's invisible possession.

She gave a lurch and I was on my own. No, don't you say such a thing. Come on in here, honey. She rearranged herself cozily as though she was on the Flatbush Avenue bus and somebody wanted to sit down next to her with a lapful of packages. She does not believe you can ask a child to get back into a bed where a nightmare's been, even if he's well awake of it. But she is a thoughtful mother, soft, the way you like her. I told myself. So Sebastian leaped over me, putting his foot precisely down on the part of me already most affronted and bereft, and slid like an er-

mine, long and elastic, right between the fading warmth of the
two of us. I considered a hundred inadequate revenges and had to
settle—such was our arrangement there, utilizing the king-size bed
as it was not, believe me, intended—I had to settle for a quick but
earnest pinch of anger aimed at my wife's near nipple, so recently, fervidly hardened to my fingers; and of course missed, as
she turned her back to us both, and delivered an unfond tweak to
the meaningless goose flesh just under her armpit.

Now what is this? I repeated to Clarette—the winy name she
walks through her sober life graced by. Weren't you supposed to
be down at recycling at eight-thirty to set up?

Oh that. A wave of the hand. How can I blame her for not hurrying to begin a day to be spent in a booth under a huge poster,
big as a billboard, that features a *trompe l'oeil* painting of one
giant-assed soda bottle with a green tree blooming inside where, in
the good old days, model ships used to lie captured—and the tremendous and portentous words around the bottle: THIS (what?)
HAS BEEN RECYCLED!!! They are actually going to tote
along to their booth, these believers, these naifs of the nonretum-
able generation, bins full of green and brown bottles, lovingly
sorted, and enough bound newspapers and smashed tin cans for
another war drive. To demonstrate what I'm not certain: But if
the craftsmen can show their crafts and the artists their art, I
guess these noble collectors have an inalienable right to make the
most of their garbage. Poor Clarette. I'm in sympathy with anyone who doesn't get out of her kimono by nine just to help them
pile it higher.

I, on the other hand, am hurrying. I argued for a rat as the
proper emblem for our beloved neighborhood, or at very least a
roach, or coupling roaches rampant, to signify endless and reliable
proliferation. But it is the spider who won on the grounds of his
picturesqueness, his ready identifiability and, not least, a leftover
black widow, or whatever the damn thing was, from a block party
on West Seventy-third Street last year. We were assured no one
from George Street could possibly have been on West Seventy-
third Street on that day; they probably checked it out door to
door with signatures on one of those clipboards.

I was not talking to Sebastian after last night but he didn't
notice, glass raised, his other-worldly Tang quaffed in the gay style

of an officer lifting a stein in *The Student Prince.* Two weeks of
silence and he wouldn't notice as long as you didn't block his view
of the tube. Nineveh was painting her nails green. She would
soon, she informed me solemnly, be painting her cheeks to match,
alternating the green stripes with pink, to look like Minnie
Mouse. She thinks I don't know anything, of course, but I do
know a couple of insignificant items, and a fairly good grasp of
Minnie Mouse's physiognomy is among them. But I don't really
know what her generation is into vis-a-vis the Ducks and Mice; for
all I know Minnie's into orange sunshine or purple snowflakes or
harder stuff and has suffered genetic damage. Far be it from me to
intrude my advice, so I finished my coffee, warned them, like a
drill sergeant, to keep it moving, all of it, especially their mother's,
and left. There was an air of excitement that made me walk on
the balls of my feet, like the first day of school or an air raid.
Maybe when the circus rolls into town you feel like this, but I was
born in the city, East Ninety-fourth Street, so we only knew the
season by the big ads in the Sunday *Times*, which my parents always answered with checks.

Fontaine was out there standing in the middle of the deserted
street. There was one bastard who hadn't obeyed the urgent signs
we had posted on the trees last night: he'd parked his frigging little Triumph right there, business as usual, in the middle of the
block just about where the cuchifrito booth was supposed to go. I
want to bust his windows out! Fontaine shouted, that earnest little chipmunk face all gnarled up. Who he think he is, he see the
signs, by order of police, how big we got to make them? He spat
accurately on the dusty fender and a thick tear washed its way
down, showing blue underneath.

The others, coming slowly out of their shuttered houses, tuck-
ing in shirttails or straightening essentially unstraightenable Mexican shirts and Pakistani caftans, gathered around. Molly had her
baby on her back. Mrs. Olsen was coming at a run. They had sug-
gestions. Release the handbrake, roll it onto the next block and
let them deal with it. Festoon it with streamers and pretend it's a
decoration. I suggested we raffle it off. A couple of kids volun-
teered to kick it to pieces. We were still standing around, just
about ready to see if Mrs. Santiago could get it to levitate, when
this kid comes striding up out of the basement where what's his

name lives, the kid who does the rug shampoo demos at McCrory's, and without a word—not one word, of apology, of good morning, of screw you, folks—he got in, turned on the ignition, and swooshed the thing the hell out of our way with a thunder of hoofbeats, I swear, shouting Hiyo Silver, and left us our pristine curb with the only the natural shit of the day huddled in it like flowers crawling back into their chinks, and we could then begin to set up the Great George Street Follies in dead earnest and not without a few firstclass second thoughts.

Now let me backtrack for a necessary instant. How did this great day, this jollity of neighbors, this togetherness so unreal and off center it will surely attract the attention of the *New York Times*, ever manage to come about? That Chico Pacheco there, public spirited though he may secretly be, with his name like a dance, is working assiduously with hard-frowning Howard Peet in his approved-pattern sport shirt open exactly to the correct half-inch under his solid-state transistorized adam's apple? (They are putting up a stage that says THE WHEEZLES AND SNEEZLES PUPPET PLAYERS.) That Doree Rosenberg, whose cunning little face this morning reminds me of nothing so much as an olive that's sat in a martini overnight, or maybe a pickled mushroom except, if you can except it, that it's the high pink Revlon must call Kindled Spirits or Effort and Enthusiasm, is tacking up on an endless pegboard the *manifestaciones folkloríticas* of her neighbors, which range from some rather terrifying photographs of noodles and—dog food is it, with all those gaping pores?—to the drawings for some medical textbook of the billion channels and locks of the Isles of Langerhans and the pink pleura of what I would take to be the left lung.

How it came about was neither simple nor inevitable but it has its own kind of semifated, i.e., half-assed, probability to it. We got one of those bonuses in the mailbox one day; long after the mail had come, some noble volunteer spirit had actually attempted to find the appropriate orifice on these houses into which to thrust a mimeographed page that announced its democratic intentions by saying MIRA! and then Attention! across the top in that carefully premeditated order. The problem, you must understand, in a "semirenovated" neighborhood is that, after having failed to determine how many souls, drunk or sober, still dwell behind those out-of-order doorbells in the rooming houses where the mailboxes have few names, let alone current ones, then you have to decide just exactly what, on the blue or gold or flayed-brick houses, is intended to be the ingathering place for mail and *New York Times*. Is it that little straw basket that clings to the entry gate on leather thongs? Or the bean pot with fitted cover, or does that hold mung-bean sprouts ripening? Or—for the casual ones who take it as it comes—are you intended merely to fling the mail through the chinks in the gate onto the sodden leaves and old political and reupholstery ads that thicken the puddles over the drain? Is the entrance, in fact, in the basement or up the broad steps beside the magnificent double doors retrieved from that castle in Transylvania? I would rather canvass the World Trade Center, both buildings on foot, than deliver flyers on George Street.

Nonetheless, somebody did it. The flyer invited all "like minded citizens" to come to a meeting at the hippest house on the block to consider finding a new alternative to the block association. Well now. That wasn't a bad idea, I had to admit, though it isn't really the way I like to spend my time. The Block Ass. did generally innocuous things with its dues: bought those apologetic infant trees out there for the convenience of the dogs, then threatened with prosecution the people whose dogs aimed with deadly accuracy for their steps or those same hypocritically offered trees; urged you to vote, go pull the red lever for any twelve out of thirteen of Ali Baba's thieves for the city judgeships; lobbied against the bus that rattles down the block merely taking people where they need to go in the—ah, ghettao down they-ah. That sort of business. Turns its back generally on the real problems, say, what's getting passed from hand to hand to vein on the corner: things too sullying to see. Clarette went to one of their meetings once and, besides being ogled by a couple of up-tight assistant treasurer types whose wives keep everything in a bun with a rat in it, apparently mortified them by trying to talk about the real grown-up traffic the kids direct. You could hear them whispering to themselves if not to each other: But it's her own *people*. How can she say such scabrous things about those little children who could be her *cousins*?

So I went to this meeting. It was in the house of a writer, a cat who gets his kicks out of having six working fireplaces (half of which he had to discover under old wallboard, scraping, tearing with his fingernails like a man escaping from a high-security cellblock) and nothing but plants and pillows in his parlor. I think he's showing off his floors, which are half Peruvian mahogany and the other half Ugandan maple, or the other way around. We all sat around indirectly on the backs of those peasant wood choppers, on Peter Max poufs in all the forbidden color combinations, sort of waiting for the water pipe to get to us, as it were, and we all agreed—in our beards and boots and clean jeans and wash-and-wear work shirts—that the gentry on the block had flubbed it. True to their instincts they had protected their own little WASP hegemony. We, ah, we were all in agreement on that. But what to do? Invite squatters to live in the vacant buildings! Start a free school in a basement! Make the parking signs bilingual! Get a giant speaker and alternate rock and Latin music on the weekends! Get St. Anselm's Mercy Hospital to do abortions! (Half the women in the room would volunteer to have one if that would help.) Push the pushers to another block! Take down the backyard fences! Have a block party whose theme will be Discover Thy Neighbor! (since you will all be untimely ripped off together).

The writer's wife in velvet knickers and a gold undershirt passed around coffee and macrobiotic petit fours that tasted like you'd had a fever for a week; maybe even been in a coma. We agreed. We passed a joint to signify our accession to our three radical points that night. The light was dim; the fire crackled richly though it was May; we had vowed as homeowners—most of us having been pushed by the Misfortunes of Economic Realities into borrowing down payments from our capitalist parents, who loved to see us crawl into that hateful bag—not to charge our tenants more than three hundred dollars a month. (If we could help it, letting conscience be our guide.) We had decided to have a multiethnic Street Fair complete with police barricades at both ends of the block to close it off even to the rest of George Street, thus indicating true inner-block solidarity (as opposed to intrablock, which comes later). We would find a cause to use the money for at our second meeting, when we could fight about how many people could relate to flower boxes, how many to gas lamps, or to arts and crafts for the kids, how many to free movies—Regis Debray? Looney Tunes?—shown on somebody's back wall. And we were henceforth to call ourselves—perhaps we could even be so incorporated, the lawyers would get to work on it—the Gowanus Liberation Front.

And here we were. My patience had been frayed close to its limits by the trouble we had with our spider, who sagged, who broke his right mooring and came perilously close to falling in the face-painting pots. Finally, looking like a magnified rubber practical joke from a Times Square novelty shop, we got it to dangle firmly but menacingly above us. The man with his trucks full of rides arrived and tried out his generators; they were so noisy the only thing you could do was play music with a firm beat over them. The teen-age girls with their hair to their behinds—these were the ones who went to the private schools where they learned the Joyous Useless Arts—hung their tie-dyed and batiked and bled-upon tee shirts on a line with clothespins: such magnificent homage to the potential of human organs exploding. Well, sure I was still horny thanks to my son Sebastian's nightmares, but that one blond girl with her twitchy little ass in pink short-shorts was shaking out and pinning up the exact unbelievable colors of the orgasm she's never had.

And so the people began to arrive, right in time for lunch. The pigs' ears sizzled, the cuchifritos and the eggplant Parmesan competed, hissing. Children walked around with luminescent dots on the ends of their noses, peace signs on their cheeks, and at around one-thirty a beer-powered man, wider than the ferris wheel, scooped a shy skinny Spanish lady into the crook of his arm and danced in dizzy circles with her. A dozen couples and a dozen singles began to whirl and shake, some of them the fantastic triple-jointed leapers who tip in three directions at once, looking nowhere, straight ahead. What does it feel like to tell your body GO and have it make its way for half an hour without you? Ah, I thought, standing at attention beside my booth, why can't I fly? Why are the soles of my feet all tarred and sticky with seriousness and the bones of my rib cage brittle, my whole life aged? Why was I born to work in the office of a publisher of high quality bad news, all of us buried under a silt of words, and not to fight and leap and twirl around in the streets, stealing breakfast from uncovered trash cans and thanking no one? Clarette was dancing alone down there in front of her boxed bottles, her pointy hips making arrows that said UP and DOWN and oh glory, her whole slick pelvis lighting up TILT. I almost abandoned my place and went down there and took her home.

So it was lovely till then—the troubles of the day minor, the pleasures ephemeral maybe but tangible: black and white and brown groups appeared to meld and separate and come together again, though of course everybody was hanging onto the friends they came with. A trampoline broke and somebody got his shoulder a little bent but fortunately it was a grownup, not a kid (which is probably why it broke). Naturally he told us he'd sue; we told him there was no one to sue. How could that be? This is happening, isn't it? It's real, we're here, it's not a dream, so there's got to be somebody to sue. Bug off, pal, wait till we're incorporated. When we become an Institution, a recurring, an annual, a perennial even, then we can begin our joyous life of constant litigation.

The puppet show, too cute for words, couldn't be heard above the music, so all you could see were flowers dancing and big wolves eating up chipmunks and then cleanly puking them up again: the moral of it all, I suppose, being that you'd better watch what you eat because some of the sweetest ickle things are first-rate poison. My own kids surfaced from time to time to tell me they'd won a quarter playing some kind of unofficial craps down in front of Luis's bodega, or a two-mill grab bag of plastic monkeys for a dime throwing darts. I told them to stick with the craps, it paid better.

I was stuck myself, now, manning the cakes and cookies. It was dreary but whoever had to bake all this stuff in July had it drearier. The crowds danced up to me and back, always in cycles, a dozen at a time or none at all. I had a kid of around eleven or twelve named Wilbert helping me, skinny, very dark, and desperate to please. His shoes were shined. He told me he lived down at the far end of the block in one of those anonymous houses across from the hospital. (When he told me that and I registered no recognition, I hastened to assure him that I didn't know half the names of anybody on our homey block, I don't think he believed me.) We made a good team, he'd take orders and shovel the stuff together, I'd take the money and make change.

After a long time, having handed out countless cookies with rainbow sprinkles and cake that was losing its frosting to the heat, he muttered something about my not trusting him with the bread. I turned to say, What bread, nobody baked bread. But, smartass that I was, he meant the coin box. Well, I told him smiling, smiling, I didn't know if you'd like making change and all, it can get a little hairy—you know.

Yeah he knew, but he said he'd like that. It would be good practice for school and all. He was glaring at me; still polite but good at a kind of incipient militant challenge under the eyebrows. I found myself wishing my foulest wish, that my wife would sidle up with her Afro, her gingerbread skin, her raisins-on-gingerbread eyes. That wish alone should get me knifed in an alley, if not in my own bedroom. I mean I would sympathize. Furthermore, as the gods would have it, splitting their fat and sloppy sides, the whole of my dear wife aspires to the approximate color of the palms of her hands, the soles of her feet. I know she sees herself being sucked one day into her pale extremities, whoosh, all gone, her toes and fingers swollen; then coming out herself, rising like a flower blooming, a butterfly emerging, a parachute springing open, all bleached and wan and happy. That best of all places, that sherry-brown buttocks, gone maggoty-white like a Rubens: like a loaf of processed Silvertop rising in a plastic bowl. That day I will divorce her.

But she did not come to me now that I needed her, my *bona fides*, good dog, good wife; she could not abandon her bottles and cans, her wooing of the nifty faggot god called Mr. Clean. I was left alone to face this Wilbert, who looked ticked off at me, his hand clenched around a muffin, about to eat it, the ultimate vengeance: borrowing and bloody well not planning to replace it with a dime, goddamn it, stealing from the people. The people Unincorporated.

But then he collapsed, went abject. Forget it, man, skip it, no shit, he said, and turned to a customer. Did he see my fear? My power? Was he getting signals from a rooftop or wrist radio, something from Muggers Central that said *Lay off, we get that ofay muhfuh later, in his sleep* . . . ?

Just to show him I trusted him, then, I let a few minutes go by, sold a couple of deflated popovers and half a banana bread to that Martin and his tired wife in a silver pants suit who leans on him always, without seeming to touch him. Then I said with such casualness the kid deserved to pistol-whip me on the spot, bend me back over the daisy-paper tablecloth and knock my teeth right out my tailbone, Hey Wilbert, man, watch the booth a minute, O.K.? Just like that. Adding egregiously, TCB, baby. Literally. Do I like to dishonor myself or just my race?

Well, I didn't want to see any more of the fair, it'd been gyrating for hours just beyond my eyeballs and I felt a little queasy, so I went up my own steps and into the dark cool of the house.

Bad move. Every minute of this day had been flushing me with the unsettled feeling that I was approaching some last divide, some boundary, some wall—ultimate. Lurid. Real. I walked into the kitchen; the hum of the refrigerator greeted me at the threshold with its reminder of all the petty inefficiencies and annoyances of this overpriced pigpen. Sometimes it got so loud you had to raise your voice. It had no light, the week we moved in the bulb shattered in my hand when I was putting in a fresh one. Three stitches. Now, when I turned I saw the very ultimate wall in front of me, the frigging emblem of this life my wife aspires to while I aspire to her as she might be if she were me: *the brick wall*, hung with geraniums and frying pans and a plastic shelf from the Pottery Barn, from which lentils and almonds peek out of portholes like stowaways. The country wall that's a dead giveaway: worth two liberal votes (in '68, one for Gregory, one for Cleaver), a lifetime subscription to the *Voice*, a good double lock on the door, Lamaze lessons, and a TV set of inconsequential size crammed in a corner apologetically (on which I watch football and she watches Julia Child and the children learn their life from Scoobydoo).

I am too bored to move. No man can leave his wife and kids for reasons like these, he can only go on dreaming and dreaming that he will. Epiphanies are still for those who deserve them: who have a streak of originality left in them, obliterate good sense and bad logic and can fall down an endless rabbit hole. Talk about epiphanies: it had never occurred to me before this minute, this very second, that all the undergraduate-essay-style cant I scribble on my reports of rejected manuscripts every endless day of my working life is real. Means me. Epiphanies are not shop talk? Editorial shorthand for We'll Take It? Will *that* be my one epiphany? My beast in the jungle had me by the throat. The reasons in my life oppressed me, they were real, but I yawned. I positively gaped with the tedium of my tedium, ennui of my ennui.

I stood wishing I were murderous—*un crime passionel*, how I wished I could be roused to cut curse words out of my wife's grudging sides, or hang my engorged sex from the chandelier alongside the Pest-strip, the way they hang the tail and ears of the bulls who couldn't make it. Watch who you calling a bull there, baby, you a tsetse fly, the refrigerator told me. I reached in and pulled out a plum. What a good boy. Are these the plums, the very ones, shrivelled in their skins and the skins whitish as though they'd been marinated a century in Milk of Magnesia, that the good Dr. Williams ate and left that note about, that makes my neck crawl for the simplicity, the bareness of the means of fucking *genius?* They are sour and mealy and Christ I really do think I want to die right now, or sleep a good long imitation. I will crawl in this refrigerator and perish like those kids who hide in deserted freezers. But this pile of the landlord's crap leaks so much you couldn't assassinate a goldfish in there. I'll strangle myself with the telephone cord, I pay enough for it. I'll drink cleaning fluid. But the voice of the medulla just goes plodding on, my refrigerator voice, advising aspirin and bed rest: You just get on with it, these things can't be hurried. Sooner or later, rely on it, you'll catch something, kid; and then you'll go out fighting and kicking.

So I poured myself a tall glass of leftover rosé that tasted exactly like the discount it was, and went downstairs and out, belching. Everybody was gathered around the middle of the block where they were auctioning off an afghan that made my hair stand on end in this particular smarmy weather. Some people had more foresight than I, or they just liked to play auction. The price was stopped for a second at twenty-four dollars, but they were going up fast, killer instincts grappling, wives beseeching husbands for permission to throttle their neighbor's bid.

The crumbs and leftovers made my table a good place to stay away from, flies dive-bombing, ants beginning to scout the turf. And of course, of course, the money was gone. The money box on its side, clean and empty as a baby's mouth, and Wilbert, my friend, my assistant, *mon frère*, has split.

Or has he? I was standing there smiling the smile of the damned, thinking, if you want to know, about Florence: a jewelry store on the Arno, near the middle, where, window-shopping for some silver to bring my mother, I met a girl once who had the tattoos of hands on her breasts. I was almost free of the First Annual George Street Miasma, tracing a finger around those fingers that were huge, that were a giant's leavings, when Wilbert came up to me looking anxious.

So we did our little dance. Where is it, pal? Where's what? You know what. Oh shit. Forgive me, O Lord with your blasted ears who haven't heard a word of me from where I float trapped in this chaos, this egg of my life, lo these many years, but these are scenes I forbear to repeat. They are too demeaning, I get wound in the coils of words, of things as they seem, of this little kid, black till he's purple, a veritable eggplant of earnestness, who ends up crying real, or at least wet, tears, saying Frankie took it, I help you find him, he down by Anthony's but he tough, man, you be careful. He cut.

We trooped off to catch Frankie, who eluded us like a Casbah pickpocket or who, innocent, was just going his way. Foiled whichever he was, we walked back silently, shouldering our way through, to report the mess to The Writer, who was masterminding this whole exasperating Victory for Togetherness, and so I got to watch a man like me, an asshole that opens and closes to all the wrong cues. I felt, I know I look like this man, this William Buckley of the lower passions, the penultimate fool (when it is the ultimate fool who will save us). He considered Wilbert weeping. Wilbert wronged. One of these deep dark children—parents recent emigres from the most desperate class of abused plantation serfs, ah yes. (Check it out.) With glasses, indicating, perhaps, an effort toward study, toward application, hope and desire. Upward, onward and off the welfare rolls forever. The thieving little bastard, does he even *live* on this block? Or does he come to play the show like the cat with the Whizzy

Whip and the rusty junior ferris wheel? I don't know, I don't care, but his face was abused, washed with his desperation: He my friend, Frankie, he take it and say Don't rat on me, man, you be sorry.

So why are you ratting? Oh I am two-faced; helplessness is two-faced, his and mine. Or three- or four-faced if it gets the chance.

I don't want no trouble sir.

Don't call me sir.

Yes sir.

The Writer was getting impatient with us now. Did I have any idea how much was gone from the till? he wanted to know.

I had no idea. Was the money real? As real as Wilbert, who is not real?

You ever been arrested? I asked this kid whose frayed shirt was sweated through, whose baggy pants rode his scarecrow hips at the danger point. I'd hate to see him in his underwear, the sight of my chunky Sebastian in his shining Jockey shorts afflicted me: my boy the color, the shape even, of a manila envelope stuffed with dollar bills.

He hesitated. For suspicion once, he told me. He didn't have to tell me that, goddamn it, he would not protect me from himself.

I shrugged and went home. Just left him there to himself, thinking what he would think, victory or defeat: his own business. I didn't clean up my crumby little table. Too much superego got me in this mess in the first place. Let The Writer come and call me a washout, all-around four-star fuckup, I was finished for the day, if not forever. Let the ants and the flies divide the spoils, invite the spider down. They are not shameful in their dealings.

So you see, that's how it happened that I walked upstairs again, this time with my face set, like a man resolved on flinging a rope over the rafters. I packed my shabbiest suitcase, a faded plaid, like a wife going home to Mama. High melodrama: tossing things out of the dresser and halfway across the room so they tumbled open in a childish mess on the bed. My own wife used and ill-married, my children pinched between my finger and her thumb, my prick the uroboros, snake with its tail in its mouth, belly to the ground, ear to the sky, let it delight itself a while since Clarette, her head in *its* own mouth, barely greets it when it comes. . . .

All my loudest shirts shouted out in the dark of the snapped-shut case; the dashiki I bought thinking it was a form of flattery; the purplish pants that shine to mock me. All my fly vines. How Wilbert would laugh, is laughing, should laugh. How he'd like to own them.

I picked up my suitcase and trucked on downstairs. I left a penciled note for Clarette and our children, who, reading above grade level, were sure to read it with her. It was hard to write. What should it be?

'LIFE IS NOT A DREAM. CAREFUL! CAREFUL! CAREFUL!'?

or   'EXPECT POISON FROM STANDING WATER'?

then again, 'I HAVE SLIPPED TOO FAR FROM THE MASK OF MY TRUE
            FACE, AND SO I HAVE LEFT THE EYEHOLES BARE'?

or   'I DREAMED THAT WE ENTERED ROME AS
            TRIUMPHANT CONQUERORS. AND I THOUGHT OF THE
            ENTRY INTO THE ETERNAL CITY. BUT I
            WAS IN THE RANKS OF THE BARBARIANS'?

But why confuse the poor girl more than I must simply by being my ordinary condescending self? She has never had a literary bent but today is the last day in the world I would want to make her regret it. So I wrote simply:

DEAR AND DARLING. THERE IS NO OTHER WOMAN.
I STOLE THE MONEY. TELL EVERYONE.

Then, an afterthought, I added the I Ching I knew I would throw if only I had some pennies in my pocket. But my pennies had gone for change at the cake and cookie stand, I had cast my last little bread upon the waters and see where it had landed me. But I knew, I knew what it would be if I were to play it out, all six throws, and Clarette likes the Ching. It speaks sense to what little power we have to choose; speaks softly to her better parts and, miraculous, doesn't mess her hair much. I put the book in the last air space in my suitcase.

NINE AT THE TOP MEANS:

The bird's nest burns up.
The wanderer laughs at first,
Then must needs lament and weep.
Through carelessness he loses his cow.
Misfortune.

Then added, though it came from another page:

No blame, no blame.

Just let the misfortune not be theirs, I thought, let Frankie, Freddie, whatever the strongbox artist's name was—if there was such a person in sneakers, on horse, running across the backyard fences—let him not maim my children looking for me. Let him not abuse my wife's fallow charms no matter how she receives him, with hosannahs or with police whistle. But let there *be* a Frankie, somewhere, somewhere else.

It was hopeless. I squeezed into my swollen suitcase the skinny Saturday *Times* Clarette would never miss. I put two more stone plums in my pocket that bulged now as if I had a gun, and I went downstairs on tiptoe, closed the front door gently, and snuck off down to the corner to learn how the Gowanus Liberation Front had already put up its gates—for inner-block security and a hint to the likes of me. But I don't take hints easily; omens yes, innuendoes never, nor rumors, nor compacts nor conspiracies. Painfully I scaled the gates, dropping my plaid suitcase, my bandanna on the end of a stick, down on the other side, happy there were no faces looking up at it astonished, as if it were a bomb. My only misgiving, as I went over the top myself, was that its weak seams were already beginning their slow disintegration from the shock of the fall.

A CHRONICLE OF LOVE

H. E. FRANCIS

H. E. FRANCIS is a Professor of English Literature at the University of Alabama in Huntsville. His book *The Itinerary of Beggars* won the 1973 Iowa School of Letters Award for Short Fiction. He is a native of Bristol, Rhode Island.

THE CLUB WANDERER IS ALWAYS IN NEAR DARKNESS. Lights burn from invisible places. A crystal globe revolving over the dance floor sends out shafts, steady as a light at sea. Against the sunken glow the band becomes four living shadows. Front spots now and then thrust them close. During breaks, the juke blinks on for ten minutes, coiling blue-green-yellow-purple-orange over the faces clustered around the tables. At the entrance three figures, two women and the doorman, come stark against the lights whenever the door swings open. Through an arch, dim lights over the bar glitter—bottles and glasses, sometimes the flash of eyes or teeth.

The dancers are dark against the lights, silhouettes whose motion the music dictates as if with unseen strings, now leaping and veering, now drifting, swaying, or standing in a quivering freeze—but always moving, moving. The pianist's arms leap, the guitarists sway, the drummer goes frenzied, the vocalist breaks into the flood. Sounds drown over. From all the country around—and all the way from Nashville or Birmingham or even Atlanta, when there is a big-time guest star—the swingers come to hear the country western of the SOUNDS.

The day he was twenty-one, Lawton Wingfield's buddies said, "Field, tonight we're carrying you to a real place. Wow! We'll cel-

ebrate this here birthday like it's the *last*. If you don't get you a
good drunk and fun and laid all to one time, we been sure miscal-
culating. . . ." And Field did. Then, come every Friday, he was
back at the Wanderer as regular as work or church, a thing not to
be omitted without breaking his new rhythm. His whole self came
to be attuned to it. Going to the club was how he knew it was the
end of work week and the beginning. That's what he told everybody: "Man, when you walk in there, it's the beginning."

(*John Paul Vincent:* When I heard Field's sick in the city, I
went; but he wasn't in no room. Mrs. Warner said he didn't
hardly stay there a minute after he come from work, got him a
shower and changed clothes, and gone—she didn't know where—
cept she knew he drank, but never said a word to him cause he
was good and quiet, paid on the button, and she knew something
was bugging him. You all right, Field? she'd say. Right as the day
I was born, was all she'd get out of him. Field never was much for
talking, after Alice. Don't believe nobody ever heard him say that
name, Alice, one time neither, after, like the name died with her
too, or her name's just for him, I don't know. Can't be far, Mrs.
Warner said, he's got no car. Had a wreck, Field did, and lost it.
But you know, she said, I don't think he had no wreck. I think,
the way he looks sometimes, I think he let that car go, just let it
go, she said. What his friend Hadley said was: he didn't even hear
sometimes; and Field told Hadley: I don't know, Had, if it was
accident nor not, it just happened like I wasn't there. I seen—But
he'd never tell what he seen. That's how come I think he didn't
have no accident. I went looking—Field wasn't far: that club one
block off, the Wanderer, that's where. Says: Well, John *Paul*,
agrabbing me, and I seen that whole place come up in his eyes
like he's not going to make it, like I was something I wasn't or
maybe all of Greenville come in with me and surprised him,
maybe like it was Alice; but in a minute he's turned on again—
gone, way out, sailing like I never seen nobody. And *skinny!* Only
I was afraid to say, but after I did: you got to take *care* now,
Field, I said. Hooo, I'm in the best shape I ever been in, not
a ounce of fat and all hard's a rock, he says, never was this way
on the farm—*feel* that. But his face was like jaundice, no matter what he said; like a ha'nt he was; and I thought, He'll die

right here this night, he ain't going nowhere or moving in about a hour, but he's on his pins, high up like a jack, and *Je-sus*, you should of *seen* that mother! I sure in a hurry changed my mind. And he didn't stop neither. He went at it till the last lick, only I don't know what happened, he all of a sudden went, passed out. We had to carry him home, they got a doctor, he said You bring him around in the morning; but there wasn't no disease nor nothing *he* could see, but says That boy's so weak he maybe won't get up again if you don't see that he gets to the hospital in the morning. The doctor began to ask about family and all. I told him too, but looked like they'd do him no good here. Only Field come round after—I sat watching him like he was going to fade out— he said You better sleep, hoss—hear? The boys pick me up for work at six. And I slept too—I didn't mean to—and when I come to he was gone. Jesus, who'd of believed it—gone to work and back and that night dancing again! I had to go to Greenville. I had to tell his folks. He couldn't go on too much like that.

Reta: Where are you *going*, Field? I'd ask him, cause he was already smiling, he was on his way—like doped up or loaded or Jesus-bit. I couldn't think of anything else to say. He looked like traveling, he'd never stop, his eyes were seeing things—he had that look—and I wanted to reach up and jerk his head down and tell him Me me me, look at *me*, but he'd study that globe or the long lights. His eyes followed like they were real and he'd lose them. He made me feel like a *thing*, just nothing. I hated him. I did, I did, I did.

Marylou: Nobody ever danced like Field. I followed him around. I'd sit and watch all night, thinking he'd ask me, but once he picked somebody it was her all the time, he most never let up, held onto her like she's his life, and dance dance dance. When the band took a break, it was the juke, and he'd even bend and bob when he wasn't dancing, aswaying, like he was rubber and couldn't stop. Sometimes it was funny—I wanted to push him like one of them toy clowns with a round bottom.

Reverend Bullard: Lawton used to come to Greenville, to the church—I'd see him from the rectory window—never when there was service, always Saturday—and stand outside and stare. He'd be there a long time, walk around the grounds, and go back and look at that door, then go away. He never set foot in the church. Perhaps he'd stay fifteen minutes, half an hour. He never looked sad, no—but quiet and natural, a bit at home even. I never went out to disturb him.

Wendy: Call me his Tuesday girl. Every Tuesday, like clockwork. And all night. How'd Field ever get to work? Who knows? He'd leave me in bed. I don't think he even knew who I was by then. Sometimes he'd slip and call me Alice. Who cares? He gave me a good time and if I had to be Alice for him to make it that good, okay, so I'm Alice.)

Friday night

FIELD:
Like it says in the Bible, Alice, I come to a city over five months now, only it ain't like you think. Oh, it's all shining all right, them neons make it so bright you see it miles, yeah, it makes a great big whale of a light in the sky, a mountain you're going to big as a promise, like driving fast to, only when you get there, it come down, you're on it and can't see *it* anymore, just a couple of miles of neons, and they're pretty, they sure are, like an invite to anything you ever dreamed could be, you know, like the sun at home daytime only this here's here, makes you feel the things are so close you can grab them. Grab what? Well, I had to find out, you gone and all, and came here. It's a stone city, and days, when the neons are gone, it's like they just died quiet come morning, and the city's not even there, not the same one, it's a whole different thing, like it's got a mind of its own and a body too, you know what I mean? And days I get a hankering for green and dirt under my feet, not cement, stone, asphalt and all—makes your feet hurt, cept when you're dancing. I'm dancing all the time now, Alice, like I'm with you and loving dancing the way you did, and I got me some prizes even, they're yours, they really are; if it wasn't for you, I'd never of danced anyway, not one time, I don't know—maybe that's a lie, but how do you know? Anyway I'm

telling you, that's how come you know. *You* taught me—remember? Daddy said no, not to go, he'd give me the farm, always said I'd be him someday and my kids me standing in that
same doorway and looking at the view, and I swear to God I can
see the view right now bigger than the ceiling and high and wide
and so fresh with air, Alice; and Momma she said I'll not have a
body to cook for f-you go, son, and that almost broke me up. I
couldn't tell them why, why I was going, and you got to hand it
to them, they didn't prize it out of me, not even try cept
Momma's hangdog look when she wants to get her way, only I
still wouldn't tell them, in their heart they know I guess, I don't
know, and I'm getting letters all the time—oh, it ain't but a hour
from here, sometimes Daddy comes in to business, I seen him
bout a month ago, and he said Son, you looking bad, you better
come home, this life ain't doing you no good, but I said Got me a
steady job in construction almost five months now, I can't go
back on that, and he said Guess you cain't if you feel that way,
son. It's that *son* got me. Daddy he don't use it like that all the
time, son son son, like he got a hankering to. Well, ain't we all?
And he give me all the news, said the Hansons moved to town,
mister got too old to keep things going; Whip McCord gone to
college—imagine, Whip!—and Bethanne McCune married ole
Jimmie Haley—*Jimmie*, what never settled down one *minute* in
his life; and Willa Mae took a job as a librarian in town; seven
boys gone to Vietnam; and Wick—you remember how he pestered
me to go with him hunting all the same times I was sneaking off
with you?—the Viet Cong got him; and all the news, only nothing
from your house—that's how come I know Momma and Daddy's
sure why I come here without one time saying it; it made me feel
better I tell you, Alice, only cept when Daddy went; he said I'll
tell Momma we had a long talk; and I give him a linen handkerchief for Momma I bought one time for when she'd go to church,
you know when she gets to hacking and one of Daddy's won't do;
and then he got in the truck, he said Better be careful, boy, you
looking mighty bad, I won't tell your momma that; and I almost
couldn't see him when he said that, but it don't matter none's
long's I can dance, I got to keep dancing, it's the time you're
there, Alice, I feel you—you know that—and you know something,
Alice—course you do!—you know that ball hangs right smack there

in the center of the dance floor, it makes colored lights moving slow, every color, and when it hits, you see faces just one sec, like it's all a dream and you drifting like water's carrying you past everything far far. Last night I sure got going good, you know, I mean that music tore right through me and made my blood sing so it's going like that rhythm abeat and abeat taking me right up there, agoing so my feet's dancing on fire and my arms touching the sky and me like getting longer and longer till my hands near touched that light and it come in my eyes and made me feel all lit up inside and about to bust into it all and—you know what, Alice! —them faces bobbed and bobbed, I got like dizzy and that light white as fire and I seen your face just as clear, it tore me up, and I reached out quick and all that music saying *Alice* and me too *Alice, Alice*, and I must of passed out, I couldn't dance any more, or I fell or something, but my whole heart's to bust I'm so happy cause I seen you, I seen your face.

Six nights a week the band plays. They give the place a soul, slow and fast, always loud, a vibrating voice that trembles everything. All the place keeps moving, the juke instantly merging into their last struck note. One of the three owners is always at the entrance, a smile of welcome. Weekends Jaw sells tickets, fifty cents cover charge, for the whole long night; and Willyjo, the doorman, a kind-faced, ox-broad man not very tall, pounds his fist into his palm rhythmically, and taps, and rolls on heels and toes, arock half the night in a partnerless dance. When the door swings out, the neon freeway pours scorching bright light in. "Hey, Freddie!" "What say, Jimbo?" "You're sure lookin' cool, honey." "Man, get a load-a that!" "You'd cream just lookin' at her!" "Which side is up?" They laugh in the warm, near air and cigarette smoke and wafted alcohol. From a side room, especially during band breaks, comes the familiar clack of pool balls. Cries, laughs, jeers fill the room—JoePeteMiriamWaltBickWillaMaeLoisJimmieMurphAngie-Roberta.

Each entry shuts a door. Outside, a hundred rooms vanish. The world recedes into deep and endless dark. The Wanderer holds its own lights, faces, past—familiar. Ben, one of the owners, smiles. "Ready, Will? Say, Gert, another screwdriver here." The bartender, Bob, knows them all inside out and backwards ("You heard about ole Harry's pullin' a gun on that drummer last night? One o'clock in the a.m. the cops come, askin' where he headed—"). And the waitresses, Gert and Eula, are faces constant as drink, despite the shifting wigs and eyes and lashes and gewgaws and rage of outfits. And the other constants are there: the half-drunk little carpetlayer hanging on the end of the bar; the NASA engineer; the Fayetteville carpenter; the long-haired, dark girl from the Studebaker place; Alton, the Vietnam vet; Paul, the bootlegger from New Hope.

Whenever Field looked around they were all there. He breathed it all in deep. "*Hey*, Field!" "Hey, Ben. Hey, Eula," he said. "Bud?" Bob said, bottle and glass ready. "And a double shot of E.T.," Field said. He relaxed—back, as if at home, a family. Light glowed. The dark burned.

(*Roanna:* Met him downtown by Grant's this one Friday morning and I don't know what but something just stopped him cold when he saw me like he thought I was *some*body—you know, somebody not *me*. He near flipped when he came to. Me, Roanna Wilcox, I said. *I* know Roanna, he said, looking like he still didn't but looking hard too, and I put it out for'm to see too. Sure don't look like no country girl right now, he said. Pure country, I said, you *know* it—he ought to, coming from right down my way there by the Piggly-Wiggly sign—and I touched his arm, quick: You doing all right, Lawton? And just that quick li'l ole touch did it, he came round, he came right close like he's going to have me right there against Grant's window, and I laughed and said Now, Lawton, and quick he said How bout dancing tomorrow night, it's Sat'dy, and we can go down to the River Club after and never stop, what say? Why, Lawton, I said. Only he ain't so dumb; this time he reached out and touched my shoulder and his hand hard and rough-skinned it just sent shivers down me. You're from my town, he said, like it was the sweetest thing. And he made it that way all night too at the club and me thinking every minute Pretty soon we'll leave, we'll go it somewhere—in the car or the grass or back of my place, or he got a place, about to die with him rubbing me like that sometimes, and when it's over, him near passing out from dancing and drinking, and fell asleep on me and me on top of him to wake him up and go at it, I couldn't stand it, and drove back home alone without a thing, Goddamn it.

Reddick Farr: His daddy was the only one came. Mrs. Warner couldn't say a word to him. I said Field wouldn't have nobody around, a loner he was since he came here, only he didn't seem alone, he had something in his head, I don't know what. His daddy just looked at him. Said How'll I tell his momma? And it Sunday too. Jesus!

Kim: Always did prefer ectomorphs, and he certainly was that. Field was on the construction crew for the new building. He told me how he went dancing at the Club Wanderer. I got the hint and couldn't resist. And he *did* dance. You're a little out of my class, he said. And you out of my orbit, I said. He laughed, a rather boyish innocent laugh too. There was something terribly moving about him. I wanted to hold him and comfort him, tell him it was all right. And in bed when he was sleeping, I did hold his head, so thin and long his face, with long dark lashes, and long brown hair. But the rest of him was all hard, wiry, all energy— maddening in bed, with a terrible impersonal drive. I felt used, with an enormous indifference by him—and I wanted that.)

Saturday night

FIELD:
Oh, Alice, I'm telling you this every night, honey, only what can I do, me not wanting to talk to nobody, everybody's you—I can't help it—I'm looking at them, but it's you. Pretty soon I'm danc- ing up a storm. I know how it is: I try—I say I'm going out with Sue, Alice wouldn't want me to just moon like this; but it's be- cause *that*—you wouldn't want me to do it—that's why I do it: if you wanted me to it wouldn't mean the same thing, now would it, Alice, honest? It's cause you *don't*. Maybe that don't make no sense, but it's the onliest way I know. Mornings—not just one time, Alice, but every morning—since you gone I been waking up like I died and come back and it ain't real. First thing, I think The bed's *real*, I ain't dead, Alice's here; and for a sec I be-

lieve it too, I leap out and get in my clothes—it's like back on the
farm with Daddy and Momma, and I know if I look out the
kitchen window I can see straight out to the sun smack on your
bedroom window just the way I could nighttime fore you put your
light out, and me watching, like it's the moon right inside your
room shining for me—you saying Field, I'm never going to pull
the shade down so's you can't stop seeing me—ever. And I ain't
—I ain't stopped *one* second since I seen you in the river. Ohjesusgod, Alice, why why *why*? Oh, don't, *don't* answer me, Alice,
I can't stand that: I know it's me, I did it, but you got to know:
I'm trying, I'll make up for it, I *will* too, Alice. You won't be
ashamed your Field's just gone and forgot with no shame for what
he done. Listen here, Alice, ain't never gonna stop till it's done,
and I reckoned with it, and it's right by you, if it takes twenty
years—hear? You *hear* me, Alice? Why don't you answer me?
Alice! I been waiting all day for your voice, just one *sound* since
last night, cause I seen your face, Alice, and now I'm waiting for
you to say it so I'll know I'm getting there cause I can hear it in
my head, I *been* hearing it day and day and day, like never stopping, only I want to hear it *out*, I'll know I'm *with* you, in the
same place, I done it, and you forgive me and we'll be together. I
work like a dog, Alice, yes—you believe it? ole Field the farmer's
son working like a dog in the city! Ain't it a joke? But I got to, I
stop one minute and you're there and then I'd of had to leave
work and start looking for you, there ain't no way to stop if you
get in my head. It's all I can do to keep you back—*Till five* I'd
tell me, *Till five*. That's all I could do, even when you was there,
say *Till five, don't think about*—I'd not even say your name, but I
heard it and I'd work harder, *Till five*, and come five o'clock I'd
be in my room and washed and changed, only now I'm not even
doing that, I just come straight here to the club and get me that
cool beer and a double shot to begin and another cool beer and,
oh man, I can say it *Alice*, like free—and you're right there. You
come floating up, far—I see you, just like you was, only you're
now, in your white dress, all of you so small, and all your legs
showing, that little mini, and all your shoulders, I'm smelling your
long black hair on me. I want to put my hand right in the mirror
and tell you Alice, come dance with me, honey. And you know:
I'm already dancing, my heart's dancing thinking about you and

you coming with that white dress, and my feet's starting. That ball of light—you see it, Alice—it hits them colors round and round, it goes and goes, and band time it beats with the band, they send the old rhythm right into them lights and pretty soon they're going right into you, like they're touching and warm, and getting warmer, and your blood goes, it begins, it starts abeating, abeating, and your blood beats, abeating; and it's your legs beating, and your toes, and your arms; and it's all of you pretty soon abeating. I got to get up. I got to go get Alice. She's sitting there in the dark. She's at one of them tables. She's all alone waiting for me. She knows I'm coming. I see her eyes, all the light in her eyes, in the dark and holding it for me, yes she is. And I go right to her close, and I feel her hand and take her . . . and quick as anything it's you, Alice, you're right there against me so good it hurts, I'm about to bust, and a minute I shiver like, standing there and swaying, swaying, and I can feel it already going right into you, my hot and my blood like my skin's yours, and you come back into me, and me into you, and you can't tell which, and then moving and swaying like we're all alone, moving round in a circle, standing still and moving; and dipping, dipping; moving and moving; and the lights going round and round till it's like carrying, the music's lifting us and carrying. And I ain't letting you go, Alice, never a time: nothing going to stop us even with you klack-klack-klacking to a fast one and your arms legs and whole body and hair swinging and throwing and flying high and your bubs shaking and hips wiggling and legs leaping, and when I close my eyes feeling you I see you just the same through my eyelids, yes I *do*, that light comes right through, I can feel it—you believe that?—and you, I see *you* in it, waiting for you to come down, your face, and kiss me, only it don't. I keep thinking it will, I feel me getting longer and longer, I try, I keep reaching only it's like I ain't long enough, but if I got up enough steam and danced harder, I could move, I'd get so light I'd float up on the music, right smack up to you, and I'd feel your face against mine; and I get afraid, Alice: comes a minute—I *know* it's coming—and it's going to make me want to cry and yell, but I can't he'p it—I think if I open my eyes, I won't see it, but if I do it'll be gone, don't go, Alice! And it's water, everything's water, I'm looking, and there's your face, and all your hair, and the willow branch almost touching it, and a leaf floating by, and you still, looking at me out of the water, and I got to touch your face, Alice, I got to put my hand in the water and touch your face, both of my hands, I can't stand it, I'm reaching and quick my voice's saying *AliceAliceAliceAliceAliceAlice*, my blood's crying it, and all of me beating, and I open my eyes and a minute it's me under, and hands reaching down, but they're mine, going like *mad* like *mad* like *mad* like *mad* and you're there and you going like *mad mad mad mad mad*, your hips and arms and legs and hair and hair and hair hair hair hair hair drum drum drum drum drum woweeeee, we going and leaping leaping and pretty soon close rubbing and sliding, sliding and rubbing, oh baby Alice you going to make me come right here on the floor, slow slow grinding slow slow grinding grinding, and I'm getting there, getting on high, I feel it riding that music, that rhythm coming with a long slow heave, long long long now, and pulling pulling, and I'm getting there slow, slow moving up, up, oh Alice I'm going to, I'm going to, going to touch, right out and reach your face that's coming down to me. And then I'm waking up it's bright light I can't stand, sun, morning sun, and the walls all dirty wallpaper, them flowers like dead and dried in a winter field gone to seed, and dark ribbons straight down the walls, and that light, and them blinds making dark bars on the floor, my eyes're wet from the sun and the night before and I got to get up quick, I wish I was dead, my head's bustin, Jake'll pick me up in a minute. Good thing I'd moved close to the club or I'd be up the creek, only Alice I couldn't stand it, thinking it's the only place I'd get to you, and here I am dancing with you again, I'll never stop, no never till I'm with you 'one minute past eternity,' yes *our song:* and there I go, it's your face coming up close to the water, only like if I look long *I'm* under and looking up and you looking down at me, it gets all twisted and I wanted and I wanted to get out from under the water and *to* you. Sometimes I want to move my arms only I can't, like the water's holding them down, I want to scream then, only the water's filling my mouth and then quick the water moves and you gone, gone, Alice, and I can't see or yell or touch, thinking I'll never see you again, about to go crazy thinking that, and thinking you're getting even for all them girls I'm dancing with and kissing and screwing, but Alice, you know something: I get dancing and get me going and feel them warm and begin to *go,*

up, high, up up up, and—I don't know how come—but I ain't
here, I'm floating, oh baby I'm going fast so fast sucked up in a
thing so strong I know I'm going to hit, I know it—going to hit
and *pow* explode and go everywhere, smithereens, and then all of
a sudden it's you: *pow* and it breaks like fireworks and then honey
it's so quiet and you come so clear, clearest light I ever seen, like
you're close as that ball turning round in the ceiling and if I reach
up I'll touch your long hair and face I love: only somebody's crying, it's my momma—yes, momma—and I say Momma, what's
making you cry? like I *know* only don't, and Poppa's standing
there with his hand on her shoulder and looking at me like when
my dog Wilbur got runned over, and I *know*: you said to me It'd
get dark forever if I couldn't see you no more, Field; you said
There's no man in this here world for me but you, Field, you
know that, Field; you said I'd not live a day without you if I
thought you *believed* Andrew Phelps ever come *near* me cept that
one kiss he snuck and me not knowing he was there, it didn't
mean a thing, I'd of run, I *did* slap him too; you said Nobody
touched me the month I was at my cousin Willa Mae's, nobody
ever would but you, Field, and the letters are from a boy likes me
but you *know* I won't look at, I swear it, I'll swear on the Bible,
I'll swear before Reverend Bullard and the whole church Field;
you said What's in my belly's yours, Field, gonna look like you,
you wait, then you'll be ashamed you ever said a word, you'll take
it all back and love me all your life, you will, just you wait and
see. And oh, Alice, I do, I love you now like never before; never
knew I'd love you so much I couldn't stand even to live without
you. I got to go where you are. I had to find the way, Alice. I
come one night and danced and there you was. You was in my
arms, apressing and agliding, like a miracle come in me, and I
knew I couldn't let you go: when I woke up it wasn't you, but I
knew I'd had you for a minute, maybe a hour, maybe all night,
and I'd get you back: so I come here, I danced, I danced, I kept
dancing, I couldn't stop dancing, I can't now: I'm getting to you,
Alice, I know I am, and I won't stop, never, till I'm with you—
you hear me? And maybe you'll tell me it's not doing any good,
but you just wait till you see this time I mean it, I do, I'll never
stop dancing till I'm in your arms forever and you can't let me go,

I won't let you, only sometimes I can't make it, Alice, you know I
get to falling, I get so weak—me—go ahead, *laugh!*—me, ole
Field, getting so weak he almost can't stand up, but something
pushes me, keeps me going till the last song and then go on like
I'm dancing out the door and in the car and in bed even and
sleeping too, it never stops, the room's still athumping when I
wake up and all day that music's pounding in me when I'm bang-
ing nails and lugging boards. Come five o'clock it gets strong,
stronger every minute, till I'm back in the dark and that light
going round and the band comes *one minute* past *eternity*; it's
like you, I'm near you, that place; like I lay my head right down
in the dark against your skin, the dark's all warm, and you say
Come on, honey, come onnnnn, Field, we'll dance, honey, and
me getting up feeling you all soft and warm and cool too agin
me, and fore I know it I'm dancing, I'm swinging and swaying and
leaping and bouncing and jerking, keeping time, keeping the beat
with you and that music and that hot air touching like it's water
and your face under water, it comes, it's looking at me, oh-jesus
it's looking at me, and if just one time you'd say Field, it's your
fault; but you never did, nobody ever accused me but me, and
Momma and Poppa looking at me so soft and pitying like looking
at my own dog, and Reverend Bullard's soft voice and all them
people and nobody not one accusing, saying a word to me but me
me me me me

   The neon sign CLUB WANDERER burns around the clock. In the
sun it fades a sickly blue and red, but with nightfall it beckons,
stark and beautiful in the empty sky. With each opening of the
door, some soul loosed from the SOUNDS spills onto the freeway. From outside, in the night traffic, you would not suspect the
seething rhythm, the collective beat like a heart throbbing deep in
the night; only the parking lot, filled to overflowing, tells you
something is happening close by. During the week it is the lone
pool player, seeking, who comes, and the isolate couple, the va-
grant drinker, the so-called perpetuals; weekends it is the lovers,
mates—couple time, rest and desire, escape and search—com-
mingled with the usuals. The regulars know that if you go away
for days, weeks, months, even years, and come back, some of them

will be there; it is the place to find them; sit long enough and the missing will walk in, no longer phantoms from the past, for sooner or later nearly all return. "How's everything on the West Coast?" "Hey, man, ain't seen you since Vegas." "Lauderdale! Too empty. Nothing doing!" The truckdrivers make the Wanderer known all over the country. "Wilson struck a hydrant on US 1, off Elizabethtown." "Heard about Field?" "Heard about Bess Wickham's shooting all the way up to Dayton." "What's Larry doing now?" "She's making it in New Orleans, got guts that girl." Inside, they wait—for dates, loan, two-timer, wife-stealer, thief, friend. Nobody is forgotten. Away long enough, he comes up in the conversation. "Can't stay away too long, it's in the blood." They have every confidence. When the moment comes, the light is burning outside, a stark, beckoning sign.

(*Walt Everst:* I got there too late. His landlady said Field just got took away—to Greenville. Had to turn me around directly and go back home.

Sue: Why was he dancin' that way, for *what?* I wanted him—yes, I did, me, and I went through all that with him, drinking and dancing. My God, I'm sick of dancing; I never want to see a floor in my life, after him. Near killed me with his dancing. *What for?* He'd not answer, he'd look through me, he'd look like I wasn't even there. It'd make me madder'n hell. Sometimes I even hit him and then he'd smile or laugh and grab me, and what could I do then, I wanted him so? I don't go near the Wanderer now. I hate that place, *hate* it.

Mrs. Wingfield: His daddy stops and stands in the fields. I see him from the kitchen. He stops work and looks, like he's waiting. Only he ain't waiting. He al'ays did. But he cain't now. He keeps lookin' into the ground, and sometimes up. Then he gits mad and works like you never seen him go. But I know he'll sell it. He's waitin' for me to put my foot down and say no. He knows I will too: he cain't stop workin' and sit. He knows that'd kill him sure. Used to be he'd look out there like it'd just go on, somebody else'd come, and somebody else, somebody he *knew*, and he'd die comf'table knowin' it was one'-a his, like he had somethin' to do with it even after he was gone. But seems like to me now he just stops and looks up like he got no place to go.)

Sunday night

FIELD: Alice, you're talking to me, baby, I know you are—there's a sound I never did hear before in that music, like somebody touched the guitars in a way not before, and the piano and the drums and all together they got a extra sound never come before, makes my blood tingle and hum, me all humming, Alice, never hummed like this before; a sound come. What you think of that? A sound—it's taking me to you, I'm riding it, I sure am, Alice, taking me to you like it's your voice in my blood trying to tell me and if I open my mouth it'll come out—I will too, I'll open it—and *you'll say it*, me talking and you talking like one sound; then I'll know I got you, I'm touching you like that ball of light come to my hand at last, and I'll kiss your face happy out of my mind, blow it, and never leave you, whole hog. Only, Alice, sometimes my hand don't do what I tell it, or my legs, I'm dancing in my head, only legs slow or dragging and arms flopping—how come?—I *can't* fall off now, honey; it's time, been too long; and Momma come last night right in the middle of the night and said Field? Field? You hear me, Field? and I was saying Yes, Momma, only seemed like she'd not hear, saying Field? and my eyes wide open's could be in the pitch black cept for the light over the city. I come to a city, Alice, and Momma's in the city atalking, Field, son, we want you home, you got to come home or there'll be nothing left-a you, Field honey, and then what'll your poppa do, going along with you the way he done so you could try yourself out and then hopefully come home and take over the way he says you're supposed to, ain't no life this city life for a boy's got so much country in him, pure country your daddy says, says How come he's wasting pure country in the city, I'd like to know. Field, honey? And Momma's right there, only my eyes filled with that big dark and I can't touch her; and it's morning and Daddy he's standing there but real, says You going to a hospital, Field, or you ain't living long, and it's the first time I ever seen like a shadow of water in my daddy's eyes, and you know, Daddy he ain't never showing it, but this time ups and shouts at me A hospital, a hospital, you hear me, Lawton Wingfield? And you know, Alice, I had to out and laugh loud's I could to hear my daddy talk thataway, for a minute it was like *you* caring; and me getting up and putting on my clothes; Alice, I had to hang onto the bureau—you believe that?—and fell, I couldn't he'p it, but had to get out fore they called somebody, I ain't going to no hospital, and it's Sunday and the sun out and burning; everything's so green I think I never seen things before, a tad of grass around the house, but them *trees* swinging over the houses with wind, like you in it, Alice, it's *that* good: and Daddy's shouting at me, and me back at him, I couldn't *he'p* it, Alice, he don't understand, I'll go back home, Daddy, but you let *me* do it, I'll decide and then pop I'll be there one day on the stoop—okay, Daddy? and him standing there, but I know he's going to do something, I know it. So I got me away, I got to Bill Wamp's place by the church and sat in the fi'ty-six Ford up on blocks, up there on Ninth Street, cause I got this thing to do, my legs are abeat with it even when they ain't moving, Alice, like dancing in my head even when I ain't dancing, it never stops, *I* ain't never stopping cause long's I'm dancing I'm with you, honey, no matter what, come hell or high water: and your face in the river, the water's over it, only I feel water, air's all water, touching, only how can I see your face and it's mine too, I feel the water, only why don't you let me have it?—you ain't never accused me, only your eyes looking out of the river at me are worse than anything, Alice; if only one time you'd say Field, I done forgive you, one time Alice, I'd maybe sleep a minute and rest and think She's beside me, I don't worry none; but everywhere I go I'm seeing your face and eyes in the sky and trees green and the sidewalk and through that there Ford windshield and working in the cement and on bricks and in the dark worse, the only thing, like your eyes are that big white light over the city come down and holding me and never letting me out, Alice honey, only please please *Say* it one time: You done it, Lawton Wingfield, you killed me, so it'll be like I got down on my knees before Momma and Poppa the first time and said I did it, I can tell it all now, I did it, I didn't mean to, and to all my buddies don't know and all the church and all the town and God even, like as if *He* didn't know too, Alice; like it's this here Sunday and

I made it to the Sunday afternoon jazz session and they're all here
—like it is, Alice—they *are* here, every one of them—and you give
me the word, just say it, *the* word, Alice, and I can throw me
down right in the middle of all that music and rhythm and pumping and tell it like it was: I killed Alice Falls, my wife even if we
didn't tie the knot yet, and I was wrong playing around like she
wasn't even mine to make her jealous and love me more and not
be able to stand one minute away from me, and thinking she'll
come round when *I* want her, and she did, she did it like I told it,
and carrying mine and me not knowing a while and then when
she says it, thinking *she* been cheating the way I'm doing and
wanting to kill her and *did*—just by walking off and telling her
I'll never see you again, I don't want to see your face, never want
to look at you, hope it's born dead and you gone with it; and
packing my things and telling them I'm going on construction in
Huntsville, I'm going there and beginning; beginning, yes, Alice,
and it was the ending; Lonnie he come telling me first thing I's in
a room and making money and thinking Maybe I'll die and never
have to think about her again cause, honest, Alice, I never
thought of anything but you on the walls and in the mirror and in
the bed till I'm thinking I can't never sleep in no small box like
this room, no box of no kind, without I'm tight in with her and
going crazy out of my mind with her. Momma said She's the
sweetest thing this world knows, why'd she do a thing like that?
and Daddy and Momma and everybody I know at the church and
then Field, How come you stayed away? old Bickley says, and me
blind with you, Alice, ready to die, and couldn't stay away from
that church one day after and that night—you know what, Alice?
—I went there—sure you remember—and slept all night right beside you, me near dead too, wishing I *was* beside both of you, and
not knowing, never knowing now, who it'd be, like me or you, a
boy or a girl, or what'd it bring with it, maybe it'd have kids and
its kids like forever, and it cut off with you in the river and I'm
me wanting to know where you done it, how—you jumped off
that Runkley bridge way up where we'd go nights? or just slip and
let yourself not move or fall? maybe you did fall? Jesus, Alice,
God help me, it'll drive me crazy you don't tell me or just come
down, come down from that light going and no don't tell me, just
yell it out It's your fault, Lawton Wingfield, just yell it out,

yellllllll, it's in my blood, I can hear it all beating, oh Alice baby, you feel that rhythm, man there never was a band like the SOUNDS, and you dancing like you never danced before tonight, like we never *was* together thisaway, so close you're ole Field hisself, and that light it's getting so bright almost to blind me but I ain't taking my eyes off it one time, noooooo, Alice, you ain't leaving me tonight, you coming down, you coming close, you going to touch down with that white face and smiling and say Field honey, I love you, Field honey, don't never leave me; and I'm going to touch your face with both my hands, Alice, you so close you'll never get far from Field again, you feeling it now, Alice? that beat like it's your heart, feel it? It's abeat and abeat, uuuuuuuuhhhhhhhhh, man, Alice, it's bout to swell right out of me, it's moving and moving, it's leaping like it's going to bust out and go into this here room, like water, your face, come down, Alice, and kiss me and tell me it's all right, just one time, please, Alice, my heart's to bust if you don't, oh man, *listen* to that, that sound, that sound like them SOUNDS *never* made before, never, no, they going to carry me, oh that sound, Alice, it's going to carry me; look at that light, look, I'm looking: it never been so bright; Alice, if I reach I'm going to touch it, and I'll do it too, Alice, make my arms stretch out I don't care how long if you'll just one time come closer, say it; I been trying so hard, Alice, I never in my life tried so hard to do anything like dancing till I can't no more and every bit of me's going to you, I can't stop cause if I do, you won't be there; I'm afraid, Alice, yes I am, I got to tell you that, without you I'd die and I don't know how, this here's the only way to get to you, Alice, and be near you and never stop without you're in my arms, oh Alice you hear that beat, it's going, it's getting there, it's moving up up up, mannnnnnn, feel it a beat beat beat, my heart's going, it's going so fast, it's making—listen to that, that sound, Alice it's coming, it's coming yes from down in me, it's in my blood, it's coming from my heart going to you, Alice; you hear it? yes you do, you do, I see it, I see your face, it's coming, Alice, jesusgod you *do* hear, you coming down, that light's getting there, I getting to it, I *am*, Alice, ohjesusgod it's beating beating abeat like never, abeat-abeat-abeat woweeeeeeeeee going, I'm going to make I'm going to come right in my britches, Alice, if you, if you . . . yessss, bust out into the air, it's going to go right through my skin and into air and sweat and water and smoke and that light, it's so bright, and you, Alice, I see you, *Alice!* yes ohmygodjesus, Alice, thank you, baby, come on, come onnnnnn, we going to make it, we going to make it together, going to *be* there, I feel it coming, it's burning up up up, oh my blood and that heart's beating beating and this whole room growing and all light and you coming down, and now, Alice honey, your face, it's so close I can touch if I reach out with my hands, yes I will, I will, my heart's beating and my head and all this room, my heart busting out into this whole room, Alice, Now, now, tell them, *tell* them I done it and I made up for it, Alice, in the only way I know how, dancing, dancing, and to get to you, tell them. I'm burning, Alice, and yes I can now I will touch you; see, honey, my hands, they're moving, my arms, they're going right up to that light, reaching to touch, I'm going to touch you, I'm going to touch, I'm going to

SEPARATING

JOHN UPDIKE

JOHN UPDIKE was born in Shillington, Pennsylvania, in 1932, and has published seven novels and three volumes of poetry, as well as over one hundred short stories.

THE DAY WAS FAIR. Brilliant. All that June the weather had mocked the Maples' internal misery with solid sunlight—golden shafts and cascades of green in which their conversations had wormed unseeing, their sad murmuring selves the only stain in Nature. Usually by this time of the year they had acquired tans; but when they met their elder daughter's plane on her return from a year in England they were almost as pale as she, though Judith was too dazzled by the sunny opulent jumble of her native land to notice. They did not spoil her homecoming by telling her immediately. Wait a few days, let her recover from jet lag, had been one of their formulations, in that string of gray dialogues—over coffee, over cocktails, over Cointreau—that had shaped the strategy of their dissolution, while the earth performed its annual stunt of renewal unnoticed beyond their closed windows. Richard had thought to leave at Easter; Joan had insisted they wait until the four children were at last assembled, with all exams passed and ceremonies attended, and the bauble of summer to console them. So he had drudged away, in love, in dread, repairing screens, getting the mowers sharpened, rolling and patching their new tennis court.

The court, clay, had come through its first winter pitted and windswept bare of redcoat. Years ago the Maples had observed how often, among their friends, divorce followed a dramatic home

improvement, as if the marriage were making one last twitchy
effort to live; their own worst crisis had come amid the plaster dust
and exposed plumbing of a kitchen renovation. Yet, a summer
ago, as canary-yellow bulldozers gaily churned a grassy, daisy-dot-
ted knoll into a muddy plateau, and a crew of pigtailed young
men raked and tamped clay into a plane, this transformation did
not strike them as ominous, but festive in its impudence; their
marriage could rend the earth for fun. The next spring, waking
each day at dawn to a sliding sensation as if the bed were being
tipped, Richard found the barren tennis court, its net and tapes
still rolled in the barn, and environment congruous with his mood
of purposeful desolation, and the crumbling of handfuls of clay
into cracks and holes (dogs had frolicked on the court in a thaw;
rivulets had evolved trenches) an activity suitably elemental and
interminable. In his sealed heart he hoped the day would never
come.

Now it was here. A Friday. Judith was reacclimated; all four
children were assembled, before jobs and camps and visits again
scattered them. Joan thought they should be told one by one.
Richard was for making an announcement at the table. She said,
"I think just making an announcement is a cop-out. They'll start
quarrelling and playing to each other instead of focussing. They're
each individuals, you know, not just some corporate obstacle to
your freedom."

"O.K., O.K. I agree." Joan's plan was exact. That evening, they
were giving Judith a belated welcome-home dinner, of lobster and
champagne. Then, the party over, they, the two of them, who
nineteen years before would push her in a baby carriage along
Tenth Street to Washington Square, were to walk her out of the
house, to the bridge across the salt creek, and tell her, swearing
her to secrecy. Then Richard Jr., who was going directly from
work to a rock concert in Boston, would be told, either late when
he returned on the train or early Saturday morning before he
went off to his job; he was seventeen and employed as one of a
golf-course maintenance crew. Then the two younger children,
John and Margaret, could, as the morning wore on, be informed.

"Mopped up, as it were," Richard said.

"Do you have any better plan? That leaves you the rest of Saturday to answer any questions, pack, and make your wonderful departure."

"No," he said, meaning he had no better plan, and agreed to hers, though it had an edge of false order, a plea for control in the semblance of its achievement, like Joan's long chore lists and financial accountings and, in the days when he first knew her, her too copious lecture notes. Her plan turned one hurdle for him into four—four knife-sharp walls, each with a sheer blind drop on the other side.

All spring he had been morbidly conscious of insides and outsides, of barriers and partitions. He and Joan stood as a thin barrier between the children and the truth. Each moment was a partition, with the past on one side and the future on the other, a future containing this unthinkable *now*. Beyond four knifelike walls a new life for him waited vaguely. His skull cupped a secret, a white face, a face both frightened and soothing, both strange and known, that he wanted to shield from tears, which he felt all about him, solid as the sunlight. So haunted, he had become obsessed with battening down the house against his absence, replacing screens and sash cords, hinges and latches—a Houdini making things snug before his escape.

The lock. He had still to replace a lock on one of the doors of the screened porch. The task, like most such, proved more difficult than he had imagined. The old lock, aluminum frozen by corrosion, had been deliberately rendered obsolete by manufacturers. Three hardware stores had nothing that even approximately matched the mortised hole its removal (surprisingly easy) left. Another hole had to be gouged, with bits too small and saws too big, and the old hole fitted with a block of wood—the chisels dull, the saw rusty, his fingers thick with lack of sleep. The sun poured down, beyond the porch, on a world of neglect. The bushes already needed pruning, the windward side of the house was shedding flakes of paint, rain would get in when he was gone, insects, rot, death. His family, all those he would lose, filtered through the edges of his awareness as he struggled with screw holes, splinters, opaque instructions, minutiae of metal.

Judith sat on the porch, a princess returned from exile. She regaled them with stories of fuel shortages, of bomb scares in the

Underground, of Pakistani workmen loudly lusting after her as she walked past on her way to dance school. Joan came and went, in and out of the house, calmer than she should have been, praising his struggles with the lock as if this were one more and not the last of their chain of shared chores. The younger of his sons, John, now at fifteen suddenly, unwittingly handsome, for a few minutes held the rickety screen door while his father clumsily hammered and chiselled, each blow a kind of sob in Richard's ears. His younger daughter having been at a slumber party, slept on the porch hammock through all the noise—heavy and pink, trusting and forsaken. Time, like the sunlight, continued relentlessly; the sunlight slowly slanted. Today was one of the longest days. The lock clicked, worked. He was through. He had a drink; he drank it on the porch, listening to his daughter. "It was so sweet," she was saying, "during the worst of it, how all the butcher's and bakery shops kept open by candlelight. They're all so plucky and cute. From the papers, things sounded so much worse here—people shooting people in gas lines, and everybody freezing."

Richard asked her, "Do you still want to live in England forever?" *Forever*: the concept, now a reality upon him, pressed and scratched at the back of his throat.

"No," Judith confessed, turning her oval face to him, its eyes still childishly far apart, but the lips set as over something succulent and satisfactory. "I was anxious to come home. I'm an American." She was a woman. They had raised her; he and Joan had endured together to raise her, alone of the four. The others had still some raising left in them. Yet it was the thought of telling Judith—the image of her, their first baby, walking between them arm in arm to the bridge—that broke him. The partition between himself and the tears broke. Richard sat down to the celebratory meal with the back of his throat aching; the champagne, the lobster seemed phases of sunshine; he saw them and tasted them through tears. He blinked, swallowed, croakily joked about hay fever. The tears would not stop leaking through; they came not through a hole that could be plugged but through a permeable spot in a membrane, steadily, purely, endlessly, fruitfully. They became, his tears, a shield for himself against these others—their faces, the fact of their assembly, a last time as innocents, at a table where he sat the last time as head. Tears dropped from his nose as he broke the lobster's back; salt flavored his champagne as he sipped it; the raw clench at the back of his throat was delicious. He could not help himself.

His children tried to ignore his tears. Judith, on his right, lit a cigarette, gazed upward in the direction of her too energetic, too sophisticated exhalation; on her other side, John earnestly bent his face to the extraction of the last morsels—legs, tail segments—from the scarlet corpse. Joan, at the opposite end of the table, glanced at him surprised, her reproach displaced by a quick grimace, of forgiveness, or of salute to his superior gift of strategy. Between them, Margaret, no longer called Bean, thirteen and large for her age, gazed from the other side of his pane of tears as if into a shopwindow at something she coveted—at her father, a crystalline heap of splinters and memories. It was not she, however, but John who, in the kitchen, as they cleared the plates and carapaces away, asked Joan the question: "*Why is Daddy crying?*"

Richard heard the question but not the murmured answer. Then he heard Bean cry, "Oh, no-oh!"—the faintly dramatized exclamation of one who had long expected it.

John returned to the table carrying a bowl of salad. He nodded tersely at his father and his lips shaped the conspiratorial words "She told."

"Told what?" Richard asked aloud, insanely.

The boy sat down as if to rebuke his father's distraction with the example of his own good manners and said quietly, "The separation."

Joan and Margaret returned; the child, in Richard's twisted vision, seemed diminished in size, and relieved, relieved to have had the boogeyman at last proved real. He called out to her—the distances at the table had grown immense—"You knew, you always knew," but the clenching at the back of his throat prevented him from making sense of it. From afar he heard Joan talking, levelly, sensibly, reciting what they had prepared: it was a separation for the summer, an experiment. She and Daddy both agreed it would be good for them; they needed space and time to think; they liked each other but did not make each other happy enough, somehow.

Judith, imitating her mother's factual tone, but in her youth

off-key, too cool, said, "I think it's silly. You should either live together or get divorced."

Richard's crying, like a wave that has crested and crashed, had
become tumultuous; but it was overtopped by another tumult, for
John, who had been so reserved, now grew larger and larger at the
table. Perhaps his younger sister's being credited with knowing set
him off. "Why didn't you *tell* us?" he asked, in a large round
voice quite unlike his own. "You should have *told* us you weren't
getting along."

Richard was startled into attempting to force words through his
tears. "We *do* get along, that's the trouble, so it doesn't show
even to us—" "That we do not love each other" was the rest of
the sentence; he couldn't finish it.

Joan finished for him, in her style. "And we've always, *especially*, loved our children."

John was not mollified. "What do you care about *us?*" he
boomed. "We're just little things you *had.*" His sisters' laughing
forced a laugh from him, which he turned hard and parodis-
tic: "Ha ha *ha.*" Richard and Joan realized simultaneously that
the child was drunk, on Judith's homecoming champagne. Feeling
bound to keep the center of the stage, John took a cigarette from
Judith's pack, poked it into his mouth, let it hang from his lower
lip, and squinted like a gangster.

"You're not little things we had," Richard called to him.
"You're the whole point. But you're grown. Or almost."

The boy was lighting matches. Instead of holding them to his
cigarette (for they had never seen him smoke; being "good" had
been his way of setting himself apart), he held them to his
mother's face, closer and closer, for her to blow out. Then he lit
the whole folder—a hiss and then a torch, held against his
mother's face. Prismed by his tears, the flame filled Richard's vision; he didn't know how it was extinguished. He heard Margaret
say, "Oh stop showing off," and saw John, in response, break the
cigarette in two and put the halves entirely into his mouth and
chew, sticking out his tongue to display the shreds to his sister.

Joan talked to him, reasoning—a fountain of reason, unintelligi-
ble. "Talked about it for years . . . our children must help us . . .
Daddy and I both want . . ." As the boy listened, he carefully
wadded a paper napkin into the leaves of his salad, fashioned a

ball of paper and lettuce, and popped it into his mouth, looking around the table for the expected laughter. None came. Judith said, "Be mature," and dismissed a plume of smoke.

Richard got up from this stifling table and led the boy outside. Though the house was in twilight, the outdoors still brimmed with light, the long waste light of high summer. Both laughing, he supervised John's spitting out the lettuce and paper and tobacco into the pachysandra. He took him by the hand—a square gritty hand, but for its softness a man's. Yet, it held on. They ran together up into the field, past the tennis court. The raw banking left by the bulldozers was dotted with daisies. Past the court and a flat stretch where they used to play family baseball stood a soft green rise glorious in the sun, each weed and species of grass distinct as illumination on parchment. "I'm sorry, so sorry," Richard cried. "You were the only one who ever tried to help me with all the goddam jobs around this place."

Sobbing, safe within his tears and the champagne, John explained, "It's not just the separation, it's the whole crummy year, I *hate* that school, you can't make any friends, the history teacher's a scud."

They sat on the crest of the rise, shaking and warm from their tears but easier in their voices, and Richard tried to focus on the child's sad year—the weekdays long with homework, the weekends spent in his room with model airplanes, while his parents murmured down below, nursing their separation. How selfish, how blind, Richard thought; his eyes felt scoured. He told his son, "We'll think about getting you transferred. Life's too short to be miserable."

They had said what they could, but did not want the moment to heal, and talked on, about the school, about the tennis court, whether it would ever again be as good as it had been that first summer. They walked to inspect it and pressed a few more tapes more firmly down. A little stiltedly, perhaps trying to make too much of the moment, to prolong it, Richard led the boy to the spot in the field where the view was best, of the metallic blue river, the emerald marsh, the scattered islands velvet with shadow in the low light, the white bits of beach far away. "See," he said. "It goes on being beautiful. It'll be here tomorrow."

"I know," John answered, impatiently. The moment had closed.

Back in the house, the others had opened some white wine, the champagne being drunk, and still sat at the table, the three females, gossiping. Where Joan sat had become the head. She turned, showing him a tearless face, and asked, "All right?"

"We're fine," he said, resenting it, though relieved, that the party went on without him.

In bed she explained, "I couldn't cry I guess because I cried so much all spring. It really wasn't fair. It's your idea, and you made it look as though I was kicking you out."

"I'm sorry," he said. "I couldn't stop. I wanted to but couldn't."

"You *didn't* want to. You loved it. You were having your way, making a general announcement."

"I love having it over," he admitted. "God, those kids were great. So brave and funny." John, returned to the house, had settled to a model airplane in his room, and kept shouting down to them, "I'm O.K. No sweat." "And the way," Richard went on, cozy in his relief, "they never questioned the reasons we gave. No thought of a third person. Not even Judith."

"That *was* touching," Joan said.

He gave her a hug. "You were great too. Thank you." Guiltily, he realized he did not feel separated.

"You still have Dickie to do," she told him. These words set before him a black mountain in the darkness; its cold breath, its near weight affected his chest. Of the four children Dickie was most nearly his conscience. Joan did not need to add, "That's one piece of your dirty work I won't do for you."

"I know. I'll do it. You go to sleep."

Within minutes, her breathing slowed, became oblivious and deep. It was quarter to midnight. Dickie's train from the concert would come in at one-fourteen. Richard set the alarm for one. He had slept atrociously for weeks. But whenever he closed his lids some glimpse of the last hours scorched them—Judith exhaling toward the ceiling in a kind of aversion, Bean's mute staring, the sunstruck growth of the field where he and John had rested. The mountain before him moved closer, moved within him; he was huge, momentous. The ache at the back of his throat felt stale. His wife slept as if slain beside him. When, exasperated by his hot lids, his crowded heart, he rose from bed and dressed, she awoke enough to turn over. He told her then, "If I could undo it all, I would."

"Where would you begin?" she asked. There was no place. Giving him courage, she was always giving him courage. He put on shoes without socks in the dark. The children were breathing in their rooms, the downstairs was hollow. In their confusion they had left lights burning. He turned off all but one, the kitchen overhead. The car started. He had hoped it wouldn't. He met only moonlight on the road; it seemed a diaphanous companion, flickering in the leaves along the roadside, haunting his rearview mirror like a pursuer, melting under his headlights. The center of town, not quite deserted, was eerie at this hour. A young cop in uniform kept company with a gang of T-shirted kids on the steps of the bank. Across from the railroad station, several bars kept open. Customers, mostly young, passed in and out of the warm night, savoring summer's novelty. Voices shouted from cars as they passed; an immense conversation seemed in progress. Richard parked and in his weariness put his head on the passenger seat, out of the commotion and wheeling lights. It was as when, in the movies, an assassin grimly carries his mission through the jostle of a carnival—except the movies cannot show the precipitous, palpable slope you cling to within. You cannot climb back down; you can only fall. The synthetic fabric of the car seat, warmed by his cheek, confided to him an ancient, distant scent of vanilla.

A train whistle caused him to lift his head. It was on time; he had hoped it would be late. The slender drawgates descended. The bell of approach tingled happily. The great metal body, horizontally fluted, rocked to a stop, and sleepy teen-agers disembarked, his son among them. Dickie did not show surprise that his father was meeting him at this terrible hour. He sauntered to the car with two friends, both taller than he. He said "Hi" to his father and took the passenger's seat with an exhausted promptness that expressed gratitude. The friends got into the back, and Richard was grateful; a few more minutes' postponement would be won by driving them home.

He asked, "How was the concert?"

"Groovy," one boy said from the back seat.

"It bit," the other said.

"It was O.K.," Dickie said, moderate by nature, so reasonable that in his childhood the unreason of the world had given him headaches, stomach aches, nausea. When the second friend had been dropped off at his dark house, the boy blurted, "Dad, my eyes are killing me with hay fever! I'm out there cutting that mothering grass all day!"

"Do we still have those drops?"

"They didn't do any good last summer."

"They might this." Richard swung a U-turn on the empty street. The drive home took a few minutes. The mountain was here, in his throat. "Richard," he said, and felt the boy, slumped and rubbing his eyes, go tense at his tone, "I didn't come to meet you just to make your life easier. I came because your mother and I have some news for you, and you're a hard man to get ahold of these days. It's sad news."

"That's O.K." The reassurance came out soft, but quick, as if released from the tip of a spring.

Richard had feared that his tears would return and choke him, but the boy's manliness set an example, and his voice issued forth steady and dry. "It's sad news, but it needn't be tragic news, at least for you. It should have no practical effect on your life, though it's bound to have an emotional effect. You'll work at your job, and go back to school in September. Your mother and I are really proud of what you're making of your life; we don't want that to change at all."

"Yeah," the boy said lightly, on the intake of his breath, holding himself up. They turned the corner; the church they went to loomed like a gutted fort. The home of the woman Richard hoped to marry stood across the green. Her bedroom light burned.

"Your mother and I," he said, "have decided to separate. For the summer. Nothing legal, no divorce yet. We want to see how it feels. For some years now, we haven't been doing enough for each other, making each other as happy as we should be. Have you sensed that?"

"No," the boy said. It was an honest, unemotional answer: true or false in a quiz.

Glad for a factual basis, Richard pursued, even garrulously, the details. His apartment across town, his utter accessibility, the split vacation arrangements, the advantages to the children, the added mobility and variety of the summer. Dickie listened, absorbing. "Do the others know?"

Richard described how they had been told.

"How did they take it?"

"The girls pretty calmly. John flipped out; he shouted and ate a cigarette and made a salad out of his napkin and told us how much he hated school."

His brother chuckled. "He did?"

"Yeah. The school issue was more upsetting for him than Mom and me. He seemed to feel better for having exploded."

"He did?" The repetition was the first sign that he was stunned.

"Yes. Dickie, I want to tell you something. This last hour, waiting for your train to get in, has been about the worst of my life. I hate this. *Hate* it. My father would have died before doing it to me." He felt immensely lighter, saying this. He had dumped the mountain on the boy. They were home. Moving swiftly as a shadow, Dickie was out of the car, through the bright kitchen. Richard called after him, "Want a glass of milk or anything?"

"No thanks."

"Want us to call the course tomorrow and say you're too sick to work?"

"No, that's all right." The answer was faint, delivered at the door to his room; Richard listened for the slam of a tantrum. The door closed normally. The sound was sickening.

Joan had sunk into that first deep trough of sleep and was slow to awake. Richard had to repeat, "I told him."

"What did he say?"

"Nothing much. Could you go say good night to him? Please."

She left their room, without putting on a bathrobe. He sluggishly changed back into his pajamas and walked down the hall. Dickie was already in bed, Joan was sitting beside him, and the boy's bedside clock radio was murmuring music. When she stood, an inexplicable light—the moon?—outlined her body through the nightie. Richard sat on the warm place she had indented on the child's narrow mattress. He asked him, "Do you want the radio on like that?"

"It always is."

"Doesn't it keep you awake? It would me."

"No."

"Are you sleepy?"

"Yeah."

"Good. Sure you want to get up and go to work? You've had a big night."

"I want to."

Away at school this winter he had learned for the first time that you can go short of sleep and live. As an infant he had slept with an immobile, sweating intensity that had alarmed his babysitters. As the children aged, he became the first to go to bed, earlier for a time than his younger brother and sister. Even now, he would go slack in the middle of a television show, his sprawled legs hairy and brown. "O.K. Good boy. Dickie, listen. I love you so much, I never knew how much until now. No matter how this works out, I'll always be with you. Really."

Richard bent to kiss an averted face but his son, sinewy, turned and with wet cheeks embraced him and gave him a kiss, on the lips, passionate as a woman's. In his father's ear he moaned one word, the crucial, intelligent word: *"Why?"*

Why. It was a whistle of wind in a crack, a knife thrust, a window thrown open on emptiness. The white face was gone, the darkness was featureless. Richard had forgotten why.

MAGAZINES CONSULTED

American Review—Bantam Books, 666 Fifth Avenue, New York, N.Y. 10019
Antaeus—Ecco Press—1 West 30th Street, New York, N.Y. 10001
Antioch Review—P. O. Box 148, Yellow Springs, Ohio 45387
Aphra—Box 3551, Springtown, Pa. 18081
Appalachian Journal—Box 536, Appalachian State University, Boone, N.C. 28607
Ararat—Armenian General Benevolent Union of America, 628 Second Avenue, New York, N.Y. 10016
Arizona Quarterly—University of Arizona, Tucson, Ariz. 85721
The Ark River Review—519 Montgomery Avenue, Haverford, Pa. 19041
Aspen Leaves—Box 3185, Aspen, Colorado 81611
The Atlantic Monthly—8 Arlington Street, Boston, Mass. 02116
California Quarterly—100 Sproul Hall, University of California, Davis, Calif. 95616
Canadian Fiction Magazine—P. O. Box 46422, Station G, Vancouver, B.C., Canada V6R 4G7
Carleton Miscellany—Carleton College, Northfield, Minn. 55057
Carolina Quarterly—Box 1117, Chapel Hill, N.C. 27515
The Chariton Review—Division of Language & Literature, Northeast Missouri State University, Kirksville, Mo. 63501
Colorado Quarterly—Hellums 118, University of Colorado, Boulder, Colo. 80304
The Colorado State Review—360 Liberal Arts, Colorado State University, Fort Collins, Colo. 80521
Commentary—165 East 56th Street, New York, N.Y. 10022
Confrontation—English Department, Brooklyn Center of Long Island University, Brooklyn, N.Y. 11201
Cosmopolitan—224 West 57th Street, New York, N.Y. 10019

Cutbank—c/o English Dept., University of Montana, Missoula, Mont. 59801

December—P. O. Box 274, Western Springs, Ill. 60558

The Denver Quarterly—Dept. of English, University of Denver, Denver, Colo. 80210

Descant—Dept. of English, TCU Station, Fort Worth, Tex. 76129

dog soldier—323 East Boone, Spokane, Wash. 99202

Epoch—159 Goldwyn Smith Hall, Cornell University, Ithaca, N.Y. 14850

Esquire—488 Madison Avenue, New York, N.Y. 10022

The Falcon—Mansfield State College, Mansfield, Pa. 16933

Fantasy and Science Fiction—Box 56, Cornwall, Conn. 06753

The Fault—41186 Alice Avenue, Fremont, Calif. 94538

Fiction—c/o Dept. of English, The City College of New York, N.Y. 10031

Fiction International—Dept. of English, St. Lawrence University, Canton, N.Y. 13617

The Fiddlehead—Dept. of English, University of New Brunswick, Fredericton, N.B., Canada

The Fisherman's Angle—St. John Fisher College, Rochester, N.Y. 14618

Forum—Ball State University, Muncie, Ind. 47306

Four Quarters—La Salle College, Philadelphia, Pa. 19141

Gay Literature—Daniel Curzon, English Dept., State University of California, Fresno, Calif. 93740

Georgia Review—University of Georgia, Athens, Ga. 30601

Graffiti—Box 418, Lenoir Rhyne College, Hickory, N.C. 28601

The Great Lakes Review—Northeastern Illinois University, Chicago, Ill. 60625

Green River Review—Box 56, University Center, Mich. 48710

The Greensboro Review—University of North Carolina, Greensboro, N.C. 27412

Harper's Magazine—2 Park Avenue, New York, N.Y. 10016

Hawaii Review—Hemenway Hall, University of Hawaii, Honolulu, Haw. 96822

Hudson Review—65 East 55th Street, New York, N.Y. 10022

Intro 6—Anchor Press/Doubleday, Garden City, N.Y. 11530

The Iowa Review—EPB 453, University of Iowa, Iowa City, Iowa 52240

Kansas Quarterly—Dept. of English, Kansas State University, Manhattan, Kan. 66502

Kineo Writing—Kineo Island Club, Rockwood, Me. 04478

Ladies' Home Journal—641 Lexington Avenue, New York, N.Y. 10022

The Literary Review—Fairleigh Dickinson University, Teaneck, N.J. 07666

The Little Magazine—P. O. Box 207, Cathedral Station, New York, N.Y. 10025

Lotus—Department of English, Ohio University, Athens, Ohio 45701

Mademoiselle—350 Madison Avenue, New York, N.Y. 10017

Malahat Review—University of Victoria, Victoria, B.C., Canada

The Massachusetts Review—University of Massachusetts, Amherst, Mass. 01003

McCall's—230 Park Avenue, New York, N.Y. 10017

The Mediterranean Review—Orient, N.Y. 11957

Michigan Quarterly Review—3032 Rackham Bldg., The University of Michigan, Ann Arbor, Mich. 48104

Midstream—515 Park Avenue, New York, N.Y. 10022

Mundus Artium—Dept. of English, Ellis Hall, Box 89, Ohio University, Athens, Ohio 45701

The National Jewish Monthly—1640 Rhode Island Avenue, N.W., Washington, D.C. 20036

New Directions—333 Sixth Avenue, New York, N.Y. 10014

New Letters—University of Missouri–Kansas City, Kansas City, Mo. 64110

The New Renaissance—9 Heath Road, Arlington, Mass. 02174

The New Yorker—25 West 43rd Street, New York, N.Y. 10036

The North American Review—University of Northern Iowa, 1222 West 27th Street, Cedar Falls, Iowa 50613

Northwest Review—129 French Hall, University of Oregon, Eugene, Ore. 97403

The Ohio Journal—164 West 17th Avenue, Columbus, Ohio 43210

Ohio Review—Ellis Hall, Ohio University, Athens, Ohio 45701

The Ontario Review—6000 Riverside Drive East, Windsor, Ont., Canada N8S 1B6

Panache—P. O. Box 89, Princeton, N.J. 08540

The Paris Review—45-39-171st Place, Flushing, N.Y. 11358

Partisan Review—Rutgers University, New Brunswick, N.J. 08903

Perspective—Washington University, St. Louis, Mo. 63130

Phylon—223 Chestnut Street, S.W., Atlanta, Ga. 30314

Playboy—919 N. Michigan Avenue, Chicago, Ill. 60611

Ploughshares—Box 529, Cambridge, Mass. 02139

Prairie Schooner—Andrews Hall, University of Nebraska, Lincoln, Nebr. 68508

Prism International—Dept. of Creative Writing, University of British Columbia, Vancouver 8, B.C., Canada

Quarterly Review of Literature—26 Haslet Avenue, Princeton, N.J. 08540

Quartet—1119 Neal Pickett Drive, College station, Tex. 77840

Ramparts—2749 Hyde Street, San Francisco, Calif. 94105

Redbook—230 Park Avenue, New York, N.Y. 10017

The Remington Review—505 Westfield Avenue, Elizabeth, N.J. 07208

Rolling Stone—625 Third Street, San Francisco, Calif. 94107

Saltillo—201 Andrews Hall, University of Nebraska, Lincoln, Nebr. 68508

Seneca Review—Box 115, Hobart & William Smith Colleges, Geneva, N.Y. 14456

Sequoia—Storke Student Publications Bldg., Stanford, Calif. 94305

The Sewanee Review—University of the South, Sewanee, Tenn. 37375

Shenandoah—Box 722, Lexington, Va. 24450

The Smith—5 Beekman Street, New York, N.Y. 10038

The South Carolina Review—Dept. of English, Clemson University, Clemson, S.C. 29631

The South Dakota Review—Box 111, University Exchange, Vermillion, S.D. 57069

Southern Humanities Review—Auburn University, Auburn, Ala. 36820

Southern Review—Drawer D, University Station, Baton Rouge, La. 70803

Southwest Review—Southern Methodist University Press, Dallas, Tex. 75222

The Tamarack Review—Box 159, Postal Station K, Toronto, Ont., Canada M4P 2G5

Transatlantic Review—Box 3348, Grand Central P.O., New York, N.Y. 10017

Tri-Quarterly—University Hall 101, Northwestern University, Evanston, Ill. 60201

Twigs—Pikeville College, Pikeville, Ky. 41501

Twin Cities Express—127 North Seventh Street, Minneapolis, Minn. 55403

U. S. Catholic—221 West Madison Street, Chicago, Ill. 60606

Vagabond—P. O. Box 879, Ellensburg, Wash. 98926

The Virginia Quarterly Review—University of Virginia, 1 West Range, Charlottesville, Va. 22903

Vogue—350 Madison Avenue, New York, N.Y. 10017

Washington Review of the Arts—404 Tenth Street, S. E., Washington, D.C. 20003

West Coast Review—Simon Fraser University, Vancouver, B.C., Canada

Western Humanities Review—Bldg. 41, University of Utah, Salt Lake City, Utah 84112

Wind—RFD Route 1, Box 810, Pikeville, Ky. 41501

Woman's Day—515 Broadway, New York, N.Y. 10036

Works—A.M.S., 56 East 13th Street, New York, N.Y. 10003

Yale Review—250 Church Street, New Haven, Conn. 06520